The Making of the Member

By Ray Burston

© 1995

During the 1980s an unsung 'Black Country' town in the industrial West Midlands was a world removed from Britain's renowned 'corridors of power' at Westminster, corridors that were overshadowed throughout by the ascendancy of one of the most formidable and controversial prime ministers of modern times.

Even so, this seeming backwater becomes the battleground for two ambitious young friends as they embark on a thirteen year quest to become its Member of Parliament – a contest that will rage instead through the 'corridors of power' of its local government and business community.

Each young man hails from a different side of town; from a different side of the political divide. And just as surely each power-hungry young man – frequently beset by personal crises of his own – finds himself caught up in the passions and combats, the triumphs and disappointments, and the intrigues and scandals that will attend that quest.

It is a quest that will prove to be the making of the Member.

DUDLEY LIBRARIES	
000000779335	
Askews & Holts	02-Nov-2015
	£9.29
GL	

To Les and Karen…

and to all those still climbing that long, 'greasy pole'…

*"Born for the universe, he narrowed his mind,
And to party gave up what was meant for mankind.
Though fraught with all learning, yet straining his throat,
To persuade Tommy Townsend to lend him a vote.
Who, too deep for his listeners, still went on refining,
And thought of convincing while they thought of dining.
Tho' equal in all things, in all things unfit,
Too nice for a statesman, too proud for a wit.
For a patriot too cool, for a drudge disobedient,
And too fond of the right to pursue the expedient!"*

*Oliver Goldsmith's "The Retaliation",
(inspired by Edmund Burke)*

PART I

1. Winter of Discontent
September 1978 – September 1979

2. The Lady's Not For Turning
October 1979 – September 1980

3. Ghost Town
October 1980 – July 1981

4. Breaking the Mould
August 1981 – March 1982

5. Rejoice, Rejoice
April 1982 – December 1982

6. Gloriana Victrix
January 1983 – June 1983

PART II

7. Testing... Testing...
July 1983 – May 1984

8. Strike!
June 1984 – December 1984

9. The Potter and the Clay
January 1985 – September 1985

10. One of Us
October 1985 – June 1986

11. Young, Upwardly Mobile
July 1986 – December 1986

12. Economical with the Truth
January 1987 – June 1987

PART III

13. The Loneliest Road
July 1987 – May 1988

14. The Golden Age That Never Was
June 1988 – December 1988

15. Scapegoat
January 1989 – July 1989

16. Walls Come Tumbling Down
August 1989 – December 1989

17. This Evil Tax!
January 1990 – June 1990

18. A Storm in the Desert
July 1990 – February 1991

19. Scandal
March 1991 – October 1991

20. The Last Hurrah
November 1991 – March 1992

21. Tomorrow is Another Day
The 1992 General Election

Part I

1978-1983

1 WINTER OF DISCONTENT

The sun had not long gone down on another warm summer night. In the stillness of the countryside a gentle breeze swept effortlessly through the tall trees that lined the roadside like a whispering phalanx. In the distance an array of headlights broke open the gathering darkness. At first almost imperceptible, gradually the punishing sound of a high-revving engine destroyed the tranquillity. A solitary car was travelling at frightening speed from out of the blackness.

In the front passenger seat, Brad had his one foot slung over the other (and both in turn jacked up by the car's dashboard). He closed his eyes and enjoyed the full force of the breeze from the open window drawing his long mane up and about, feeling the freedom of speed as the car hurtled down the highway. Meanwhile, Carl, the driver, gripped the wheel and scanned the terrain that advanced into the beams of his powerful driving lamps.

'Who killed the music?' wondered Craig from his eerie on the back seat behind them, his handsome face momentarily illuminated by the lights of an oncoming car.

Carl glanced away from the road. He fumbled in the console, removed the dead cassette from the stereo, and felt around in the glove box for another offering, bringing it up briefly to within reading distance. Vaguely discerning the title, he pressed it into the stereo, which swallowed it with a reassuring clunk. After a brief pause, music poured forth from all four corners of the vehicle. Then Carl took the car into a bend, the tyres squealing but just gripping the road. Craig thrust himself back down into the rear seat and into a darkness relieved only by the lights of the occasional passing car, his eyes glazed in contemplation as he noted to approach the familiar collage of houses, shops and factories which banished the black for swirling shades of floodlit amber. Where did he fit into the scheme of things?

"*...NO FUTURE... NO FUTURE...*" went the hellish song. Craig was just one more member of a 'punk' generation; an angry young man feeling for the answer, but sensing that perhaps there was no answer.

To be sure, Craig William Anderson had never been his father's 'favourite' son, though his father loved him and his influence was heavy upon him. Above all, his father's military background had moulded Craig's early life and shaped his perceptions. Thus in the year that China had 'fallen' to the communists his father, Leonard Anderson, had been summoned to serve King and Country in Her Majesty's Royal Air Force; the year of the Coronation had been the year Leonard had met and fallen in love with a charming young girl called Patricia, Craig's mother; the year that Sputnik shocked the world had been the year that Stephen, his eldest son, had been born; and the year that Macmillan had romped home at the polls the year that Len, Pat and the infant Stephen had followed the RAF to Aden, then a prosperous entrepôt at the foot of Arabia, guarding the Indian Ocean. Then – in the year of the U2 crisis, and of Belgian flight from the Congo; of the Sharpeville shootings in South Africa, Barricades Week in French Algeria, and young senator called Jack Kennedy began talking about a 'New Frontier' – Craig himself had been born.

Meanwhile, the car screeched onto the car park, and Carl and Brad, together with their still-contemplative companion, headed off towards the sound of loud music drifting from the gaudy neon edifice. Walking through the double doors of the *Tropicana* nightspot they were quickly caught up in that familiar hedonism of hot, perspiring youth. Eventually, they emerged from the dense pack of humanity swarming around the bar to gather on one of the mezzanine balconies that overlooked the dance floor, itself swept by revolving lights that picked out bodies swaying to the beat.

Before too long, the lads were eyeing up three girls who had not long previously discovered a gap on the swathe of youngsters that lined the opposing balustrade and were now posing there, looking alternately to the boys and to each other, sensing that tonight was going to be a good night at the *Tropicana*. Both groups occasionally smiled across the room. Meanwhile, Craig edged in close to Carl to offer advice on how to proceed. Whatever plan of attack had been agreed upon, the decisive blow was pre-empted when the DJ suddenly upped the tempo and the girls hurried down onto the floor, still glancing back to see if the lads were watching.

The house shook to an electrifying thump hammered out through the scattered nests of speakers as people swarmed onto the floor in the seething mass of colour, movement and emotions. The boys knew that a change of tactics was required. They leant on the balcony and, with preying eyes, watched as the girls weaved about to the rhythm, captured by the beams that spun randomly to search out every corner of the dimmed and cavernous room.

Craig's eye gradually settled on one of the three beauties, a slim and attractive blonde. He observed how her neatly blow-waved hair glistened in the light, her shapely body perfectly tuned to the nuances of the beat. Brad was by now also singling out his target, and returned the smiles that she occasionally offered him as all three girls looked up to see if they still commanded the lads' attention. For several minutes her tall, dark figure meandered in and out of the other revellers, her high heels bearing a slender frame, her tight denims faithfully reproducing the full beauty of her lovely long legs.

When the music died, the girls moved away and ascended the carpeted steps that led once more to the balcony. The lads signalled to each other with their eyes. Then the pack moved in for the kill. By now, a new song was blaring out, and only by speaking directly into the girls' bejewelled ears could introductions be made. From the smiles and laughter it could be discerned that whatever banalities had been spoken had evidently fallen like seeds on fertile ground. Soon laughter spread infectiously and a pairing took place.

Amongst the throngs surging out at the end of the evening, the three couples cut a path arm-in-arm to Carl's ferocious looking car – one of many revving up to leave the *Tropicana's* floodlit car park. Exhaust fumes swirled up into the crisp late-night air while ostentatiously-customised Escorts and Cortinas queued up at the exit, growling to be away and off for the back seat *amour* of the drive home. Carl whipped his beaten old charger into life and, with a squealing of tyres and much smoke and noise, the monster raced through the archipelago of remaining parked cars to reach the open road. Letting the clutch up suddenly, the huge wheels spun violently before gripping the asphalt again. Regaining command, the car hurtled off down a wide dual carriageway, engine throbbing as Carl demanded all the power it could deliver.

Carl hung on to the wheel as he picked out the road ahead. His girl was flung back into her seat, momentarily disbelieving he had made the car perform some of the manoeuvres it just had. In the back, Craig and Brad were huddled together with their respective trophies on a seat manifestly not made for four. There were giggles and laughter as all parties twitched and fumbled to find a degree of personal comfort, Carl's erratic driving throwing them about with abandon. Eventually Brad nestled his nose up to the ear of his girl, pulling her body close in to his own. Craig was meanwhile locked in an amateurish kiss with the blonde, their heads moving about, trying to counteract the movements of the car as passing lights danced over their faces and pulverising tunes from the Clash and Elvis Costello pounded from the car stereo. Otherwise, he sensed himself drifting off into a daydream once more.

Aden had not been the only happy memory of strange and distant lands that this son of a serving NCO had tasted. Though the Empire and its dotted collection of military bases were fast retreating, the opportunities for overseas postings were still there. In the year that the heavens had opened on the crowds at Woodstock the Andersons settled in Bahrain in the Persian Gulf. These were to be the final years of the British presence 'East of Suez' and, symbolically, the final posting of the Anderson family before his father had decided to quit the Royal Air Force for good. Politically, the eyes of their country had also been turning towards events closer to home. The government of Harold Wilson (and Edward Heath's administration that unexpectedly followed it) now had mounting problems to tackle: balance of payments crises, inflation and militant trades unions. It was from this point on that Craig remembered becoming cognisant that, like all fathers, his own inevitably set great store on the achievements of the eldest son. He had sensed that Stephen's comradeship had been giving way to some healthy competition.

If Britain's horizons had shrunk, so had Len Anderson's; as if he knew that the day when they would find themselves back home on a rainy street amidst the solicitude of life in 1970s Britain would not be too far way. They had resolved to enjoy the lazy, swaying palms and sea-swept beaches while they lasted. The Andersons would soon say farewell to Bahrain, and the flag would come down on another happy memory as a Royal Marine band played a last farewell. And so once again Craig now found himself mulling over better days, albeit in the back of a car speeding back into the unremarkable town that had been his home ever since.

His girl nudged him and he returned to reality. By now, the familiar landmarks of Gunsbridge's outer suburbs were passing by. The town was a pretty uninspiring sprawl of urban industry and housing estates. However, to its south and west, middle-class estates with elegant-sounding names like Amblehurst and Little Worcester had sprung up. From here, it was only twenty minutes drive into Birmingham and Wolverhampton along the fast motorways that criss-crossed the Borough, and which had aided the growth of this leafy commuter belt. Meanwhile, to the east of the town were the tower blocks of large, soulless council estates like Tower Park, Berksham, and the infamous Scotts Estate – from where on a clear day one could view the whole vast jungle of factories, motorways and urban dereliction that characterised this half of town.

During the seventies, the Council had tried to improve the town. A new concrete-and-steel shopping mall had not long been opened, where one could window-shop for an afternoon amongst imported palm trees instead. Craig and his family had settled in the Lower Henley district, an area of both council and owner-occupied dwellings just to the south of Gunsbridge, but close enough to the motorway to be within a comfortable drive of the giant car factory just over the borough boundary where his father worked as an electrical engineer.

It was along the deserted carriageways of one of these motorways that the car sped, the lamp standards blanketing the road and its flanks in a kind of eerie orange daylight. Veering off into Lower Henley, the car pulled up in front of a set of traffic lights that flashed superfluously at this late hour. As Craig emerged from the back of the car, his girl craned out through the window of the passenger door to offer him a long, exaggerated kiss. Then Carl and his impatient machine raced away, leaving only a disappearing smile from his latest 'conquest' to remind Craig of his night out.

Brad watched Craig wander off in the direction of his home – *virgo intactus* for one more night at least! Though he lived on the opposite side of town to his friend, the two had met at the sprawling sixth-form college that they both attended in the centre of town. They hung around together, bound loosely by their shared musical passions and by their unrivalled ability to pull women, a tribute to their good looks and imposing statures. Brad knew Carl, who had 'wheels' – a priceless advantage in a town where the buses all stopped after eleven.

After depositing his remaining buddy, Carl sped away once more, leaving Brad and his girl alone upon a very different kind of sleeping estate. Carl's manner of exit had set the dogs barking, but the chorus soon died down. In the distance the sound of an overnight freight train rippled across from the far side of the Scotts Estate. As the couple walked arm-in-arm, a police car cruised away at speed, the occupants scanning warily like scouts sent out by an army of occupation. This was the seedier side of town.

To be sure, the year 1960 had seen another baby boy entering the world, this time in Gunsbridge's grim and unsung maternity hospital. For Robert Bradleigh (or 'Brad' as he inevitably came to be dubbed by his peers) there were to be no long sea-swept beaches or palms swaying in a hot, sultry breeze. His mother had bore him when she had been only eighteen (and his father had not been much older). It was destined to be a teenage romance that would go the way of so many. The couple had lived with his mother's parents until the strain could be borne no longer, and his father quit on the day that that aspiring young president had been gunned down on Dealy Plaza. His father was seldom to be seen again throughout Brad's lonely childhood.

His mother, Yvonne, had soldiered on, though most of the rearing of the infant had fallen upon his doting grandparents. Yvonne, a buxom, attractive girl, had thus been able to recapture a portion of the youth she had left behind in that fateful year. She would dance and sing in the pubs that dotted this grimy industrial town. Vivacious and popular, few would have guessed that she had hidden within her the bitterness and cynicism of one who had suffered the shattering of so many young dreams on the unforgiving treadmill of love.

Brad had been as protective and supportive as a young boy could be, cast as he often had been between his mother and her lovers, in a man's world where passion had often given way to emotional violence. He had always tried to remember only the happy memories: glimpses of his mother through the bedroom door setting her hair and putting on her face, pretending to be Dusty Springfield as she mimed to a tinny-sounding transistor radio, an orchestra of nail varnish bottles cluttering up her dressing table. His grandparents had offered him emotional support and what little sense of security could be garnered from this imperfect situation. And he could recall how he would gaze out of his bedroom window late at night to observe the lights of the town spangled like stars on the horizon; or lying on the mat in front of their little black-and-white television, engrossed by those Gerry Anderson puppets. One of nature's loners, on warm summer evenings, whilst the others played, he would dream about being a Thunderbirds hero who, damning fear and faint hearts, rescued the weak and the vulnerable from the clutches of certain death. Of such seeming trivialities was his childhood fashioned.

Thus it had been with sadness that he had followed his mother to set foot in her new council flat in the year that Neil Armstrong had set foot upon the Moon. Fourteen storeys up, it had been cast amidst a sprawling grey wilderness, built without feeling way out on the fringes of town. This quiet, introspective child soon became the victim of bullying at the vast comprehensive school he had attended; until, in the year that Ted Heath went down to defeat at the hands of the miners, he one day discovered a combative streak in his character and nobody ever pushed him around again. The experience had reinforced his intense concern for the underdog, and tempered it with the knowledge that justice sometimes required a touch of mendacity if it was to win the day.

So where was he heading, he asked himself metaphorically as he strolled through this unforgiving quarter, arm-in-arm with this girl whose name he couldn't be bothered to recall? Academically, he was gifted like so many working class kids whose genius is often left unrequited. More so, he had begun to appreciate that only by utilising his brain to the full was he ever going to escape the prison of ignorance and low expectations that had trapped his parents. Therefore, he had chosen to stay on at sixth-form college. The 1970s had been a tumultuous time as the 'Sick Man of Europe' tottered on the knife-edge amidst successive economic and social crises. But whilst the hopes and dreams of ordinary people were crashing down all around him, his grandfather had helped steel him to keep the flickering flame alight in the hope of better things to come.

Reaching one of the blocks of tall grey flats on the estate, the two lovers stopped, and Brad cast his arms round her waist and pulled her tight to him. They embraced beneath the humming, fluorescent-lit board that spelled out the name of this particular block. He brushed her flowing hair back from over her eyes before sinking his tongue into her mouth. She gently shadowed its every peregrination as he poured his passion into her. They locked in this intense sparring for several minutes. She gasped impatiently while he caressed her and she excited him in turn before bringing it all to fulfilment. Then they both fell silent again and she rested her head on his big broad shoulder.

"I'd best be going now", she whispered. "You've got my number?"

Brad tapped every pocket before deciding that he had. Whether or not he ever used it again was another matter. Like so many of his 'conquests', he'd have to sleep on the decision. She had a nice body though!

She strolled into the foyer of the block, pressed for the lift, then turned around and waited. They exchanged some final glances before the lift arrived. Then its doors closed, the light in its tiny window vanished and she was no more. Brad turned away and headed off into the night.

****

As he sat surrounded by his books, Craig could hear the sound of his father washing upstairs. He had his college work to complete that he had neglected from the previous night, so he sat pensively at the dining room table, sucking the end of a cheap plastic biro. He knew his father was seldom in a good mood when he came home from work. Indeed, truly that factory seemed to bring out the misanthropist in him. And as his father descended the stairs, the greying hairs protruding from the borders of his vest, Craig noticed him offer his son an ominous glance before switching on the television and pressing for the channel with the latest news. Then he disappeared back into the kitchen, leaving the set buzzing with the week's biggest story.

It was fully expected that Prime Minister James Callaghan would go to the polls that autumn. Throughout 1978 the economy had stabilised after the traumas of the previous three years, and Labour was holding its own in the opinion polls. They would never have a better opportunity to halt Conservative ambitions of government. Craig sucked his pen once more as he watched Mr Callaghan telling the glitterati of the trades union movement however that there would be no election that year, delegates looking on aghast while he teased them, singing "There was I, waiting at the church..."

Craig had always taken an interest in politics, eagerly soaking up all the information that his 'A' level courses in Government & Politics and History provided him with. Meanwhile, his father had re-entered the room, curious as to what his son had found so fascinating about a TUC Conference.

"In my day we would never have tolerated the country being run by the trades unions?" said his father – a statement that Craig knew was a warm-up for what was coming next. "...And you need smirk, my lad!" His son tried to look innocent as he awaited the coming tirade. "...Some of us had to work long and hard to give you the best in life, and all you do is fill your head with that bloody noise. Listening to Queen won't get you to university!"

Craig had to decide whether to respond. Knowing his father's opinion about the sort of music he listened to, and knowing his inability to reason about preconceived views, he decided that discretion was the better part of valour. He donned a studious demeanour and sunk his face back into his books. Even so, he was amazed. His father evidently displayed some interest in the posters on his bedroom wall other than to criticise them for the way the drawing pins ruined the plaster. Stephen had always been able to decorate his room with pictures of Jaguars, Nimrods and Tornados, to say nothing of the way he dotted the ceiling with his carefully crafted Airfix models frozen in flight. So it always bugged Craig that the impunity his brother had acquired never extended to the gallery of rock legends that covered his own bedroom walls.

Craig had always tried to please his father, only lately asserting a limited form of independence. However, he never possessed Stephen's unrivalled ability to twist his father around his little finger. It was probably something to do with the vague sentiments Craig had expressed to the effect that he would not be taking up a career in the RAF. Why could his father not understand that it was not that he was unpatriotic; nor that he was turning into some long-haired weirdo? In fact, Craig was rather proud of his well-groomed fair hair – even if he did comb it up the middle.

****

Built in the late sixties from the Brutalist trinity of glass, steel and concrete, Gunsbridge College of Further Education was a pretty dehumanising sort of structure. With its mass of tube-like interconnecting corridors joining each block to the other, it rather resembled some sort of futuristic space station, though the graffiti and the damp streaks running down the outer walls helped to bestow upon it a more earthly ambience. Critics of the town's comprehensive education system like to joke that academic standards in the Borough were maintained in spite of the College, rather than because of it.

Craig sat at his usual desk, books and pencils ready for the next dose of erudition. The lecturer was meanwhile prodding at the bulky overhead projector that sat on his desk, and which shone at a bare patch of tangerine-emulsioned wall. His attention was momentarily caught by Brad, who strolled in with a motley collection of ring binders and textbooks slung under his right arm, as well as a chewed red biro propped behind his ear. Flashing a greeting at Craig with his eyebrows, he offloaded his cargo of knowledge on the desk immediately behind and sat down as the lecturer rose to address them.

"Now I hope you've all completed last week's project on the role of the monarchy in the British Constitution. You can leave your papers on my desk afterwards. Today, we will be continuing our look at the role of political parties in the British parliamentary system by looking at the history and philosophy of the Conservative Party..."

The lecturer manoeuvred his assortment of acetates onto the projector and settled into a detailed monologue on his chosen topic. Making notes as it proceeded, Brad would periodically stare out of the window for a few seconds before receiving inspiration and frantically scribbling a few more paragraphs. Craig too, would sometimes gaze at the rain-sodden view of the town available from this floor of the building before doing likewise. After about a quarter of an hour, the lecturer summed up and invited questions and comments, voices from the room discussing the salient points: was the Conservative Party still a class-based party? Was Mrs Thatcher taking the party too far to the right? Could the Tories govern the country without provoking the unions?

"But sir", Craig insisted, "Mrs Thatcher has spoken the truth when she says that the unions have acquired too much power and used it too selfishly. Most people think the TUC has more influence on events than the Prime Minister!"

"That's a valid point." The lecturer said, changing his posture as he leant on the edge of his desk. "Even many in Mrs Thatcher's shadow cabinet are worried about the effects of breaking the 'Butskellite' Consensus." He turned to address the class before continuing, "Do you remember what we said the 'Butskellite' Consensus was?" Brad lifted his pen in the air and sat himself up in his chair.

"Sir, it was the unspoken understanding that in return for the Labour Party continuing to run a mixed economy and maintain Britain's nuclear weapons, the Conservatives would not undo Labour's policies on the welfare state."

"Very good, Robert", said the lecturer before turning to Craig to permit him a rejoinder.

"But sir," he continued, "It's not Mrs Thatcher who has broken the consensus. Surely Labour, by their policies on nationalisation, are the ones who have broken the agreement?"

"I can see the *Iron Lady* has a staunch defender in Gunsbridge, Craig!" the lecturer joked in a mildly patronising remark that even so injected a little humour into the debate, the class rippling with amusement. However, Craig was undaunted.

"And it is ridiculous to say that Mrs Thatcher will provoke the unions. Is not even Mr Callaghan unable to prevent them from dictating their own terms? Or to act without *their* permission?" he insisted sarcastically.

"Very true" the lecturer admitted, "The Prime Minister is having great difficulty persuading the TUC to accept his anti-inflationary pay strategy."

Brad made the final contribution. "Sir, it's not a question of the unions accepting the Tories' policies. The British people won't accept them when they see precisely what she has in store for them. I'd give her eighteen months before either they or her own party reject her."

This was the first time that the two lads had perceived which side of the political fence the other might be sat upon. They had never been close friends; Brad was too mercurial to be anyone's 'close' friend (and, indeed, as far as Craig knew, he didn't really have any close friends). Both boys made a mental note not to discuss politics, given that that was one subject they evidently didn't have in common.

****

Thinking he'd heard the front door open, Craig had wandered over to the window. It was yet another bitterly cold day outside. Yet seeing no one, he returned to spread himself out on top of his bed, reading the newspaper that his father had brought home from work. Once more he found himself following with interest all the comings and goings of the Government as it battled to maintain its credibility.

Through the grim winter of 1979 the weather had deteriorated. Snow had hung around on the streets for weeks on end, seeming to emphasise the feeling that Britain was frozen in crisis. For indeed, this infamous 'Winter Of Discontent' seemed to have descended upon the hapless Callaghan government like a blinding storm, with the strikes and the weather having attained a sort of symbiosis, especially in the media... *"BRITAIN UNDER SNOW... PICKETS CAUSING PROBLEMS... RAIL STRIKE GOES AHEAD... WORST WEATHER FOR SIXTEEN YEARS... PORTS CLOSED... PETROL CRISIS WORSENS... HOSPITALS UNDER SIEGE... BRITAIN UNDER SIEGE... TWO MILLION FACE LAY OFF... BREAKDOWN BRITAIN..."* ran the headlines. All the time, militancy by the well-known acronyms of the trades union movement had left Mr Callaghan's anti-inflationary strategy in tatters, permitting Mrs Thatcher to tempt the nation with her alternative to a Britain that seemed ungovernable. "Crisis? What crisis?" the Prime Minister was meanwhile misquoted as saying.

Suddenly, Craig became intensely aware of someone watching him. There, at the portal, stood the fine erect figure of an airman, his impressive blue uniform smartly pressed, his cap under his arm and a radiant smile on his face. At a sudden loss for words, Craig marvelled at this unexpected appearance of his beloved brother. Stephen advanced towards him and laid his arms around his little brother, burying Craig's head in his hands.

"I hear you've been trying to land without your undercarriage!" said Stephen, a cryptic reference to the bad atmosphere that Craig's increasingly strained relations with his father had created, and which even now he could sense pervaded the Anderson household.

"How did you get here?" wondered Craig.

"Mum told me that you and Dad had had 'words'. Anyway, I was 'passing through', as they say."

Whatever, Craig was not sorry he was home. He and his brother had often shared their feelings. Stephen certainly had plenty of tales to tell. After some minutes however, he got down to basics, insisting, "You know, it's high time you made up your mind what you want to do."

"It's okay for you. You've always known what you wanted to be." Craig replied evasively, sitting back on his bed.

"But there are things you care about. What about politics? You've always spoken your mind on the things you believed in. Either way, you've got to learn to be your own man."

"That's all very well. Dad's positively drooled over you. He's backed you all the way!"

"I know that. But let me tell you this. At one time, this caused me some pretty serious heart-searching. But I remembered my first flight as a cadet in the Air Training Corps. I was fifteen at the time. It was only a little Chipmunk trainer – a bit of a boneshaker really." Stephen mused, Craig watching his eyes glaze over as he lifted them heavenwards, continuing, "But it was a tremendous sensation. I could feel the elements; feel the G-forces pressing on me. I could look straight down on fields and farms and villages. I knew from that moment on that I had to fly. Nothing in this world would ever stir me more than cutting through the clouds, or slicing along valleys at the speed of sound. From then on, I determined that it was flying or nothing. That's why, when I resolved to become an RAF officer, I did it for me – and not Dad."

Craig shrugged his shoulder in agreement. He couldn't really do otherwise after such soaring eloquence. And besides, he respected his brother above any other mortal. At the dark moments of life, Stephen had always been there to pull him through, ever exuding confidence in him.

"I don't know much about politics, but I imagine that it's like everything else in this life: if you want it badly enough, you'll sacrifice everything to get it. Everything in this world will weigh down on you in order to make you forget it, and to be like all the other mediocre people in this world who merely plod along. That's Dad's trouble; he's what you might call an 'armchair politician'!" Stephen mused, Craig nodding in agreement.

"But don't you see! You're in danger of falling into the same mode of thinking. All these late nights and dolly birds; it's not the real 'you'. I believe somewhere inside, you've lost faith in yourself. I know that college is boring, and that girls are more fun. But like I said, if you want it, go get it. Forget Dad, forget the girls, forget college – or at least forget that it's boring. Just concentrate on getting the qualifications necessary to make your dreams a reality. Map out a rough route to get you to your goals and go after them, adjusting it as you go. But don't ever lose sight of the ultimate prize."

Again, Craig could not better his brother's advice, so he said nothing. However, Stephen could sense he needed one more convincing argument in order to sustain his attack. He pointed to the inscription of the badge on the breast pocket of his tunic. "Look at that! You know what that says?"

"*Per Ardua Ad Astra*," answered Craig, translating the Latin motto without hesitation, "To reach for the stars."

"Absolutely! And that should be your goal: to reach for the stars. Your dreams may seem just as elusive. Your goal may seem just as far away. But reach out and grasp it. And never settle for anything less!"

"Anyway, I'd best be making tracks. You're not the only person I've come home to have 'words' with." Then Stephen tapped his nose, winked, and whispered, "Old flame, you understand!" Then he stood up, straightened his uniform and set his cap.

Meanwhile, Craig smiled to himself to observe how his brother wore the uniform of Her Majesty's Royal Air Force with pride, even in the indifferent environs of his younger brother's disorganised bedroom.

"Don't forget to write, 'Action Man'." he nodded at Craig. *"Per Ardua Ad Astra...* nothing less!"

Stephen saluted as he made his way down the stairs. Craig eased himself off the bed and wandered back to stare out of the window. He watched his brother don his greatcoat and trudge out into the sleet and the wind, making his way past a group of people on the picket line outside the council yard at the end of the street. Craig couldn't help contrasting the smart, purposeful comportment of his brother with the dishevelled and dispirited statures of the pickets huddled around a smoking fire kindled in an old oil drum, one of whom leaned wearily against a crudely painted banner which demanded that the Government 'END LOW PAY NOW'. Craig watched him mutter some cynical remark at Stephen as he brushed past. Stephen just smiled and made his way off up the street. It seemed that here, in microcosm, were the very qualities of pride, spirit and endeavour that had created for Britain the greatest empire the world had ever seen, side-by-side with the qualities of pettiness, cynicism and selfishness which were now in the process of bringing the country to its knees.

Meanwhile, the pickets were stopping cars, interrogating the drivers before officiously waving them away again. Here was socialism, Craig thought, announcing its failure for the world to see. The country was desperately sick. Surely only Mrs Thatcher seemed to have the courage to tell the patient that there was only one really effective cure on offer.

****

His mother said she trusted him, though Brad couldn't help wondering if it was sometimes indifference rather than trust. When he saw his mother giggling on the sofa with her latest 'flame', he knew that he had long since ceased to be her prime preoccupation. Instead he drifted into his bedroom, donning the headphones of his stereo to escape with the Boomtown Rats, the Police, Ian Dury, or some of the other bands that were making it big that winter. Then again, he paused and lifted the needle from the turntable, returning to his college folders. "*It's a Rat Trap, Billy*" went the song – but Brad was determined to break out of it.

Eventually he heard his mother mumble farewell to her latest boyfriend and start to get herself ready to head off for the Dickensian factory in town where she worked, earning the limited wage that kept the proverbial wolf from the door. She shouted a farewell to her only son from down the hall. Then she too was gone.

Important as it was, Brad simply couldn't summon the energy to renew his studies now that he was on his own again. He grabbed the headset from behind his bed once more. While filling his head with music, out of the corner of his eye he spotted a little old man dressed in an old raincoat, a bushy scarf and a tartan cloth cap.

"Granddad!" he exclaimed, "Take a seat!"

The little old man laid down his shopping bag and dragged a chair across the room. Sitting down, he removed his cap, shaking the moisture from it. "I wasn't expecting you", exclaimed his startled grandson.

"The door was open so I wandered in. I thought I might find you listening to that racket again!"

His grandfather was breathless after the walk from the bus stop, but was soon piecing together what it was he had popped over to say. Closer than a father, Brad always valued to his grandfather's counsel and listened to him respectfully – even when he lectured him sternly about his taste in music.

"Anyway, I heard you were studying politics, so I've brought you these." he then offered, feeling round in his bag and pulling out some old dog-eared books.

"What are they?" Brad enquired, thumbing inside for clues.

"Books on politics. Or more to the point, books on socialism. Tawney, Crosland, that kind of thing." he insisted.

Brad was amazed. He knew his grandfather had always been a Labour supporter. Now though, as he fingered through some of these treasures of political philosophy and social history, he shook his head in wonderment. "I didn't know you were into all this. You kept this secret well."

"I was one of the leading lights in the local party. That was in Attlee's day. Things were different then. Hitler had just been defeated and we were coming home in triumph. We felt we had a whole new world to build. It was like a clean page; we could start all over again. We weren't going to have all that claptrap from Churchill; nor were we going back to means tests and mass unemployment. From now on, it would be different: homes and jobs for all, free health care, people before profit."

"What went wrong?" Brad enquired, still leafing through the assortment of tomes he had just acquired.

"I guess I just lost the fire. Your grandmother never showed much interest, so I guess I let it slip. I still watch events, though. As I see it," the old man continued, "it's up to you young ones to make sure you build on all that's been set in place. We never really built on what Attlee, Bevan and Morrison gave us. There's still not real justice. People grow up in ignorance and squalor; live, get married and die in the same. All the time, the rich get richer and the people at the bottom are still at the bottom – outsiders looking in on a society where every man just looks after himself."

"I'm afraid if Mrs Thatcher ever becomes prime minister it'll get worse."

"Ar', lad. We can always find money for new missiles, but never for a decent wage for hospital workers, for instance. It's all so unjust. No, I've done my bit. It's your turn now, son. If you want your children to do better than you and your mum have done, you've got to stand up. We need people like you. You've been through it all; you've seen where it all ends. Don't let them grind you down. Stand up and show them that there is something better than throwing it all away down the pub... or on pop records!"

Brad could see the wily old fox was reading his mind perfectly. So much of what his grandfather had hoped to achieve were dreams he himself cherished. More than ever, he was becoming cognisant that the goal of making something better was the very blood in his veins.

"I'm pleased to see you're into your studies", his grandfather said, himself paging through Brad's scribbled notes, lifting his nose and examining the contents through his bifocals. "You stick at it, son. That's my big regret. We didn't have the opportunities that you youngsters have got now. In my day, it was either the factory or the army. I wish I could have studied all this."

Meanwhile, his grandfather continued to thumb through the notes until his eyes alighted on something that caught his interest. "Here, she's a good example – Emmeline Pankhurst; the Suffragettes braved imprisonment and ridicule. I only wished your grandmother – and your mother for that matter – had studied them and learned a thing or two!"

Quite so, thought Brad. However, he couldn't help enjoying the irony that the two most important women in his grandfather's life had been so indifferent to the horizons that the Pankhursts had opened up, whilst he feared that one who had benefited to the full from the enfranchisement of women might soon be leading the country off in directions that were complete anathema to the old man and his beloved protégé. Brad determined, there and then, never to let any woman stand in the way of his dreams.

****

The coach sped down the motorway into the drizzle, its occupants trying to while away the journey cracking jokes, playing cards, or just staring out of the windows at the cars and lorries passing by with lights twinkling in the rain. To them it was just another day; yet for two of these passengers today held the promise of being a different day – a special day. As the coach finally turned along Whitehall and the lecturer stood up at the front, issuing instructions, they knew that much alright. At last Big Ben came into view as they passed alongside the Cenotaph. Dodging the cars and the ubiquitous red buses, the driver found a convenient spot to set down his passengers, the students gathering up their coats and filing off the vehicle.

Suddenly, it was there in front of them! The great palace stretched out before their eyes, firing their imaginations. It seems so different to how it looked on the television, when interviewers had inevitably used it as the backdrop to their latest bulletins from Westminster. For Craig and for Brad though, the Houses of Parliament had lost none of their ethereal majesty, even when enveloped in mist and spitting rain. Their eyes were lifted up to its imposing spires – symbolic of the glory and tradition of this historic corner of London. Meanwhile, the lecturer watched with a sense of accomplishment as his two star alumni savoured the architecture. His gratification was all the more sweet because such interest and awareness as they had shown seemed so rare within the apathy and inertia of the College.

Once the policeman on the door had ushered them in, the lecturer halted them again in the Central Lobby. Meanwhile, Craig was caught up in the bustling ambience of this great crossroads of Parliament, where MPs, journalists, researchers and tourists all ambled together. Suddenly, an impressive character with receding white hair strode over to meet them. His dark suit was immaculate, his regimental tie exactly set in place. He smiled and shook hands with the lecturer, his self-confident charm and wit instantly putting everyone at ease.

"Good morning, ladies and gentlemen." he opened, clasping his hands together in delight, "My name is Sir Edgar Powers, and I'm the Member of Parliament for Gunsbridge South..."

The students listened politely while he outlined some of the duties of an MP and the places the students would be visiting, along with liberal sprinklings of history relating to the buildings. Then he led them all off to marvel for themselves at this treasure trove of eight centuries of evolving democracy.

"And where do you come from, young man?" Sir Edgar enquired of Brad as they traversed the corridors, Sir Edgar walking erect with his hands folded behind his back.

"The Scotts," replied Brad nervously, aware that Sir Edgar had always been one of the Conservative Party's more respected backbenchers.

"Ah, I know it well." the wizened MP announced, although Brad couldn't say he'd seen too much of Sir Edgar on the notoriously rough estate. "And what brings you to show an interest in politics?"

"I'm interested in the use of power in order to advance the conditions of ordinary people; to create a more just society. I want to concentrate on my exams first. Then I'll consider joining the Labour Party, I suppose." he continued, perhaps realising that he had not displayed a surfeit of tact.

Full of grace, the venerable member responded reassuringly. "And very wise too. Completing your exams, that is," he inserted by way of a qualifying grin. "You won't go far in politics unless you know what you're talking about. Too many politicians on all sides just gabble on about nothing of any great substance; but the ones who are respected are the ones who can advance their case wittily and coherently; and, I might add, make it understandable to the man in the street. You've got to educate yourself before you can educate others!"

Such sage humility impressed Brad. For a fleeting moment, Sir Edgar had crossed the chasm and proffered the wisdom of years, wisdom acceptable to the young man with so many ideals to express. The old Etonian and the young lad from the council estate had found common ground. Having overheard their conversation, the lecturer meanwhile smiled and savoured the accord.

Sir Edgar continued to mill about the group, ever radiating warmth and welcome. Craig was bringing up the rear, eagerly reflecting on the beauty of each corner of this glorious palace. Sir Edgar drew alongside and commenced a conversation. "You evidently enjoy what you're seeing." he observed.

"It's beautiful; so many centuries of history. If these walls could talk, they would certainly tell us a story!"

"Yes, indeed. Men have fought and sometimes died to create our free institutions. It's all left its mark on the 'Mother of Parliaments'."

Sir Edgar then listed some of the poignant dates and events that had shaped those institutions, and how this great House had played its part in the creation of British democracy. Inevitably, he couldn't resist asking Craig why he was so fascinated by it all.

Craig paused before opening his heart to someone who he knew would understand. "I think we stand at an important crossroads. I believe only Mrs Thatcher can see that clearly."

"You should consider joining her upon her great crusade," Sir Edgar counselled. Then he answered his own inchoate question when he ventured to note that "No doubt exams come first; and I don't blame you. But we would value your support. You are right. I believe that the nation does stand on the precipice. It has taken a long time for our country to accept that our problems require a pretty radical solution. Tell me, where do you live?" Sir Edgar asked. Then he fumbled in his breast pocket for his diary. Scanning the pages, he alighted upon a contact. Fumbling some more for a spare piece of House of Commons notepaper, he scribbled a number down and passed it to Craig.

"He's the local councillor for your ward – George Franklin. You'll like him; he's quite a jovial chap – and he's also president of the local ward association. Just give him a bell when you're ready and he'll introduce you to other people who think like you."

"My father calls me right-wing." Craig beamed innocently.

"Then you're in good company!" joked Sir Edgar *sotto voce* (and behind a shielding hand!). Then he quickly cast aside his conspiratorial demeanour and proudly surveyed his impressive young acquaintance. "Unfortunately, I can't say George is a desperately political animal. But he'll look after you nonetheless. Just say Edgar sent you!"

With that, Sir Edgar squeezed Craig's arm and headed off to the front of the line to brief the group as they prepared to enter the House of Commons. Taking their seats in the Strangers' Gallery, both Craig and Brad felt something well up inside them. Although it seemed smaller and more Spartan than the House of Lords, the Commons had a very functional air about it nonetheless. The day's session had just started up after Prayers, and a member was on his feet addressing the chamber. Other MPs reclined on the long green benches that lined the House to carp or cheer as the mood took them.

Craig tried to imagine what sights and sounds would have filled the House during some of the more memorable occasions in its history: Disraeli and Gladstone sparring over the Sudan; Joseph Chamberlain excoriating Irish home rule; Churchill rising gravely to address the House after the fall of Dunkirk; or Enoch Powell savaging Edward Heath for railroading both Britain and the Tory Party into the European Economic Community.

Brad savoured how many great social reforms had first been set in motion in this chamber. The sense of history was overpowering. The seeming tedium of today's debate couldn't suppress that. Indeed, the sense of destiny positively infected him. Here it was that Keir Hardie had turned the eyes of the nation towards the rising power of the working classes. Here it was that Ramsay MacDonald had addressed the House as the first Labour prime minister. Here it was that Attlee, Bevan. Morrison, Cripps and Dalton had introduced the bills that had reshaped post-war society. Brad ached to think that he could have been a part of those historic moments.

Craig looked across the Gallery and both their eyes met. For one brief moment, the two teenagers stared intensely at each other: one mind tasting the prospect that a Conservative victory would soon put an end to the Labour's apparent fudging and bumbling: the other feverishly casting about for ways of advancing the stalled socialist vision. Both boys yearned to be a part of the coming wielding of power. Neither was certain of how exactly that yearning would be fulfilled, but knowing that, ultimately, it must surely end somewhere on one of those benches that spread out below them.

Their eyes separated again and they looked down into the chamber. Behind the Speaker's chair, MPs were milling about, gossiping to colleagues, trying to imagine how the no-confidence vote would fall later on – for these were to prove to be the dying days of Mr Callaghan's tormented government. Meanwhile, the two young men searched around for familiar faces. Most of all, they tried to picture how they themselves might be received, rising up with order paper in hand. Then the Speaker would look their way and utter above the uproar, 'I call the Honourable Member for Gunsbridge South...'

****

The coach pulled up outside the darkened college and the two lads braced themselves against the chill wind advancing the dusk along. Brad, then Craig, bade the lecturer good night and headed off into the town. Ever since they had started to fathom out where the other one stood on matters political, their conversation had become more laconic. Increasingly too, there had been fewer late night parties. A mood of sobriety and study was now the order of the day. They walked for several minutes existing on only small talk.

Eventually Craig suggested they head for one of the local pubs in the town centre. As they wandered through the doors, the place seemed equally sober – quieter than they had seen it in a long time. Instead there were just a few couples seeking intimacy in the secluded alcoves facing away from the bar. A lone kid in a bomber jacket pumped coins into the fruit machine, the sound of coins rattling in the hopper as he hit the occasional jackpot. Meanwhile, Craig strolled over to the jukebox, now standing strangely silent in the corner of the room, and looked up and down the selections. Brad joined him with the drinks, but neither one availed themselves of the songs on offer.

"You thought any more about your future?" probed Craig as they both drew up a table instead.

Brad responded only vaguely. Several minutes then elapsed between conversations. Meanwhile, both lads looked around at the fixtures or stared into their glasses, thinking of things to say. They realised that they had each changed. The days of carefree fun were over. Their paths were diverging. Craig mentioned that he was trying for university.

Eventually they came to the bottom of their glasses and left for the bus station. Brad liked Craig; he was a likeable, inoffensive sort of kid, though often naive with it. For his part, Craig admired Brad for his basic rectitude, though he thought he had detected a disingenuous streak in him on occasions. Still, it was Craig's nature to always look to the best in people. He wished Brad every success with his 'A' levels.

A pair of idling buses was waiting to take what few people there were home. Craig checked the destination blind and boarded the bus for Lower Henley. Across the way, Brad boarded the bus for The Scotts Estate. Wiping the condensation from the window he looked out across the tranquil terminus, the failing sunlight reflected in the rippling remnants of rainwater puddles left from earlier showers and now iridescent from mixing with the oil deposits. With a perhaps a tinge of regret Brad waved to Craig across the concourse. Craig similarly waved back. Then the two buses, like their solitary passengers, departed – each for their separate destinations.

****

THE GUNSBRIDGE HERALD
Friday, May 4th 1979
Evening Edition   -   Still only 7p

THATCHER TRIUMPHS
Margaret Thatcher today became Britain's first ever woman prime minister after leading the Conservative Party to victory in the General Election. The new Parliament comprises 339 Conservative, 268 Labour, 11 Liberal, and 4 other members, giving the Tories a forty-three seat majority...
NO CHANGE – SIR EDGAR FOR SOUTH, TERRY JOHNSON FOR NORTH

Incumbent members Sir Edgar Powers and Terry Johnson were returned once more as Conservative MP for Gunsbridge South and Labour MP for Gunsbridge North respectively...
NO CHANGE – LABOUR HOLDS COUNCIL
Labour have held onto Gunsbridge Council, maintaining their three-seat majority after a surprise victory in Barnwood ward, a robust challenge from candidate

Micky Preston snatching the seat from the sitting Conservative councillor. In the other upset of the evening however, Labour lost their chairman of finance when Tory candidate Mrs Elizabeth Gainsborough narrowly scraped home in Lower Henley ward...

NORTH SEA BONANZA STARTS FLOWING IN
Chevron Petroleum UK today announced that their Ninian Field oil platform has started production at 80,000 barrels a day. Expecting to quadruple production by 1982, it is predicted that Britain will soon become a net exporter of oil...

****

"He immatures with age", Harold Wilson had once wittily observed. However, Brad thought not as he sat towards the back of the dismal little hall, absorbing every dramatic, yet penetrating outburst from this master orator. Indeed, immaturity hardly seemed the mark of this voice calling from the wilderness.

Antony Wedgwood Benn had been one of the brightest stars of Harold Wilson's first administration – the quintessential youthful technocrat. However, by the time Wilson had returned to power in 1974, Benn had become an increasingly disillusioned *bête noire*, his views shifting ever-leftwards until the party leadership had exiled him to the fringes of the Labour movement.

He now passionately purveyed his message to the small, dedicated band of brothers who formed the nucleus of Gunsbridge South Young Socialists, cadres enthralled by his charge that Wilson and Callaghan and the 'unelected' echelons of the party had 'betrayed' the cause, having failed to offer the British people the alternative of 'real socialism'. He damned both the sordid schemer in the Gannex raincoat and the avuncular bumbling of his successor, and called upon the faithful to rise up and reclaim their party and seize the levers of powers for themselves.

Brad could have thought of better ways of passing a lazy summer evening in this meeting comprising all of a dozen assorted souls who, from their indifferent attire, were probably misfits all. It had not made walking through that door any easier for this tall, dark loner, who was otherwise wary of strangers. Hence by sheer force of will had he entered within and sat himself down in the anonymity of the rear of the hall, waiting for some sign that might justify such an act of spiritual exertion.

Yet it was now plain that he had not exerted himself in vain. Benn and his injunctions now lit up his consciousness, throwing everything into perspective at last. Inklings he'd often had about politics, and of wanting to do something to change things, were now energised by the powerful rhetoric of the former minister. Brad felt the urge to soak up more of this elixir; to work to secure socialism and justice now that the new dark age of Thatcher-style Toryism had descended upon the nation – albeit only temporarily, he was assured. After all, Benn reminded his audience, was not capitalism in crisis?

The meeting finished and the motley band of revolutionaries began to disperse into huddles to furiously debate the dialectics of the class war according to Comrade Benn. Brad was tempted to join in; yet huddles were not his scene. Painfully self-conscious, he stayed rooted in his seat, mulling over what had been said.

"You like what he says?" someone asked him. Brad turned about to observe a brawny young Asian guy sat a row or two back to his left, his hands in his pockets and his feet stacked on one of the fold-away chairs in front of him. The questioner then stood and motioned towards the front of the hall and their guest speaker, still shaking hands with his admirers.

"You want to learn some more?" he enquired again in his imperfect English, urging this apprehensive young recruit to forsake the succour of his own foldaway chair

****

Craig often rode for miles on his faithful racing bike in order to be alone with his thoughts. Today, a sunny afternoon's ride along the pleasant banks of the Birmingham-Gunsbridge Canal had brought him to the Thomas & Clifton Steel Works, where the disused waterway wound its way through the heart of this imposing and perversely majestic factory. Smoke was meanwhile drifting into the clear blue skies above. A quick spin in low gear brought him up onto the old cast-iron footbridge that offered vistas of the seething furnaces where white-hot rolled strips issued forth to be grappled and cooled by workers braving the Dantean heat. Like those strips of cooling steel, the young cyclist felt his own life had also passed through some kind of crucible.

In the intervening weeks Craig had phoned the number Sir Edgar had given him and been introduced to Gunsbridge South Young Conservatives. Small in number, they were nevertheless enthusiastic activists, and Craig enjoyed their discussions and debates. Conversely, the first meeting of the Lower Henley ward committee had not proved quite so riveting though. Most of the night had been taken up by a vigorous debate over precisely what kind of cheese the local ladies' branch should provide for the cheese and wine evening. So this is the dynamic force that was all that stood between Christian civilisation and the dark age of socialism, thought Craig as he observed the apocalyptic struggle to agree whether to procure some Stilton! However, he had found himself persuaded by Elizabeth Gainsborough (one of their new councillors – and a determined and attractive woman), that Gunsbridge South Conservatives weren't a bad lot after all. Craig had proved partial to her motherly touch, and now felt he was ready to go out and spread abroad the new optimism that Mrs Thatcher's victory had ushered in.

Before cycling on, he gazed one more time at the humming iron works. Across the way, quaint little industrial locomotives hauled out loaded up flat-wagons of Thomas & Clifton's wares, ready for the long haul to their final destinations. He was quietly confident that the 'Sick Man Of Europe' would soon be on the road to recovery, and that – with Mrs Thatcher at the helm – Craig William Anderson, Great Britain (and maybe even the Thomas & Clifton Steel Co Ltd too!) were also on the road to realising their full potential at last.

2 THE LADY'S NOT FOR TURNING

"The train now standing at platform eight is the..." said the announcer as Craig dashed across the crowded concourse of Victoria Station, hauling behind him a large, battered suitcase that had evidently seen sterling service on many overseas travels. Finding a carriage, he threw open the door, slung his luggage inside and climbed aboard. Then the guard blew his whistle and the train slipped out. A short burst of rooftops filed past the window until, having secured his luggage and made himself comfortable, Craig relaxed. Meanwhile, the River Thames slid past.

"You're lucky. It's a few minutes late," chuckled a voice sat opposite. Craig, still regaining his breath, looked up.

The voice belonged to an attractive young girl in her late teens. A bright red band swept her shiny dark hair back as she looked up from a folded paperback she had been reading. "You look as if you're returning to college," she proceeded to surmise.

"First year actually."

"So am I. Where are you heading?"

Craig explained, and it transpired they were both making for the same university. "What are you studying then?" he enquired of his new acquaintance.

"Spanish. And I'm also doing philosophy. But it's the Spanish that I want to major on. You see, I was brought up in Argentina. My parents were missionaries over there."

That's an unusual occupation, thought Craig as he tried to puzzle out what he found most attractive in her. She was certainly good looking; indeed, natural beauty, he opined to himself – clear skin, sparkling eyes, the kind of diamond white smile that toothpaste manufacturers would have paid a fortune for. Then she offered him that disarming smile once more and introduced herself.

"I'm Nicola Branson; or Nikki as everyone calls me."

"Craig Anderson," grinned the latecomer, reaching over to shake her hand, her smooth feminine digits slipping gracefully into his own. Then they talked further before she returned to her novel and Craig gazed out of the window at the scenery sailing swiftly by as the train left the suburbs of London behind.

The city streets soon gave way to the rich meadows and idyllic villages of the South Downs. Little halts sped in and out of view with the batting of an eyelid. Before too long, the train was hurtling into the suburbs of a large city, with the seagulls circling overhead telling Craig that the coast was not too far away. He stared down at the busy streets nestling under a tall, curving viaduct that carried other trains across and into the impressive arches of the terminus station. The brakes ululated and slowly brought the train to a halt.

"May I help you?" he enquired of his fellow passenger, who was otherwise gathering her belongings together.

"I think I'm okay, thanks all the same," Nikki replied, heaving at her own bulky suitcase. Craig, however, was not prepared to accept that for an answer, so set his own luggage down on the platform before returning to help Nikki move her case.

He managed to locate a trolley and lifted their belongings onto it. They both strolled together around the fine old station to a local train waiting on an outer platform, finding a vacant compartment and boarding. Then the train drew quietly out of the station, the electrical pick-ups arcing in bright blue flashes as it snaked its way over onto a branch line for a short journey, during which time they exchanged some more small talk. He pondered that she would probably be the first of possibly hundreds of girls he would meet at university. If they were all as stunning as Nikki then he would consider the frugal life of the last few months to have been more than rewarded.

The train pulled into what seemed like yet another sleepy suburban halt when suddenly almost every door along the entire length of the train swung open and young people of every race and colour poured out. Luggage was swung about awkwardly before they all converged on a hapless ticket collector. Craig and Nikki looked at each other with mock trepidation and prepared to jostle through the narrow bottleneck that led them through the station to where other youngsters were standing about on a grassy embankment. Then Nikki noticed two girls holding up a card with 'NIKKI BRANSON – CHESHIRE' hastily scribbled on it.

"There's my welcoming committee. See you around some time," She said, making off towards her friends.

The two girls jumped up and down in excitement as Nikki strode towards them. Then all three embraced and welcomed each other, laughing and exchanging all the latest gossip. Meanwhile, Craig pushed through the crowds until he saw ahead of him a short, curly-haired boy with steel-rimmed glasses, and who held out a sign above his head by which Craig picked him out: 'CRAIG ANDERSON – WEST MIDLANDS'.

"That's me," said Craig, enlightening his own rather less demonstrative one-man welcoming committee.

"What? Craig Anderson? Gunsbridge South Young Conservatives?" said the boy. Then he thrust a hand forward. "Jonathan Forsyth of the University Conservative Association. Pleased to meet you, old chap! Sir Edgar Powers contacted me," he then continued, Craig allowing his new friend to help him with his luggage. "He told me to look out for a bright young man with blond hair who would add sheen to any student union debate."

Craig was quite taken aback, both by Sir Edgar's kind forethought and the compliment that accompanied it. Meanwhile, they continued on towards the modern redbrick buildings that formed the campus, walking through the arches into the main piazza.

"I think you'll find we're quite an active bunch," Jonathan insisted. "We're pretty effective in making sure that the lefties don't have things all their own way. Mind you, it's not just the socialists. There's the CND people, the radical feminists, the anarcho-syndicalists – you name them, they all hate us with a passion. But we don't care. We know what we believe in and we're confident that we have a prime minister who is going to stand up to such people."

Jonathan gave Craig a brief summary of the campus geography before leading him to his dormitory on the second floor of one of the blocks sited on a hillside overlooking the main administrative and teaching centre. Opening the door, he threw Craig's bags inside. Craig, meanwhile, was animated in an instant by the tremendous view the room offered across the sweeping Sussex countryside.

"Yes, all the first-year students seem to wind up in this block. The 'admin' people probably think the view will prove inspirational," Jonathan noted, gathering his breath.

"I can see I'm going to like it here," Craig enthused, still transfixed by the panorama that was so unlike anything he'd ever seen from his own bedroom window.

With that, Jonathan closed the door and left Craig to unpack. The 'new boy' was still captivated by the views however, and couldn't help feeling that he'd 'arrived', as it were. From here whole new vistas would spread out before him just as surely as the magnificent rustic scenes that filled the window were so different from the assembly of rooftops and garages that he had observed at home. Dreams and reality seemed to walk hand in hand, and he pondered all the opportunities that the experience of university would open up for him. '*Map out a rough route... Don't lose sight of the prize...*" his brother's words kept coming back to him.

****

Menace hung thick in the air. On one side of the road stood a massed crowd of chanting and banner-waving demonstrators; on the other, a solid phalanx of police. Trouble seemed likely to break out at any moment. Police officers on huge imposing horses patrolled the no-man's-land in between.

Craig stared out of the window at the gathering conflict. He was always appalled that the freedom of people to express their views should be threatened by this sort of intimidation. He watched the chief police officer enter the no-man's-land and fire off a volley of garbled instructions through his megaphone. The crowd responded with jeers and catcalls, and the officer withdrew back into the blue line to consult again with colleagues.

"Don't let it get to you, old chap," said Jonathan, coming over to see what all the fuss was about. "I've known them mount worse demos than this, especially when we invited Sir Keith Joseph to come and speak. Come and sit down; you're making the place look untidy."

Craig returned to the front of the hall to where some of the lads were running a final test on the acoustics. A young girl was meanwhile ensuring that the table on the stage had a jug of water and a cluster of glasses to hand.

"Stewart, have you issued a pamphlet on each of the chairs yet?" yelled Jonathan anxiously to an innocent-looking fellow in a blue blazer, who looked at the bare chairs and could offer only a blank expression in return. "Well, we'd better do it now. He'll be here in any minute!"

"It should be good tonight," Craig reassured him as he took a wad of leaflets from Jonathan. He followed his friend up the aisles, laying one on each chair.

"I'll say. This guy is supposed to be close to the PM. Indeed, he's rumoured to be in line for the Cabinet before too long," Jonathan replied in between licking his fingers to make separating the leaflets easier.

"I just hope he gets past Rent-a-Mob," his trailing colleague worried aloud.

"Look! He's arrived!" shouted another boy, poking his head around the door.

"Quick! Let's get everything ready!" Jonathan snapped, everybody rushing to battle stations.

Outside a sleek silver Jaguar sped up on the tail of its police escort. Pandemonium broke out as the demonstrators surged forward and the police line raced in to contain them. Flour bombs impacted on the uniforms of some of the officers, who slowly pushed the mob back onto the far pavement.

"MAGGIE-MAGGIE-MAGGIE.... OUT-OUT-OUT.... MAGGIE-MAGGIE-MAGGIE.... OUT-OUT-OUT...."

"MAGGIE!" the ringleader cried.

"OUT!" came the chorus.

"MAGGIE!"

"OUT!"

"MAGGIE-MAGGIE-MAGGIE!"

"OUT-OUT-OUT!"

Slowly a clearing was established and the chief police officer waved the VIP through and into the hall to a rapturous reception from the assembled audience, though not without some booing and hissing from elements at the back of the hall. The debonair young guest waved back to his supporters as he was led to the stage and took his seat, along with Jonathan to his right and Craig to his left. The hall fell quiet, permitting Jonathan to introduce the guest.

"Thank you, my friends. I know that, like me, you have come here tonight because the reputation of our guest has advanced ahead of him."

"Yeah, reputation for crucifying the working classes!" interjected a heckler from the back, who Jonathan pretended not to hear.

"...A reputation for speaking the truth and applying an uncommon foresight in analysing just what this country needs to do in order to reverse its decline. Oliver Lyons first entered Parliament last year as the member for Manchester South West. As a writer and a journalist before that, he came to prominence early on as one of the prophets of free-market economics and, as he put it, 'lifting the state from off the backs of the people'. Never one to mince his words, I'm sure tonight we'll all go away very much enlightened by what we will hear. Ladies and gentlemen, may I present to you Oliver Lyons MP."

Oliver Lyons stood up, thanked the chairman, straightening his jacket, and then waited for his audience to be still. Meanwhile, photographers manoeuvred rapidly beneath him, their flashbulbs momentarily drenching his elegant and imposing presence.

"Thank you, Mr Chairman," he commenced, pausing to position his notes on the small lectern in front of him. "As we sit here tonight in this illustrious university, I think we all know deep down in our hearts that our nation has reached one of those critical turning points in its long and glorious history..."

He continued to build on his dramatic opening and outlined all those areas of national life where Britain had fallen behind, his audience listening intently. Occasionally a heckler would dispute a fact or yell out an expletive, only to be castigated by the MP's supporters. Meanwhile, the object of the hecklers' insults continued to expound his shopping list of ideas, banging the table to emphasise his rhetoric, excoriating previous administrations that had lacked the courage to tackle the nation's woes. The audience cheered and applauded enthusiastically. Pausing, he then entered into a tirade against his opponents, reminding them that, "Even as I speak, the Labour Party is drifting irrecoverably to the left. In has come the hard, uncompromising ideology of Tony Benn and the Militants. This is the *real* face of Labour!"

The audience cheered again, drowning out the contrariness of the hecklers. Returning to the point, the speaker continued his speech before closing on a rallying note to the faithful, the audience rising almost to a man to offer him a long standing ovation. As he sat down, Jonathan remained standing to remind the audience that there was a limited time for questions before their guest had to dash off to another engagement. At this point, an attractive young girl in a long dress and bright-coloured scarf stood to her feet and confronted him.

"Mr Lyons, you conveniently forgot to mention that implementing your 'vision' is leading us back to the mass unemployment and poverty of the 1930s," she barked at him indignantly, her deep, mellisonant voice straining and her delicate fingers splayed backwards as she tried to emphasise her point. Craig recognised her as Alannah James, a fellow first-year in his economics class; a very bright and articulate student from a wealthy, middle-class background.

Oliver composed his thoughts and replied, "You are right in intimating that we cannot reverse the socialist legacy without some pain. But we have known for many years now that things just could not carry on in the manner we have been accustomed to. I'm pleased that the Prime Minister has signalled her determination to grasp the nettle now in order that real prosperity will be created later on. And, my dear, I think she deserves our full and wholehearted support for that stand!"

After pouring all his fire into the reply, he sat down, leaving his supporters to cheer once more and the hecklers to defiantly dismiss him with abuse. Alannah seemed clearly less than satisfied with his answer, but pursued the matter no further. After a few more questions Jonathan pronounced the meeting closed, and the hall slowly emptied, leaving behind just a handful of Tory activists to congratulate the MP on his peroration. Craig introduced himself, clasping Oliver's bronzed hand firmly.

"You were superb. That's the message they need to hear," he enthused.

"Thank you," said Oliver with a smile, looking this dashing young student in the eye inquisitively. Meanwhile, Jonathan interrupted, informing the MP that Craig was one of the more electrifying orators in the student union debates, of whom the world would no doubt be hearing more in years to come.

"That's good," said Oliver, observing Craig's obvious embarrassment. "I trust we'll meet again some day." he bade him before his impatient police escort moved in and motioned him towards the door and the sound of the mob baying with fury outside.

"You will," hinted Jonathan as he disappeared out of the room. He winked at Craig, "...You will."

****

As the door opened, it allowed the lively sounds of the little village pub to escape, the crowded student dive vibrating to the sound of laughter and debate. Craig and some friends emerged and walked back together towards the sprawling campus. Spring was in the air and the nights were getting warmer.

"So Martin thinks it's time to try a little *reflation*, does he?" roared Jonathan, employing his usual sarcasm.

"I just think Maggie's taking it all too far," quipped Martin, trying to defend his solitary stance. He was a tall, gangling lad, whose acute acne had forced upon him a certain reticence, though he now felt sufficiently roused to take issue with some of his friends' radical remarks. He waved his huge hands about furiously as he tried to make himself heard above the derision of his peers.

"I just think we've kicked a hornet's nest," he continued, trying a metaphor instead. "Unemployment is soaring away. And by screwing down the money supply and cutting back on public expenditure in the middle of a recession I think we're in danger of having a revolution on our hands. And we're absolutely massacring our country's industrial base!" he insisted, resigned to being in a minority of one.

Otherwise, the lads reverted to plotting their nascent political careers. They had each talked on diverse occasions about their desire to step onto the ladder of power. Jonathan, as always, exuded confidence. He was mapping out the perfect route through a safe constituency and into Parliament, through the Cabinet, and into Number 10. However, the others knew that politics was a 'greasy pole', and so hedged all their sentiments about with plenty of 'ifs' and 'buts'. Craig, too, accepted that the path was likely to be littered with dashed hopes.

Entering the main piazza, Craig thought he could hear music drifting from a hall further down the campus. Wandering towards the sound, as they drew closer, the lads could at last peer through the windows at a group of students huddled together around an ensemble of guitars, their hands raised in adoration, their voices full of joyful emotion.

> *"Were the whole realm of nature mine that were an offering far too small,*
> *Love so amazing, so divine, demands my soul, my life, my all."*

"Sounds like the 'Holy Rollers' are having a knees-up!" groaned Jonathan contemptuously. He broke into a few off-key verses of their hymn, delighting the others with his condescending tomfoolery.

Craig said nothing. Instead, he trained his eyes on the gathering and suddenly picked out a face he recognised. Yes, it was Nikki; smiles and tears mixed together as she sang along to these gentle melodies, her arms raised and her eyes closed as lifted her head heavenwards as if in adoration of someone or something.

"Groovy, eh, Craig?" said Jonathan, now waltzing around the piazza with a mock partner. "Be careful, Craig. They're a right nutty bunch, that lot!"

"Yes, not thinking of joining them, are you?" suggested another boy. "You're better off sticking with us Tories!"

"No. It's just that I know that girl." Craig meanwhile explained, continuing to watch Nikki singing with her whole heart, sheer joy appearing to radiate from her face.

> *"All to Jesus, I surrender...."*

****

Craig found the lecture such a drag. He couldn't concentrate at all. He chewed his pen, stared out of the window, doodled on his folder or just watched Alannah James busily scribbling down notes. Occasionally, she would look up and smile back at him politely. Nice girl, he thought: attractive, intelligent. Shame she was a 'Red'! The lecturer was meanwhile debating Keynes' theories of full employment, a debate that Craig would normally have waded into fearlessly with his forthright views; indeed, Alannah was doing just that. Today though, something was dominating Craig's thoughts to such an extent that, for once, his heart seemed elsewhere other than politics. As the lecture finished and students filed out of the room, he gathered up his books and struggled to point himself in the direction of the door, holding it open as Alannah passed through and thanked him.

Taking his lunch in the refectory, Craig found himself lazily scooping at his food with his fork, mixing it together to try to make it look more appetising than it actually was. He took his time and lingered on each mouthful, daydreaming away.

Then suddenly, as he had secretly hoped, she walked in, wearing a pleasant patterned summer dress with just a light, homely cardigan hanging loosely over her shoulders. The sun caught her as she passed by the window. She noticed Craig upon sweeping past his table on her way to the servery.

"Hiya!" she said with that innocent voice which always seemed to melt him. "Can I join you?"

Craig rose rapidly to pull out a seat. Indeed, the celerity of his reflexes momentarily surprised her, leaving her gaping down at the waiting chair.

"Oh. You are a gentleman. Thank you," Nikki exclaimed as she sat down, laying her books to one side.

"What can I get you?" he enquired, self-conscious about appearing nervous in front of her. All his coolness seemed to disappear, for it felt as if he was learning the art of courtship all over again – and it showed!

"Oh, nothing much. I'll have a yoghurt and a fruit juice, please. I'm a great believer in light lunches," she joked, dipping into her bag for her purse.

"No. This one is on me!" Craig insisted, and darted off to the servery. He returned moments later with the desired order, which looked decidedly Spartan beside the clutter of plates, dishes and other goodies littered about his own tray. Nikki thanked him and daintily peeled back the foil from the top of the carton. Craig watched her savour the first delicate spoonful.

"I didn't know you were... er... a Christian," he said, struggling to make his observation land as gently as possible.

She flashed her big brown eyes and drew the spoon back from her mouth. "How did you find out?"

"I saw you the other night having a sing-song... er... I mean... er..."

"You mean our weekly praise and worship service."

"Er...yes, one of them," he stuttered.

She smiled, coyly taking another mouthful. "Yes, I suppose it does seem like that if you've never been to one before. It's really about letting God know what you feel about him. I've known about Jesus since I was knee-high, but then there came a point in my life when I suddenly realised that I loved Him too... for myself, I mean."

Craig looked at her totally mystified, maybe recalling his colleagues' admonitions about these people being 'nutters'. An academic brew of politics, philosophy, comparative religion and sociology had certainly never prepared him to handle a statement quite like that. As such, he felt clumsy as he spoke.

"My parents took me to church occasionally too... well, sort of. My parents never really talked about it much, you see. But you seem so... caught up in it."

"I suppose I am. But when you love someone, you want to let it show," she noted, almost seductively.

"Quite!" said Craig. Nikki smiled, sensing that he had clearly run out of things to say.

"I hear you're one of the leading Young Conservatives on the campus," she commented. "You see, word spreads around here. You've spoken out about the demonstrators. It would appear that most of them hate you. But then the demonstrators don't always like us either, mainly because the Christian Fellowship has spoken out against abortion. So we both seem to have ended up in the same boat, so to speak."

"Indeed. I don't agree with abortion either... er, if you know what I mean," He looked her up and down as she rested her soft, cherry lips on the edge of the plastic cup, sipping silently. "I suppose you don't sleep around either... I mean..."

She withdrew the cup and tried not to laugh at Craig's awkwardness and embarrassment. "No, we don't sleep around," she assured him graciously. "It doesn't mean we don't often feel the desire to. But it's not the way. And besides, it creates more problems than it solves: one man, one woman, together – for life. That's the way God intended it to be."

"I guess I agree," said Craig, who, though he approved of such a noble sentiment intellectually, at that moment felt desperately guilty as her lustfully observed her sit back in her chair so that the full beauty of her sculptured breasts could be made out through the outline of her dress. In fact, his mind raced feverishly as she looked him in the eye. Was she drawing him on? Was she just marvelling playfully at this bumbling idiot who was drooling over her? Was she being irritated by his slowness in making his feelings known?

"Hi, Nikki, who's your friend?" enquired a voice.

They both looked up in surprise. Then Nikki's stared up fawningly at a well-built young man, who bent down, kissed her tenderly on the lips and pressed her shoulders lovingly.

"This is Craig. He's a first-year in history and economics," she said, watching Craig's 'bubble' visibly pop before his very eyes. Then she continued, "Craig, this is Steve, my boyfriend. He's doing his final year in law," Then she turned to this 'Steve' guy, saying, "Craig is that YC I told you about – the one who has put the backs up all those left-wingers with his speeches at the student union debate."

"Oh yes, you told me," said Steve, congratulating Craig and shaking his hand (evidently oblivious to the fact that this was also the same YC who had just come within an ace of chatting up his woman!). "I really admire Mrs Thatcher for her guts, although I think her economic policies are really messing up the country."

Craig grinned politely, trying to take umbrage at the sort of dumb statement he'd expect from an apolitical, sandal-wearing 'Jesus-freak'!

"You'll have to come along to one of our meetings", Nikki invited him, resting her sleek feminine arms around Steve's waist. "Then you'll understand all about the Christian faith."

"Anyway, Nikki," Steve continued, full of excitement, "I hope you haven't forgotten that Max from the Pentecostal Fellowship is over here today. He's giving the second part of his talk on Romans 8 if you want to come along."

"Sure!" she enthused, grabbing her things and finishing her fruit juice. "Thanks for the lunch. I'll see you around sometime," she called back to Craig.

Craig watched them disappear through the door. After another affectionate kiss, the couple strolled off, arm-in-arm, under the swaying blossoms of the trees in the piazza, Nikki's hair trailing up in the gentle April breeze. Who's Max? What's a Pentecostal Fellowship? And who or what is Romans 8? Craig thought to himself as he turned around and stared at the messy remains of his lunch. He pushed the tray away, propping up his chin with his arm. Then he bashed his fist down hard against the formica table, the sound of the plates jumping with the shock causing heads to turn on some of the neighbouring tables. Love, like politics it seemed, evidently had doors that shut as well as opened.

****

The summer of 1980 saw the popularity of the Mrs Thatcher's new government begin to nose-dive, with unemployment climbing to reach the giddy two million mark. All across the land, factories were closing and dole queues lengthened as the gentle breeze of monetary restraint combined with an overvalued pound and a world recession to send a veritable tornado ripping through British industry. New music from bands like Joy Division, UB40 and the Specials came into its own as youth desperately tried to express the frustration and alienation of a life without hope on the dole. At Westminster, eager critics called in desperation for the Government to execute a discreet 'U-turn'. Countering them, a girl called TINA

("There Is No Alternative") became the darling of the young Turks in the Conservative Party to whom Mrs Thatcher increasingly turned.

All this should have united the Labour Party in a single-minded endeavour to present itself as the alternative to what even one of the Prime Minister's own backbenchers satirised as "a dose of 'A' level economics". Instead, Her Majesty's loyal opposition chose to fall apart. In May, Labour's Wembley Conference met and approved an infamous commitment to further wholesale nationalisations. At that same conference, David Owen – Labour's promising former foreign secretary – was savaged by delegates for voicing support for the British nuclear deterrent.

In November of the previous year, the moderate Labour statesman Roy Jenkins had spoken prophetically of the need for a realignment of British politics back towards the radical centre. David Owen had been dismissive at the time, as indeed had his colleague and fellow Labour ex-minister, Shirley Williams. Now with the left attacking with a vengeance, Owen and his like-minded friends began to ponder Jenkins' words anew.

****

"Thank you, Mr President. In proposing this motion, I think the time has come to evaluate precisely what quality of learning the system of state education in this country has bequeathed to our children."

On such a sententious note did Jonathan Forsyth rise to address his peers on the motion put before the Debating Society by the University Conservative Association, namely: "that this Society considers the enforced closure of good grammar schools to have been seriously detrimental to education in Britain."

Craig sat next to him, watching this superb orator in full flow: witty, urbane, inevitably sarcastic, but always erudite. Over on the far side of the hall, he noticed their opponents honing their tactics for a rebuttal of Jonathan's claims. At their head was Alannah James; hair like silk and a body that would turn any man's eye. She reread and amended her notes, occasionally looking up to offer Craig a mischievous smile, for he was doing likewise. Despite her politics, Craig liked Alannah. She was refreshingly different to so many of her comrades in that she still possessed the human touch. It was unusual for her not to greet Craig whenever they passed each other by on the campus (unlike her other sour-faced socialist colleagues). More to the point, she certainly knew her stuff, and spoke eloquently and movingly in those deep, haunting tones that had become her trademark during these debates. As she swung into action, Craig couldn't help wishing that his fellows possessed such a shrewd, cerebral and charming member on their own side.

Of course, the debate was irrelevant in so far as comprehensive education was now a *fait-accompli*. It was all good fun though, and Craig felt the adrenalin pumping as his turn arrived to demolish Alannah's arguments, more so when he spotted Nikki sitting up in the gallery absorbing the power and thrust of his oratory and watching intently as the debate progressed. If words of passionate deliberation could melt a girl's heart, then Nikki's must have dissolved by now! If only, he thought. Indeed, he found himself increasingly and exclusively addressing both Nikki in the gallery and Alannah across the table: two women who had caught his eye during his first year. As he launched into his final condemnations, he had that funny feeling come over him that both of them might yet be playing very influential roles in his life, though he was unsure exactly how.

"Mr President, to conclude on a lighter note, I must say that I always find it one of life's more amusing paradoxes that some of the most vigorous advocates of the levelling of all our schools into one homogenous system are often the very people who have benefited most from selective education; one thinks of people like Tony Benn or Shirley Williams, for instance. Perhaps this esteemed body will bear that in mind when offering credence to the arguments so cogently advanced by my opponent, the former alumni of one of the country's most elite girls' schools!" Craig concluded, glancing cheekily at Alannah.

Grasping the significance of Craig's little pun, a ripple of amusement hummed amongst the students, though it soon turned into loud, thunderous merriment when eventually Alannah riposted across the table to him, "Mr President, someone who has achieved great things in the comprehensive system should not decry its role in fitting him to be one of the more inspired debaters of this illustrious university. I refer, of course, to the former alumni of Lower Henley Secondary School!"

Craig could not better such a deflating rejoinder. Meanwhile, up in the gallery, he noticed Nikki amidst the riotous commotion, observing that she, too, couldn't resist a chuckle or two. He looked back across the table at Alannah.

"*Touché*, Miss James," he whispered graciously, "*touché*!"

****

It had certainly been a turbulent party conference. The 'wets' and the 'dries' had faced each other all week at Brighton across a chasm of mistrust and disdain. Some delegates had expressed unease at the hard line being pursued by the Prime Minister (as did certain ministers). However, there was one young man who would have none of this. In an act of supreme self-will, he requested permission to speak. To his great surprise, it was granted. Walking nervously up to the rostrum from the back of the conference centre, he anxiously glanced at his hastily scribbled notes, cleared his throat, and poured out his heart to the largest audience he had so far addressed: stop listening to the faint-hearts; stick to our policies; defend our convictions. That was the powerful message of this defiant delegate from Gunsbridge South.

Craig's speech was in earnest, and brought the Conference to its feet as he strutted back to his seat. The Prime Minister applauded him too, whispering to an adjacent colleague some words that those in the hall took to be nothing but complimentary to the fiery young man with the blond hair.

In her keynote speech at the end of the week, Mrs Thatcher rounded on her critics, saying, "This Government is pursuing the only policy which gives any hope of bringing our people back to real and lasting employment. We shall not be diverted from this course. For those waiting with baited breath for that favourite media catchphrase – the U-turn – I have only one thing to say: you turn if you want to. The Lady's NOT for turning!"

3 *GHOST TOWN*

As the sun sank slowly over the horizon, aimless smoke drifted from the huge cooling towers of the Sizemere power station. Brad stretched the baggy sweat shirt over his head and looked out from his fourteenth-storey bedroom across the factories and warehouses that littered the northern vistas of Gunsbridge, now silhouetted against what was left of the fading sun. This was a grimy, unsung town, so typical of many that had grown from nowhere to prosperity on the back of an industrial revolution that had turned the West Midlands into the workshop of the world. All kinds of factories nestled across the bleak, grey landscape; but mostly the large engineering companies that provided such basic manufactures as machine tools, castings and automotive components – the staple products of any proud industrial nation. Criss-crossing it all were networks of railways, motorways and canals to transport them to markets that once spanned the globe, but were now contracting mercilessly as the bleak winter of recession set in without quarter.

Brad heard his mother getting ready in her bedroom down the hall. The cheerful songs that she once hummed were no more. Now it was just the painful silence of one who had lost all hope of finding meaning to a dreary and unexciting life. Her job had been a useful source of income and gossip that helped her to feel a part of the world in which she existed. Now that was no more. She had been the first of several batches of redundancies from another ailing company, which in the end had made no difference: within months the order books had evaporated and the company had gone into liquidation – yet another established name from the Gunsbridge Chamber of Commerce disappearing into history. The town's unemployment rate accordingly rose a percentage point or two.

"You off out?" she called, hearing her son making his way down the hall. "Party business?" she guessed aloud.

"Sure," he replied, grooming himself in the mirror. "I'll be back about eleven."

She crossed the hall into the bathroom, her bathrobe knotted tight around her waist and her curlers set in place. Brad gave her a tender kiss on the cheek and shut the door behind him. Descending in the lift, he caught the familiar odour of male urine. Then he marched out across the windswept no-man's-land of The Scotts Estate.

It had always been a rough estate – a dumping ground for 'problem' families. Over the last year or so, things had grown worse; to the poverty and deprivation was now added an incipient despair as the number of households with a jobless head had overtaken the number in work. The crime and graffiti had more menace to it now. The police seldom patrolled in less than pairs, even during the day. To be sure, The Scotts Labour Club was an equally sad looking building. Built in the early sixties, at the same time as the rest of the estate, it had not been immune to the vandalism and neglect that pervaded the area. On the steps that led up to it a group of lads sat about smoking. They fell silent and looked up as Brad approached, warily moving aside to let him pass.

He entered the lounge and propped himself up against the bar. The bar tender was busy checking the pumps, his beefy arms revealing the story of his life by way of a gallery of tattoos that chronicled girls he had known and ships on which he had served. Meanwhile, over in one corner, an old man stood watching his companion sizing up a challenging shot on the pool table, chalking his own cue and supping from his emptying glass. In another corner a television mounted high on the wall beamed out pictures of Russian helicopters strafing Afghan villages. Then everyone's attention turned to observe the arrival of Sharif Khan, his bushy black moustache twitching as he looked around for a familiar face. Seeing Brad, the well-built Asian flashed his eyebrows knowingly.

Brad had been in the Labour Party just over a year now and felt confident that he had gained sufficient knowledge of the procedures and complexities of the local party to be able to hold his own in debates. Meetings were never very well attended; but amongst those who did – especially those who, like Brad, felt they were living in desperate times – there had developed a kind of conspiratorial fanaticism; from this small 'cave of Adullam' (and indeed others like it up and down the land) a mighty blow was about to be struck to place the party once and for all on a footing for war with their class enemies. They were only a few in number but, like Brad, they were determined that the compromises of the past would not be repeated. It was time to purge the party of its time-servers, technocrats and anti-socialist elements. Brad agreed that the party leadership had badly betrayed the cause. Along with Sharif Khan, who had taught Brad the in-and-outs of the local management committee, they had now almost captured control of both the ward and of Gunsbridge South constituency. It had often been an unsavoury task. Yet Khan had warned him that, in this world, one was often required to be a little devious if one wanted to achieve ones goals. Somehow such words seemed to accord with Brad's own philosophy in life.

Gradually others arrived, and the small group headed upstairs into a stuffy little committee room, taking their seats beneath a stark strip light that hummed monotonously. Meanwhile, a flattering portrait of Jim Callaghan hung slightly unevenly on the main wall, the only dash of colour in a room of flaking grey paint. Rod Turner, the chairman, tapped the ashtray on the table, declaring the meeting open. Gradually, as he spoke, the room began to fill up with cigarette smoke as delegates eyed each other up warily.

"Right, comrades," he said, turning over his agenda, "can I take it that you approve the minutes of the previous meeting?"

He looked to the assembled activists as they muttered in agreement. His wiry grey hair and his weathered physiognomy, as well as his oil-stained fingers, all attested that he was a working man and proud of it. To be chairman of his constituency management committee was perhaps the supreme accolade of almost half a century spent organising local Labour and trades union activity in the Borough.

Brad doodled on his notes while the secretary reported on the social events in hand. Fund-raising wasn't his scene, however much he recognised that no political activity could be successfully undertaken without money. Whilst the secretary was listing the events, he stared around the room at those present, trying to ascertain what thoughts might be passing through their heads as they smoked, supped, scribbled or shuffled on their seats. He turned first of all to Khan; deep in thought as he stared down at his papers. Brad liked Khan. He was rough-and-ready, and – despite his thick Kashmiri ascent – very articulate. He had taught Brad what books to read, which articles to study, and had ensured Brad's own socialist convictions were thereby seasoned with a healthy dose of his own.

Next to Khan was Gary Bennett. Hair dishevelled, eyes sparkling with malicious intent, he was fidgeting with his biro, anxious to get to the meaty part of the business. Brad admired his keen intellect, although there was something unreal about him. He possessed very little sense of humour; and even less tolerance for those who happened to disagree with him. Unmarried and unemployed, he was also unimpeded by any commitments that could act as a brake on his ruthless pursuit of political power. Brad didn't dislike him, but he did distrust him; as indeed he did the secretary, Frances Graham – a not unattractive woman, despite the fact that she too never smiled!

Brad had a soft spot for the chairman. Though Rod Turner was of the 'old school' of Labour activists, Brad considered him honest and fair; and that his heart was undoubtedly with the interests of the working people of his home town. Brad also knew that, precisely because he was dismissive of all this far-left nonsense, his days were numbered. Eyes that watched him from around the table also itched to thrust daggers into his back: for Rod Turner, almost alone, had stood his ground against persistent sniping by the others that he was too reactionary and insufficiently zealous to the cause he had spent a lifetime serving.

Finally, Brad's gaze rested on one of Rod Turner's few consistent supporters. Though Jennifer Allan and Rod Turner disliked each other personally (a feud dating back into the mists of time, and to which Brad had yet to satisfactorily discover the precise origin), she also detested all these johnny-come-latelies. Brad disagreed with her politics, but knew she had a solid reputation as a first-class ward councillor and council committee chairwoman; not assets to be discarded lightly – least of all by her electors.

At last, the chairman cleared all the trivia out of the way and glanced down ominously at the agenda. "Now we come to the question of mandatory reselection, which will be raised at the conference next week. I propose that the mandate from this constituency is that we oppose it because I don't..."

Before Turner could finish, several angry voices interrupted and made the rest of his sentence inaudible. Amongst the scramble of voices, Gary Bennett thrust himself forward and presented his case.

"That is out of order, Chair," he screeched. "You have no right to presume that this is the view of the rank and file of this party. I recommend a resolution, namely that this committee strongly endorse the mandatory reselection of all parliamentary members as a step towards improving the accountability of the party's representatives." Several delegates clapped and cheered as he added for good measure, "I also say, let's put that resolution to the vote."

Brad nodded his agreement, although, with the Chairman waving his hands in a vain attempt to restore order, he wished the others would at least let him have his say and be done with.

"Listen... listen..." he watched Turner plead, "The local party must have confidence that a member will act as his conscience dictates. Remember, comrades, we are talking about fellow socialists here after all, who have..."

Again, these pleas were drowned in uproar as the comrades screamed abuse and banged the table.

"We've all heard that before..." yelled one.

"What about Healey's cuts!" suggested another.

"Stuff consciences!" grumbled Bennett, "What about the wishes of the rank and file!"

"Rank and file, lad!" gasped Turner, apoplectic with rage. "What do you know about the 'rank and file'? Forty years I've worked for this party. Don't tell me about the rank and file when you've been..."

Again Turner was silenced by the delegates, who roared abuse and stamped their feet, chanting for it to be put to the vote. The chairman banged his ashtray on the table. Calling for order and desperately searching across the smoke-filled room, he counted to see if it was worth the risk of putting it to the vote. He didn't look confident, his eyes darting from head to head. He had hoped that a nice pleasant evening would have tempted more members out to brave the abuse and the tedium, but he realised now that it had been a forlorn hope. The activists smelt blood and were baying all around him.

"You're behaving like children!" screeched Jennifer Allan from the back, momentarily silencing the pack. "How are we going to convince the voters when you behave this way..." she continued. Again, taunts and jeers greeted her counsel of moderation.

"What about socialist policies...? Put it to the vote... Join the Tories, where you belong...!" they cried.

"Alright, alright!" screamed Turner, tossing out a compromise. "We will instruct our delegates to..." though again his words were drowned out amidst screams of righteous indignation.

"I move a vote of no-confidence in the chairman," proposed Khan provocatively.

Turner went pale. As the applause grew more intense, he knew he had held back the tide as long as he could. Once more, they had plainly mustered more firepower than he had, and he reluctantly bowed to their demands.

"Okay, okay. We'll vote on the resolution," he sighed, the dwindling cigarette in his hand twitching nervously. "Those in favour, please show."

The secretary counted the hands as Turner gazed about to see who had the willpower to defy his tormentors. "Those against," he continued resignedly, noting how Jennifer Allan alone held her arm erect.

"The resolution is carried, seven votes to two."

The room erupted into loud cheers, though Turner tried not to show his dismay and attempted once more to call the meeting to order. For the remainder of the meeting he was reduced to a sad shell of a man.

Later, when the meeting broke up, the delegates filed downstairs into the bar. Brad, glad to breathe in some fresh air, swept back his hair and shook his head in relief. The internal feuds seemed to be becoming more vitriolic, more personal, and distinctly rowdier. Still, he took comfort in the fact that at least some positive decisions were being made on policies. Sharif Khan dropped his hand upon his shoulder.

"Not tiring of the 'Revolution'?" he joked, slapping Brad's shoulder fraternally. "You know, for years they've ignored us. Now they can't any longer. Our moment has arrived."

Brad strolled out across the car park and noticed Rod Turner fumbling with the keys for his grubby old Morris Marina. "Can't offer you a lift home, can I?" he offered, the door finally opening with a squeaking jerk.

"No. I'm okay. It's only across the way. Thanks all the same though. No hard feelings for my supporting that resolution, eh?" Brad smiled emolliently, "Only you know my feelings on the question of accountability."

"Yeh, sure," grunted Turner magnanimously. "That's politics. It's what it's all about, lad."

"I'm grateful to you for nominating me as Young Socialist delegate to the conference," Brad continued.

"No sweat! Listen, I'm impressed by you, son. You've got a keen mind, gallons of energy, and I think you can go a long way. Remember this, though," he cautioned. "There are a lot of our people who don't give a damn about resolutions on this, that and the other. All they care about is that the party remains true to them: to their hopes and fears. That's why I say: don't get mixed up with that rabble. They represent nobody but themselves. I believe you're smart enough to see that. It's the people that win you elections – and unless, God forbid, that lot ever gain power, that's the way it's gonna' stay. Have a good time in Blackpool, eh!"

He started up the engine with much clattering and smoke. Then the car sauntered noisily up the road with its nearside tail lamp flickering on and off. Brad tutted in amusement. Rod Turner was one of life's great survivors, with so much wisdom dwelling in such an unschooled man. Brad wondered how much longer he could cling onto office now the dam was finally cracking apart.

****

The 1980 Labour Party Conference in Blackpool was where all the pent-up frustrations of the years poured forth. The left was seeking to wrestle control away from the parliamentary party and the leadership, and hand it back to the grassroots membership. The *leitmotiv* for this was the allegation of betrayal of socialist principals by successive Labour governments. All these charges came gushing forth from delegate after delegate in a public display of venom not witnessed since the turbulent conferences of the Gaitskell era. At one point, Jim Callaghan even despairingly cried, "for goodness sake, comrades, stop arguing!"

The star of the show – indeed its *prima donna* – was undoubtedly the irrepressible Antony Wedgwood Benn. Always a compelling orator, he now tore into the record of the Labour government of which he had been a member. To Conference cheers, Benn went on to outline his blueprint for a future Labour government, including common ownership across huge swathes of British industry – all to be implemented within days of a Labour government taking office.

The New Year brought further acrimony. Delegates gathered at the special Wembley Conference in January to finally thrash out a formula for the controversial task of electing the party leader. Jim Callaghan had since stood down; and, in a bitter contest, the expected favourite, the combative former chancellor-of-the-Exchequer, Denis Healey, was passed over in favour of veteran party rebel, Michael Foot – in whose lap the whole controversy now fell. After Wembley, the so-called 'Gang of Four' – David Owen, Bill Rodgers, Shirley Williams and Roy Jenkins – met at Owen's flat in Limehouse and declared that "the need for a realignment of British politics must now be faced." Indeed, the belief that the Labour Party had been lost irretrievably to the left came as a particularly bitter blow to Shirley Williams, who noted that "the party I loved and worked for no longer exists". In March, the 'Gang of Four' resigned their Labour whips, and the new Social Democratic Party was born.

****

Brad was late arriving in the stuffy committee room, the chairman having already commenced his opening remarks. He smiled apologetically and sat down on a spare seat next to Sharif Khan. The chairman continued his introduction.

"I think you all know why we're here, comrades. The task has fallen to us to choose a man or woman who will represent Gunsbridge South for the Labour Party at the next election; and who, we hope, will be one of many candidates returned to enable Labour to form the next government of this country."

Several members muttered agreement and the meeting settled down, Rod Turner referring them to their briefing notes, informing them that "The selection committee have now narrowed down the short-list to just two candidates. First of all, I will call Mr Derek Hooper."

"Now for some real talking!" grunted Khan, who glanced around the room eagerly. Brad, too, sensed excitement rippling through the room.

Brad took the opportunity to look around at the composition of the meeting. Despite the best endeavours of Turner to rally his supporters together, from quick mental arithmetic it appeared that Bennett had again mustered greater numbers, including some people that Brad had not seen before, but who, from their assortment of provocative lapel badges and dour expressions, he imagined were of Bennett's persuasion. All this was probably with the connivance of the secretary, who always used her office in a very partisan manner.

As they discussed this between them, Derek Hooper entered the room. Though not of great stature, he had that aura of impatience with human frailty about him that Brad could have imagined of Savonarola or Robespierre. Attired in a tweed jacket with a small, tightly knotted red tie, he strolled up to the front and sat down. Brad did not know Hooper that well, except that he was one of the councillors for Tower Park ward in Gunsbridge North constituency. However, his reputation had gone on ahead of him: he was already well known for his fiery left-wing views and for his covert activities with something they called the 'Militant Tendency'. Indeed, his extreme views not only provided rich propaganda for the Conservatives of Gunsbridge, but also rallied the left in the town, who warmed to his caustic rhetoric. Invited to address them by a less-than-enthusiastic chairman, he soon worked himself into form, his words resonating sharply round his slightly protruding front teeth. He would occasionally glance accusingly at Jennifer Allan, sitting a few rows back from the front, who glared back at him equally defiantly. Several members cheered, though the chairman just looked away nonchalantly. Then Turner started to drop not-so-subtle hints that he was outstaying his welcome. Hooper therefore wound up on a rallying call to defy the Government by all possible means. Then he sat down, pleased that many of the assembled members were applauding rowdily. The Chairman meanwhile invited questions from the floor. Bennett and Graham asked him supportive questions on his commitment to what they nebulously called 'grassroots sensitivities', Hooper seldom responding with anything other than a prolix reply.

"I'll allow one final question to Councillor Hooper," Turner informed them all, mindful of the advancing time. Several hands went up, including that of Jennifer Allan. Turner acknowledged her. He knew that Hooper was anathema to everything she believed in, so he awaited her question with great interest.

"Councillor, if you had to choose between accepting the democratic system and pursuing your socialist vision, which one would you forsake?"

"Your question is highly hypothetical, Councillor," insisted Hooper, going on to prevaricate at length until Jennifer Allan politely requested that he give a direct answer.

"Alright!" he conceded, for being succinct required great discipline of him, "I believe that the working class has suffered an appalling setback with the election of Thatcher. She has heralded in the most right-wing government this century, one that is dedicated to smashing all the hard-won victories of the Labour movement. I make no secret that I believe that, if the working classes of this country are to survive these acts of social vandalism, then they cannot deny themselves any avenue of attacking the Tories, discrediting their schemes through political strikes, mass demonstrations and other extra-parliamentary activities. We must not let them triumph."

His clarion call brought a noisy ovation from Bennett, Khan and others. The Chairman brought the meeting back to order and the steward led Hooper away, the interviewee raising his fist in salute as he was applauded all the way to the door.

The second candidate was Councillor Joe McAllister, the Deputy Leader of Gunsbridge Council, and ward councillor for Sizemere – again in Gunsbridge North. From the moment he entered the room, Brad picked up on a feeling of coldness descending upon the meeting. McAllister stormed in bearing his notes, leering superciliously and impatiently at the assembly through his heavy-rimmed spectacles. He neither smiled when the chairman introduced him, nor laughed at Turner's amateurish attempts at humour. Finally, he was called upon to speak.

"Well, of course my friends," he boomed sententiously. "You see before you tonight a man who has spent nearly thirty years serving this town, five of them as deputy leader of your council. So I probably qualify uniquely to speak on behalf of the people of this borough..."

The membership switched off mentally once McAllister began cranking up his tedious monologue, boasting of his record of civic achievement: an old folks' home opened here; a fire station opened there. Brad yawned and leaned over to observe Khan, whose eyes were also glazing over. His friend had told him of the time that McAllister had personally intervened to prevent Khan from standing as a candidate in a council ward. Brad had heard from other sources too, how McAllister had used his position to get rid of both party workers and council officers whom disliked. Mean, vindictive and masterfully devious, he ran his own ward like a personal fiefdom, despite sporadic guerrilla warfare from the small, but determined left-wing opposition in Sizemere.

"Rumour has it that the Leader of the Council has pulled strings all over the place in order to get McAllister on the short-list, if only to get him off his own back," intimated Khan.

"What about Turner? He hates McAllister's guts!"

"Forget Turner. He's been told to shut up and do his job if he wants to keep his seat on the top table."

The chairman eyed up Brad and Khan discussing the long string of enemies that McAllister had accumulated in the party. Brad, sensing Turner's irritation, broke off such tittering and tried to look attentive as McAllister continued droning on at length. When, at last, the unsmiling hopeful sat down, he answered several questions from appreciative older members, who knew the name even if they had never met the man. Even so, he still managed to belittle one little old lady with an answer that showed a superciliousness bordering on rudeness. If that was how he treated his supporters, how would he deal with his enemies? Brad raised his hand, eager to find out.

"Councillor, will you be voting for Tony Benn in the deputy leadership election this autumn?" he asked him.

"No, son," McAllister snapped condescendingly, "I will *not* be voting for Tony Benn! And I'll tell you why I won't be voting for him. He is devious, arrogant..."

"That's rich coming from you!" yelled someone from the shadowy recesses at the back of the hall, to which a hail of guffaws flowed forth.

After McAllister had completed his verbose reply, the Chairman thanked him and drew the session to a close. Thereafter, Bennett and the others slow-handclapped McAllister as he headed for the door, Brad unable to resist joining in. As he did so, he noticed the departing councillor staring at him, McAllister perhaps making a mental note of Brad's face for future reference.

"Say, that's your cards marked," Khan teased him. "Anyway," he insisted, looking around the room as the ballot papers were being issued. "This is a beautiful situation. I do believe we have this one in the bag!"

Normally, Khan knew that a leading local councillor would be odds-on favourite in a seat like Gunsbridge South, which, though Conservative held, was easily winnable with a favourable swing and a good deal of hard work. Yet he could point out at least a dozen members who McAllister had, to his knowledge, made implacable foes of – either by his mendacious dealings or his acid tongue. Meanwhile, Brad glanced down at his own ballot paper, pondering it for a moment. Then he put a cross discreetly against Derek Hooper's name. He folded it up and handed it to one of the scrutineers just as the room began to buzz again with gossip and intrigue. Rod Turner stood up to loosen his tired joints and mopped his brow before lighting up another cigarette. He briefly conferred with the party official who was sitting to his right. Then the result was passed to him. He seemed to be straining to find his voice as he rose to announce that, of the eighty-two votes cast, Derek Hooper had received forty-two votes, and Joe McAllister forty.

All hell broke loose, with Bennett, Khan and the left rising to their feet to celebrate the triumph of their man. Amidst the pandemonium, Jennifer Allan stood up and fought to make herself heard above the din.

"This hardly represents a mandate from this party," she screeched. "I have been told of long-serving members who only received notice of this meeting yesterday. And who are all these people at the back who I've never seen before? What has the secretary got to say about that?"

"On yer' bike, granny! This is a democratic decision!" someone shouted. Frances Graham said nothing, but just beamed condescendingly at the councillor.

"The decision is therefore that Councillor Derek Hooper is adopted as the prospective parliamentary candidate for the Gunsbridge South constituency," said Turner. "...And God help us!" those close to him heard him mutter.

While the celebrations continued, Rod Turner stared down blankly at his creased agenda before ripping it up and stuffing it in his jacket pocket. Then, under his nose, he saw a note drop. He looked up slowly to observe Jennifer Allan bearing a truly mortifying expression of disgust on her face. She said nothing, content to just burn holes in him with her vexed, blue eyes. Then she turned and strode out the meeting just as a jubilant Derek Hooper was being led back in by his supporters. Turner unfolded the piece of paper, perhaps sensing just what was inside.

****

THE GUNSBRIDGE HERALD
Wednesday, June 3rd 1981
Evening Edition - Still only 10p

WE FIGHT TORIES OUTSIDE PARLIAMENT, SAYS CANDIDATE
In a keynote speech to the local trades council yesterday, Labour's new prospective parliamentary candidate for Gunsbridge South, local councillor Derek Hooper, called upon the gathering to defy the Government "on every front", including 'extra-parliamentary action'. With Labour's poll-standing having slumped from 46% in January to only 30% now, his comments will only cause Michael Foot even greater headaches as he seeks to rebut charges of left-wing infiltration into the party...
OWEN LAUNCHES LOCAL SDP
Dr David Owen was in town yesterday to address the inaugural meeting of Gunsbridge Social Democrats. Led by former Labour councillor, Jennifer Allan, the new branch has recruited over a hundred members so far, including two other Labour councillors who have defected in the past month...
MORE FACTORIES CLOSE
Another local employers, the Thomas & Clifton Steel Works, has called in the receiver after suffering a serious slump in orders. It is thought unlikely that the two thousand jobs at the plant can be saved...
SHERGAR BEATS 'EM ALL!
Top racehorse Shergar has won the Derby by a spectacular ten lengths, the greatest margin this century...

****

As soon as he wandered into the hall, Brad was pummelled by the booming music and the flashing lights of the weekly youth disco at The Scotts Labour Club. He used his elbow to open the door into the servery whilst precariously balancing several boxes of crisps and chocolate bars that he had just bought from the nearby cash-and-carry. Entering in, he placed them on the table and tried to regain his breath.

"No, Brad, I want the crisps over there!" said a diminutive young lady as she turned away from her pubescent customers to momentarily instruct Brad on precisely where she wanted each item stacked.

"Next time, Helen, you can do the carrying and I'll play barmaid," Brad gasped, re-sorting the boxes.

Helen Bone continued to hand out the lemonade to the kids queuing up with their fifty pence pieces and crumpled pound notes. Brad leant against the table and watched her perform this labour of love, for he'd often had his eye on her. Though not superficially of outstanding beauty, she was one of those girls who the more a boy studied her, the more her less obvious charms became visible. Her dark shoulder length hair shook about as she darted from one side of the servery to the other, pouring drinks. Brad admired her slightly oversize posterior, just able to make out her panty line through her flimsy trousers as she bent over. Very nice, he mused lustily.

Driven to distraction, he looked out instead at the wild, good-humoured fun of the kids bopping away to Spandau Ballet, Adam and the Ants or the Human League. Girls danced, and boys congregated in the shadows that swept along the walls, a few skinheads smoking covertly up the corner. Brad delighted in such youthful fun. The school-leavers of Gunsbridge didn't have much going for them: unemployment was still rising inexorably, and factories were either closing or laying off workers; and the sprawling comprehensive schools had ill-prepared these kids for a life in the tough and competitive technological era that was beckoning. Yet theirs was an uncomplicated life, for all its uncertainties. Brad, however, felt it incumbent upon him to concern himself with the weightier issues confronting these working class kids, for the fortunes of the party that sought to better them were sinking fast.

The advent of the Social Democrats had hit both main parties hard. The Conservatives were still struggling through the barrage of condemnation that had accompanied Sir Geoffrey Howe's bleak 1981 budget in March. Shortly after that, Brixton in South London had exploded in an orgy of violence, riots greeting a heavy-handed attempt by the police to clamp down on street crime. Labour had proved incredibly inept at exploiting the Government's predicament; nothing seemed able to halt the party's steady decline in the face of its own internal divisions. Many local party members quietly defected to the SDP, although Rod Turner had remained loyal, hoping that the ascendancy of the left would prove to be just a transient affair.

"A little help wouldn't go a miss, you know!" shouted Helen.

Brad turned around to see her on the verge of being overwhelmed by the outstretched hands of the dozens of youngsters waiting impatiently. He strolled back inside and started to help out, taking orders and trying to use his stature and imposing voice to restore a touch of decorum to the drinks queue.

The kids respected him immensely, despite the occasional cheekiness from some of the more witty extroverts. Brad was touched by their plight, and considered it worth the loss of a Tuesday night (and having to put up with Helen's frantic hectoring) just to see a little joy brought to their faces. Bennett and Khan had thought him crazy to sacrifice valuable time that could be spent on Militant's more ideologically pressing matters. To be sure, Brad had gone along to one or two of their meetings, where they had invited some obscure speaker to address them on the prospects for revolutionary consciousness amongst the Nicaraguan proletariat. He decided that serving *Vimto* at the Labour Club disco was distinctly less soporific! He was all for raising the consciousness of the working class, but considered that such tedious gatherings were beyond the endurance of most youngsters, and that by offering them more animated weekly activities he was probably doing more to make them feel that someone was interested in them and their problems than any number of Militant publications or speeches.

Brad didn't specifically proselytise; yet many of the youngsters knew who he was and what he believed in. One of the lads who had showed some interest in the Labour politics was Colin, a skinny, spotty teenager, who appeared to be something of a loner. With the evening now drawing to a close, Brad noticed him standing up the corner of the room – pensive and alone, staring at an attractive blonde girl who was in the process of racing out of the room in the arms of one of the more dashing lads. Brad knew from piecing together threads of conversations that Colin had had his eye on this girl for several weeks. Yet evidently the lank-haired, unassuming kid just wasn't her type. Brad could sense that the bottom had just dropped out of Colin's world.

The room started to empty during the few minutes it took for the DJ to sign off, so Brad strolled over to him as he leant idly against the wall, his long, baggy parka helping to disguise his gangling frame.

"Can't give you lift home, can I?" he said, jingling the keys to his new car. Colin nodded approvingly. Meanwhile, Helen had completed the last bit of tidying up and grabbed a box full of the things she wished to take home.

'Brad's new car' was a misnomer. The 'car's new owner' better described the relationship! Helen and Colin descended the steps to the car park and piled into the old black Mini. Starting the engine, its distinctive whine filled the still July evening.

"Any joy on the job front?" enquired Helen of their heartbroken passenger.

"Not really," the lad muttered laconically, the glow from the streetlights racing over his face. "I've got two interviews next week."

Brad and Helen wished him well, although Colin didn't exactly exude enthusiasm. Was it that he didn't care? Or was he just too shy and inarticulate to say he cared? Brad glanced at him now and then in the rear-view mirror and dearly loved to know the answer.

"Wonder what's going on here?" pondered Helen as she made out swirling blue lights up ahead.

As they drew up closer, they could see more clearly that police cars had drawn up on the car park of a run-down suburban shopping centre. Racing out of their vehicles, the officers charged after a group of about fifty youths who were in the process of looting the contents of several shop fronts that had been broken into. As the officers approached, some of the youths turned and ran; but others started throwing bottles, bricks and any other item of debris that could be fashioned into a suitable projectile. Temporarily halted by the volley of missiles, the officers dived for cover, some helping injured colleagues into the shelter of shop doorways.

"What the hell's going on?" declared Brad in amazement. "What is this country coming to?"

Just then, a fleet of large, heavily armoured police vans drew up. Out leapt police reinforcements in riot gear. Without pausing, they lunged towards the rioters, who dispersed in haste, the police grabbing the ringleaders. Several fights broke out, both sides seeming to cast off restraint. Brad braked sharply to avoid a bunch of youths, who ran in front of his Mini trying to escape arrest. The car squealed to a halt just a split second before ramming one particular robust and mean-looking kid. He banged furiously on the bonnet before continuing his getaway. Brad was momentarily dumbstruck by the expression of rage carved on the guy's face as they eyeballed each other fearfully. Then two or three police officers raced up in hot pursuit, frantically waving Brad's car out of the battlefield.

"It's getting more like the United States everyday!" declared Helen, clutching desperately at her chest.

"What do you expect with twenty-five percent unemployment in some parts of this town," Brad protested, checking in his mirrors to confirm that the danger had past. He noticed Colin staring out of the rear window, apparently unmoved by all the excitement. Perhaps he knew all along that this was just waiting to happen. Perhaps he even knew some of those involved in the looting. Meanwhile, in the distance Brad could just make out flames flickering from the scene of violence they had just left behind.

Dropping Helen off at her flat shortly afterward, Brad turned and headed back to the Scotts Estate, this time with Colin occupying the front seat, from where Brad lectured him, shaking his head with avuncular disgust that this was what three million unemployed was leading them to.

Colin said nothing at first, but then intimated that "They've talked about this for days. They're bored; they're frustrated. They just want some excitement."

"Funny concept of excitement: burning someone's shop down!" Brad opined.

"They don't care. They've got nothing to lose really, have they?"

After he had dropped Colin off, Brad turned the radio up. The big story on the eleven o'clock news was that the Toxteth superb of Liverpool was now burning fiercely. For the first time ever, a British police force was employing tear-gas to break up rioting. Other reporters from around the country were phoning in their stories of incidents breaking out in Manchester, Birmingham, and in other large cities. It seemed like the entire nation was being plundered by angry teenagers.

"...And a late item just in," the radio crackled, *"is that Sir Edgar Powers, Conservative member of parliament for Gunsbridge South has collapsed after leaving the Carlton Club this evening. News is still patchy, but it's believed that Sir Edgar, who is sixty-one, suffered a heart attack, and has been taken to a West London hospital. We'll keep you posted on that story as further reports come in..."*

Shame, Sir Edgar was such a pleasant chap, Brad recalled – even if he was a Tory! Then he thought no more of it and looked forward instead to climbing into bed at the end of a truly bizarre evening. He sought comfort from the late-night music show during his journey home, though he could find none...

"Why must the youth fight against themselves...?
Government leaving the youth on the shelf...
No jobs to be found in this country...
Can't go on no more – people getting angry!
This town's 'comin' like a ghost town!"

4 BREAKING THE MOULD

Craig was lying on his bed and sucking his pen when he thought he heard a distant noise drifting in through his open bedroom window. Thinking nothing more of it, he continued scribbling away, the sunlight filtering in and casting a long beam across him. Then he heard it again. Leaping up, he craned out of the window to observe two cars pull up in Snowdon Avenue. Out of them emerged a dozen well-attired young men and women wearing large, conspicuous red-white-and-blue rosettes. The suspicions Craig harboured about their politics proved correct when a car with a tannoy speaker attached to its roof suddenly came into view. Plastered with posters and balloons, it cruised leisurely around the bend and into the tree-lined avenue.

"GOOD AFTERNOON, LADIES AND GENTLEMEN. THIS IS JENNIFER ALLAN, YOUR LOCAL CANDIDATE FOR THE SOCIAL DEMOCRATIC PARTY, SEEKING YOUR SUPPORT ON POLLING DAY IN THE GUNSBRIDGE SOUTH BY-ELECTION. THE TORIES ARE DESTROYING THE COUNTRY, AND LABOUR IS DESTROYING ITSELF. NOW IS YOUR OPPORTUNITY TO VOTE FOR A BRAND NEW START. VOTE FOR MODERATION. VOTE SOCIAL DEMOCRAT..."

Craig was unimpressed. He was even less impressed when he saw a motorcade of journalists and television reporters following the SDP cavalcade. As the canvassers spread out and started knocking on doors, the television crews moved in to film those bewildered housewives who opened those doors to suddenly find themselves caught up in a news item. Craig noticed his mother peep from behind the downstairs curtains to see what all the fuss was about. She watched a telegenic young woman in a business suit stroll up the drive and make for the front door. Craig leaned back inside, unsure whether to race his mother to the door.

"Mrs Anderson?" enquired the canvasser, smiling at Pat as she dried her hands on her apron. "I'm calling on behalf of Jennifer Allan, your Social Democrat candidate in the forthcoming by-election. I just wondered if we could look forward to your support," the girl beamed.

"Well, we normally vote Conservative – that is, my son and I...."

"Lots of people are telling us that they used to vote Conservative, but now they're switching to us in great numbers," the girl continued in her refined and dulcet tone, evidently assuming Pat would be doing the same.

"But Mrs Thatcher is..." Pat insisted, trying to protest that she had not entirely abandoned the faith. Craig listened in horror through the open window, regretting that he had not sprinted down the stairs fast enough.

"Yes, we know," the girl continued, intercepting Pat's sentence, "you think she is going too far this time. That's why we believe it is essential that you vote for a moderate centre party. Oh, by the way, how does your husband intend to vote?"

"Why don't you ask him?" said Pat, drawing her attention to an Austin Princess just pulling onto the drive. Meanwhile, Len Anderson had just lumbered out of the car when a news team scurried up the drive. Pointing at Len, the presenter beckoned his cameraman to film the encounter, the soundman duly bringing up the rear and thrusting a huge, fluff-covered boom at him.

"Excuse me, sir," shouted the canvasser across the bonnet of the car, "I'm from the Social Democrats. Will you be joining your wife and son in voting for Jennifer Allan next week?"

"Jennifer who?" grunted Craig's father, looking alternately at his wife, the presenter, his cameraman and soundman, the bonny young canvasser and (palpably fuming behind the upstairs curtain) his son – all waiting for some earth-shattering revelation.

"Will I hell as like! I don't vote for anyone. You're all as bad as each other. We only ever see you at election times. And, hoy! You!" he bellowed at the cameraman, "Get off me' bedding plants!"

The girl beat a subtle retreat, thanking Mr and Mrs Anderson for their time. Thereafter, the camera team hurriedly followed after her whilst once again Jennifer Allan's car swept up the street broadcasting her message of change.

****

Brad cast his eyes around to see if all members of his team were present. Then the troops dispersed to knock doors along the steep, winding hill. Brad started off up the road and headed towards some grim-looking maisonettes further up towards the crown of the hill, thrusting a wad of garish red leaflets into Colin's hand. He was heartened that Colin had of his own volition come forward to offer his services to the campaign, and smiled while the taciturn young lad gazed down at Hooper's portrait on the front before turning one over to study one of the candidate's less provocative messages on the back. Then he rammed the wad into one of the long, cavernous pockets in his parka, causing the coat to sag on one side.

Morecambe Road was one of the older council estates in the town, and consisted of mostly red brick houses; some with well-kept gardens, others with pieces of rotting cars scattered on overgrown lawns. Every now and then, old men in string vests could be seen perched on home-made garden gates castigating the children playing in the street on their battered bikes and skateboards. Meanwhile, housewives scurried about in slippers and curlers. Most houses were identified by the numbers daubed on the front with paint that had been left over from decorating the bedroom. A few, however, had gone upmarket, with fancy mahogany doors and ornate plaques bearing pretentious-sounding names like *Tralee, Chez Nous* or *Koinonia*. Arriving at the top of the long hill, Brad and Colin climbed the steps of the maisonettes and commenced canvassing.

"Excuse me, Missus'," said Colin, addressing the housewife in the mini-skirt and tight-fitting top who peered round the door of the first house. "We'm calling from the Labour Party. Will you be voting for us next week?"

"The Labour Party? Yeh, of course. We always vote for the Labour mon', doh' we, Ken," she said, turning fawningly to a big, hairy hunk of a man, who wandered down the hall with odd snippets of toilet tissue blotting up the mishaps that had occurred whilst shaving. He looked Colin up and down before grunting his laconic reply.

"Yeh... we do... always... for the Labour mon'."

The dishy bird smiled and eased the door shut. Meanwhile, Brad rattled another letterbox a few times and leant back on the railing of the veranda, admiring the view out over towards the town centre. After no obvious signs of response, he rattled it again.

"Awright', awright'... Ah' bay' deaf, yow' know!" protested a voice from down the hallway. Not an auspicious start, thought Brad. Then he waited while a collection of bolts and chains were unlocked and the door swung slowly open.

"Yes, whatcha' want?" muttered a little old man with no teeth, who stared Brad in the face impatiently. "... 'n before yow' start, Ah' bay' interested in buyin' no bleedin' '*Watchtower*' magazines!"

"No, I'm not selling anything," Brad insisted, trying to sound professional. "I'm calling on behalf of Derek Hooper, who's your local Labour candidate in next week's by-election. I'm calling to see if we can rely on your support, or if you need any help to get to the polling station."

"Need any 'elp!" he grunted dismissively. "Coach and hosses' bay' gunna' stop me from gettin' down there!"

"Oh yes, you'll be voting for us then?"

"Votin' for 'im! Yow' must be bleedin' jokin'. I wouldn't vote for that pigeon-brained pillock if yow' paid me! Ar've been Labour all mah' life, but it cracks me up t' see dick'eads like 'im runnin' the party. On yer' bike, son, I'll be voting SDP – mek' no mistake about it!"

The little old man slammed the door shut and muttered some profanity as he headed back down the hallway. Brad stood there, totally stunned, before shaking his head and ticking his register accordingly. Then he tried another door further down the corridor.

"It breaks my heart, young man," warbled the woman who peered around the door. "I always used to vote Labour. But now? I'm sorry – it's all gone too far for me; all these council grants to gays and lesbians? And what about banning our nuclear weapons?"

"These are just malicious stories spread by the *Sun* and the *Daily Mail*," said Brad, a trifle disingenuously. Even so, she looked unconvinced. The door slowly started to inch shut, and Brad detected that she would not be voting his way.

All six team members finally met up at the chip shop at the bottom of Morecambe Road. Helen reappeared bearing bags of greasy, steaming chips, and they all sat down on the wall outside to rest their aching feet and wounded prides.

"Much success?" asked Brad of his colleagues as he delved inside a bag to pick out some morsels.

"I'd say pretty disastrous," interjected Helen, her mouth filled with chips. "There's an anti-Thatcher vote out there, but I'm not sure we're receiving it."

Just then, they saw a car turn into the estate, the blue-white-and-red balloons blowing about merrily... *"VOTE FOR JENNIFER ALLAN. LABOUR IS FINISHED. THEY CAN'T WIN. VOTE FOR THE SOCIAL DEMOCRATS..."*

The team dissolved into paroxysms of rage, everyone yelling out 'traitor, traitor', whilst Colin gave the car a conspicuous two-fingered sign as it cruised past. Jennifer Allan and her helpers in the back just waved confidently as they passed by. People in the houses opposite peered round their curtains to see what all the commotion was. Tomorrow, perhaps the opinion polls might buck up. Perhaps.

****

Craig opened the gates and cast his eyes up at the loving devotion that had gone into cultivating the verdant lawn and surrounding flowerbeds. He was sure he would find a favourable response here. And so, the gravel crunching and shifting beneath his feet, he marched up to the front door, past the Mercedes basking proudly on the drive, the fading sun showing off the best of its sleek, metallic lines. Then he gave the ornamental knocker a hearty wrap and waited for a reply. Down the hall, he could see a plump male figure through the frosted glass heading his way. Then the door inched open and a dapper little man in a smart designer sweater folded his arms and focussed his gaze on Craig's prominent blue rosette, puffing away on his pipe as he did so.

"Can I help you, my good man?" he enquired briskly.

"I'm calling on behalf of Simon Zygowski, your Conservative candidate in the coming by-election. I wondered if we could look forward to your support."

"Let's see. If I said I had the *Guardian* delivered each morning, what would that tell you?" he quizzed Craig.

"I guess it would tell me that you were a person who held views to the centre-left of British politics."

"Got it in one, old chap," he said, tapping Craig's shoulder patronisingly, "got it in one. Now piss off!"

And with that, he returned inside and closed the door, leaving his seething interrogator to wander back down the drive, though as Craig brushed past the Mercedes he couldn't help wondering how such opulence would have fared had Michael Foot been prime minister!

****

The Town Hall was filled with expectation as folks started to arrive and stake out for themselves what looked like the best seats from where to observe the proceedings. The hall soon began to fill up with people all gaily bedecked with different coloured rosettes who had come to count the votes in the Gunsbridge South by-election.

"Is this seat free?" Craig heard someone enquire. He looked up to observe a young, fair-haired girl in corduroy trousers and an expensive woollen jersey beaming down at him hopefully. He quickly spied out her red-white-and-blue rosette that said simply *BREAKING THE MOULD – GUNSBRIDGE SOUTH 1981*.

"Be my guest," he replied obligingly, shuffling himself along to make room.

So this is the kind of person who votes SDP, he thought to himself; although he felt strangely at ease sitting next to such a charming young lady, whose easy banter and chirpy feminine mannerisms appealed beyond his political prejudices to his eye for a pretty woman. Meanwhile, Craig also observed an old acquaintance across the room that he had not seen in a long time, interested to spy out the bright red rosette that he bore pinned to his black leather jacket. Yes, that was Brad alright, he mused, perhaps not so surprising after all. For Brad's part, it also strangely came as no surprise to see his old school friend sitting opposite: after all, hadn't he seen his face on television during last year's Tory party conference! He acknowledged Craig warily before heading back to where the counting girls were sorting the first boxes to arrive.

Once they had arrived, everyone tried to see if a trend was emerging from the faces of the ballot papers. There were plenty of Labour votes, although there was a conspicuous SDP presence too. Brad noted down the figures on his returns sheet and showed them to Derek Hooper, who had wandered over to watch the process that he was confident would soon sweep him into Parliament. The Labour candidate folded his arms smugly and chatted away to his supporters about arrangements for the celebration party they intended to hold back at their headquarters.

Attention, meanwhile, was switching to some of the other candidates now walking in. Simon Zygowski strolled in, accompanied by his agent, his mannerism hinting that he was not wholly confidence of success. Smart, youthful and relaxed, he greeted his party workers and toured some of the other tables to shake hands with the counting staff. Jennifer Allan also toured the tables expectantly, aware that she was being consciously shunned by the Labour supporters whispering behind her back as she strolled past them. And engaging in that quintessentially British pastime, other 'fringe' candidates had paid their deposits in order to seize a fleeting chance of being a media star. Indeed, Screamin' Lord Sutch (of Monster Raving Loony Party fame) was there, looking out for the odd vote that might perchance have passed his way.

"I see you're a Tory," remarked the girl who had sat next to Craig, observing his rosette. "I'm with the SDP myself, as you've probably guessed. Well, tell a lie – I'm a member of the Liberal Party really. But, well… you know: sometimes it pays to team up with like-minded people. I'm Jane Allsop, by the way," she then enlightened him, finally offering Craig the long, slim hand of friendship, which he tentatively shook. "Anyway, what's a good-looking guy like you doing hanging round with the Tories?" she scoffed playfully, although Craig wasn't entirely sure whether to feel feeling flattered or patronised by her back-handed compliment.

For what seemed like hours, the counters delved into the wads of votes, segregating them by candidate. Brad looked at his watch. It was coming up to midnight and still Hooper's victory was not quite in reach. Hooper himself was fidgeting anxiously with one of his many lapel badges as he watched the SDP vote trailing not far behind. Simon Zygowski was also on edge, and paced along the long tables filled with papers. His vote seemed unable to break through decisively. Finally, shortly after the town clock had struck one o'clock, the returning officer gathered the agents together once more. Then, clearing his throat, he mounted the stage and read out the result.

"...Being the returning officer for the constituency of Gunsbridge South announce the result of the by-election for the said constituency is as follows: Allan – Jennifer Rosemary (Social Democratic Party), 27,011 votes."

A huge cry rippled through the hall as Jennifer Allan's supporters gave her a rousing cheer and danced up and down. Several Labour supporters booed and heckled. They were not expecting an SDP vote of that magnitude.

"Hooper – Derek Manston (Labour Party), 20,903 votes."

Derek Hooper's supporters roared in righteous indignation at the returning officer, who begged for calm. The police moved in discreetly behind some of Hooper's more crazed hotheads, who were plainly in the mood to thump someone.

"It's that old bag. She's a traitor!" screamed one.

"Yeh, she's a traitor... We'll remember this, sister!" retorted another.

"Zygowski – Simon John (Conservative Party), 20,322 votes..."

"She's in! She's in! She's done it!" screamed Jane Allsop to her friends, who joined her leaping into the air and dancing.

Craig didn't feel much like singing or dancing. He smiled across at his party's candidate, dejection and pain etched all over his face. The only consolation was that the Labour supporters were also jumping up and down – only with fury instead!

"I knew that Hooper bloke would be our undoing," Helen charged as they drifted out onto the Town Hall car park. Brad unlocked the passenger door of his Mini to let her in.

He paused before confessing that "He's certainly gave the opposition plenty of rope with which to hang him."

After such a drubbing, conversation remained distinctly muted between the two disappointed party workers. Periodically Brad felt disillusioned with politics (usually when Labour were doing badly in the polls), and he felt an attack coming on as he drove Helen home. Finally, the little black car pulled up outside Helen's apartment block.

"Off home?" she enquired coyly.

Brad smiled. Where's else would he be going at just coming up to one o'clock on a wet, autumn morning?

"Fancy coming in for a while?" she continued.

Brad contemplated how this most loyal of fellow comrades was suddenly offering him the perfect antidote for his melancholy. He leaned over and kissed her tenderly on the lips.

"Why not," he then replied. Then he pulled his keys slowly out of the ignition.

****

The SDP-Liberal tide showed no signs of receding: twenty-three MPs who had stood as Labour candidates in 1979 finished the year taking the SDP whip in the House of Commons. In October, the Conservatives lost Croydon to the Liberals in another by-election. In November, Shirley Williams brought the SDP triumph in the Crosby by-election. The *Times* reported that Mrs Thatcher was now the most unpopular prime minister since records had begun. And so sure were their supporters of the inevitability of their cause that David Steel, the leader of the Liberal Party – the SDP's electoral allies – felt confident enough to tell his party conference to go back to their constituencies and prepare for government. The bandwagon seemed unstoppable.

Meanwhile, a world removed from all this, a bunch of Argentine scrap metalworkers had hoisted their country's flag over an abandoned whaling station on an obscure little island called South Georgia, eight thousand miles away. While Conservative MPs mulled over their bleak prospects for re-election, a Royal Navy vessel was quietly despatched from the Falklands Islands to investigate.

5 *REJOICE, REJOICE*

Craig wandered into Lower Henley Conservative Club to find everyone in the small cosy lounge room glued to a television set that was mounted over the bar. Even Eddie, the barman, looked up whilst pulling pints. The reason was not hard to discern: the nation had awoke to find a tiny piece of itself called the Falkland Islands under foreign occupation, soldiers of Her Majesty's armed forces being disarmed on the lawn in front of Government House while their Argentine captors looked on. A strange new flag fluttered in the stiff South Atlantic breeze, and a new conqueror now held these windswept, sparsely populated islands in an act of aggression that was as brazen and insulting to the regulars gazing up at the television set as it was unexpected.

"Bastards!" grunted one, almost crying in his beer, "the complete and utter bastards!"

"They can't be allowed to get away with this," mumbled another.

"Never mind, folks, we've got work to do; an election to win," they were reminded by Elizabeth Gainsborough, an elegant, well-spoken lady, who was chairwoman of the local party in Lower Henley. Therefore they all took their seats over in a secluded alcove. Then Elizabeth, a woman every inch as steely and determined as the prime minister whose taste in fashion she followed, crossed her legs, opened the folder she had brought with her, and started to hand around copies of the minutes of the previous meeting. Craig took a copy and passed the others along, observing his colleagues in the Lower Henley party as he did so.

Tony Clare puffed on his cigarette and bit his nails as he ran through his copy. As chairman of Gunsbridge South's YC branch, Craig had had a good deal to do with this chain-smoking kid with the greased-back hair, although he couldn't say he'd found the experience edifying. He held views that were so right-wing that he was in danger of becoming *plus royaliste que la Reine:* even Mrs Thatcher would smart at the prospect of privatising the police, Craig thought as he watched him load another cigarette into his mouth.

Gerry Roberts, by contrast, had become one of Craig's closest political friends. Oozing self-confidence, he was one of those dashing young men for whom the advent of Margaret Thatcher had proved a heaven-sent opportunity to put his spirit of enterprise to good use. Ever resourceful, the thirty-year old businessman had proved to be an asset without equal to the local party.

Of the others gathered around, Lucy Lambert was a cute, little soul. Short, septuagenarian and rather doddery, she studied her minutes through the bifocals chained around her neck, drawing the document in closer to pick up on the some of the finer points. Completely apolitical in any intellectual sense, Craig liked her for her immense practicality with some of the more humble chores of political life in the ward, such as stuffing envelopes with election literature, making tea and typing memos. Meanwhile, Joan Knight was the Trojan horse for the local residents' association, where her ultimate loyalties probably lay. However, she was a useful source of gossip and intelligence to the local party about how feelings were running on her estate. She read her minutes with aquiline precision, just in case she had been misquoted. Next to her sat the Taylors, a husband and wife duo. Joe was an easygoing car salesman; his wife, Jean (who definitely wore the trousers!), had an irritating tendency to fire off equine guffaws at the least provocation (like one of Tony Clare's unfunny jokes for instance).

The last character Craig's eyes alighted on was George Franklin, one of Lower Henley's three local councillors (the others being the superlative Elizabeth Gainsborough and a Labour chap whose name was only ever mentioned in contempt). George was one of those irrepressible characters whose verbal diarrhoea was only made tolerable by his totally inoffensive disposition. Hopelessly at sea as far as matters of High Tory doctrine, he nevertheless kept the confidence of his party because of his impressive reputation as a practical, people-orientated councillor. If you wanted your street light fixed or a sheltered flat for your elderly parents, George was the man to see.

"Right, ladies and gentlemen, can I take the minutes as read?" insisted Elizabeth, opening the meeting. Nobody disagreed, so she moved on.

"Right. As you know, George Franklin is up for re-election this time, and I believe we must all give him our best efforts in order to see him re-elected."

The committee concurred, George chortling his appreciation as the chairwoman continued running through all those items that even so needed squaring up: posters, leaflets, canvassing, and so on. Each of these tasks was then delegated out to whomever she deemed appropriate for the job. With such concise direction, Craig ('volunteered' – as usual – for several of these tasks) could see that nothing was going to stand in the way of any campaign organised by Elizabeth Gainsborough.

****

"Just rejoice at that news and congratulate our forces and the Marines!" snapped the Prime Minister impatiently to the reporters scrambling over each other. As a battery of further anxious questions came at her about the stunning recapture of South Georgia, she waved her hands dismissively, *"Rejoice...rejoice..."*

"Four of the usual beverages for my good friends and me; plus whatever you're drinking, Eddie," cried Gerry as he burst in through the doors of Lower Henley Conservative Club fresh from an evening 'on the doorsteps'. Eddie, distracted from the televised footage of the 'Blessed Margaret', lined up some glasses in readiness.

"Tonight we know we're onto a winner," Craig assured him eagerly, following in behind.

"Too right. The Prime Minister is less and less 'that old cow' and more and more the greatest Englishwoman since Boadicea," claimed Elizabeth, daring to infer that a bovine metaphor could ever have been warranted to describe her beloved leader.

"I'll be blowed!" staggered George Franklin, bringing up the rear. "It's amazing what rounding up a few Argies can do for your electoral prospects. That reminds me, did I ever tell you about the time in North Africa when Monty bought me a beer?"

Eyes darkened as George started to answer his own question. The others sensed another lengthy yarn coming their way, and knew from experience that their jocular candidate had a legendary ability to talk the hind legs off a donkey, especially if conversation revolved around his years in the Western Desert. And now someone had inadvertently started him off again!

"Yes, I'm sure you have; but I dare say Craig hasn't heard it," interjected Gerry, motioning towards the washroom. "Call of nature!" he explained.

"Now you mention it, I think I need one too!" added Craig, hastily charging after his colleague. Instead, George turned to Elizabeth and proceeded to recount at length his pivotal role in Rommel's defeat.

"'Monty bought me a drink in Cairo'. I ask you!" Gerry marvelled once safely out of earshot. Then he changed the subject, noting, "I hope all the slogging of the last two years is behind us now. It certainly feels like we've turned a corner. Hey, I say," he then turned to Craig, changing it yet again, "you know that we've still got to sort out a new candidate for this constituency – probably later this summer. I thought your name ought to be on the shortlist."

Craig was taken aback: being Member of Parliament for Gunsbridge South had been his waking dream throughout his days at university. But it was a tall order to secure the nomination, especially as Craig was but a mere lad of twenty-one.

"I'm too young!" he gasped. "Besides, I'd need to cultivate the 'Maywood Heath Mafia' first," he continued flippantly, referring to the local constituency big-wigs who held all the main offices in the Association, and who nearly all hailed incestuously from the most wealthy and powerful of the Gunsbridge South wards.

"You've a lot more admirers than you think. And they don't all begin and end in Lower Henley," Gerry assured him. He cupped his hands, lit up another cigar and held the door for Craig. "Think about it!" Gerry demanded of him as he wandered past, Craig unsure whether he was being entirely serious.

****

Elections are seldom other than wearisome affairs, and Craig had found the afternoon's canvassing run particularly tiring. Stomping up the stairs as he returned home, he noticed someone milling about in the spare bedroom. Entering his room and crashing out on his bed, he thought nothing more of it. Then he thought again. Could it be? He bounced back up off the bed and peered out behind his bedroom door.

"Steve!" he exclaimed, beholding his brother crossing the landing. "What brings you home from Germany?"

"I only arrived here just after lunch. You must have just missed me. How is the Young Tory, anyway?" his brother teased him playfully. He then started jabbing at Craig in order to stimulate some fight out of him. Craig enjoyed the rough-and-tumble and gave a spirited defence, retreating gradually before Stephen outsmarted him and placed a half-Nelson around his neck, forcing him to the floor.

"What's going on up there?" yelled their mother up the stairs.

"Nothing, Mum," replied Stephen innocently, "Just teaching Craig how to show respect for an officer!"

There was time to exchange sibling gossip before their father returned from work and the family assembled around the dining table. Pat served up the meal before finally sitting herself down to partake of it with the others.

"So when did you find out you'd be caught up in this Falklands thing, son?" enquired his father.

"Yes, you mean this is it?" said Craig with a tingle of excitement.

"Nobody's said anything: where, when or how. But I can't think where else we'd be going. After all, any attempt to recapture the islands will need air support."

"I just wish they'd settle it. I can't really believe they want to fight over a few ridiculous lumps of rock," said Pat, shaking her head.

"Let's hope so," Len concurred. "Either way, I'm sure the RAF won't let the side down," he gleamed with pride in his elder son. Craig couldn't help wondering if ever his father would gleam with pride at the sight of his other son one day rising at the Despatch Box. Perhaps not, he thought, and carried on dissecting his pork steak.

Afterwards, the family relaxed in front of the television. Craig was chuffed to see the news carrying a feature on the political situation in Gunsbridge, where a possible change of control of the Council in next week's local elections was the source of media interest. Shortly afterwards, tapping his brother's shoulder discreetly, Stephen suggested they go for a drink. Craig agreed, and so they drove out to one of their old haunts in Amblehurst.

"This place has changed," muttered Stephen as he gazed about at the happy crowds chatting above the sonorous melodies of ABC and Simple Minds. "It was all spit-and-sawdust when I last set foot in this place; none of these video jukeboxes."

"Ah well, that's progress," Craig reassured him. Indeed, the youthful frivolity of the Friday night crowd was almost infectious, everyone flushed with their week's money. How incongruous, Craig thought, that lads of similar ages and backgrounds were at that very moment heaving about in force nine gales at the other end of the Earth, waiting for the order to lunge against minefields, machine guns and barbed wire.

Gradually the throng grew until conversation was impossible. Both brothers drank up and left, their seats promptly claimed by a group of young girls dressed up to kill. Skipping the nightlife, both brothers agreed instead to take a walk up on the hills that rose up gently to the west of the town. On a clear day, all of Gunsbridge could be viewed from here. Craig had brought his first girlfriend here, and suspected that every other young man in Gunsbridge had probably done the same in their time. Now though, only the whistling wind kept them company, along with a thousand and one tiny lights dotted along the horizon. An imposing albino moon glowed like a jewel over the town they knew so well.

"I don't know about you, but I think that wherever I go, I'll never find such a beautiful sight as this," said Stephen as he surveyed the man-made constellation. "The factories and offices: they all look so different from up here."

"It's our town," replied Craig. "We grew up here. Look, there's our old school over there," Craig pointed to the outline of a darkened building.

"Yeah," Stephen mused. "It seems like an eternity since I was there, kissing Jane Bissell behind the boiler room. Wonder what she's doing now," he smiled wistfully, bracing himself against the breeze that gusted across the exposed escarpment. "Anyway, how about you? Has Maggie not welcomed you into the Cabinet yet?"

"I'm still mapping out my route. Whatever, I want you to know that I appreciate you. I can honestly say that you've been the true inspiration in my life. You've always urged me on; you've never ridiculed my beliefs, or what I'm doing. Maybe one day it'll pay off."

"It will. Look at me: I've spent five years of my life learning how to be the best pilot I can. You do the same with your dreams. Give your heart and soul to what you believe to be right, and then you'll find an opportunity will arise that you are uniquely created for. Take it and never look back, no matter what people say. I seem to remember giving you a Latin lesson once upon a time."

"*Per Ardua Ad Astra*?" Craig reminded him.

Turning to his little brother, Stephen looked into his anxious eyes, "Here's another: *In Omnibus Princeps*; our squadron's motto: 'First In All Things'. Don't put yourself down. Always be the best in the things you need to do."

****

Just after four in the morning of May 1st 1982, a lone Vulcan bomber woke Port Stanley with bombs that rained down on the Argentine garrison to the east of the town. Hopes for peace were further torpedoed – literally and metaphorically – when the submarine *HMS Conqueror* sank the Argentine cruiser *General Belgrano* the following day. However, revenge was swift: on May 4th a single Exocet anti-ship missile fired from an Argentine navy jet gutted the destroyer *HMS Sheffield*. The real war had begun in earnest.

Three weeks later, British troops finally stormed ashore in San Carlos Bay. For the next few days, the fate of the entire operation depended on the skill and resolution of the British in beating off many stubborn attacks by enemy aircraft. Later that week, the key garrison of Goose Green was retaken after a ferocious battle. Time was fast running out for the beleaguered Argentine occupiers.

****

On June 15th 1982, something real, if intangible, appeared to have come over the British people. For the first time for so long, they had achieved something of which they could be singularly proud; something soul-stirring, something thoroughly unambiguous. '*BRITAIN IS ONCE MORE A NATION OF CONFIDENCE*', observed the *Daily Mail*. Thousands of miles away the previous day, thousands of bedraggled and demoralised Argentine troops had finally surrendered, along with the hopes and illusions of their countrymen. Their rout, and the victory of the British forces, had been stunning, spectacular and complete.

Out for a breath of the fresh air, Craig continued to gently pedal his faithful cycle along the familiar towpath of the deserted canal, sensing somehow that a watershed had been passed. Britain was back, proud and self-assured; and Mrs Thatcher herself seemed to personify this resurgence. The reality – unemployment, social tension and political friction – remained; but for most people in those first heady days of summer, the symbolism of renewal would matter more than the substance. And why not? thought Craig: it was very agreeable to witness the British propensity for self-denigration cast aside for once by pride in a job well done. Why, George Franklin had even held onto his Lower Henley seat – and the Conservatives had captured Gunsbridge Council to boot! The eerie tranquillity of the surroundings Craig now wandered through brought to mind this theme of renewal, and so he decided to cycle up to the vantage point of that old cast-iron footbridge and ponder it further, leaning back on his saddle and resting his hand on the parapet as he did.

The Thomas & Clifton Steel Works had once employed thousands of men and despatched its manufactures the length and breadth of the Empire. Now all was very still, the rusted corrugated cladding of its silent foundries hugging the silted-up canal and casting their long, distorted reflections across the becalmed olive green water. The furnaces were all extinguished now, the wharf abandoned to a flotilla of ducks that meandered in and out of the lush reed beds. Corroded cranes hung motionless overhead like haunting reminders of another age. Across the way, a solitary black-and-white cat gingerly stepped over the rusted rails and frayed sleepers of the overgrown wagon sidings, the sweet singing of the birds momentarily causing it to look over its shoulder before hurrying across the deserted marshalling yard.

Nothing could ever resurrect this once-proud foundry, one of Britain's many contributions to the industrial revolution. Yet however obtusely, maybe victory in the South Atlantic might just prove some sort of turning point in the long, slow decline of British prosperity, of the bleak industrial recession that had claimed so many illustrious names, even of the nation's perception of itself. Such a turning point had been a long time coming. Craig took one last look at this peaceful scene before departing, suddenly partial to the thought that, perhaps for himself and for the quaint little country that he loved so much, a long awaited new era might just be about to begin.

****

"Sit down, son," insisted his father abruptly. Yet Craig was intrigued when he noticed his mother locked in a vacant expression, sitting motionless on the settee. And he was startled by the sight of someone attired in air force blue sitting once more in his father's favourite armchair.

"I'm afraid it's bad news," the officer confirmed. "We have been informed that your brother has been listed as missing in action. He was on one of the final sorties over Port Stanley. We suspect his plane was damaged by heavy flak and that he crash-landed somewhere out at sea. Search and rescue units scoured the area all day but without success. With the weather closing in, the odds of finding anything were pretty remote."

There was a heart-rending silence that engulfed the room. Craig swallowed hard. His father bit his knuckles and said nothing. His mother tried to fight back intruding tears.

"I'm sorry," said the officer, painfully conscious of the invidious task he was performing. "It was a particular cruel tragedy. He had served valiantly on countless missions, frustrating the enemy defences. To be his squadron's only loss of the entire conflict, well..."

The officer grew ever more conscious of his intrusion into private grief. Len thanked him for his trouble and led him away while the family absorbed the loss of such a promising young member, stolen forever beneath the waves of a faraway ocean. As Len returned, Pat wept uncontrollably into his shoulders. Craig was in a daze, the weeping of his parents becoming mere background noises. A hole in his spirit was gaping open, nerve endings frayed, emotional power vaporising as it drained out of him. He stood up and drifted towards the door. For one brief moment though, his father's eyes locked onto his own. Len had lost his favourite son. Would he ever love Craig as he had Stephen? Could Craig ever take Stephen place? The remaining son disappeared up to his room, knowing that both he and his father wanted to say something profound to each other, but somehow just didn't know how.

For hours, Craig just stared at the ceiling. Occasionally, he would cast a glance over at the pullout map of the Falkland Islands hanging on his wall, souvenir from one of the jingoistic magazine articles that had followed the progress of the Task Force. What was once known only as a staging post for Antarctic explorers was now the graveyard of hundreds of young men cut off in their prime by the vagaries of geopolitics.

As darkness gathered outside, Pat put her head round the door. Seeing her son still awake, she slipped into room, drew the curtains and sat down on the bed beside him. Gently stroking the wavy hair of the man, she whispered to the boy inside. The little boy reached out and drew unto her, protective arms closing tight around the child. The infant began to weep, the mother feeling his every tear soaking into her. Crying without restraint, the baby ached for the comfort of his mother, who now responded with tears of her own. The man who would presume to all the power, glory and prestige of the highest office in the land now craved for the succour of her womb, fearful that he was truly on his own from now on.

****

"Take a seat. He'll be with you shortly," said the pretty young thing who had escorted Craig into the reception area. She glanced at him coyly before taking her own seat and resuming the typing of a long memo, pausing occasionally to answer the telephone. "Good afternoon, Bus Engineering Ltd..." she would chortle.

Craig would have dearly loved to watch this charming young lady at work, but guessed it would only embarrass her. Therefore rummaging through the collection of magazines on the low table in front of him, he flicked through the pages and found himself engrossed in an incisive story on the fighting in Lebanon, where the victorious Israelis were now at the very gates of Beirut. Or at least they were when that edition had been published. Since then, events in the Levant and elsewhere had moved on. Meanwhile, the intercom buzzed and the girl took the call, acknowledging it and gracefully making her way over to Craig.

"Mr MacDonald will see you now," she said. Craig set down the magazine and followed her through the mahogany door that led into an austere panelled office.

"Ah. Craig Anderson. I'm Frank MacDonald, pleased to meet you," enthused a stocky, middle-aged man, sporting a distinct, no-nonsense Yorkshire accent. "Sit yourself down, lad."

Craig had been overjoyed to graduate with distinction. Now he had begun the task of making use of the letters he could attach after his name. He fancied himself in political research, but slowly came round to the view that, whilst it would superbly complement his political ambitions, nonetheless it might make him too introspective. Besides, he wanted to see how the wider world of industry and commerce worked. Thus had he decided he'd try his hand at a career in marketing. After all, if you can successfully sell nuts, bolts and widgets, he thought, selling a political programme shouldn't be too hard!

So here he was inside one of the biggest names in bus and coach manufacture. Bus Engineering Ltd – or BEL for short, as the huge illuminated letters on its front offices reminded the world – was also one of the biggest local employers, situated as it was in a factory on the northern side of the town. The post of marketing executive sounded interesting.

"So that in a nutshell is your task," said MacDonald, leaning back in his chair as he rounded off his monologue. "I trust you'll enjoy working here. By the way, if you've got a few minutes, I'll show you round the plant."

"Why not," Craig concurred, sensing he was going to enjoy working for BEL.

MacDonald escorted him out of the office block and over the way into the factory. Upon entering, Craig (who had never set foot in a factory before) was amazed at the cacophony of sounds that echoed around the cavernous building. Welding guns flashed and machines chattered, stacker trucks raced round with warning buzzers tootling, and machine presses stamped away rhythmically. A 'ghetto-blaster' blared out Duran Duran above the noise as brawny workers whistled away and darted about the shop floor.

"This is where the body panels are stamped and welded into a framed vehicle," he said, pointing to the huge presses churning out side frames, underframes, roofs and other miscellaneous panels. Conveyors hoisted them along until further machines lined them up ready for welding robots to join them all together. As Craig scanned down the long assembly line, he gradually watched bits of steel come together as a body shell.

"This plant used to be appallingly inefficient, you know," said MacDonald speaking above the din. "Then this guy from America came over: Rex Schumacher. He took this factory and turned it upside down. It was painful: jobs were lost, management overhauled, capacity slashed. But he managed to improve the profitability of the group, and slowly we've been able to claw our way back from the brink."

Craig was impressed. He watched the finished bodies move down the line and into the paint bay. Here the bodies were electro-coated, primed and then spray-painted by operatives in lint-free overalls, all anonymously clad in masks and hoods like monastic mendicants. This was British industry in all its raw splendour, busy creating the nation's wealth.

"This building is where the final assembly takes place," noted MacDonald, leading Craig along the main production line. Craig stood in awe, surveying the long assembly tracks stretching off in the distance as far as the eye could see. The bodies moved inexorably down the line; first, the running units were married to them; then an army of production workers scrambled in and out, fitting interior panels, seats, glazing and electrical looms. On the outside, other workers bolted on wheels, lamps and other items.

"And this is the finished product!" MacDonald beamed proudly, inviting Craig aboard a completed poppy-red single-deck bus. "As you can see, our new total quality programme is really paying off," he noted gleefully. Then he inexplicably changed the subject. "I noticed on your CV that you're into politics," his new boss probed him

"Yes," Craig admitted. "I'm active in the local Conservative Party."

"Ah, Maggie's minions! Mind you, Mrs Thatcher has given us a hell of a ride over the last few years, but I think we're through the worst of it. It's helped knock us into shape. These workers..." he continued, pointing to the military precision with which they affixed parts to the vehicles, "In the past, when we wanted to change the production process or introduce new methods, it used to be a nightmare wooing the unions. Then, as I said, this Schumacher fellow came in and gave the workforce an ultimatum: either accept that things have got to change or this plant is finished, and your jobs with it. And they've done it! We've increased productivity, improved the quality, and now we're winning back customers who'd given us up for dead. We're confident that we've learned from our past mistakes. Schumacher has big plans to break into new export markets – and that's something that you'll be getting involved in."

Craig was impressed. And if, through his hard work, he could enrich himself and bring jobs and prosperity to his hometown, he would consider himself to have been amply rewarded. He took one final look down the endless miles of assembly line churning out vehicles. It was a challenge he felt he was now ready for.

****

"Ladies and gentlemen, the result is very clear," announced Geoffrey Earl, the association chairman. "Mr James Whitney is duly selected as our new prospective parliamentary candidate."

The victorious candidate was led in to claim his prize, the room tingling with goodwill towards their new champion, which he now skilfully exploited in order to set his campaign off on the right note. There was an enthusiastic applause. Indeed, James Whitney's whole personality was truly magnetic, and he seemed to charm everyone who crossed his path. His wife, Eleanor, had also won over the constituency with her ability to complement her husband perfectly. In addressing the party faithful, James masterfully dismissed the policies of the opposition parties, deriding their pretensions. All of which was plainly what the good Tories of Gunsbridge wanted to hear. Craig was encouraged too. As James descended from the stage and merged himself into his delighted supporters, he stole his hand as he passed his way.

"Great stuff!" he cried.

"Thank you. You're Craig, aren't you?" James recalled, placing the face. "I'm always on the look-out for energetic YCs. Any good at writing newsletters?"

"I did some writing for the Conservative magazines at university."

"Good. You can be the editor of my newsletter for this constituency. How does that take you?"

Before the prospective member could answer, James and his wife were hauled over to meet some members of the 'Maywood Heath Mafia', and Craig had found himself landed with a job.

"Never mind writing articles for someone else," said Gerry, who had overheard it all. "You should have been in his shoes now! This constituency belongs to the likes of someone like you," he charged, not wholly in jest.

"Maybe," Craig replied, shrugging his shoulders, "But obviously not this time."

6 *GLORIANA VICTRIX*

He lifted his weary head and tried to make out the fluorescent digits of the alarm clock: 5.50am. Outside all was dark and peaceful. He lay back on his pillow and contemplated snatching a touch more sleep. Then he sensed a string of gentle fingers slowly rising up the inside of his leg. He closed his eyes and savoured the sensation. Then, casting his head sideways, he brushed her hair back from over her burning, appetitive eyes and moved closer to her, her mouth receptive to his every salutation, waiting for him to be a part of her. Somnolence followed frenzy until at 6.45am the alarm on the bedside radio came on. Brad raked his hand through his long black hair and teetered over to the window. Pulling the curtains back, he looked out into the street at the cars and buses splashing through the slushy layer of snow that had fallen overnight. He switched on the light and returned for his trousers, his ear half cocked towards the radio.

"US and French troops in Beirut have today... more attacks by Shiite militias... talks involving the Syrians... Meanwhile, at home, the House of Lords have affirmed the findings of the Boundary Commission into the redistribution of parliamentary seats..."

Interesting, thought Brad, wrestling with his socks; it would mean that The Scotts ward would transfer from Gunsbridge South constituency to Gunsbridge North in order to take into account all the population shifts in the town since the boundaries had last been fixed. This would make Gunsbridge North even more solidly socialist; but it would also conversely make Gunsbridge South harder to win from the Tories.

"...The SDP member of Parliament for Gunsbridge South, Mrs Jennifer Allan, has announced that, following a debilitating stroke last month, she will not be seeking re-election for another term. A spokesman for the local SDP-Liberal Alliance said that a selection procedure to choose a new candidate would be undertaken shortly."

Brad was by this time trotting off to the bathroom. Returning, he noticed that Helen had shuffled around on the bed, still deep in sleep. The quilt had been discarded and her substantial posterior lay exposed. Brad couldn't resist smacking it firmly, the milk white flesh quivering as the slap broke her dreaming. Helen tried to ignore him, scratching about for the quilt to haul back over her and that her lover snatched from the bed. It was no use. She rolled over, sat up, and grabbed her nightie, still in another world. Eventually, she arrived at the bathroom on autopilot. By the time she had transformed herself, Brad was busy preparing breakfast, so she sat down to study the free offer on the cornflake box.

"I suppose you've read this crap!" Brad asked, flicking a piece of paper at her which he had discovered lying on the kitchen worktop.

"Yes. I found it in the letterbox last night. It's about that bloke that the Tories have chosen to fight this seat."

Brad carried on frying his bacon and gritting his teeth in contempt. "It's full of nonsense about what they have done to cut taxes, fight inflation, and save us from the Russians – the usual line."

"It's very professional though," Helen remarked, spooning in the cornflakes as she admired the illustrations.

"Hmmn. I dare say it's been written for him by some YC jerk fresh from college!" Brad snarled dismissively.

He sat down and ploughed through his fry-up, observing Helen between forkfuls. He had been living with her for nearly a year now and had found her witty and immensely practical, if often independent-minded and stubborn. He knew she felt strongly for him, and that the bonds were getting stronger each day. Five years older than him, she had given herself unreservedly to him – not least by sharing her homely little flat with him.

This, in turn, had prompted Brad to open himself up to her a little; for this young man – so bold and outspoken in his political convictions – nonetheless maintained his innermost feelings like cards close to his chest, only rarely allowing a glimpse of the real Brad that dwelt inside. As Helen glanced back across the table, she was all the time subconsciously searching out yet more intricate pieces of the jigsaw with which to piece together a more complete picture of this complex personality. However, she could see her lover was becoming uneasy at this subtle interrogation and so she quickly changed the subject.

"Do you think our new candidate has much of a chance?" she quizzed him.

Brad was non-committal, shrugging his shoulders ominously. Spurned in their first choice of Derek Hooper to fight the seat again, the Militants had successfully schemed with other malcontents in the party to manoeuvre the selection in favour of some obscure welfare rights advisor who hailed from the same 'bedsit polyocracy' that traditionalists like Rod Turner held in such utter contempt.

"I'm surprised you never put yourself forward," Helen noted coyly.

"The thought had crossed my mind: there lies power; and with power comes the ability to influence events: to change attitudes; to give hope to people like Colin. You know, that kid's still without a job – eighteen months after leaving school! There must be millions of kids like Colin up and down this land stuck on dead-end

YTS placements by this Tory government. Meanwhile, it suits the Tories' purposes to have a pool of unemployed kids to keep wages down and workers tame. That is the biggest injustice of all, and it masquerades as sound macroeconomic strategy! I want to grab the levers of power in order to end that sort of immorality," he vowed, turning to Helen, who hadn't quite been expecting such forthrightness in response to a throw-away remark.

****

The counting was coming to an end, and one-by-one the results were announced. The Conservatives had lost one seat to the Alliance. However, there was no sign of any swing to Labour, and they remained confident of retaining control of Gunsbridge Council.

Craig looked across the cavernous Town Hall at Brad and his Labour colleagues, huddled in conspiratorial secrecy. He guessed they had had a bad night. Earlier in the year, the Bermondsey by-election had produced a shocking defeat for Labour at the hands of the Liberals. Now the local elections would not be offering much comfort for Mr Foot either.

"I therefore declare," the returning officer annouced, "that Elizabeth Alexandra Gainsborough is duly elected as councillor for the ward of Lower Henley."

Elizabeth cast her arms high in triumph and thanked her supporters, who cheered and applauded as she rejoined them. After a burst of unenthusiastic heckling, the Labour supporters withdrew to lick their wounds, while Elizabeth was escorted by her colleagues to the waiting reception at the Conservative Club across the road. There she joined others of her re-elected friends in a profusion of blue rosettes, cheering as they watched other results now coming in from around the country.

"Splendid performance, darling!" remarked Peter Brereton, the Leader of the Council, advancing towards her.

He kissed and hugged her tightly, together basking in the applause of the room. Not to be left out, Craig also embraced his local councillor, who responded with less than her usual formality, kissing him on the cheek and squeezing him maternally. Craig always enjoyed the approbation of his female colleagues, however expressed.

"My friend," said James Whitney, grabbing Craig's arm and shouting above the din, "those newsletters are helping me no end. I've had scores of people comment on how professional they are. I really think we're getting the message across."

Two compliments in one evening! Craig could feel his head swelling. Feigning modesty, he chose instead to draw up a chair and console his friend Councillor

Des Billingham, who had been narrowly defeated by the Liberal Party's youthful new candidate in Foxcotes ward.

"She's a cunning wench, that Jane Allsop. I'll give her that," said Des morbidly contemplating his undoing. "Only a few votes decided it; and this evening I discovered why.

"Apparently she got hold of a copy of the highways department's rolling maintenance programme a few weeks back, showing that several roads on the Thornton Estate were on the cycle to be resurfaced. So she went round expressing shock at the condition of their worn-out roads, promising that she'd do something to have them renewed before the week was out. And, lo and behold, round come the council road gangs to lay a shiny new surface. I couldn't understand why people were saying what a splendid girl the Liberal candidate was. That was until today, when someone told me how quickly she'd arranged for the resurfacing of the roads she'd promised!"

Craig shared Des's sense of bitterness: yes, Jane Allsop – it was she, he recalled, casting his mind back – that chatty wench! He made a mental note to watch out for her in future.

****

Mrs Thatcher, addressing the Scottish Conservative Conference, had boldly set the theme, proclaiming "in four short years, Britain has recovered her confidence and self respect... Now the choice facing the nation is between two totally different ways of life". Meanwhile, Michael Foot, who – for all his sincerity – was still scoring low marks in opinion polls, replied "the Tories promised us jobs, prosperity, tax cuts, industrial peace and law and order. We might not have believed all their promises, but no one could have conceived that they would create such disasters." Then, to the scribbling of incredulous journalists, he continued to proclaim "if Labour had stayed in office we could have become one of the most prosperous nations in the world!"

'Boadicea' or 'Worzel Gummidge' – the country was now being asked to decide; for on May 13th, Parliament was dissolved, and the 1983 General Election was underway.

****

"Howzat!" exclaimed Craig, and he thrust a copy of the latest newsletter under the nose of his candidate.

Unwinding at the campaign offices, James Whitney lounged back in his chair and scanned down the offering. He rested his feet on the desk whilst, over on the other side of the office, Elizabeth Gainsborough perused the local paper for stories about the election. Geoffrey Earl puffed on his pipe and crept up behind James, reading Craig's literary masterpiece over the candidate's shoulder.

"Very good. This is what we need. Look..." he said, offering up the sheet to Geoffrey for closer scrutiny. The crusty chairman raised his glasses and read down the proof copy with a hint of scepticism in his manner.

"*Labour's Defence Policy: Surrender By Another Name...*" he mused on the title.

"How many do you think we should run?" enquired Craig, resting on the edge of the desk.

"What do you think, Geoffrey? A thousand? Two thousand...?"

"You'll need more. Maywood Heath alone will swallow that number."

"I wasn't thinking of delivering in Maywood Heath," said Craig.

Geoffrey dropped his glasses back onto his bulbous nose, detecting something amiss. "What? That's our best area, lad!" he asserted, damning the youngster's impertinence.

"The previous issue on tax cuts, nationalisation and the economy was targeted at our best areas: Maywood Heath, Amblehurst, Little Worcester," Craig reminded them, whilst at the same time reaching over for a copy of the relevant issue to display before them. "This issue, as you can see, majors on defence, which is Labour's weak issue. This is divide and rule."

"There are no votes for us on the council estates. Or not many," maintained the Chairman obdurately.

"Maybe. Maybe not," confided Craig. "But obviously there are votes there for Labour. That is unless someone casts doubts in the minds of their traditional supporters about their policies. And that is what I want to do: pick up on the things that will most alienate ordinary, patriotic working class voters from the Labour Party. So irrespective of whether it gains us votes, I want to destroy the credibility of the socialists amongst their own natural supporters. At best, they may vote for us as the party of strong defence. At worst, they will stay at home in protest; or, alternatively vote for the SDP – and so split the anti-Tory vote. Either way, we win."

"There you are, Geoffrey; a party chairman-in-the-making!" insisted James, full of praise for Craig. Geoffrey huffed, but grudgingly caved in to the candidate's subtle ribbing at the way that the stick-in-the-mud 'Maywood Heath Mafia' were always putting down the bright campaigning ideas of his zestful protégé, no doubt regarding him as that cocky little so-and-so from Lower Henley!

Thoroughly impressed, James leapt up to study the summary of the polls that his team had pasted to the office wall, speculating that "Either way, my friends, we mustn't be complacent. This Allsop girl could yet come up from nowhere and derail us."

"Yes, funny choosing her to be their parliamentary candidate," Geoffrey mused, "And so soon after her council triumph. Either they've given up on this seat, or they possess great confidence in her vote-winning abilities," he chuckled dismissively, not so sure it wasn't the latter. He wandered over to Elizabeth to see how the papers were covering their endeavours.

"There's been some good coverage of Norman Tebbit's visit," she mused aloud. "...Oooh, look! There's me!" she bubbled, pointing to a glimpse of her distinctive hair style in the background of some photo-shoot, the 'Chingford Skinhead' otherwise captured sharing a joke with the Leader of the Council.

****

Immediately that the car pulled up the kids from the estate cheered, although precisely what for they had yet to discover. Who was this mysterious visitor? Was it Annie Lennox? Or perhaps Boy George?

Well, not quite. Yet as Michael Foot emerged from the car and waved his stick high over his head like Moses urging the Israelites off to the Promised Land, the crowd was enthusiastic even so. Ushered inside, he was shuffled into a packed hall of applauding well-wishers who had come to hear this veteran campaigner rally them to the most critical campaign he would fight in a long and tempestuous political career.

"Michael, this is Terry Johnson, sitting MP for Gunsbridge North," said the local party chairman, introducing the worthies who would flank him on the stage. "...And this is Melissa Templeton, the candidate for Gunsbridge South... and with her Robert Bradleigh. They'll be escorting you around this afternoon."

"So you're my minders, are you?" the Leader joked as he shook their hands fraternally.

They all sat down, ready for the meeting to begin. Brad was quite moved at the thought of being only feet away from the man who in just over a week could be the new prime minister. In the time it took to formally open the meeting, he glanced over to receive a reassuring smile from Labour's wizened leader.

Terry Johnson had been the Labour MP for Gunsbridge North since 1964. Now in his late fifties, he had seen off scores of lacklustre challenges to this rock-solid Labour seat over the years, as well as the inevitable reselection procedure recently which, though they had put the fear of God into a good many sitting members, had been effectively seen off by this big, blunt, bearded Black Country bloke. His cockiness was legendary, and riled Conservative backbenchers as much as it had the Militant pretenders in his constituency. Now, however, he used all his jovial charm to kick off the day's business on a high note before handing the microphone over to the man they'd come to hear. And so Michael Foot rose to implore them to help end four years of Conservative misrule.

The Leader was at his best, both witty and urbane. Brad couldn't help but be impressed at his passion and conviction, but cognisant also of the fact that, for all his incredible human and intellectual qualities, in the age of the 'presidential' election campaign and the instant televised image, this septuagenarian orator was not quite what the media gurus were looking for. Indeed, he cast his mind back to their amusement at this doddering scribe walking his dog over Hampstead Common; or their mockery over his appearance at the Cenotaph wearing what they had cruelly dubbed a 'donkey jacket'. He contrasted these with the purposeful images of the Prime Minister, resolute and regal, that the Tories always seemed to manufacture. And so the party was stuck with Michael, who now poured out his heart, passionately expounding his commitment to Labour's lengthy and controversial manifesto – the "longest suicide note in history" as one Labour wag would dub it – that had to date brought down upon his party so much derision.

When the meeting was over, the stewards passed the buckets round to beef up party funds. Mr Foot was meanwhile whisked off for some local photo opportunities. Melissa took him on a walk around a local old folks' home, where he chatted happily with an earthy resident who he was told had once met Nye Bevan, the mention of whose hallowed name caused the Leader to stop and converse at length on the subject of so many of his best literary works. The Leader toured the town's job centre, promising them a Labour government committed once more to rediscovering the lost elixir of full employment.

Finally, Brad took the Leader on a visit to one of the constituency's biggest council estates. Three years of hard work in Gunsbridge South had taught him where the real support could be found and he now led the Leader up to some of Labour's most vocal well-wishers. The press corps gathered round as neighbours came out into the street to see what was going on. Someone started up a chorus of *The Red Flag*, prompting the Leader to join in the singing of this anthem to the brave new world that they had pledged themselves to create.

Racing back home after the Leader departed, Brad almost flew through the door on wings. Helen wanted to pour out the latest gossip from the office. He, himself, was never one for conversations that majored on apolitical trivia – less so when he had more consequential matters on his mind. Finally, aware of his state of excitement, Helen switched on the television and they sat down together to await the evening news.

The headlines majored on the Prime Minister hobnobbing with world leaders at an international summit in the United States, with Mrs Thatcher dominating the proceedings in all her majesty. There then followed coverage of the day's other election claims and counterclaims. Finally there was a brief item about the Labour leader's visit to Gunsbridge, which consisted of snippets of Mr Foot's hectoring speech, his reminiscing about Bevan, shaking hands with two jobless skinheads, and warbling the *Red Flag* on a run-down council estate, surrounded by a huddle of housewives in curlers and waifs with their shirts hanging out. Where was the passionate repudiation of Thatcherism? Where was the promise to bring hope to the young, the elderly and the vulnerable? Where was the genuine joy of a group of ordinary people who were heartened that someone so important should deem to descend upon their forgotten neighbourhood and articulate their fears and aspirations? Or was it just that Labour appeared to be so rooted in images of the past?

****

After about an hour of scrutinising ballot papers, Brad felt goggle-eyed, and excused himself from Helen and Rod Turner in order to drift off into the foyer. As coincidence would have it, from the opposite side of Gunsbridge Town Hall, Craig also made his way to the drinks machine in the foyer, hoping to wake himself up after a long day on his feet. Brad caught him trying to make sense of the instructions as he searched for change with which to propitiate the machine.

"Got no tens?" he enquired. Delving into his pockets, Brad handed Craig a few. "...Here... and mine's a white coffee with sugar while you're at it."

Craig smiled, noting his friend's resigned expression. Gazing back into the hall at the counting now well advanced, they both chatted together while the Conservative 'pigeon holes' where being crammed full of ballots papers. A victory for James Whitney could only be a few more minutes away. Even so, the tentative exchange had a pleasant feel to it. It was the first time either one of them had had chance to make conversation with the other since those far-off days at college. Knowing the other's adverse political affiliations had not made for such an encounter previously. Yet now the time felt ripe to at last establish a *rapport*. Brad paused before reminiscing.

"Remember that day trip to the House Of Commons?" he enquired wistfully, leaning back against the doorpost. "Meeting Sir Edgar, and all that?"

"Yes, I do," replied his old friend. "I guess that's what started all this off."

"Yeh. I remember sitting there in the Strangers' Gallery and thinking 'I want to do that'. I guess I still do, crazy though it seems."

"I know the feeling. Do you think you'll ever make the big time?"

Brad stood erect once more. "Oh yeah. I'll do it. I don't know when, or how, or where; but I'll do it. And you?"

"Yep..." Craig affirmed, "One day."

For one brief moment this could have been the *Tropicana* back in those halcyon summers when unemployment of just over a million could rock a government, trades union bosses had gulped beer and sandwiches at 10 Downing Street, and defeating Argentina had entailed nothing more sinister than scoring in the World Cup. So much had changed, and the boys had changed with it. No more the carefree teenagers cruising about town, breaking hearts as they went. Now they were rapidly transforming themselves into fighting politicians; ready for the day when they would lay everything on the line to hear their own names read out across some crowded town hall on such a night as this.

"Here's to it!" Brad toasted the prospect, gently raising his little plastic cup.

They each the bade a simple farewell to the other before making their way back to their respective colleagues – strange tribes ranged across different sides of the hall, different sides of a gaping ideological chasm.

"...Being the acting returning officer for the constituency of Gunsbridge South announce the result of the election for the said constituency to be as follows..." Everything then fell silent as the returning officer read out the results slowly and solemnly... "Allsop – Jane Elizabeth (SDP-Liberal Alliance), 13,747 votes."

A cheer went up, although Jane's team knew she had failed to win on a vote of that size, respectable as it was. However, Craig couldn't help but notice a furrowed brow appear beneath her fine golden crown, as if to discount defeat and remind her opponents that they had not seen the last of her yet.

"Templeton – Melissa Jean (Labour Party), 13,253 votes."

Brad felt like crying, despite the brave cheers of his friends. It was an appalling result, made all the more galling by the derisive laughs from the Tory side.

"Whitney – James Jonathan Robert (Conservative Party), 33,705 votes... I therefore declare that the said James Jonathan Robert Whitney is duly elected..."

Nobody was listening. Craig was too busy hugging his fellows, lifting Elizabeth Gainsborough clean off her feet! Labour supporters gnashed their teeth, but the jubilant Conservatives just carried on trying to take in the sheer magnitude of their victory. Finally, James Whitney strode purposefully up to the microphone.

"Thank you, Mr Returning Officer, and your staff. I would like also to thank all my loyal team, including... especially Craig Anderson for all his hard work in editing my campaign literature."

"Tory lies, all of it!" yelled Sharif Khan indignantly.

James just grinned and ignored him; tonight's victory tasted sweet, and he could afford to be magnanimous. Meanwhile, Craig took an exquisite delight in the dubious mumblings amongst the 'Maywood Heath Mafia' that James's endorsement of his campaigning YC had caused: one up for Lower Henley, he chuckled to himself!

"Tonight, my friends," their new MP continued, "I have no doubt that we are on course for a historic election victory. The last four years have been tough, controversial and often painful. But now with inflation back down and the economy set for steady growth, I believe we are entering a new era of opportunity and hope, for which we can all be grateful to our superb prime minister..."

Homage paid to their *gloriana victrix*, James moved away from the microphone and held his arms high in triumph.

"FOUR MORE YEARS! FOUR MORE YEARS! FOUR MORE YEARS!" came the chant from a Conservative Party that sensed its most exciting days still lay ahead.

Part II

1983-1987

7 *"...TESTING, TESTING..."*

During her first four years in office, Mrs Thatcher had set herself the goals of taming inflation and halting the 'ratchet effect' of socialism. Yet if the *cri-de-coeur* of those first years had been to arrest the dead hand of the State, then the landslide victory she had just achieved would now signal a new departure: namely to start driving that 'dead hand' into rapid retreat; to advance the cause of enterprise and individual endeavour. One of the principal means for achieving this would be the first of a series of privatisations, along with firm control of socialist-controlled big spenders in local government.

The scale of her victory was truly breathtaking. Not since Attlee had swept the board in 1945 had any prime minister surveyed such a trouncing of their foes. The parliament that had been returned comprised 397 Conservative MPs, 209 Labour, 23 SDP-Liberal Alliance and 21 others, giving the Government a majority of 144. For the Labour Party, the election had been nothing short of a catastrophe, with the party scoring its lowest share of the vote since 1918, finishing only marginally ahead of the Alliance. Michael Foot bowed out, and the Labour leadership passed to Neil Kinnock. "Just remember how you felt on that dreadful morning of June 10th," he had reminded his flock during his first speech as leader. "Just remember how you felt and think to yourselves: June 9th 1983 – never, ever again!"

That summer the pressure on the Government from the so-called 'peace' movement mounted – rekindled of late by the imminent arrival of American cruise missiles at RAF Greenham Common. Therefore, in one of her shrewder moves, Mrs Thatcher had appointed Michael Heseltine as her defence secretary to head off the challenge from the Campaign for Nuclear Disarmament. Debonair, dramatic and well-versed in the art of image politics, the tall, bronzed figure with the flowing blond locks seemed heaven-sent for helping the Government recapture the moral high ground in this increasingly shrill debate. The sight of the man they called 'Tarzan' strutting before the television cameras in a combat jacket whilst touring missile bases besieged by women 'peace' demonstrators seemed to signify that one of the thorniest political nettles of the eighties was about to be well and truly grasped with both hands.

Yet by the time the year was out, the CND revival had passed its high point. By this time too, the Russians were losing the will to outpace the Americans in military spending. The Soviet economy was as moribund as its ailing leadership, and was increasingly unable to match the United States weapon for weapon; especially now that Ronald Reagan, America's hawkish president, had announced plans for a multi-billion dollar 'Star Wars' weapon system that threatened to render Soviet missiles obsolete at a stroke. As far as the Cold War was concerned, the more discerning communists began to sense that the 'writing was on the wall'.

****

"So this is what all the fuss is about?" commented Brad, surveying the vista beneath him.

"Yes, this is it. Trescott Park. And that's all that's left of the old Thomas & Clifton Steel Works," said Micky Preston as the wind rippled through his long, grey mane. "I can remember when five thousand men worked here."

The two men stood on the embankment that overlooked what was left of the once impressive foundry. Over the vast moonscape of demolished brickwork and tangled debris, bulldozers trampled about, levelling the site as they went. Over in isolated corners, bonfires flickered while workers gathered up odd bits of timber and threw them onto its funeral pyre. Where once there had stood great furnaces seething with white-hot ore, now there was only barren earth. Where the main gate had once had stood – where, upon the sounding of the five o'clock siren, workers would stream out each evening – now a solitary eight-wheeled lorry waited to turn out into the traffic, loaded up with rubble destined for some landfill site. Where once had been two dozen or more railway sidings busily worked by grimy little shunting locomotives, now there was nothing except a couple of dull grey Portakabins that stood in as site offices. From out of one of these a lone foreman braved the biting wind to empty out the contents of his mug before wandering back into the warm, closing the door behind him.

"It's quite sad really," Micky sighed angrily.

The bearded councillor for Barnwood ward had become one of Brad's closest colleagues now that his political career was about to shift up a gear: for Lower Henley branch had kindly asked him if he would like to stand as the candidate for the ward in the municipal elections due the following May. Their only sitting Labour councillor, Stan Taylor, had been deselected after increasingly bitter wrangles over his close personal friendship with one Harry Conway, a millionaire property developer known to be interested in the potential for developing this derelict site into an American-style shopping mall. It was that that had clearly roused the two onlookers.

"That's assuming Conway gets planning permission," Brad cautioned optimistically.

"He will," replied Micky with more than a hint of cynicism. "Peter Brereton is one of his golfing partners. The Conservative Group is being well-and-truly softened up to approve it: fifty acres of retail park, ten thousand free car parking spaces – all within ten minutes of the motorway. It'll devastate the town centre."

"What about the jobs Conway says he'll create?"

"What jobs? Part-time, low paid jobs for checkout girls? They're not real jobs. Besides, once he's got his foot in the door, he'll be after that land over there too," said Micky, pointing out a desolate field rising up in the distance. "The Council owns that land. My bet is that if we don't take control this year, the Tories will sell that land to Conway. Then his retail development will double in size overnight. As you can see, it's vital we get you in to stop this monstrosity from spreading."

The two men drifted back over to Micky's old brown Austin Allegro and headed off back towards town. While Micky hummed to the radio, Brad sank into a daydream once more, staring down at the ring on his finger, an act not entirely prompted by the fact that Helen now had his baby growing inside her. He had tried to spend more time with his new wife whilst he still had time on his hands. And he wanted to be a loving father – come what may. He knew from painful experience how desolate life can be without a real dad to call your own.

As they passed by the imposing Victorian edifice of Gunsbridge Council House, Brad knew that only a few weeks separated him from possibly taking his seat in the council chamber. He'd already drafted his election address and ran through it once more while Micky was waiting at the traffic lights.

> *My fellow electors,*
> *I am deeply honoured to have been chosen to represent the Labour Party in your ward. Many people are very concerned about the way the Tories have neglected local services in this town. The Social Services budget has been frozen, council house rents raised, council staff sacked, and their jobs given to 'cowboy' private firms. And this is just the beginning!*
> *That is why I am asking you to support me. Along with other Labour councillors, I will work to restore the Tory cuts, and prove once again that the Council can provide caring services to all its citizens. Your vote can make the difference, and if you cast it for Robert Bradleigh, I promise you I'll work to look after your interests and the well-being of this town.*

They pulled onto the car park of Lower Henley Workingmen's Club. As Micky went to lock the car door, he paused, reopened it, and hauled out a folder that he secured under his arm. "We might as well make this a working visit," he muttered aloud.

"Long time, no see," said Joy, the aptly-named barmaid who greeted them, her ample cleavage resting on the bar like ripe fruit on a barrow stall as the two men entered into the smoke-filled bar.

Micky reached for his wallet before ordering, adding that "Actually, Joy, you can do us a favour."

He then proceeded to open his folder and run his fingers through the assortment of documents. "Where do you live?"

"Why? Are you planning on paying me that visit you've been promising?" Joy chortled, oozing innuendo as she presented the beers on the bar top and leant forward to observe Micky shuffling his paperwork, Brad catching a pleasing eyeful of her infamous 'melons'.

"I need some signatures for Brad's nomination form. Molson – Joy Patricia?" he confirmed, scanning down his registers, still not party to his candidate's visual delight. Maybe he'd seen it all before, Brad mused.

"What is your candidate going to do for me in return for this little favour?" she enquired coyly, winking at Brad, who was not quite able to avert his gaze away before she caught him fantasising over her size 40-DD bazookas.

Micky completed the details on the form. "Here, sign just there. And by the way, is Jimmy Dearn about?"

"He's over by the dart board," Joy advised them, scribbling her moniker on the form.

"I'm very grateful," Brad smiled. Meanwhile, Micky led him off in the direction of their next acquisition.

"Then pop by and see me when you're out canvassing next. Don't forget, will you," Joy cried after him.

Brad mused on the prospect... but it was too mind-blowing! Now he knew why she was known as the 'Siren of the Smoke Room'! He concentrated instead on searching out Jimmy Dearn, a slim, weathered figure, who he located trying to nail the 'double-top'. A straight-talking bricklayer, he had been in the party many more years than anyone could remember. Yes, of course he'd second this fine young man, he declared.

Brad was humbled. Micky sought out more workers from around the snooker tables and the bar. Excusing himself for interrupting their games or conversations, he introduced Brad to them, extolling his dedication to their cause, and asking for their support for his nomination. One by one, they cheerfully affixed their crude signatures to his form. These ordinary, decent working class folk then wished him all the best, and expressed their gratitude that someone was prepared to fight for their dignity. Moments like this were what made the lonely, difficult road of politics all worthwhile.

****

It was a bright, sunny Friday outside, so that when Brad and Micky Preston walked through the door of the electoral registration office the interior seemed terribly dark and dingy. Up the one corner sat a clerk typing out some memos rather amateurishly, and it was to her that the duo now addressed themselves as they laid their documents down on the reception counter.

"Is Eric Tucker about?" enquired Micky.

"I'll just find him," she droned, screwing the top back on the Typex bottle.

With that, she disappeared, returning some moments later with a squat, middle-aged man with his shirt sleeves rolled up and his glasses perched on his head, who checked through the papers diligently, making sure everything was in order. Time seemed to stand still in the office, the clock ticking monotonously away above the vague mumble of the traffic outside. Eric's trusty clerk pushed a few more keys on her typewriter before pausing again to correct another error with the magic white fluid.

"Any news on who the Tory candidate is?" enquired Micky as an aside.

"We've not had the Conservative nomination papers yet," Eric confessed, "but I suspect they'll put forward that Herbert Parsons chap again. They usually wheel him out when they have difficulty filling a vacancy."

"Ah, bumblin' Herbie Parsons – the original 'pressed' man!" Micky roared, "I wouldn't lose any sleep," he then chuckled to his bewildered candidate. "He's seventy-four, has a nervous twitch, and is as deaf as a post!"

Just then the door creaked open, and amidst the sudden burst of sunlight and the thunder of a passing lorry, in swept two figures silhouetted like gunfighters lined up in the portals of a saloon bar. In place of a six-shot, one of them bore a folder under his arm.

"Good morning, Eric. I've come bearing the nomination papers of the Conservative candidate for Lower Henley."

As the door slowly shut and the blinding rays were banished back outside once more, Micky finally recognised the Buddha-like countenance of George Franklin. The two figures moved forward and the councillor laid his documents on the counter, coolly announcing, "Gentlemen, this is Craig Anderson."

"Greetings, Brad," the youthful candidate smiled.

"D' you two know each other?" murmured Micky.

"You could say that," replied Brad calmly. The entry of his old school friend into the fray had suddenly given the contest a very interesting turn.

"I don't suppose there'll be any further nominations," Eric noted. "Besides, they've only got until midday. So that makes you two gentlemen the only candidates. Everything looks in order, so may the best man win!" he joked, looking up briefly to see why the noise of the traffic was rushing in again through the open portal. Indeed, they all looked round. Two more figures stood silhouetted by the sunburst, this time pleasantly recognisable by their distinctive feminine curves. The door closed and the two young blonde lasses casually wandered in.

"Councillor Miss Allsop, this is a pleasant surprise," Eric chirped as she laid her papers down on his counter.

"Eric, meet Candy Rawlings," she announced, the others looking on with a mixture of surprise and unease, "the Alliance candidate for Lower Henley ward. And I intend to be her agent!"

The male quartet that ranged either side of her didn't know quite what to do or say. Certainly the entrance of a third candidate into the fray had upset all their equations. And with the gregarious, dynamic councillor for Foxcotes running the show, could they be sure that her winning combination of a keen eye for publicity and an intense pursuit of local concerns wouldn't suck votes away to her beaming candidate?

"Cheer up, lads," Jane smiled jovially, observing their dismay, "it could have been worse. You could have been sharing the ballot paper with me!"

****

"Surprise, surprise! They're back from the printers."

"Ooh, good. Let's have a look, Craig," said Elizabeth Gainsborough, snatching the brown paper parcel out of his hands. Tearing open the wrapping, she grabbed a handful of leaflets and started handing them round.

"Hey, isn't he handsome!" swooned Jean Taylor as she opened out the large photograph on the front of the big A3-sized address. "He looks like that George Michael fellow that our Tina's got plastered on her bedroom wall," she then guffawed, much to Craig's obvious embarrassment.

"You'll really charm the ladies, that much is for sure," bubbled George Franklin as well.

"Never mind the mug shot, let's have a read of his personal message," suggested Gerry Roberts. He turned a leaflet over and read it out aloud.

> *Dear Electors,*
> *This is the first time I have ever fought an election as a candidate, and I am immensely proud to have been chosen to represent Lower Henley for the Conservative Party.*
> *Over the last two years, your local Conservative council have been taking great strides towards making the Council more efficient. For instance, the efficiency audit we conducted in the Social Services Department has enabled us to provide better care without increasing the budget. We have reduced the excessive subsidy given to the Housing Department, and have contracted out many everyday council services, enabling us to limit this year's rates rise to a mere 2% - well below inflation!*
> *Our record is an impressive one. I would therefore be honoured to serve as your local councillor and help ensure that this Borough continues to enjoy some of the best local services around.*

"Very good, Craig," Joan Knight congratulated him. "The Labour Party has got a fight on its hands!"

Craig was grateful for his colleagues' approbation, although it still couldn't smooth away the doubts he was battling with. Sure, he could win Lower Henley given a favourable swing; but that was just the trouble – he wasn't sure whether he wanted to win it!

As the committee began to pour over the minutiae of the campaign, Craig wasn't really listening. Instead his mind wandered, thinking back to how Herbert Parsons had fallen ill at the last moment, and how nobody could be found to stand for the party in this highly marginal seat. There then followed a frantic hunt to find any old name to stick on the ballot paper. Was there no one else willing enough (or mug enough!) to take on the task? Well, there was always Craig....

Thus had Craig allowed himself to be persuaded by George Franklin's appeals to the higher good of the party. And so, with only a day left to go before nominations closed, Craig was hastily proposed, seconded, adopted, and whisked down to Eric Tucker's office, still wondering what he'd let himself in for. It would be good experience if ever he decided to enter Parliament, George had reminded him.

Indeed, that was probably its only saving grace. He had hoped to apply to join one of the selection weekends, where party workers take groups of parliamentary hopefuls away for a few days in the country and put them through their paces. Those that pass are then successfully included on the 'Approved Candidates List', and thus come recommended by Conservative Central Office – a priceless advantage when looking for vacant parliamentary seats to be adopted for. It looked as if he'd have to shelve his plans for the time being. The fate of Gunsbridge Council could stand or fall on the decision of a handful of voters in a seat like Lower Henley.

****

"You're very privileged to have me, son," Rod Turner teased the young candidate. "I'm only here 'cuz this is a seat we must not lose!"

Brad was heartened by his support, but he knew something that Rod Turner didn't. Moves were afoot to ease Rod out of his job as chairman of Gunsbridge South general management committee (or 'general committee' as the party now insisted on calling it – 'management' smacked of elitism!). This veteran had passed his sell-by date, and was proving ever more incapable of standing up to Bennett and his Militant cronies.

Brad had just about had enough of all the hectoring, backbiting and posturing of the Militants. Much as he respected people like Tony Benn, he was becoming more disillusioned with the hard left, which he once considered his natural home in the party. Labour could ill-afford the haemorrhaging of good party workers; alienated and disgusted by the tragic-comic antics of the Militants, who still kept badgering committees to pass dotty motions that only served to give the local Tories another source of rich copy at Labour's expense. Indeed, as Brad canvassed doorsteps on the Heronmore council estate, he knew only too well how badly their childish naivety went down. Meanwhile, Rod Turner had just returned down a garden path after interrogating a dishy dolly bird in a bathrobe, who now waved sweetly as he closed the gate behind him.

"How come you always find the best doors to knock?" exclaimed Brad. "That old bat back there just tore me off a strip!"

"Ah, well," he grinned, "it's always the candidate's prerogative to canvass the 'dogs'!"

Brad was not amused. He made off up the path of the next house, one of those irritating variety where the front door is actually located up the back alley! Opening the gate, he tiptoed into the yard and rang the doorbell, waiting for a response. Meanwhile, out of the corner of his eye, he thought he spotted a shadowy figure looming. Looking round, he suddenly noticed that rather a stocky-looking bull terrier had poked its head round the wall and was eyeing him up and down. The dog growled menacingly.

Gingerly, its prospective meal started to retrace his steps towards the gate. Likewise, the Staffie began to shadow him, gradually quickening the pace. Brad then sprinted pell-mell up the path and over the front gate, though not before the fleet-footed hound had sunk his teeth into his new trousers. The animal just would not let go. Struggling with one leg still cocked over the gate, Brad finally lost his temper and clobbered the evil mutt over the head with his clipboard, upon which the dog withdrew back up the path with a piece of Brad's trouser leg as a souvenir.

"What happened?" gasped an alarmed Rod Turner, noticing his exposed shin.

"Candidates prerogative!" Brad barked back. "I got the 'dog' – literally this time!"

****

"Ready?" shouted Craig from beneath the bonnet.

"I think so," muttered George, fiddling under the dashboard.

Craig took that to be a 'yes' and released the crocodile clips onto the battery terminals. A few sparks flew, and the tannoy set mounted on the car's roof oscillated loudly before George tuned the set in correctly.

"TESTING, TESTING... FOUR AND TWENTY VIRGINS CAME DOWN FROM INVERNESS..." he chortled bawdily down the microphone, scandalising a diminutive old lady who was waiting at the bus stop over the road.

"Where shall we go first?" Craig asked,

"Let's try Heatherfields," his agent suggested. "That's a new estate. There should be a good few votes there."

As the car cruised along the main road that ran through Lower Henley, Craig couldn't resist pressing home his credentials. *"GOOD EVENING, LADIES AND GENTLEMEN, THIS IS CRAIG ANDERSON, ASKING YOU TO COME OUT AND VOTE FOR ME – YOUR CONSERVATIVE CANDIDATE..."*

Entering the modern, brick-built estate, the two vote-seekers suddenly found themselves escorted by an honour guard of cheeky kids on chopper bikes who, as Craig urged the neighbourhood to vote Conservative, echoed his clarion call with one of their own to vote Labour! One kid, sporting a baseball cap that almost submerged his head, mounted the pavement on his bike and rode alongside the car.

"'Ere, mate, mar' dad votes Labour!" he called out to Craig, who was resting his arm on the open window of the car as it cruised along.

"Never mind, kid, I'm told it's curable," he replied, a trifle irritated. *"DON'T FORGET TO COME OUT TONIGHT AND VOTE CONSERVATIVE!"*

"No. Seriously!" insisted the kid, dodging in and out of the pedestrians walking up the avenue. "'E sez' yow' lot am a right bunch o' tossers!"

"Listen, son," Craig snapped, "haven't you got any homework to do?"

George drew the car to a halt as he came to the end of a cul-de-sac. Then he hung his head out of the window and beckoned the kids over. "Would you like some badges and stickers?" he asked them all.

"Watcha' got, mate?" they screamed excitedly, and scrambled amongst themselves for an armful of Craig's unused campaign material – posters and all.

"This is Craig Anderson. Now you go and tell your mums and dads to come out and vote for him," George admonished them cheerfully.

The lads scurried off, dutifully plastering their T-shirts, caps, bikes, and any other available surface (including someone's garden gnomes) with stickers bearing Craig's smiling face. This enabled Craig to broadcast in peace once more.

"DO THE RIGHT THING. COME OUT TONIGHT AND VOTE FOR CRAIG ANDERSON, YOUR LOCAL CONSERVATIVE..."

Even so, he thought he could make out the sound of another muffled admonition drifting over from the other side of the estate.

"VOTE LABOUR AND STOP THE TORY CUTS. THIS IS ROBERT BRADLEIGH ASKING FOR YOUR KIND SUPPORT... VOTE LABOUR!"

He knew he was right. He saw another car, a little black Mini, heading up the avenue with a loudspeaker strapped to its roof.

"ONLY A CONSERVATIVE COUNCIL WILL KEEP YOUR RATES BILL DOWN!" Craig insisted.

"ONLY A LABOUR COUNCIL WILL IMPROVE LOCAL FACILITIES!" came the reply.

"VOTE ANDERSON – CONSERVATIVE!"

"VOTE BRADLEIGH – LABOUR!"

"HI, BRAD..."

"HI, CRAIG..."

The two cars sailed past each other at just the spot where one man was washing his car on his driveway whilst another was tending the roses in his front garden. Both looked up at the spectacle. The man washing his car waved at Craig, and pointed to the large Conservative poster in his bedroom window. His neighbour, wielding an insecticide spray, put his thumb up to Brad, and pointed to the poster of Brad hanging on his garage door. Both men then gave the other a disgusted look before returning to their respective chores.

"Wasn't that the Tory candidate?" asked Donna Tromans, one of Lower Henley's young Labour activists, who was endeavouring to steer Brad's quirky little car whilst he fumbled with the makeshift amplifier.

Up ahead, a gang of kids were waiting in ambush so that when she veered off up a leafy avenue (and while Brad was beseeching the estate to turn out and vote Labour), the pubescent cyclists yelled "Vote Conservative!" and weaved about on their bikes behind the car. One kid sporting a baseball cap that almost submerged his head – bedecked as it now was with 'CRAIG ANDERSON' stickers – mounted the pavement on his bike and rode alongside, teasing the newcomers.

"Yow'm the Labour bloke, ay' ya'?"

Brad feigned surprise and glanced behind him at the big Labour poster gummed to the car's rear quarter window. "So this rumour that they teach kids how to read at your school is true then," he muttered sarcastically.

"Our Mom votes fer' the Conservatives, like!" proffered their pursuer.

"Does she now? Evidently she never learned anything at school either then!" Brad quipped with even more sarcasm. *"STOP THE TORY CUTS... VOTE LABOUR TONIGHT...!"*

"No, seriously," the kid interjected. "'Er sez' the Labour Party 'm a right bunch o' dickheads!"

Brad was relieved when they finally reached the main road, there to be finally left in peace. Travelling up the wide boulevard, they passed the 'Hare and Hounds' public house, where the beer garden was full of happy drinkers enjoying the superb sunny evening. Brad thought this might prove a useful place to pick up last minute votes.

"GOOD EVENING, COMRADES, THIS IS ROBERT BRADLEIGH, YOUR LOCAL LABOUR CANDIDATE, REMINDING YOU TO CAST YOUR VOTE THIS EVENING BEFORE THE POLLS SHUT..."

A meaty wench sitting on the wall with her friends stood up, spread open wide her black leather jacket and displayed her T-shirt to them, the words *FRANKIE*

SAYS severely distorted by the curvature of her massive, wobbling bosom as she pointed to her preferred candidate and *RELAX* – his one-word manifesto! Brad gasped: not even Joy's were that colossal! His face turned sour, however, when another bunch of cyclists, this time wearing evil-looking helmets, appeared on *their* bikes – huge, growling 750cc beasts!

"I think we'd better quicken the pace," he warned Donna as the bikes formed up into a convoy and drew alongside. The car jerked stiffly as Donna rediscovered the accelerator and clung to the wheel for dear life.

The bikers closed in and started taunting Brad and Donna, tearing off the posters from the car. When they reached the Amblehurst Road they noticed a police car waiting idly on the roundabout, perchance to nab a speeding motorist. Perhaps less from respect for the Queen's Peace than from the fact that its decor was now in shreds anyway, the bikers began to peel away and leave the hapless activists alone. Meanwhile, Donna drew the car up to the Give Way sign, where she promptly stalled it. Meanwhile, a little Volvo gaily festooned with orange balloons appeared travelling in the opposite direction.

"VOTE CANDY RAWLINGS... SOCIAL DEMOCRAT/LIBERAL ALLIANCE..." it boomed as it passed them by.

****

Both candidates were by now extremely tired, so it was just as well that the last of the votes were being counted and a result was not far away. Craig stood with George Franklin, watching the nail-biting finale approach. Brad was flanked by his wife and a pensive-looking Micky Preston.

Craig had worked hard on this campaign, despite his apprehension lest he win it! Brad, meanwhile, was struck by just how amicable the campaign had been. Oh, that all campaigns could be run that way, he mused. It was not beyond the realm of possibility that they could be facing each other again on a night such as this, perhaps when a greater prize was at stake, and they would both be sorely pressed to conduct the campaign with a little less equanimity. And who could tell where the determined Jane Allsop would turn up again!

Helen watched while her husband and the other candidates and agents debated the figures with the returning officer. They had already ordered one recount, which had overturned an apparently narrow Conservative victory. After much haggling and posturing, it appeared that the second recount would have to suffice. The returning officer led them to the stage to announce the final tally for the Lower Henley ward.

"Anderson – Craig William (Conservative Party), 1562 votes."

Gerry, Elizabeth and the Lower Henley crowd applauded his stalwart service over the last few weeks. He had certainly put enough of a fight in to beat the formidable challenger that the local Labour branch had put forward.

"Bradleigh – Robert (Labour Party), 1588 votes."

It was not to be. The Labour supporters were jubilant. Brad struck a defiant fist into the air. The Conservatives mourned their failure to take the seat: 'if only I'd canvassed a few more roads', they knew Craig must be thinking to himself (Craig, meanwhile, breathed a quiet sigh of relief!).

Candy Rawlings had polled over a thousand votes; so a small cheer went up, the attractive young blonde girls waving to their faithful followers, once again having picked up disaffected voters at the margins. Craig and Brad had fretted throughout their campaign about the competition these eager young ladies represented. However, by now Brad was feeling elated and put these cares behind him, confidently walking up to the microphone and launching into some old rhetoric about Labour being closer to power, even though with virtually all the results in Gunsbridge now in, it looked unlikely that Labour had damaged the Conservatives enough to take control.

Craig returned to his disappointed colleagues while his victorious opponent was carried off shoulder-high to rejoin the celebrating Labour team. He was relieved that the agony was over, and determined to spend the weekend in bed to recover. Before he could do so, however, a handsome well-heeled gentlemen with sweeping dark hair and a well-tailored suit grabbed his arm and smiled at him as he made for the door.

"I just want you to know, Craig, we're grateful for all you've done. The effort the socialists have to put into defending this seat has probably diverted their energy from fighting in other vulnerable wards. You've taken the heat off the rest of us."

Craig was grateful that his endeavour had at last brought him to the attention of one of the most powerful men in the Gunsbridge South constituency party. Councillor Peter Brereton – this tall, eloquent figure – fastidiously surveyed his fiefdom from his Maywood Heath power base. Craig had up until now been a mere foot soldier in the party, though he had often tried to catch the Leader's eye. It appeared now that he had at last succeeded, and could count himself amongst the ranks of the senior party workers. Equally true though, the higher one climbs, the stiffer the competition becomes; so Craig took a final look around the Town Hall, picking out potential rivals.

On his own side, some of the 'Maywood Heath Mafia' were chatting away, laughing and joking together. Had his near-victory finally convinced them of the sincerity of his endeavours? On the Labour side, Brad was still being held aloft, ducking under the doorway as his supporters carried him out. Craig was determined that, if he were to ever face his socialist contemporary again, the result would be very different to that of tonight. These were his known rivals; but how many other equally ambitious young men and women were waiting up and down the country to fill one of the few hundred posts that marked the first rung on the ladder of a parliamentary career? Meanwhile, Jane Allsop smiled to her well-wishers across the hall on her way out. Could he ever entirely discount the challenge of the centre parties?

Craig was satisfied that tonight he had proved his mettle in combat, so to speak. He had meanwhile set himself another goal on his 'rough route' to power: to be securely adopted for a parliamentary seat in time for the next general election. For that, he needed to prepare the ground now. Leaving the Lower Henley campaign behind him in the closing hours of that pleasant May evening that was precisely what he was determined to do.

8 STRIKE!

"All be upstanding for the Worshipful Mayor of Gunsbridge!" the cry rang out, and the grand oak doors were thrown open wide. Into the august council chamber, with its grand chandeliers, the Mayor and his train were ushered to take their seats at the head of the waiting councillors.

As they plodded through a succession of orders and petitions, Brad quite fancied himself now in the role of an elected representative. He would dearly have loved the thrill of also being a part of a victoriously re-elected Labour council. Yet when Councillor Peter Brereton rose to move business, he was still entrenched as leader of the controlling Conservative Group – albeit with just a slim, two-seat majority. Labour were frustratingly close to power. Yet there would be no local elections in the Borough next year. Therefore, provided Brereton could keep his members disciplined, punctual and in perfect health, he was safe for two years.

After Brereton sat down, the Mayor called on the leader of the Labour Group, Tom McKerrick, to speak. Brad was vaguely acquainted with McKerrick, who represented Tower Park ward in Gunsbridge North. Stocky, greying, and drifting into his sixties, he was a retired railway guard, who had elbowed his way up through the Labour Party and now provided a forceful sparring partner for Brereton, displaying a mastery of the details of his brief and a cutting humour that helped to break the tension of long, heated debates.

"These are your friends and enemies for the next four years," whispered Micky Preston.

"Some of them must have been hired from the mortuary!" replied Brad, grinning. "Anyway, who they are?"

"Let's start over on our side," said Micky, leaning forward to view along the benches. "Next to Tom McKerrick, that's Joe McAllister, the Deputy Leader."

"I've had the misfortune to cross swords with him before," said Brad.

"Yeh, right son-of-a-bitch. He'd knife his grandmother to advance his own cause. I hate him. I think most of us do. The man's evil, make no mistake."

McAllister looked their way, leering through his thick-rimmed glasses. Then he noticed Brad, the new councillor only too aware that the Deputy Leader had not forgotten his role in his failure to realise a parliamentary career.

"Next to him is Frank Collins, our shadow chair of Education."

"Who? That short bloke there?" enquired Brad of the diminutive, wiry-haired Einstein-look-a-like.

"That's the one. The Tories call him the 'Poison Dwarf' because he gets their backs up. He gets our backs up sometimes too; but he's a good firebrand socialist all the same. Further round is Maureen Tonks. She's shadow chair of Community Services."

"What does Community Services do? I noticed I'm on that committee."

"Parks, libraries, youth clubs, community centres – that sort of thing. Anyway, next to her is the infamous Derek Hooper, of course. The Tories say they hate him, but really they love him: he's a gift to their propaganda machine. And that guy waiting to speak is Walter Pugh."

The Mayor called out his name, and the podgy, bald-headed man rose to address the chamber. "Mr M-m-m-m-mayor, I gorra' say this ay' right. T-t-t-time after t-t-t-t-time the Government 'ave changed the g-g-g-goalposts in this g-g-g-game. It p-p-p-p-plays havoc with our b-b-b-b-b-b-b..."

"B-b-b-budget?" quipped one of the Conservative councillors.

"B-b-b-bananas?" suggested another, a cruel if timely interjection that flushed a roar of amusement from out of the Conservative benches and provoked a rebuke from the Mayor. Micky, meanwhile, continued his *tour-de-horizon*.

"Behind us is Roz Young. She's also into all these dotty causes. Therefore she's another gift to the Tories," he sighed, moving on to review the Conservative side. Just then a diminutive man with no hair, except for two bushy white locks over each ear, stood up, the Mayor permitting him to reply to a point.

"MrmayorireallydofeelthatIhavetotakeissuewiththecouncilloroverhisblatantattempt toconfusetheissue!"

"What's he on about?" exclaimed Brad. Indeed, Tom McKerrick and some of the Labour shadow chairmen cupped their ears, straining to pick up the salient points of the Ulsterman's garbled, rapid-fire response.

"That's Spencer Fitzgibbon. He's the Tories' chairman of Finance. Or Spencer 'Fitzgibberish' as we prefer to call him!"

"Somrsthatcherisrighttosaygoodriddancetothecountycouncilsthegoodfornothingtal kshopsdoesthatanswerthegentlemens question?" Probably not, but the tongue-tied councillor sat down anyway. Micky resumed again.

"Next to Brereton, that's Mike Rotherwood. Don't ever take him on in debate without doing your homework first. He eats unwary comrades for breakfast! ...George Franklin you know – a bit of a buffoon, but he's harmless enough... and Elizabeth Gainsborough you've probably also seen before too. She's a bitch, but she's a smart bitch; someone else you don't provoke unless you know what you're doing."

Pausing, Micky pointed to a tall, looming figure with a handlebar moustache. "That's Dick Lovelace – ex-Royal Marines, and a real hang-'em-'n-flog-'em Tory. He'd have us all believe he's just a straight-talking politician; but like the rest of us, he's a schemer at heart – not so much a 'Cockleshell Hero' as a 'cock'n'bull' one! ...And finally that jerk over there, that's Neil Sharpe. He's one of their new members. In fact, he's the only young blood the Tories have got now that you've seen off that Anderson chap."

"And of course," Micky concluded, reclining back in his seat, "no commentary on this council is complete without reference to 'Goldilocks' over there: the thoroughly deadly Councillor Miss Jane Allsop."

"Yes, I've read about her in the papers," Brad confided, watching the deceptively innocent-looking young Liberal making notes, pausing to suck her pen while she allowed her thoughts to congeal. She momentarily glanced up at Brad, looking him up and down with a calculating stare before completing whatever it was she had been scribbling.

"Look at her. Inside that pretty little head there lurks one of the most cunning minds in this chamber. Never fool yourself into thinking that she's just a dumb blonde, because she ain't! You'll find that out soon enough," Micky assured him, aware that the Mayor was becoming impatient at their constant whispering. "She works bloody hard at local level, and knows how to use the press with devastating effect. Thank God there's only one of her – so far at least!"

****

They called it the Battle of Orgreave: a pitched battle fought across the rolling meadows of South Yorkshire. A telegraph pole was uprooted and hurled at the massed ranks of police. "HERE WE GO, HERE WE GO, HERE WE GO...!" chanted their tormentors, charging down the lane brandishing sticks and other makeshift weapons, only to be scattered by mounted policemen across golden cornfields swaying lazily in the warm spring breeze.

Never could two more unyielding forces have faced each other across the divide. On the one side, a government led by a prime minister with an enviable reputation for toughness, and who was no longer prepared to keep on pouring taxpayers' money into the bottomless coffers of the nation's loss-making coal industry. On the other side stood Arthur Scargill, the imperious and uncompromising president of the National Union of Mineworkers – the man who had forced Edward Heath's government to cave in to the power of his legendary 'flying pickets' over ten years earlier. Indeed, this life-long Marxist saw his members as the Praetorian Guard of the Labour movement; shock troops who could succeed where everybody else had failed in slaying the Thatcher juggernaut. However, many trade unionists were not happy with the way the miners' strike was being handled. In particular, Scargill had refused to call a national ballot of the NUM membership to endorse the dispute. This had not impressed the East Midlands miners in particular, who had therefore determined to continue working regardless, prompting hundreds of flying pickets from the Scargill's Yorkshire strongholds to swarm south, terrorising Nottinghamshire pit villages.

The Government harboured no doubts about its resolve. To ministers, Scargill was the personification of evil – a dangerous demagogue who simply had to be defeated, whatever the cost. Planning for just this kind of eventuality, the power stations had been ordered to amass huge stocks of coal, and plenty of non-unionised transport firms stood ready to haul still more from those collieries whose members also sought to defy their president. Battle was therefore joined in the most violent and bitter industrial dispute in living memory.

****

It had been a boring meeting so far; all that kept the assembled councillors awake was the approach of the most controversial item of that evening's business. First, however, they had to listen to one of the less mellifluent councillors droning on about the need to relocate a bus shelter in order to placate some aggrieved residents. Finally, the Mayor called on Roz Young to move her controversial motion. At last, the councillors sat up in anticipation.

"Mr Mayor," the dour left-wing councillor snarled, "we deplore the recent action of this Tory council in refusing the use of the Town Hall by Gunsbridge Trades Council Miners Support Committee. It is part of the ongoing assault by the Tories on the basic freedoms and trades union rights of working people..."

Tom McKerrick sat expressionless at the head of the Labour benches. Like all good socialists, he had a tremendous respect for the miners themselves and the hardships they were facing. Yet he could not help but reflect on the most poignant comment on their struggle: the old Great War metaphor – 'lions led by donkeys'. Sadly, in his heart, he had to agree.

"...So I say, support the miners. Shame on this Tory Government. Shame on this petty, vindictive Council!"

"Mr Mayor," fumed Peter Brereton, who rose to put the controlling group's case, "so long as I'm leader of this council, I will not allow our civic buildings to be used by any organisation that supports a man who takes funds from nasty Middle-Eastern dictators, the same dictator who also finances IRA terrorists that only weeks ago came within an ace of assassinating our prime minister and her cabinet at the Conservative Party Conference in Brighton!"

The debate switched back and forth, and became gradually more heated. Thus it was in an atmosphere of increasing menace that Brad rose to make his own contribution, stung by something that had been said.

"…I, too, abhor the violence that has marked this dispute. But unlike them, I am also prepared to condemn the violence done to peoples' livelihoods by this Tory government..." he reminded the Conservative side.

His comments prompted visible anger from the Conservative benches. He had spoken before in various committees, but never in the chamber itself. It was his 'maiden speech' as such. As passion rose within him, he soon shed any sign of nervousness and launched into his opponents with frightening ferocity. However, he became increasingly exasperated by interruptions from aggrieved Conservatives. Tempers were visibly shortening.

"What about the hardships of the working miners?" somebody shouted, drowning Brad out once again. He doggedly tried to finish his speech, but some unfavourable references to the conduct of the police brought howls of indignation from the Tories.

"Mr Mayor," exclaimed Neil Sharpe, rising to his feet just as Brad was working up to his finale, "How easily Councillor Bradleigh glosses over left-wing plans to undermine the rule of law in this country. Why, he's worse than Hitler."

The accusation created uproar in the chamber – both sides hurling barbs at each other. Frank Collins and Dick Lovelace exchanged angry words. Suddenly a punch was thrown. Councillors dived in to separate Brad and Neil Sharpe, though Brad managed to ram his fist into the Conservative councillor's face. The two new boys were then drawn apart, each restrained by members of their own side. The Mayor had them both ejected from the chamber, and called for an adjournment for fifteen minutes. Meanwhile, in the tumult that descended upon the chamber nobody noticed the lads and lasses from the press gathering in around Jane Allsop, who eagerly summoned them over to a corner of the foyer.

"Like I said, gentlemen," she eagerly proclaimed to their hurried scribbling, "this is indicative of the farce that both Conservative and Labour have reduced this council to. Of course, the Alliance would...."

****

THE GUNSBRIDGE HERALD
Friday, November 30th 1984
Evening Edition - Still only 15p

'HE'S WORSE THAN HITLER' – ANGER ERUPTS IN COUNCIL CHAMBER
Fighting broke out in Gunsbridge council chamber last night when Labour councillor Robert Bradleigh and Conservative opponent Neil Sharpe came to blows over a motion condemning the decision of the Tory-controlled council not to permit the Town Hall to be used for a rally at which miners' leader Arthur Scargill was due to speak...
TYPICAL TORY-LABOUR ANTICS, SAYS COUNCILLOR
The Alliance councillor for Foxcotes, Jane Allsop, has condemned last night's commotion as a 'typical Tory-Labour farce', and contrasted it with her own assiduous work in fighting for better street lighting in Avon Road and a new children's play area on the Cullmore Estate...
CABBIE KILLED IN PIT DISPUTE
A South Wales taxi driver has become the latest victim of the increasingly desperate miners' strike, after a concrete slab was dropped through the windscreen of his car as he was taking a strike-breaking miner to work...
SHOPPING 'MECCA' TO OPEN SOON
The first phase of the massive new Trescott Park Shopping City is now complete, well ahead of schedule. A star-studded official opening is planned next week, says the centre's press officer, Stan Taylor. Brainchild of millionaire property developer Harry Conway, it is predicted that when complete Trescott Park will rival Birmingham as the major shopping attraction in the West Midlands...

****

The little boy gurgled contently while Brad tenderly rocked him. In the background, he could hear Helen idly singing along to the stereo as she was preparing the meal. Then Brad lovingly held him close to him, watching as he pondered every feature of his father's face. Brad carried him over to the glowing Christmas tree that nestled snugly in the corner of the lounge, the tiny fairy lights beaming softly to offer a glorious, heart-warming sensation of Christmas: peace on Earth and goodwill to all men. Oh, that it were only so, Brad thought, cherishing the awe and wonder with which the tiny infant beheld it all. Oh, that he would never have to grow up into a world of cruelty, injustice, pain, suffering and evil. Oh, for that utopia where some benevolent deity would mend every broken heart and wipe away every tear!

  To be sure, Mark Alexander Bradleigh was the son he had always longed for, and whom he now tenderly brushed his nose against, the little lad chuckling merrily before Brad's big beaming eyes. He was determined that, for his son, history would not be repeating itself. He was adamant that Mark would always possess a father who was there: there to help him learn the skills of football; there to help him fix his bike; there to teach him right from wrong; there to comfort him when it seemed he didn't have a friend left to turn to. Yet what sort of world would he inherit? Brad grieved despairingly. Would it be one where unemployment, hunger and deprivation were not merely passed over as regrettable side effects of an otherwise opulent consumer society? Yet everywhere the political right and their all-pervading philosophy of capitalism and individualism were in the ascendance. In November, Ronald Reagan had been re-elected President of the United States by a huge landslide. All across Europe, even nominally socialist governments were emulating the style of free market economics to which Margaret Thatcher had given her name.

All around contradictions abounded. Britain was about to enter the era of high earning 'yuppies' in the City; and yet thousands of mining families were facing Christmas with little but charity to comfort them. The Western world was entering into one of its longest periods of economic boom; and yet, nightly, in affluent living rooms, the television sets buzzed with apocalyptic images of emaciated Africans caught up in famine, war and pestilence. Brad tried to think how he could explain to his son why the world he was likely to inherit was so bereft of morality and justice. However, for now Mark was untroubled, content to be held tightly by his father's loving arms.

Just then Helen re-emerged from the kitchen to put their baby son to bed. Meanwhile, Brad continued the setting of the table, taking out a bottle of wine from the fridge.

"Merry Christmas!" Helen bade him once they had sat down, reaching out towards him with her glass, which she clinked against his own.

Neither one said much for some moments, both deep in their own train of thought. Helen looked up occasionally at the man she had promised herself to, considering just how little she'd actually seen of him lately. Out most nights on either council or party business, even the odd nights they had in were often interrupted by phone calls from people having problems getting any sense out of a council department. Still, she had walked into all this with her eyes open, and tried to accept it was the price she had to pay for having a husband who was a public servant (a high profile one too, following his controversial debut in the council chamber).

Helen was not the only one who wondered what had happened to the partner she had fallen in love with. Brad considered that Helen's affectionate and loving nature had always been one of her finer points. However, since the birth of Mark, something imperceptible had changed about her. The most obvious answer was that it was the lingering effects of the severe post-natal depression that had wreaked havoc with her first few months of motherhood. That was now passing, and he noticed that she seemed more chirpy and relaxed than he had seen her for a long time. Yet he felt that something had changed; he didn't know what it was, though he knew he didn't like it. The tenderness they now enjoyed together across the meal table was just the eye of a storm that would surely be returning. He lifted up the bottle and refilled her glass.

"That reminds me of something I want to tell you," Helen chipped in. "I've found myself a nice little job. The video rental shop in Gunsbridge is looking for a part-time manageress."

"I thought you weren't returning to work."

"It'll do me good. The money will come in useful too."

"Well. Let's hope you get the job then," said Brad, who had his doubts, but smiled approvingly all the same.

****

After all the violent confrontations of the bitter dispute, Arthur Scargill and his depleted band of striking miners had lost one more battle of their long sojourn against economic reality. Despite the longest coal strike ever, the generating stations were able to safely power the country through one of the coldest winters for years. Sadly for those still on strike, victory had vanished over the horizon and out of sight for good. This dawning reality prompted even more miners to drift back to work. Finally, in March 1985 – fully a year after the strike had begun – the last defiant strikers marched back to their pits behind their traditional colliery bands. Their once-formidable union, which had a mere decade earlier brought a government to its knees, had now been reduced to a pitiful shadow of its former self – defeated, divided and forgotten.

Nigel Lawson, Mrs Thatcher's erudite new chancellor-of-the-Exchequer, considered the cost of defeating the miners to be a 'good investment'; and perhaps, viewed dispassionately, it was indeed so. Trades unions now preached moderation and were often as eager as employers to raise productivity and profitability. The biggest privatisation programme in history was now underway, with once-anaemic state firms being snapped up by eager new shareholders across the land. Ironically for the Labour Party too, the defeat of Scargillism ushered in a new age. Increasingly, Neil Kinnock would be projecting himself as his own man; sympathetic towards – though independent of – the once all-powerful trades union powerbrokers. These were to be the first tentative steps towards the creation of a new forward-looking Labour Party.

'ARTHUR SCARGILL WALKS ON WATER,' the president's humble pickets used to chant loyally. Yet the days of his kind of industrial blackmail were over.

Far from walking on them, Scargill and his schemes for revolution and class warfare now vanished unceremoniously beneath the waves.

9 *THE POTTER AND THE CLAY*

The hotel was much as Craig had expected – a rather pleasant stately home that had found a new lease of life as a much-favoured conference venue. Turning off the main road, he cruised past the grazing deer towards the car park, marvelling at this fine country mansion and how it dominated the surrounding fields. Dusk was now closing in fast, and a chill wind forced him to pull his jacket tight around him as he made his way to the entrance hall, laying his bag down and presenting himself to the reception.

"Craig Anderson?" someone asked, strolling up to him. "Hello, I'm Virginia Dettinger from Central Office. I trust you had a good journey down."

A tall, attractive and mature woman offered him her outstretched hand. Her dark hair was immaculately trimmed to border on her collar and danced neatly against each shoulder in turn as she explained politely that she would be chairing the interview sessions.

"Anyway, when you've unpacked, we're all in the sitting room; so just wander in, and I'll introduce you to everyone. Oh, and dinner is served at seven."

Craig climbed the wide spiral staircase, from where corridors seemed to depart in all directions, each one liberally adorned with old masters depicting the ancestry of the house before its hey-day of aristocracy gave way to the arrival of vulgar commercialism. Locating his room, he played with the key until the lock clicked and permitted him to enter in, fumbling for the light switch as he went.

Tasteful, but not excessive, the room was prepared without fault for his arrival. Neatly folded sea blue towels by the wash basin, watched over by a large ornamental mirror that bore his polished image as he glided past to draw the curtains, where he lingered momentarily to appreciate the exquisite beauty of a night owl hooting from the woodlands behind the estate. Then he switched on the television and tuned in to the news, which majored on another gerontocratic Soviet leader who had departed this life to join Marx and Lenin in that great revolution in the sky. This time the succession had skipped a generation, alighting instead upon one Mikhail Sergevich Gorbachev. Mrs Thatcher had recently met with him and been favourably impressed. "We can do business together," Craig recalled she had commented by way of another one of her immortal shopkeeper's metaphors.

He set out down the stairs, dressed in a smart blue blazer and tie. Passing a mirror, he couldn't help pausing to see if the thing was straight. After all, first impressions count, and he still couldn't help fretting that something, somewhere, would let him down. He continued along the corridor to his appointment with destiny, opening the door and peering round, unsure whether he'd entered the right room.

"Ah, Craig. Come on in and sit down," bade a stout gentleman in a dark jacket and air force tie, who was propping up the fire place – a glass of scotch in his one hand and a pipe giving off a sweet aroma in the other. "I'm Sir Colin Eccles of the National Union. And this is David Corbett, managing director of Royle Industries – he's our friend from the world of business for the weekend."

"Pleased to meet you," said the tall, suave businessman, shaking Craig warmly by the hand.

The room was lit just nicely, with a huge, roaring fire giving the little gathering a very cosy, informal ambience. Several people stood chatting in groups or relaxing over drinks in some of the large crafted armchairs that fanned out from the fire place, over which a large ancestral portrait hung, its patrician subject gazing down omnisciently on his assembled guests.

Meanwhile, Sir Colin summoned over the waitress. In the intervening moments, the crusty old aviator probed innocuously to learn more about this latest arrival. "I see you're from Gunsbridge," he bellowed, "Sir Edgar Powers' old seat. I knew the old blighter well. We both went to Eton together."

Such 'old boy' chumminess didn't put Craig wholly at ease: Lower Henley Secondary School wasn't quite in the same league! All the while he could sense that the eyes and ears of the leaders were twitching, eager to pick up clues that would indicate what sort of candidates this month's session had washed up.

Sir Colin eventually alighted upon a further member of the assessment team. "This is Oliver Lyons MP," he informed him, introducing a familiar face into the conversation. "Oliver, this is Craig Anderson from Gunsbridge."

"Haven't I seen you somewhere before?" asked the dashing parliamentarian, slipping his hand into Craig's.

"Oliver is our guest MP during this weekend," Sir Colin reminded Craig. "As you no doubt know, he's minister of state at the Home Office. He's also clinging on to one of the most marginal seats in the North West, so he'll know what to look for when assessing your campaigning skills."

Craig was at ease now. At last, someone who he knew would judge him by what he could do, rather than the West End club his father dined at. There was hope for the meritocracy yet!

Just then, Virginia called them to attention and announced that dinner was served. The party made its way to the restaurant, making acquaintances as they went. Craig spotted several other familiar faces from his old university: lo and behold, it was Jonathan Forsyth and Martin Radbourn (whose acne had sadly not improved with the passage of the years).

"So you're in the business of flogging buses, are you, Craig?" commented Jonathan, still as playful as ever. Dressed in his smart black suit and little blue dickie-bow, he had matured physically, and now looked the sort, as Craig suggested, competent to trade commodities in the City.

"Sure am, old chap," Jonathan asserted. "Can't wait for 'Big Bang' next year."

"How about you, Martin? How are you making your way in the world?" Craig enquired.

"Investment analysis. For a company of merchant bankers, actually."

It sounded fun, Craig thought. It probably spelt money as well. Meanwhile, the waiters and waitresses hurried about serving up a glorious country roast. Then Virginia outlined to them the agenda for their stay. She also reminded them that, after tonight, they would be divided into different teams and referred to only by the number printed on the badges they had received when they had arrived. Craig discovered that he wasn't the only candidate from Gunsbridge.

"I'm Neil Sharpe. Nice to have a fellow Midlander at the table," a brawny dark-haired colleague informed him. After swapping anecdotes, Craig then went on to introduce himself to a bright young thing that he'd noticed once or twice amongst the dozens of hopefuls milling about in the sitting room.

"I'm Brenda Shore, by the way," she responded, introducing herself. "I'm chief press officer for a leading multi-national chemicals conglomerate."

Delving some more, Craig discovered that she was a quite highly paid executive. So why give it all up for a pay cut and a four-year renewable contract?

"I need kicks. PR's exciting, but it's not the ultimate thrill. I'm active in the Greater London YCs, so I thought I'd try the thrill of rousing the voters on the hustings; and then perhaps a ministry in the government."

Craig admired ambition, though this girl was clearly aiming for the stratosphere. He tried to pretend that he was unimpressed by the calibre of Brenda and some of the others high fliers in his group, called appropriately enough 'Blue Team'. So how would Craig shape up? He was confident, or so he thought. He'd read up his Conservative Research Department briefings on current political issues; and he'd faced real, live electors on the doorsteps of a tough Midlands town. Either way, he was determined to give them his best performance: for once he was on the 'approved list' he would have the pick of the seats up for selection in the run-up to the next election. That indeed, was a prospect worth fighting for.

****

Elizabeth Gainsborough was about to untie the skimpy negligee from around her shoulders, and reveal all her mature loveliness... Then the alarm call announced seven o'clock. Craig opened his eyes to greet the new day, cursing the premature ending of a most pleasant dream. He dressed, and then wandered down to enjoy a sumptuous full English breakfast, washed down with fruit juice and much conversation about what the day held in store. Then the team were thrust in front of a video camera, set up to see how they could project themselves on that most critical medium – television.

Oliver Lyons played inquisitor-general. He proved to be as skilful at bowling awkward questions as he was at batting them on *Panorama* or *Weekend World*. Indeed, he played a most forceful devil's advocate, Craig relieved that he had stood up to such a rigorous cross-examination at all. The afternoon session was equally gruelling, with each candidate offered ten minutes to outline a convincing argument in favour of why the others should share their political aspirations. Then the assessors (as well as the other candidates) asked all kinds of searching questions designed to see how well their colleagues stood up in debate.

It went without saying that Martin Radbourn, being the course 'wet', had the most challenging session, with the Thatcherites amongst the group (almost everybody else) grilling him mercilessly on his vision of a greater partnership between both sides of industry. Assessors definitely applauded the skill and patience with which he defended himself.

"Number Thirty, you're advocating further radical measures to roll back the state," asked David Corbett of the self-assured Brenda Shore, "but others are just as sincerely crying 'enough', let's consolidate what we have..."

"It's a natural reaction to change, but let's view it in perspective. Our overseas competitors are still way ahead of us..." she continued assertively.

Just as Brenda had the ability to wrestle with these awkward conundrums, equally Neil Sharpe gave a splendid defence of his plan to reform local government finance. Jonathan Forsyth also fearlessly defended the canon of Thatcherite truth, although his usual propensity to argue rather than debate showed through once more on several occasions. Meanwhile, Craig became bogged down over his support for closer European co-operation, although he fought back tenaciously against Jonathan, Neil and the 'Little Englanders'. Impressive stuff: the assessors marked him up accordingly.

That evening, over drinks by the roaring fire, the candidates unwound and recovered from their ordeals. Indeed, as the evening wore on, all the hopefuls began to feel a sense of common bonding; as if they were the chosen few, hand-picked by Providence to be the principal actors in some mighty cosmic drama. Craig's eyes glazed over as Martin reminisced at length on their old university days. He tried to imagine how these characters might one day lead the Conservatives to future election victories.

"The Prime Minister, Craig Anderson, today finalised his new cabinet, which will include Martin Radbourn as Foreign Secretary, and Neil Sharpe as Chancellor-of-the-Exchequer. Also amongst the new line-up was Party Chairwoman Brenda Shore, who has won considerable renown for her combative performances against the Labour frontbench. Meanwhile, Jonathan Forsyth is to take over at the Home Office..."

"I say, chaps," cried Alexander Horrocks, one of the weekend's less inspiring no-hopers, peeping round the heavy, braided curtains that kept out the draughts, "it looks like the old white stuff's coming down outside. Anybody fancy building a snowman?"

Craig tried to think where he might fit this incurable buffoon into his ministerial team, stretching his sense of fair play to the limit. Minister without portfolio, possibly! Member for the Chiltern Hundreds, the more devilish half of him protested!

They all gathered round to watch the tiny flakes gently gathering on the lawn in front of the window. Outside the chill breath of winter still gripped the countryside, the fresh fall of snow sprinkling itself across the cars parked on the drive. Inside, the hopefuls ruminated upon their performances during the long, tiring day, warm and cosy as they returned once more to gather around the quietly flickering fire and ponder what trials tomorrow might bring.

****

The final breakfast gave way to the most interesting trial of all: a group debate on a controversial topic. By picking the subject of abortion, the assessors had probably picked one of the hottest potatoes of all, and they eagerly scribbled notes and comments on their clipboards as the debate raged across medical ethics, women's rights, and the value of human life. Jonathan Forsyth and Brenda Shore lined up on the pro-choice wing, whilst Craig and Martin Radbourn led the pro-life forces. The others drifted from camp to camp depending on how the debate was progressing,

"Abortion is a terrible reflection on mankind's amorality. Appallingly indignities have been visited on those who were viewed as less than human, and thus considered disposable," asserted Martin.

"I don't think that in a society that talks of freedom of the individual we can then turn round and say to a woman, 'no, you do not have control of your own body and its reproductive processes'," countered Brenda fiercely.

"To close our minds to the plight of thousands of women who will then be forced to have back-street abortions is simply not an acceptable statement of compassion in a civilised society," Jonathan reaffirmed passionately.

"Compassion!" roared Craig indignantly. "How can we say, as a society, that we have 'compassion' when over a million innocent unborn children have been slaughtered? What's more, there has been no need for this carnage: the majority of these would have been perfectly healthy children! The freedom we're talking about is rather the freedom to decide the fate of another distinctive human life. That is not a freedom to be abused with indifference, as it has been our shame to have done over the course of the last two murderous decades."

The assessors said little, except to throw out the odd inflammatory comment to keep the debate moving – not that it needed it! They were overawed by the way Craig and Martin, and Brenda and Jonathan, argued their respective corners coherently, forcefully and imaginatively. The assessors soon had sheets full of notes about how each candidate would square up in parliamentary debate. Exhilarated, the group dispersed for lunch.

"Marvellous performance!" said Virginia, discreetly congratulating Craig in the corridor.

The final session after lunch brought each individual before the assessment team, who then started to prise them open one by one to see what was really inside; and why they felt they should be accorded the honour of representing their chosen party at the highest level.

Craig's turn came around quite early in the proceedings. He entered into a small interview room, where Virginia, Oliver, Sir Colin and David sat facing a dark, swivel chair, which Virginia invited him to make himself at home in. It was rather like *Mastermind*, Craig tittered to himself as he eased himself into the chair, though he thought he'd better not share his amusement lest he be marked down as lacking that treasured ingredient of all good Tory MPs – *gravitas*.

"Now, Number 25, just spend a few moments telling us why you think you'd make an excellent member of parliament. What has led you to put yourself forward before this Selection Board?" asked Sir Colin slowly and purposefully, eyeing up his prey over the top of his half-rimmed glasses.

Craig calmed himself and then spent two or three minutes outlining how he'd become interested in politics at school, how he'd been active in debating at university, his work in two elections – and, indeed, his own candidacy in a local government election. He finished with a peroration on his conviction that the Conservative philosophy of free markets and consumer choice was vital to the process of making the country prosperous and enterprising.

"Are there any particular skills that you feel you could bring with you if you were to be selected?" probed Virginia, following on from her colleague.

"I work in an important manufacturing industry. Virtually all my life I've lived in a town that depends critically on manufacturing to secure its prosperity. I would like to feel that I would fight manufacturing's corner, either in the House or in Cabinet."

"I see," muttered David Corbett, doodling on his notepad, "Don't you feel you're a bit young to be starting out on the road of politics? You're barely twenty-five, not married, and have no family. Would it be fair to say that, as such, you have little feeling for the hopes and aspirations of everyday people and their families?"

Craig was starting to feel the pressure as the panel began to delve into his personal situation. He answered David as best as he could, asserting that he appreciated all the basic human desires, and had proved during his local election campaign that he could empathise with these, and articulate them into his priorities for action.

"Watching you over these last few days, I get the sensation that you're slightly on edge," Oliver dissected him cuttingly. He looked Craig directly in the eye and told him, "I sense that all your life you've had to fight for recognition of your own achievements. The reason I think you're uneasy is that, for whatever reason, all eyes are now on you. It's almost as if you're trying too hard. You've put on a great performance this weekend. But every now and then, it stalls. You seem to be subconsciously looking over your shoulder to see if there is someone there to commend what you've done, to tell you not to worry, and to keep on doing it."

Craig was mortified and froze up, unable to adequately answer him. Oliver pressed him again, asking him to comment on whether he thought that was an accurate description of his predicament.

"Politics is a dirty business and it's a tough business," the MP contended. "Part of the job of this panel is to sort out the talkers from the doers, the dreamers from the fighters. Anyone can talk or dreams about being an MP, but talking and dreaming won't sustain someone through a difficult campaign, or protect you from the haranguing of the media and the opposition. You've had it easy so far, if I may say so. I want you to convince me that when the heat is on, you can stop talking and dreaming, and start doing and fighting."

Swallowing hard, Craig commenced his defence, confessing that "Over the last few years I've had to learn to justify my convictions, and ask myself whether I want to take all the punishment fate can dish out at me; to fulfil my ambition to enter Parliament. You seem to think I'm still asking myself that question; and maybe in the more difficult moments I am. But in the cold light of day, I'd say, yes, I do want to represent the party I love as an MP. I'll find the strength to take the knocks, I know I will!"

Oliver had the information he required and pressed Craig no further. Craig was relieved. Then it was Virginia's turn to cross-examine him.

"Do you have a girlfriend at the moment?"

"No, I don't."

"Is that because you spend so much of your time involved in politics?"

"That. Plus my career."

"Don't you feel that once you're a candidate, you'll never find the time to get to know a young lady?"

"Maybe. Who knows?"

"Does that worry you? I mean, the thought of living life on your own."

Craig paused in a moment clouded with terror. If he said no, she'd either mark him down as a liar, a closet homosexual, or both.

"Yes," he muttered, "I mean no. One has to take what comes in this life. You've already said politics is a rough and dirty business, but it also requires a total commitment of body and mind in order to succeed. Maybe a wife would complement that struggle; or maybe I'm better off on my own. Again, I don't pretend to know the answer to that one. But either way, I'll do it. That remains my intention!"

Craig wandered from the room shell-shocked, instructing Martin Radbourn rather lamely that he was the next to be interrogated. Regaining his composure over a drink at the bar, he thought about Oliver's assertions. He was sure he didn't lack confidence: after all, self-doubt is a common human emotion – even the PM admitted that occasionally she shed a tear or two!

He had already handed in his thousand-word submission on how to run a successful campaign, and was confident that it was a political and psephological masterpiece. With that done, there was nothing else left to do now except hope.

Meanwhile, Neil Sharpe wandered into the bar, equally shell-shocked from his interrogation.

"Tough time?" Craig asked him.

"A nightmare!" he sighed wearily. "I think they've poked at every skeleton in the cupboard. They dredged up that wretched punch-up in the council chamber. I knew that would come back to haunt me!"

"It's okay. I think everyone – with the possible exception of that pillock Horrocks – is convinced that we've all sunk ourselves. Maybe that's part of the process."

Craig's gallows humour induced a grin out of Sharpe. One day these two men might be rivals for the same prize. For now though, they were both two exhausted and demoralised brothers, sharing a common affliction in that, in a few hours time, the assessment team would be making judgements that would determine who would, and who would not, be offered the chance to fight the next general election for the Conservative Party.

****

"Right chaps, I think we have all the information on Blue Team that we need. We'd better commence the dreadful deed, starting with Number 12. Fail?" asked Virginia without enthusiasm.

"Fail," was the collective reply. Alexander Horrocks was doomed. The group quickly flipped over to their more ambivalent notes on Neil Sharpe.

"Now Number 20 did cause me some heart-searching," said Sir Colin, donning a pained expression. "I've got to say he's a smart chap, but I sense something of the wild man within him."

"I know what you mean," David concurred, "very clever, very precise, very cool – then every now and then, kerpow! He blows it! I think we saw that yesterday, didn't we Oliver?"

Oliver nodded as he lounged back in his chair. "He's definitely got a short fuse. That said," Oliver quickly continued, "I wouldn't want to write him off for all time. He's got the potential to make it big."

"Shall we defer him for consideration at a later date?" suggested Virginia.

"I think that course would be very wise, my dear," Sir Colin concluded. With that, Neil Sharpe's application was put on ice. It might well be too late before he received another favourable assessment with which to contest the next general election. How easily fate deals such rogue cards to those who stake their alls on the outcome of such a game as this.

"I don't know about you," maintained Virginia, "but I think Number 23 is bright, but far too abrasive."

Once again Virginia and Oliver disagreed, Oliver using his parliamentary experience to illustrate how useful a combative figure like Jonathan would be at getting under the skins of the Opposition. After all, Norman Tebbit had turned baiting the Opposition into an art form!

"What about his relations with his constituency party?" Virginia demanded of her colleague. "That requires a degree of tact and finesse that this young man plainly doesn't possess!"

"I know; and that's why I love him. He doesn't care: he just tells everyone what's on his mind. Anyway, it hasn't done me any harm!" Oliver joked. Gradually, he eased the team around to his point of view, and Jonathan Forsyth was passed as approved to represent the Conservative Party.

"Number 30?" said Virginia, in a tone of voice pregnant with expectation.

"She's a winner – no hesitation! One of the best I've seen," affirmed David.

"Woman prime minister number two!" noted Oliver flippantly.

"Pass?" enquired Virginia, going through the formalities.

"Without any doubt at all!" confirmed Oliver. Brenda Shore received unanimous approbation.

"How about Number 29?"

No one said a word for a few seconds before Oliver chipped in, "I hate his politics; but the kid is good."

"Yes, defends himself well. Very intellectually supple, and thinks about what he's saying. Anyway, who knows; one day the heart and soul of the Tory Party might once again swing his way," noted Sir Colin, his closing remarks obviously horrifying Oliver. Meanwhile, Virginia flicked over Martin Radbourn's sheet; the polite, One-Nation Tory sailed safely over the water to the start of a career on the parliamentary ladder.

"Lastly, Number 25. Quite an impressive young man, I'd say," enthused Virginia.

"Yes, he's very good; and he's very handsome. You know – the sort the television cameras chase after!"

Sir Colin's comments brought Oliver into the fray. "I like him; he's a charmer, of that there is no doubt. He enjoys politics, and has taken it all in his stride so far. But what I said about him this afternoon still stands. I think he tends to be unsure of himself. I think he could crack."

Oliver and Sir Colin gradually grew quite voluble as they debated whether Craig was too nice to be a politician. The meritocratic MP maintained that Craig had yet to make any enemies, judging from what he had gleaned of him over the weekend. The crusty old Etonian countered by inferring that one didn't need to be a bruiser to be an effective politician – something that Oliver found very hard to accept.

"Just look at him during the debating sessions. It was as if a fire was ignited within him. What an orator! Oliver, he's got all the potential," Sir Colin insisted, defending the lad from Gunsbridge against the MP's sniping.

Virginia allowed the debate to progress until, deadlocked, she intervened. "It's no use. We have to make a decision. Do we fail him? Do we defer him? Or are we going to be generous? I hope we will, because I tend to agree with David. I say approve him, and let the constituencies weigh him up for themselves." (To which David agreed).

"Pass him. We won't regret it!" said Sir Colin, without hesitation. "Besides, his father is ex-RAF!" he then joked.

"It would be nice to have a unanimous decision," said Virginia, smiling forgivingly at their errant MP.

"I suppose he did shine – for all my criticism of him... Go on, I'll pass him."

"Thank you, gentlemen. That's Blue Team out of the way," sighed Virginia with relief. "May I suggest we adjourn to the bar for a few minutes. Then we can come back and have a look at Red Team..."

****

Politicians, someone once said, are born to be either warriors or conciliators. There was little doubt that, by any measure, Margaret Thatcher was a warrior, who seemed to only give of her best when slaying dragons, real or imaginary. She had already taken on the cabinet 'wets', Argentine revanchists, CND and Arthur Scargill. During the summer of 1985, it was becoming obvious that a new challenge to her government was rekindling that old fire within the Prime Minister's breast: for having wreaked havoc upon the Labour body politic, the

Militant Tendency now began to bare its fangs at the Government itself. Their chosen battlefield was to be the Byzantine world of local government finance; their chosen champion, Liverpool City Council – led by one cocky, overweening young Militant councillor who went by the name of Derek Hatton.

Hatton had first come to fame in 1983 when Liverpool had successfully defied the Government over the constraints it was imposing upon populist municipal spending programmes. However, two years later Mrs Thatcher unveiled a new weapon against spendthrift local authorities: rate-capping. In addition, auditors had started proceedings to surcharge Liverpool's Labour councillors. As the news sunk in amongst the voters that their municipal services were on the line, the Militants who controlled the council began to look increasingly culpable and exposed.

****

Craig was sitting in his warm, cosy flat, debating whether to feed Dire Straits or Tears for Fears into the hi-fi. Then the doorbell sounded. Dutifully, he lifted himself out of the armchair and made for the front door. Fiddling with the catch, he discovered two girls standing outside.

"Good morning, sir, we're from Gunsbridge Elim Church... Craig?"

"Nikki?"

"You two know each other?" asked the other girl, observing how her companion had been completely taken aback by the handsome young man who had emerged to see who was there.

"Don't just stand there! Come on in!" said Craig, opening the door more generously as he bade them enter.

As he ushered them into his lounge, Craig was still trying to wake himself up properly, for he was sure this had to be the start of another of his erotic dreams. Here was the girl he had once adored, who was now five years older – and more beautiful than ever. What's more, she was entering into his parlour, removing her coat at his instruction, and bringing an equally appealing young companion with her. Taking their jackets and hiding them away in some cupboard, Craig still expressed surprise as he offered them a drink.

"So what brings you here?" he shouted from the kitchen, "I thought you had departed for foreign parts."

"I did," cried Nikki, snuggling into Craig's settee. "I've spent the last two years in Spain. In two weeks time, I'm taking up a mission post in Mexico. Until then, I'm in your area for the crusade at the Town Hall. That's why we're touring the estate, inviting people along."

"Oh, that thing. Yes, I saw something about it in the papers," said Craig, returning with a tray of coffees. At last he was convinced that this was indeed reality; he was not dreaming.

"So who's your friend?" he asked.

"Craig, this is Elaine Joyner; she's working with me from Gunsbridge Elim Church. Elaine, this is Craig Anderson; an old friend from my university days, who I haven't seen in years."

Craig concurred with a nod, "And if I may say, you have become more beautiful with the passage of time."

"He always was the charmer – even then. I think that's what first impressed me about him. He was the only boy who ever made my ego positively swell," she laughed, Elaine sharing her friend's amusement.

"Tell me, are you still into all this politics?" she asked before turning to Elaine to elaborate that "Craig was a leading Young Conservative on the campus. He was quite a good speaker in the university debates."

"Yes, for all my sins, I'm still active. I hope to be selected for a parliamentary seat before too long. So what will you be doing in Mexico?" he enquired.

"I'll be working as a teacher with the same missionary organisation that my father once served with."

"So I see you're still into this Christianity thing," said Craig.

"I'm working full time there now. It's what I guess I always believed I'd do," she replied, staring Craig in the eye.

"So Craig isn't a Christian?" said Elaine, starting to latch onto the nuances of this peculiar friendship. There was no answer, both Craig and Nikki looking at each other longingly, conscious that each of them had a different definition of precisely what constituted a 'Christian'. That said, what did she feel for him? he thought, watching that soft smile break out across her angelic face. She was asking the same kind of questions of him.

"Are you still going out with Steve?" Craig asked her directly.

She thought for a moment before begging him, "Steve who?"

"That jerk, I mean guy, you were going out with at university."

"She thought a bit more. "Oh, that Steve! Oh no, we parted long ago. I'm a free woman now; which is probably just as well, seeing that I'm never in one place long enough to worry about boys."

Elaine watched the two friends recall old times, and began to feel something of a gooseberry. Nikki described her adventures in Spain, and what had led her to decide to spend a further two years in Mexico. Craig told her about his attempt at winning a council seat, and his recent grilling to get on the 'approved list'.

"Anyway, thank you for the coffee. I suppose we'd better be continuing our rounds. Otherwise nobody's going to be hearing the 'Good News'."

"What Good News is this, anyway?" Craig asked.

Nikki prompted Elaine, who pulled out a leaflet from her bag and offered it for Craig's perusal. *"Come and hear the Reverend Felix Stevenson describe how Jesus can transform your life,"* he read out verbatim from the cover. Flicking through the contents briefly he seemed impressed.

"When's he in town?" he enquired.

"The end of September. For four nights," Elaine informed him, referring him back to the front cover.

"So are you coming?" said Nikki, nudging him playfully. "We wouldn't want you to miss out on such a treat!"

"I might. I tell you what. I'm in need of someone to escort me to our constituency president's annual dinner next Friday. I hate going on my own. If you'll be my companion for the evening, then I promise I'll sit on the front row of your 'crusade'. How about it?"

The two girls looked at one another as they stood in the doorway ready to leave. Elaine had by now gleaned that Craig definitely had eyes for her friend, and suspected that – whatever Nikki might have intimated to her about the importance of being single in her chosen vocation – the feeling was definitely mutual.

"Okay, it's a deal!" she grinned, to Craig's evident satisfaction. Love, like politics it seemed, turns up all kind of surprises.

****

Craig drove around the corner and located the house he was looking for. *Deo Gloria* was just a little terraced property nestling up a quiet side street, but it fitted the description he had been given. So switching off the ignition he climbed out of the little blue Rover, straightened his dickie-bow, and pulled his jacket together. Then he wandered up and tapped on the door. The diminutive Elaine poked her head around the half-open portal.

"She's nearly ready. I'll go and tell her you're here."

After ushering Craig inside she ran upstairs, leaving him in the living room with two of her fellow lodgers, who were sitting on the floor drinking coffee from mugs with silly cartoons on the side, and who suddenly expressed great interest in this dashing new arrival.

"Oh, by the way. Craig, this is Rachel and Esther," cried Elaine just before she disappeared at the top of the stairs.

Both girls smiled at him, offering him a spot on the settee next to a silky black cat that was purring gently. He offered the animal a few introductory caresses, which it didn't refuse.

"She's spent hours getting herself ready for this evening, so she's evidently looking forward to it very much," said Rachel, who shuffled about on her delicate little posterior, pulling her legs tight under her.

Craig smiled, and then looked around to see what the ambience of the room was telling him about the occupants of the house. It was lovingly decorated in shades of grey and pink and Laura Ashley, as perhaps only three girls living together could do. On the walls were framed sketches of a suitably religious character. A shelf full of Christian books sat under the stairs. A record player softly played devotional themes....

> *"Take my life, a living sacrifice, knowing it's the least that I can do.*
> *Make my life a living sacrifice, holy and acceptable to You..."*

Still, it was all very homely. The cat obviously wouldn't countenance being anywhere else right then. It lay back and stretched out, its claws emerging and then retreating back into their sheaths as it dozed off once more.

"Nikki tells us you're going to be our next MP," said Esther. Craig mumbled something, modestly explaining that it wasn't quite as easy as all that. The girls listened with interest until they heard the bedroom door close upstairs. Then a pair of long, sleek legs began to appear through the gaps in the banister of the staircase that led straight down into the living room.

Craig stood up slowly, Nikki elegantly descending the stairs to stand before him in all her regal majesty. Her dark, shoulder-length hair glistened under the sympathetic lights of the small room, as did those lips and eyes. A black and gold evening dress started just off her shoulders and ended just short of her knees, where a pair of black stockings took over and continued all the way down her gorgeous legs to terminate at a pair of black, high-heel shoes. A small bracelet and a tiny watch hung on each delicate wrist, and she clutched a small, strapless handbag ready for her prince to escort her to the ball.

"You look more beautiful than I have ever seen any woman look before," sighed the 'prince', as if in a trance. He was thus indifferent to the amusement that his disbelief was occasioning to Esther and Rachel.

"Don't forget, Craig. Return her safe home by midnight otherwise she'll turn into a pumpkin!" they tittered. All of which prompted Craig to drift gently back down to Earth, trying to hide his embarrassment.

"You've no idea how honoured I am to be with you tonight," he insisted as he chauffeured her into town.

"I have. I can see it in your eyes. That's one of the reasons you always impressed me. You have a very honest face. I think we need more honest and upright men and women in politics."

Craig was flattered. Momentarily taking his eyes off the road to look her up and down, he continued, "I'm honoured, above all, that you've evidently taken a lot of time to look as good as you do."

"It was quite a challenge, I can tell you. The bulk of my wardrobe is up at my parents' place. I'm only down here for two weeks with Felix Stevenson. I certainly didn't think I'd be requiring an evening dress. So I borrowed Esther's. The make-up is Elaine's; and Rachel very kindly did my hair for me."

"So you travel about a lot with this 'Reverend' fellow?"

"I shall be flying out to Mexico shortly, but until then I'm working as a member of his evangelism team."

Craig escorted Nikki inside the plush hotel, where they joined the glitterati of the Gunsbridge Conservative establishment gathering to enjoy one of the highlights of their social calendar. Meanwhile, Craig eased Nikki's coat away from her exposed shoulders, handing it to the cloakroom attendant.

"Our president's evenings are always terrific occasions; and this year will be no exception. Our guest speaker is none other than Nigel Lawson..."

"Not *the* Nigel Lawson?" she exclaimed.

"Oh yes. Our president doesn't do things in half measures. I'm not sure whether we're more honoured to have the Chancellor-of-the-Exchequer as our guest speaker; or whether the Chancellor's more honoured to be speaking at a function organised by our illustrious president!" he joked.

"Hello, Craig, who's your lovely lady friend?" enquired Gerry Roberts, who bumped into the duo as he cruised past in his best dinner jacket and bright blue dickie-bow, his latest stunning young blonde piece gripping his arm.

Craig introduced Nikki to Gerry, and also to Elizabeth Gainsborough and her husband; to his friend George Franklin, whose wheelchair-bound wife was making one of her rare public appearances; and to Peter Brereton and his wife, all of whom were charmed by Nikki's pleasant banter and her graceful demeanour. Finally, they all filed past the toastmaster and into the banqueting hall.

"...Mr Craig Anderson and Miss Nicola Branson...," the room then filling with excitement as the toastmaster called out, ".... Ladies and gentleman, the Right Honourable Mr and Mrs Nigel Lawson MP..."

Seated at the top table, the committee welcomed their esteemed guests. After grace was spoken, the gathering then assumed their seats. Then the waiters and waitresses began the mammoth job of serving everyone. Craig and Nikki were seated next to Elizabeth, with Gerry and his girlfriend positioned opposite.

"I have to tell you, Nikki, I was worried about young Craig, here," his best friend joked. "Past twenty-five and still on the shelf. Yet I knew when he finally alighted upon a companion for his lonely old age, he'd choose the very best. And, behold, the lad has not proved me wrong!"

"You say the nicest things," Nikki beamed, her diamond smile making its debut. All through the first course, Nikki chatted away without a care in the world, explaining why she was in Gunsbridge, and the mission she was engaged upon. Far from intimidating or boring her listeners, as Craig had feared, they actually found it fascinating, all agreeing amongst themselves that it was nice to find a young lady who was prepared to stand up for her beliefs and ideals.

Craig was content for once just to be a spectator, watching his superlative companion in action. How incredibly disarming she was; yet how deep, how discerning, how gracious and, always, how beautiful. Craig knew then – if ever he had possessed any doubts – that he had to have this girl at his side, whatever the cost.

"We really must do this more often," he insisted to her *sotto voce*.

Nikki thanked him for inviting her, but remained non-committal. Small-talking some more, he still could not coax out the words he hoped to hear.

Banging his gavel, the president stood up and waited for silence to descend upon the room. He commenced his vote of thanks before introducing the Chancellor to them in grandiloquent terms. Their guest speaker then rose to the applause of the local party before launching into a speech outlining the Government's determination to continue working an economic miracle – that, whilst laced with occasional wit and humour, was all the same a masterpiece of Lawsonesque precision.

"What's a PSBR?" whispered Nikki during the course of the Chancellor's peroration.

"Public Sector Borrowing Requirement," Craig replied, still glued to the Chancellor's every word.

"Oh," said Nikki, making it plain that she was none the wiser.

Craig broke his concentration and offered her a fuller explanation. "How much the Government is in debt."

"Oh. And what's the Exchange Rate Mechanism?"

"It's... well, it's sort of... I'll tell you afterwards!"

Finally, the Chancellor sat down to hearty applause. The chairman signalled his intention of permitting a few questions, several petitioners seeking to milk Lawson's keen mind for economics, and to whom the deft little Chancellor gave suitably precise replies. Craig was fortunate enough to catch the chairman's eye as it roved the hall. He introduced himself and stood up to cross-examine the Chancellor.

"Mr Lawson, is it not possible that, as the economy starts to improve, we may well find that our domestic manufacturers are unable to fully satisfy demand? Therefore, is it not inevitable that we will incur a balance of payments deficit, as well as a return to inflationary pressures?"

Craig's question impressed the Chancellor. However, he proceeded to try to put Craig's fears to bed with a discourse on the new contribution of service industries to the nation's economy, as well as the new regime created by deregulated financial markets. Craig couldn't help noticing some of the 'Maywood Heath Mafia' tittering amongst themselves, no doubt delighting that this impetuous little whippersnapper from Lower Henley had been put in his place. He winced, and felt all the old insecurities flooding back. He sat down, looking to Nikki for reassurance.

For what it was worth, Nikki wasn't tittering. She had observing how Craig had lost none of his oratorical flair, only improved on it with practice. She felt so much for this dashing young man; yet he remained sadly outside the will of the God she believed had called her to other things. Sooner or later he would have to hear about these things for himself. So when the Chancellor finished his reply – and she watched Craig appear to bask in the congratulations and commiserations of his peers for almost, but not quite, confounding their guest speaker – she felt so sad that she had at last come so close to finding the boy of her dreams. However, the tickets to Mexico were booked; and that, she knew, was that!

The journey home was filled mostly with Craig trying to enlighten the innocent Nicola on the complexities of the Government's economic strategy.

"Your heart is very much into your politics, isn't it?" Nikki had to confess.

Craig shrugged his shoulders. "Only as much as yours is into all this Jesus business."

"I suppose it is," she mused resignedly. "Does it worry you that I'm a Christian?" she asked him bluntly.

"Why should it? We all need some reference point in life. You just seem more sure than most."

"I think a lot of you, Craig. All the while I was at university I could see you liked me and that you were very patient. You're so different from other boys. Yet I..."

"You bet I like you," Craig enthused, cutting her off in mid-sentence "And tonight has been one of the most memorable evenings of my life. You make me feel so proud, so lucky to be in your company."

Nikki wanted to explain further, but Craig's ceaseless flattery was getting the better of her. So she reclined back into the seat, and passed most of the journey watching the suburbs of Gunsbridge flash past, occasionally turning to smile at her effusive admirer.

It was just past eleven on the little clock on the facia of the car when Craig switched off the engine. A solitary streetlight illuminated rather poorly the tiny house where Nikki was staying, and where the occupants had evidently retired to their beds. Neither one said a word until Craig slowly turned to stare into Nikki's eyes. She waited for him to edge closer towards her. Then she had to let it happen. Those same sparkling eyes closed, and she formed her mouth ready for him to alight upon it with warm, cushioned lips. She trailed him with each turn and twist of their mouths, tenderly expressing their silent longing, Craig's dreams finally realised in the simple power of a kiss. Breaking apart, he slowly progressed down her long, exposed neck, pecking gently before returning back up to explore each feature of her face with greater vigour and frequency. She was motionless, party to all he cared to delight her with. Bracing her arms around his shoulders, she pulled him tight unto her, and started exploring him for herself, lingering upon a final deep kiss. Then they inched apart as slowly and wilfully as they had chosen to come together, staring into the other's wistful eyes.

****

There was certainly a carnival atmosphere about Gunsbridge Town Hall when Craig walked in with Nikki by his side. This time it seemed so different from the many election night dramas he had witnessed over the years. Background music was slowly easing the audience into a spiritual frame of mind as they gathered to take their seats in the huge hall.

"Jesus, we enthrone You, we proclaim You our King,
Standing here in the midst of us, we raise You up with our praise..."

Over the stage there now hung a large, brightly coloured banner proclaiming *'JESUS CHRIST IS LORD'*. Occasionally, people would bump into someone they knew, hugging and embracing each other like a long lost brothers or sisters.

"Jesus, Jesus, Jesus is the Lord, Jesus is Lord God Almighty,
Who was and is and is to come. Jesus, Jesus, Jesus is the Lord..."

Once inside, a handsome young man with a disarmingly laid-back demeanour glowed charitably and welcomed the couple as they strode up to him.

"Hiya, Nikki, who's your friend?" he enquired.

"This is Craig Anderson from Gunsbridge South Young Conservatives. I know him from my university days."

"Ah, yes. I remember receiving one of your election leaflets through my door. I never forget a name or a face," he said, Craig astounded that someone could still recall his campaign long after others had forgotten.

"Craig, this is Pastor Scott Eversley of Gunsbridge Elim Church."

"Pleased to meet you," said Craig, shaking his hand. It also amazed him too that such a boyish figure could conceivably head a church.

The couple took their seats whilst the choir opened with some rousing hymns and choruses. Craig hadn't witnessed such enthusiastic singing at a religious service. There was dancing, arm-waving, and weeping breaking out all around him. While he shared his hymn sheet with Nikki (and went through the motions of pretending to sing along too) he thought he could sense her feet also tapping away to these jazzy spirituals.

> *"I'm forgiven, now I have a reason for living,*
> *Jesus keeps givin' and givin', givin' 'til my heart overflows..."*

Nikki evidently appreciated the words, so Craig leant over towards her. "What's this forgiveness that they keep singing about?" he asked.

"It's the forgiveness of Jesus when He died on the cross," she replied matter-of-factly.

"I thought He'd done that; that we were all forgiven. They seemed to be saying that there's more to it than that."

"And so there is. In order to become a Christian, we, as individuals, need to accept that forgiveness, believe that He died for us personally, and confess to others that we believe that to be so."

Mumbo-jumbo, thought Craig as he tried to make sense of all this. He was baptised; he believed in a god. What more need he do? So instead, he turned his attention to more pressing matters.

He had an interview coming up for a safe seat out in 'the sticks': the kind of majorities that they weigh rather than count! Though he knew the competition would be tough; and though it was a rural constituency (and Craig didn't know one end of a sheep from the other!), nonetheless he tried to be optimistic. In addition, the post of chairman of the YCs was up for re-election, and Craig had made the decision to stand for a second term. It could be one more time-consuming chore, or it could be a useful entry on his CV; one more forum for befriending other Young Conservatives from around the country, many of whom were the sons and daughters of important officers in constituencies that he was hoping to be selected for. At work, he had recently been promoted to a senior management post with the responsibility for establishing potential markets overseas. In fact, as the towering, monolithic of Felix Stevenson stood up to commence his sermon, Craig wondered how the hell he'd found the time to come and listen to the Gunsbridge 'God Squad' in the first place. Then he looked at Nikki. There was the reason, and he manoeuvred his hand snugly into her own, to which she responded by opening her fingers and locking their hands firmly together. It felt so natural that, for the first time in several minutes, he felt sufficiently at ease to actually make an effort to listen to what the commanding Reverend gentleman was saying.

"So I tell you my friends that no matter how secure you think you are, without Christ you're only muddling through this life. You can be religious, or think you are; but it will avail you nothing. You can do good works, and be a fine, upstanding member of your community; but it will not alter your condition of separation from God. Jesus made it plain in John's Gospel, saying, *'I tell you the truth, that unless a man is born again, he cannot see the Kingdom of God.'* And this goes to the very heart of our condition because we..."

So Craig was deluding himself, was he? Still, there were times when even he wondered whether it was all worth it. The prize goes to the swift, the cunning, and even the ruthless. After all, no one would ever remember a politician who failed honourably – least of all his detractors amongst the 'Maywood Heath Mafia'.

So many times it had seemed that Craig had done just that. He had had his share of disappointments, sure; but that wasn't the context he was thinking of. Politically, he could claim a sound record of achievement. Personally though, there was manifest evidence of failure in his life – not least his utter inability to ever reconcile his father to all that he held most dear. This alienation hurt, for it cut deep to the very heart of him. If a man cannot enjoy the confidence of his own father, then does that not somewhere undermine his ultimate confidence in himself? He longed to impress him, to receive the accolade of his recognition. Throughout his life he had turned to his brother; then to his peers; perhaps now to Nikki; when all along the one he really wanted to turn to was his father.

"...But I say that reconciliation between God and man, between the Father and his children, is now complete; for it says in Luke's Gospel, *'And the curtain of the temple was torn in two, and Jesus called out in a loud voice 'Father, into your hands I commit my spirit''*. That torn curtain symbolised the separation that existed between God and man. By offering his blood, Jesus has ended that separation for all time. No longer need you bear your guilt and sin and shame, for Christ has set you free. And *'if the Son has set you free, you are free indeed'*!"

Nikki looked for Craig's response. He returned the glance. "He's good this guy!" he then acknowledged, adding tritely, "I could learn a thing or two from him for when I'm on the hustings!"

Finally, Reverend Stevenson concluded with an appeal for people to come forward and accept Jesus into their lives. Craig had seen such things on documentaries about overbearing American tele-evangelists, but he'd never witnessed such a phenomena first-hand before. It was a touch unnerving, not least because it was so unlike the stereotype he'd fixed in his mind. Reverend Stevenson did not hector his listeners, nor call down hell, fire and damnation on those who, like Craig, had the audacity to remain in their seats. All the time a beautiful soloist was softly singing in the background...

"Jesus, You are changing me, by Your Spirit You're making me brand new,

*Jesus, You're transforming me, that Your loveliness might be seen in all I do.
You are the potter and I am the clay, help me to be willing to let You have Your way,
Jesus, You are changing me as I let You reign supreme within my heart..."*

'The potter and the clay': an interesting analogy, Craig mused. Meanwhile, the preacher spoke gently of the love and humility of Jesus in laying down His life. He asked his listeners to come forward if they wanted to acknowledge that sacrifice in their own lives. Craig felt an affinity with such selflessness – who wouldn't? But he still remained in his seat while the Reverend closed in prayer. He gripped Nikki's hand just to remind himself what the hell he was doing on a wet Wednesday night standing with his eyes closed, surrounded by a bunch of people weeping 'alleluia' and 'glory' while some seven-foot preacher was laying his hands on people and calling out to some 'holy spirit'. Love, like politics it seemed, really does lead one into the most surreal situations. He glanced round and noticed Nikki humming along, eyes closed and tears just visible on her smooth, tanned cheeks. 'The potter and the clay': it bore thinking about, and he duly filed it away at the back of his mind, looking down at his watch.

"What now?" he commenced with the leading question.

Nikki shrugged her shoulders. "I'm open to suggestions."

"Good. Then there's a little restaurant I know just across the way. I just thought we could celebrate what remains of our week in style before you fly out."

Outside it was raining quite heavily. Nikki erected her umbrella, and they both huddled underneath, dashing along the street and through the deserted shopping arcade. Reaching the cosy little bistro, Craig opened the door and they disappeared into the half-light. Only a handful of people were out on the town on such a rotten night, just as he had hoped. Within no time at all they were escorted to a waiting candlelit table.

"Craig, the last few days have been fabulous. You've spent all your money on me. I feel so guilty that..."

"Say nothing! I'd willingly blow the lot for you. And as for Mexico – well, I can't pretend I want you to go. I think a lot of you, well, er... go on, I'll say it – I think I love you," he confessed unashamedly. "It's not just a spur of the moment thing. I adored you at university. I've often thought about you since. And when you knocked on my door the other day, well... it was a dream come true..." Nikki waited while Craig struggled to finish what he was trying to say, mumbling "...I know: your God is calling you to go. I understand. I know what it's like to have some inner conviction driving you on. But I want you to know that I really do believe my life will be the poorer without you."

Nikki shared the same inner feelings, but couldn't bring herself to say so. She thought she noticed a tear steal away down Craig's cheek.

"You'll be okay," she countered unconvincingly. "The future belongs to dynamic young men like you. I have no doubt that you'll go far in whatever you do. Just don't try to do it in your own strength. We're all human; we're all fallible. It's only when we learn to lean on someone higher than ourselves that we discover the real power that fashions us to do all the things we believe to be right."

Craig knew precisely what she was obliquely trying to say – 'the potter and the clay' and all that jazz! However, all his thoughts now turned to the fact that he had only a few more days left before his dream girl disappeared off to foreign parts. They traded on each other's backgrounds until the evening was finally through. Then the time came to escort his princess back to her lodgings. While Nikki excused herself to go to the ladies' room, Craig used the opportunity to settle the bill. Waiting for his companion to return, he couldn't help noticing a couple and their friends enjoying their wedding anniversary at another table. It must be nice to have someone to buy nice things for, Craig thought. He had now mapped out his life to position himself for the success he yearned for. All that remained was to find someone with whom he could share it. Further tears stole away unnoticed in the half-light for a goal that would elude him still.

10 ONE OF US

A truly awful miasma was hanging over the 1985 Labour Party Conference in Bournemouth. Maybe Neil Kinnock felt that way too. In the meantime, Sharif Khan, who was sitting next to Brad, was becoming fatigued, for the Labour leader had been droning on for rather too long in all his fulsome Welsh prose. Then, all of a sudden, Brad sat up. The miasma had gone, and a palpable thrill was descending upon the hall.

"You start with far-fetched resolutions," Kinnock noted impatiently. "They are then pickled into a rigid dogma... and you end up in the grotesque chaos," he continued, "of a Labour council – A LABOUR COUNCIL – hiring taxis to scuttle around the city handing out redundancy notices to its own workers!"

Pandemonium broke out for a few brief seconds before Kinnock's tirade hit home. Somewhere in the auditorium Derek Hatton was jabbing his arms about in righteous indignation. Some of the worthies of the National Executive Committee stormed off the platform in disgust. Yet, Militant heckling aside, somehow the conference floor reasserted itself.

"YOU-CAN'T-PLAY-POLITICS-WITH-PEOPLES'-JOBS!" the Leader of the Labour Party insisted, his emphatic words greeted with enthusiastic applause. Brad stood to his feet to cheer him on, Khan trying to pull him down, but realising that it was no use. The dumbstruck Kashmiri sank back into his seat with a look of incredulity written all over his swarthy face.

"The people," Kinnock reminded the conference in dramatic and measured tones, "will not – cannot – abide posturing. They cannot respect the 'gesture generals' or the Tendency tacticians... Life is too real to mistake conference resolutions for accomplished facts, or mistake individual enthusiasm for a mass movement."

In the foyer afterwards, Hatton tried to hold back a circle of news correspondents who were bunching around him, insisting in his strident Scouse tones that "The line he was taking against Liverpool Council was an absolute disgrace... and a travesty of justice!"

"Bollocks!" cried Brad, overhearing him as he shoved past the outer ring of Hatton's ensemble on his way out into the fresh air. Khan chased after him, snaking through the crowds of excited delegates swarming from the hall.

"Are you crazy?" he screeched at his comrade, finally drawing level with him at the exit onto the Promenade. "He's just snubbed good working people in there – all to win a few plaudits from the Murdoch press!"

"Come on, Sharif," Brad groaned intolerantly, "you've seen the crap we've had to swallow over the years: all those ridiculous motions on this, that or the other that end up changing sweet nothing."

"It makes no difference! Kinnock is destroying the last chance we had of making Thatcher choke on her miserable local government reforms. And you have the gall to clap him!"

Yes, I clapped him! Sometimes some things just can't be left unsaid. And I desperately want us to get this mess out of our system."

Each time Khan halted him, Brad merely carried on along the seafront, his black mane carried up by the wind and occasionally across his granite face.

"I just hope you change your mind before the selection committee sits down to decide who'll be fighting your seat next time," Khan yelled after him.

Brad stopped, turned about, and marched back up to him. "Is that a threat? Is that a threat?" he demanded, eyeballing the stocky Asian defiantly.

"We want a councillor who knows where he stands when the Tories attack working people," Khan spat at him.

"Is that a fact now? Well, let me tell you something, mate!" Brad spat back. "People have had it up to here; they're through with all these childish games. What they want is a strategy for winning the next general election – not a roll-call in Heaven stating that 'thou said the right things on committee'! Stuff all that! The days of your sour-faced friends going round sabotaging all the hard work of the dedicated men and women of this movement are numbered. And you, my friend, if you possess half as much brains as I have always credited you with, will be well advised to do likewise. Otherwise it'll be four more years of Thatcherism. How does that grab you, mate?"

Brad had made his point and carried on walking, the noise of the sea crashing on the deserted beach drowning out his parting expletives. Khan was mesmerised by the drubbing he'd just received from someone who, though so promising, had now turned out to be so unreliable – definitely not 'one of us'. Brad seemed not to care. He would not look back. Like his party leader, he had crossed his Rubicon, and had his mind firmly on other battles that lay ahead.

****

The meeting had been going for over forty minutes, Mike Rotherwood – the Deputy Leader of the Council, and Chairman of the Education Committee – battling to keep the business running smoothly. However, Brad could see that Rotherwood was plainly a worried man: a looming agenda item on tonight's business was the controversial closure of Barnwood Primary School. Despite falling school rolls, axing the crumbling Victorian school was not going to be popular. Inevitably, petitions had been drawn up by anxious parents. Brad could hear the chants of 'save our school' coming from a sizeable demonstration on the steps of the Council House below.

"Where's Dick Lovelace?" Rotherwood whispered impatiently to the Chief Education Officer, who at first offered him a blank expression.

"He phoned at three and said the AMA meeting in London had finished. He was just jumping into his car," he intimated. "Thinking about it, he's probably stuck on the M1. They're digging up the section just north of Luton."

That was all Rotherwood wanted to hear! "Why the blazes didn't he take the bloody train then?" he fumed.

"If I could have the Chairman's attention, it would be appreciated," jibed Frank Collins, Labour's shadow chairman, sarcastically. Rotherwood sat up and tried to appear unflustered, though secretly gritting his teeth at the petulant little councillor. Satisfied, the man the Tories dubbed the 'Poison Dwarf' sank back into his notes and continued his verbose monologue. "As I was saying, while the Labour Group has no great problem with..."

Rotherwood was hoping that each extra minute of Collins' wordy rumination might just usher the stranded Councillor Lovelace through those grand oak doors, above which the clock was ticking away. Finally, Collins said his piece, and the deed could be postponed no longer. The chairman reluctantly moved on.

"Next item: proposed closure of Barnwood School, Chief Education Officer to report..."

"This could be a very interesting meeting," whispered Micky Preston to his fellows. While the officer ran through the facts and figures behind the closure plan, Micky performed some quick arithmetic and elaborated further. "There are seven of them; Lovelace is evidently missing for some reason; and their sole councillor in Barnwood is bound to abstain, given the strength of local feeling on this matter. So with seven on our side there's no reason why we can't vote this item down. That'll be one in the eye for the Tories!"

"Mr Chairman," insisted Micky, turning to address the committee. "As a ward councillor, I say there is no justification in closing a good school..."

Micky gave his usual blunt, but powerful rebuttal of the Conservative case. Suitably fired up, Brad followed in with a fusillade of his own, charging that the reason Barnwood Primary School was in such a bad way was that it has been deliberately neglected by its Tory council. When was the last time it had been given a good lick of paint? he asked.

"When indeed, Councillor Bradleigh," Rotherwood fired back angrily, "Remind me of the last occasion a Labour administration gave the school 'a good lick of paint'. I realise that you were probably still in nappies at the time, but if you care to research your facts you'll discover that when your own party was in control they, too, listed Barnwood Primary down for –and I quote – 'potential rationalisation'."

Though aggrieved at such condescension, Brad remembered Micky's exhortations about doing one's homework before taking on the quick-witted Tory deputy leader. Now he knew why! Finally, with argument exhausted (and still no sign of his missing councillor) Rotherwood was obliged to put it to the vote.

"Six votes in favour, Chairman," noted the committee clerk, counting the hands.

"Those against?" Rotherwood enquired.

Hands duly went up on the Labour flank of the oval committee table. However, Roz Young and Derek Hooper did nothing. Frank Collins gave them a questioning glance, but still they sat motionless with their arms crossed.

"What the hell are they playing at?" Micky hissed. "This is my bloody school in my bloody ward!"

"Five votes against, Chairman," the clerk observed.

"Abstentions?" Rotherwood concluded, self-satisfaction now blossoming all across his face. His own Barnwood councillor thereupon salved his conscience, but was unexpectedly joined by Derek Hooper and his feminist ally.

"Three abstentions, Chairman. The vote is therefore carried."

Rotherwood breathed deeply, and his colleagues chattered amongst themselves excitedly. Frank Collins sunk his head into his hands. Meanwhile, the deed done, the two dissenters gathered up their papers and left. Micky Preston was still livid, and so decided to follow after them. Brad thought he'd better pacify his friend to prevent fisticuffs in the foyer, and so darted out as the committee moved on to discuss less heady business.

"Are we in the same bloody party or what?" Micky demanded of Hooper, having apprehending him some way down the hallway.

"Were we in the same party when the Group ignored a resolution passed in the wards about the desperate need for anti-racist and anti-sexist education in our classrooms?" Hooper gnashed, jabbing his finger at his pursuer. "We warned you in the pre-meeting that..."

"For crying out aloud, comrade, that's a side issue. The local papers will maul us if we start embarking on such gestures. Our job is to get ourselves back in power. This school closure business was a real, tangible issue for the voters out there and something we could have hammered the Tories on. And now you've gone and blown it. Are you stupid, or is there something inside you that has a death wish on this party?"

Brad managed to placate his colleague before it came to blows. Thus the two left-wingers were permitted to exit the building. "I'll tell you this much," Micky assuring him, "those bastards'll pay for tonight."

"The vibes I'm getting is that a lot of comrades want this whole Militant thing stopped," Brad concurred. "The trouble is there's every chance that they could finally stitch up control of the organs of the party."

"Wrong!" Micky insisted adamantly. "We must go out and rouse our 'silent majority' – all those quiet, hard-working people who have been barracked, abused and intimidated over the years. Control of the party and the Council is at stake. I've let Turner know that I'm putting myself forward for the vacancy of constituency chair. The idea is to create as broad a front as possible, and deal those cretins a blow once and for all."

Brad was becoming an enthusiastic intriguer and was quite taken up with the challenge of extinguishing people who he increasingly regarded as parasites feeding on the Labour's good name. The Militants had been absolutely committed and mendacious in their control of the party for so long. Now it was time to use a bit of that mendacity to turn the tables and rebuild the Labour Party around the sort of people and ideas that he felt happier with.

****

The poor little lad was turning this way and that, the accusations flying around him whilst he sat in his highchair amidst the mess he'd made of his breakfast.

"What was I supposed to do? I tried to phone you!" Brad insisted, pacing backwards and forwards, trying to locate his favourite shirt.

"Well you evidently didn't try hard enough!" Helen snapped back. Scurrying out of the kitchen, she noticed that Mark's rice cereals were going in every facial orifice aside from his mouth, and were also liberally sprinkled across the floor. Losing her patience, she ran back for a cloth to mop up the disaster.

"I've told you. They needed my vote. I tried to call and tell you I'd be late," Brad grunted with increasing fury.

"You know Monday night is my aerobics night!" Helen yelled.

"Yes, I know; but some things are more pressing than fighting your flab!"

"Everything's more pressing if it involves that bloody council!" Helen fumed, yanking the bewildered infant out of the chair and putting his coat on. Sniffing in the direction of his posterior, she sensed the inevitable! Removing his coat again, she held him at arms length and trotted off to the bathroom, grabbing a nappy on the way.

Brad knew he was getting nowhere. He genuinely felt sorry; but Labour had succeeded in blocking a further controversial property development by Harry Conway, although the brash tycoon would probably win his planning application upon appeal. Therefore, Helen had missed her night out for little more than a symbolic victory. A pyrrhic victory too: for his marriage had bore one more blow inflicted by the burdens of civic duty.

To be sure, Brereton and his band of Conservative councillors could not hold out much longer. The least Brad would be hoping for out of all this was a vice-chairmanship upon Labour's return – another step on the ladder of power. Even so, now that he was a family man he was required to tread very carefully: party, council, wife, son – occasionally he slipped, and the price of a moment's loss of touch was a lashing from Helen's blistering tongue. Appeals to her proletarian sense of solidarity cut no ice, her sense of political destiny increasingly dulled by the chores and dramas of motherhood.

She finally zipped the baby snugly inside his coat and gathered together her things. "Are you coming?" she boomed to her husband.

He emerged from the bedroom with his jacket and briefcase. Then together they made their way out into the crisp, December morning. The chill of winter soon hit them, forcing Helen to pull the infant tight up to her. Opening the doors of the frosted-over car, she started the car and strapped the child in. Meanwhile, Brad scraped off what he could of the generous coating of ice.

"I won't be able to give you a lift into town for much longer," Helen informed him, trying to put their little fracas behind her. "They want me to help out at one of their branches in Birmingham. I'm covering someone on maternity leave."

"I'm sorry about last night," said Brad, manoeuvring for reconciliation while they queued at traffic signals.

"Forget it," she sighed, leaving matters there. Then she turned down a little side street and stopped to drop off Mark with the childminder. Brad used the interlude to observe the bin men at work. Getting rid of these private refuse collectors would be a priority if Labour retook the Council, he noted.

"I'm not getting at you, Brad," Helen maintained, restarting both the car and the conversation. "It's just that holding down a job and looking after Mark is pretty demanding. All I ask is a little understanding every now and then."

Perhaps the love light was still glowing. Brad always was awkward when showing his feelings. Sure, he could make love to a woman with gusto (although Helen wasn't often after passion nowadays – with or without gusto!). Yet so often the little niceties of love escaped him. Perhaps he was just made that way. He always was one of life's loners, and opening his heart – even with the one he loved – frequently required great acts of self-will.

****

"I have resigned from the Cabinet, and will be issuing a full statement later today."

With those few, brief words to waiting journalists, defence secretary Michael Heseltine had walked away from Downing Street, leaving the bombshell called the 'Westland Scandal' to explode with a blast that would rock the very foundations of Mrs Thatcher's government.

Despite a certain symbiosis over the years, there had always been a feeling of animus between Margaret and Michael. He disliked her imperious style of cabinet government; and she distrusted his lingering Heathite instincts – definitely not 'one of us'. Yet she had given him his first taste of high public office and had called upon his dashing media image to soften up the brash image of her administration. This uneasy relationship had now been broken over the fate of an obscure West Country airframe manufacturer.

Westland Helicopters had hit hard times; its management were looking for outside help to bring in the necessary finance to safeguard the jobs of its workforce. As Britain's sole manufacturer of battlefield helicopters, the defence secretary rightly felt he had an interest in the fate of the company. And, as an ardent European and an advocate of that most unThatcherite concept called 'an industrial strategy', Heseltine felt that Westland ought to be encouraged to enter into a consortium with other European helicopter manufacturers, which would offer some prophylactic to the dominance of the American aerospace conglomerates. What had led from there to his dramatic walkout had been his impression that the Prime Minister was deliberately rigging the Cabinet agenda to exclude such considerations. She felt he was dangerously overstepping the bounds of collective responsibility by such blatant touting of his pet scheme. After a judicious leak of ministerial letters intended to undermine Heseltine's credibility, he had gathered up his papers and stormed out.

On January 13th, industry minister Leon Brittan, who had faithfully defended the Prime Minister's corner in opposing the Euro-consortium, rose in the Commons to deny his department had covertly sabotaged Heseltine's scheme. However, Heseltine had written proof to the contrary. Later that day, Brittan was forced to return and apologise for misleading the House. By now, however, keen noses were tracing the scent back to Downing Street, asking what part the Prime Minister had played the nobbling of her errant colleague. Her most treasured halo – her reputation with the voters for plain speaking and honest dealing – had been shattered beyond repair.

****

Trade could hardly be described as brisk. Perhaps it was the snow that still lingered; or perhaps there was a good film on television tonight. Either way, there weren't many customers about. Over in the 'televisions for sale or rental' corner, half a dozen new models flickered away to the latest video from the Pet Shop Boys whilst the other half a dozen flickered with dramatic coverage of the loss of the *Challenger* space shuttle minutes into its launch.

Meanwhile, someone dropped in some returns so that, checking them back into stock, Helen almost didn't notice a tall, balding man slip in and begin to browse the shelves. Something about him unnerved her. Then it became clear that she knew him from somewhere. Now where exactly? Was he one of Brad's Labour friends? Was he one of Brad's Labour enemies? Then it clicked – he was one of those Tory councillors. She'd seen him at various civic occasions. What was his name? She dipped her head slightly as he glanced over her way on his peregrinations from 'Comedy' to 'War & Westerns'. She edged up to the one-way glass security panel where she could observe this customer undetected. Then she watched him drift over to the 'Horror & Adult' section. Eyeing the titles, he would occasionally take one down and peruse its lurid covers. He seemed particularly interested in the erotic films that haunted the top shelves. Finally, he took some titles up to the counter and waited while Helen's assistant checked out his selection, all the time his eyes scanning about like someone intensely aware that secrecy was the essence of the operation. He loaded his tapes into a bag and wandered back out into the afternoon breeze.

The computer menu was still up when Helen returned, and this enabled her to track the loans in detail. She was right. He was who she thought he was. '*Lusty Linda's Lovers*', '*Swedish Sauna Club*'; bizarre choices for an upstanding councillor to be making off with, she thought. With some *leger-de-main* on the keyboard, Helen brought up a full history of all the titles issued against his card: *'Naughty Adventures of Sarah', 'Stranded in Bangkok', Danish Students Go Hiking'*. Interesting, she mused. Very interesting!

****

"...AndsoitgivesmegreatpleasuretoofficiallydeclarethiscentreopentotheseniorcitizensofGunsbridge!"

With that, there was applause. Then James Whitney MP helped the Mayor pull the cord and haul the miniature drapes back from across the plaque that declared the day centre for the elderly opened by His Worship the Mayor, Councillor Spencer 'Fitzgibberish' on February 24th 1986. It also informed everyone that Councillor Peter Brereton was Leader of the Council, and Councillor Mrs Elizabeth Gainsborough was the Chairwoman of Social Services, all of whom were now bunched in around the polished plaque by local news photographers anxious to preserve this historic moment for posterity.

Brad, as shadow vice-chairman, and Joe McAllister, as shadow chairman, were not invited to partake of the official photographs, although McAllister couldn't resist collaring reluctant reporters with his opinions of how this or that feature of the architecture would have been altered had Labour been overseeing the project. Brad, himself, raised a wry smile at the sight of Peter Brereton and Elizabeth Gainsborough crooning together whilst diplomatically shooing McAllister away, determined that this occasion would generate maximum publicity for their beleaguered Conservative council.

"Not joining in the 'freebie'?" someone asked. Brad turned around to observe some dapper young black guy in a polo-necked jumper and tweed jacket sharing his aesthetic appreciation of the murals decorating the foyer. "From my recollection, you must be Councillor Bradleigh. You've spoken to me on the phone on numerous occasions," the mysterious figure reminded him. "John Powell, political correspondent on the *Gunsbridge Herald*. Pleased to meet you," he smiled, offering Brad his ebony hand.

"Ah, so you're John Powell," said Brad, snapping his fingers. "It's nice to be able to put a face to a voice. I've wanted to thank you for the coverage you've given me lately."

"No problem," the suave Powell assured him, urging Brad along to join the queue for the buffet. "There's not much real news in this town: street lamps that don't work; school bazaars; garden fêtes; pigeon droppings on the town clock – nothing that an aspiring newshound like me can get his teeth into. That's why I need you guys to keep pumping me real stories. It's nothing political – your friends Brereton and Whitney do it all the time."

"I'll remember that. I dare say Brereton and Gainsborough will be milking this one for all it's worth."

"Come, come, Councillor. Can you blame them?" said Powell tongue-in-cheek. "Your side have really dragged them over the coals over their policy on social services. You can't deny them the sweet pleasure of the publicity that goes with opening this day centre. Some might even say that that the money for it has been found at all is the fruit of their policy of running a tight ship. Anyway," Powell continued, fumbling in his jacket pocket, "here's my card with my number on it. Like I said, any interesting stories, don't hesitate to call me. Newspapers work to tight deadlines. And we wouldn't want to delay a good story, would we?"

Brad smiled, grateful for a hotline to the headlines. Then he filed the card away in his own jacket pocket and started loading up his plate with a selection of savouries before wandering over to a quiet corner to consume them. As he did so, he noticed a red-haired young lady stroll up to him.

"It's a superb building, isn't it?" she opined in a mellow estuarine accent.

"I recognise you. I've seen you sitting in on Committee... Erm... I can't think of your name..." he stumbled.

"Never make a politician if you can't remember names!" she chuckled, offering him her hand. "Wendy Baker, team leader for Social Care in Gunsbridge South," she reminded him. "I've watched you learning the ropes for some time now. Anyway, take heart," she mumbled *sotto voce*, "I know I shouldn't say it, but you won't have the Tories to worry about much longer. Today could well be their swansong," she smiled knowingly, Brad smart enough to be able to gauge where her sympathies truly lay. It tempted him to probe her further.

"Tell me," he requested, "the Social Care team – you deal with children mostly, don't you?"

"That's right: fostering, *guardian ad litems*, secure placements, that sort of thing. I have a lot to do with Councillor Franklin," she noted, pointing out the big, jovial councillor from in amongst the crowd, "he's chairman of the Children's Services Sub-committee. We've been working to try and provide better nursery provision."

"Some hope while Elizabeth Gainsborough runs this show," Brad hissed contemptuously.

Wendy had to agree. "I'm afraid she's running this department into the ground. And as for George Franklin: well, he's a nice enough man; but he's completely under her thumb."

Just then, the object of their scorn spotted Wendy and grabbed her arm, offering to introduce her to some bigwig on the local health authority. Not wishing to offend her political masters, she reluctantly parted company with Brad and followed her chairwoman over to the other side of the room, leaving him on his own once more.

By now, the buffet was beginning to look decidedly patchy, with passing councillors and officers helping themselves to what was left. Swiping the last of the vol-au-vents, Brad couldn't help overhearing George Franklin boring some hapless officer with his account of how Rommel had been remorselessly pushed back to Tripoli, probably a spin-off from some conversation the diminutive officer had had the misfortune to strike up over recent friction between the Americans and Libya's Colonel Gaddafi. Poor bloke! Brad thought, watching the officer desperately trying to disengage himself without appearing impolite. He'd found out the hard way that George Franklin was always droning on about the most ridiculous things. Still, there was no denying that, for all his garrulousness, he had a personal vote in Lower Henley. Brad's task would be to mobilise his forces to oust Franklin in the elections just a few months away: not an easy task, but one that had to be done if Labour were to retake control of the Council. And that was something that Brad wanted desperately.

****

It was probably the most well attended meeting that Brad could remember. He never realised that Gunsbridge South Labour Party had so many members. To be sure, he knew just by looking at some of the people trailing through the door that Bennett had also roused his cronies. However, a new secretary – Stewart Henderson, a lawyer from Amblehurst – had succeeded Frances Graham. He was considerably more vigilant in checking off the names on the party's membership register for some of them to get much further than that self same door. Pouring over the membership rolls, he spotted several irregularities and flagged them up to Rod Turner, who was now putting his foot down where bogus trade union affiliations or dubious addresses were being offered. Shame he hadn't done the same a few years back, Brad mused.

"Hi, stranger. What's your poison?" said the barmaid as she attempted to snap Brad out of his daydream. "You never did come up and canvass me."

"I guess I knew you'd always support me, Joy," he joked upon being presented with another pleasing vista of those marvellous mammaries.

"Never take your electors for granted. I still believe in having personal visits by the candidate so that I can examine his qualities for myself!"

Every councillor's fantasy, Brad pondered. "Anyway, how come you're working up here now?" he continued.

"They need a pair of hands. And I just happen to have a truly divine pair."

She wasn't kidding either, for they were nestling together just nicely in her tight-fitting top. She lifted Brad's order over to the bar and then winked at him suggestively. Blood pressure rising, he decided to shuffle himself out of the way of those still awaiting service, returning to where Helen was sat.

"You know that woman?" she asked, having noticed him chatting to her before.

"Not really," he replied evasively. "Anyway, are you ready for tonight's fireworks?"

Rod Turner banged his ashtray, already half full of dog-ends, and urged them all to take their seats. The room was soon filling up with that mixture of tobacco smoke and tension that Helen always loathed about these occasions, Turner wading through several items of business before moving on to the local government elections.

"Now will all branches submit to the secretary the names of their prospective candidates in the May election. He's still waiting for a response from Lower Henley ward, correct me if I'm wrong," he requested, shielding his eyes from the bright stage lights and peering out into the murkier recesses of the room, a cigarette smouldering slowly between the fingers of his raised hand.

"Lower Henley has selected Colin Tyler," Brad intimated, looking over at his youthful prodigy and rejoicing at how far he'd come from being a shy, gangling teenager to now feeling confident enough to offer his name forward to fight this highly winnable seat.

Henderson duly noted this. Turner tried to move on to the next item of business, only to be arrested in mid-sentence by Gary Bennett, booming, "Excuse me, Chair, but I think it remiss of us to have an agenda item called 'local elections' and not discuss the manifesto for fighting them. What about our anti-sexism strategy...?"

"Comrade, you know that the Leader of the Council is still in consultation with his shadow chairmen..."

"Stuff the shadow chairs, what about some input from the rank and file!"

Some of Bennett's crowd cheered, but his call brought groans from the remainder of the assembly. Even so, Bennett was determined not to be palmed off with obfuscation by a chairman he detested.

"If he's gonna' keep hijacking the meeting like this, I'm gonna' thump him!" muttered Helen to her husband. The secretary intervened.

"Chair, the position is very clear. The Leader and his committee shadows have to sit down and pour over all the relevant details before the draft document is ready for submission to the general committee; who, in turn, will transmit their findings to the branches."

"Comrade," Turner boomed contemptuously, "you have heard the secretary's opinion. You are therefore out of order. Please sit down." Bennett was unconvinced and wanted to protest further, but Sharif Khan urged him to sit down and save his fire for later.

"Next item of business – to elect a new chair," Turner continued. "We've received three nominations in: from Councillor Preston, from Mr Gary Bennett... and a late nomination from Councillor Mrs Maureen Tonks."

The room was thrown into confusion. Certainly Micky and Brad were not expecting, nor had they any inkling of, Maureen Tonks' intervention; to that end, their intelligence network had failed them. The matronly figure sat broodingly watching Micky creep over and squat beside Brad's table.

"Why is she putting up?" Brad wanted to know.

"I can only imagine it's because she doesn't trust us," Micky opined. Both he and Brad were, after all, men of the left. Perhaps someone of Maureen's persuasion found it difficult to accept that there was a difference between 'left' (as in Micky Preston's 'left') and 'left' (as in an unreconstructed Trotskyite firebrand like Bennett). "Anyway, sit tight, brother," he recommended. "Just hope the secretary has swotted up his rulebook."

"Councillor Preston has fifty nine votes; Mr Bennett sixty four; and Councillor Mrs Tonks fifty nine," announced Henderson. Helen asked Brad where the meeting went from there.

"Another ballot. And somebody's got to do the decent thing," Brad sighed.

Meanwhile, Micky had plucked up the humility and courage to wander over to Maureen's table. Along with several other party workers, he began thrashing out an acceptable compromise. Brad guessed Maureen would be advised to stand down, Indeed, before too long it appeared plain that a deal had been struck.

"No sweat, comrade," he assured Brad emolliently. He elaborated no further, and returned to his chair.

Thank God, Maureen had seen sense, Brad noted to his wife. It also opened the way for himself, as Micky's chief sponsor, to be nominated and accepted for the position of vice-chair of the local party – a largely nominal post, but a symbolic one which he coveted nonetheless, given the support Brad had offered his friend in successfully rousing all these dormant party members. Everyone filled in their ballot slips for a second time, just waiting to avenge the years of Militant silly games. How sweet, Helen observed, for the boot to be on the other foot for once!

"Councillor Preston has one hundred and seventy votes and Mr Bennett seventy five," Henderson informed the meeting slowly and purposefully.

Brad led the cheering, the cries of Micky's supporters drowning out the protests of Gary Bennett, who screamed, "Half these people never turn up to any meetings. We're the activists who keep this party going. What a fine way to repay such dedication!"

"Oh, shut up! They never turned up because they were sick of you lot monkeying about all the while!" shouted Helen in a fit of indignation. She never did like bad losers, Brad noted. He, himself, was delighted. Now the real work of remoulding Gunsbridge South Labour Party could begin, with Micky and himself leading the team.

"One further formality, comrades," said Henderson, gradually bringing the meeting back to order. "The position of vice-chair is also vacant. Councillor Preston has indicated that he wishes to nominate Councillor Mrs Tonks. We do have further nominations from Councillor Bradleigh and Mr Sharif Khan."

"Sorry mate," murmured Micky to his protégé as he drew up behind him. "It was either Maureen on the ticket or Bennett in the chair!"

It didn't make it any easier to bear. Of course, he could fight on alone – Helen said she'd second him. However that would only risk splitting the anti-Militant vote once more. He was thus left to ponder his invidious position. He could neither blame Micky, nor afford to lose his patronage. Reluctantly he signalled to the secretary that he was withdrawing his nomination and supporting Maureen Tonks. Voting got underway, but it was a mere formality. Brad tried to be philosophical about it all.

"Right," said Micky, triumphantly assuming the chair and setting the tone, "there's gonna' be some changes around here from now on...!"

****

Brad was unable to concentrate. Therefore, Helen soon found his arm curling around her shoulder, and her ears starting to be nibbled. After all, it was their first evening in together in absolutely ages.

"Not now, Brad. I'm watching this," she mumbled vaguely, without even taking her eyes off the television. How many times had he heard that one (or variants of it) over the last year or so? Reluctantly, he backed away. Moments later, the commercial break came on, and Helen lifted herself from off the sofa. Brad heard the sound of the kettle being switched on.

"Oh, by the way," came the voice from the kitchen. "I've got something for you." "It's in my bag, over by the wall. The grey folder..." she called out, eyeing his peregrinations from a distance. "...That's the one."

Brad took out the folder and began to flick through the pages. "What is it? ...'*Dutch Lovers Bare All*'...!" he gaped. Perhaps Helen was in the mood after all! Meanwhile, Helen rejoined him on the settee.

"And before you get any ideas – No!" she affirmed abruptly. "Anyway, it's a list I've compiled of films that someone has rented out on his video card this year."

"Must be a bit of a lad..! Not...?" he then gasped in disbelief. "...Where did you get this?" he exclaimed.

"My four week stint over in Birmingham," she replied, sipping her coffee.

"That would explain it. He'd never be able to walk out of the store in Gunsbridge with this stuff under his arm. It's dynamite!" said Brad, wading through the printout. "This could put the skids under the Tories for sure."

"It will when I tell you that, my curiosity aroused, I followed him home one day. Not only does he frequent a strip club up town, but he also cruises round the 'red light' district. What was it he said in the paper the other night about children needing the security of growing up in an atmosphere of 'family values'? All this certainly puts a new light on such sentiments," she observed, poking her glasses back onto her nose properly as if to highlight her indignation. She never did like hypocrisy, Brad recalled.

'Who's a clever girl?' he smiled mischievously. All through the remainder of the programme, he paged through the print-out, with its dazzling new revelations. Finally, Helen marched back out to the kitchen with her mug, before retiring for the evening.

She had, knowingly or otherwise, offered him the information to destroy the Tories and determine the fate of one critical seat on the Council – and one or two seats were all that stood between Labour and control. The devil in him told him to use his newfound information to the full – after all, the Tories would. Remember that time when a Labour councillor had suffered a mix-up while claiming his expenses? Hadn't Brereton's bunch slaughtered him in the press? Now Brad had the weapon with which to wreak his revenge upon the hated Tory leader. Vainly, virtue tried to argue that perhaps this man was not so much a menace to society as just pitifully human – nothing more. Finally, the conscience suitably numbed, Brad dropped the folder on the table and scoured his jacket pocket until he found what he was looking for. Pausing, he stood by the phone, studying the little card. Then he dialled and waited while the call was routed.

****

It was first light in the southern Mediterranean on the morning of another calm April day. Planes taxied about eerily, creating sinister silhouettes against the backdrop of the rising sun. The deckhands strapped the expensive war machines into the catapults, just as they had done a thousand times before. Except today would be no exercise. The afterburners glowed and the turbines thundered, and the deckhands scrambled out of the way. Then suddenly, the first flight of attack aircraft roared off down the huge flat deck of the mighty carrier. Banking steeply, they disappeared off over the blackened horizon.

The previous evening – against the counsel of many of her colleagues – Mrs Thatcher had given her blessing to another flight of warplanes that had discreetly departed their bases amidst the lush Oxfordshire countryside. These fearsome warplanes now rendezvoused with their navy colleagues and penetrated Libyan airspace, about to remind their unsuspecting hosts of the awesome severity of United States airpower.

****

He had been trailing his quarry for over thirty minutes, the time it had taken the councillor to make the journey from his pleasant home in Amblehurst into Birmingham's seedy 'red light' district. Now he watched the car slow to a crawl and its driver wind down the window to commence a brief conversation with one of several young girls lining the kerbside on this murky night. Thereafter, a leggy black girl jumped into the car and it moved off into the traffic. Powell put his own car into gear and stayed just far enough behind to avoid suspicion while they wound their way along the run-down inner city streets, past boarded-up shops, tramps rummaging through overflowing litter bins, drug addicts crashed out in shop doorways, and police vans patrolling about warily. Birmingham still had plenty of prim, desirable neighbourhoods – but this wasn't one of them!

Finally, the car stopped outside a grubby-looking tenement block located down a dingy side street. Powell noticed an upstairs light come on, and the curtains being drawn. He looked at his watch and decided to nestle down into his seat. He must have waited for what seemed like an eternity before her customer eventually descended the stairs, pulling his coat tight around him before driving off.

Moments later, the girl also descended into the street, casting her eyes about in the eerie stillness. Powell flashed his headlights, and she wandered over, the clicking of her heels echoing down the dimly lit street. He watched the swaying of her hips as those lovely legs approached his car. She handed him the tape. He drew out his wallet and fumbled inside. No words were exchanged while his thick ebony fingers counted the money. Then he handed her a wad of crumpled twenty pound notes. She blew him a kiss and stuffed the money inside her cleavage. Then she turned and strolled back across the street. Powell, having that which he so prized, saw no reason to linger any longer in this less-than-salubrious quarter.

****

THE GUNSBRIDGE HERALD
Wednesday, April 30th 1986
Evening Edition   -   Still only 17p

COUNCILLOR IN CALL-GIRL SCANDAL
Cllr George Franklin, Chairman of Gunsbridge Council's Children's Services Sub-committee, has been tracked down visiting call girls, writes our special investigative report, John Powell. When challenged, the 67 year-old councillor for Lower Henley admitted having a liaison with a prostitute called 'Cindy'. The Children's Services Sub-committee is charged with overseeing many of the Council's most sensitive juvenile responsibilities...
TORIES IN DISARRAY

Sex scandals have thrown local Tories into disarray in the run-up to next week's municipal elections. Already battered by the Westland Affair and the backlash from the Libyan bombing, it is widely expected that control of Gunsbridge Council will switch to Labour after next Thursday...
REACTOR FALL-OUT SPREADING
Radioactive fallout from the Soviet nuclear reactor at Chernobyl is now spreading out across Scandinavia, raising fears that whole swathes of Europe may be contaminated in the aftermath of the horrific explosion...
TRESCOTT PARK PULLS 'EM IN
The new multi-million pound shopping centre at Trescott Park drew huge crowds over Easter, according to the centre's press officer, Stan Taylor. Local police also reported long tailbacks of traffic on the West Bromwich Road...

****

Brad had been to dozens of counts at Gunsbridge Town Hall, as indeed had his old friend Craig Anderson, who he noticed staring pale-faced at the results now coming in. Ballot box after ballot box seemed to confirm a Labour landslide. Blame Mrs Thatcher's support for the attacks on Libya, blame Westland, blame four years of Tory parsimony with the Council coffers, or blame the scandals; it didn't really matter any more. Power for Labour was just an hour or so away.

Brad began to wonder whether it had really been necessary after all to use Helen's 'dynamite' to cripple Colin's opponent. Either way, the deed was done, though he was still haunted by images of the distraught councillor attempting to flee the cameras as he left the Council House amidst a battery of screaming reporters. He had fought to suppress any guilt he harboured that the jovial face that seemed incapable of conveying anything other than mirth had been for once bereft of that jolly grin.

He had not had chance to speak with Craig as he had done on previous occasions; to exchange small talk about the old times. In fact, nobody seemed to have much to say about anything. Even Labour candidates, whilst mouthing the usual triumphalist statements as they claimed their seats, seemed vaguely downbeat. George Franklin was not at the count, conspicuous by his absence. His colleagues had lost the will even to jeer the Labour victors deriding their record. Finally, it was the turn of Colin Tyler to nervously take the stage and hear the returning officer announce the result for Lower Henley.

"...Which is as follows. Franklin – George Ronald (Conservative Party), 1005 votes."

Watching Colin fidgeting with his thumbs whilst standing rigid beneath the stage lights, Brad didn't mind betting that, given the sudden demise of George Franklin's vote, Jane Allsop and her Liberal friends weren't kicking themselves for failing to field a candidate.

"Tyler – Colin Eric (Labour Party), 1445 votes. I therefore declare..." the officer continued. Meanwhile, Colin smiled to his cheering colleagues, and was encouraged to take the microphone for his public-speaking debut.

"Thanks... er... well... I wanna thank the voters fer', er... votin' fer' me... And, er, the counters fer', er... countin' the votes... And, er... er... I wanna thank my Labour Party friends, including Brad, er, I mean Councillor Bradleigh, fer' helpin' me win today."

Brad was touched. It was not exactly Lawrence Olivier reciting the rallying cries of *Henry V*. Yet give him time and the lad would no doubt work himself into some kind of oratorical style. Meanwhile, the Conservative supporters brooded silently as they made for the door. They would almost certainly not be celebrating, Brad thought, watching Craig march off, his hands in his pockets. Just then, he noticed a dark figure in a mackintosh standing by the exit making notes while another result was read out over the microphone.

It was Powell. Seeing the reporter smile politely to the Conservative crowd as they left the hall, and observing the downtrodden expression on Craig's face as he disappeared into the corridor, suddenly the cock crowed thrice! Brad suddenly regretted that he had betrayed George Franklin to the inquisitorial prying of the media. He continued watching uneasily until Powell looked his way. Unsure how to interpret the journalist's curious stare, he turned away to Colin, who was by now back down on the floor of the auditorium with his own supporters.

****

The councillors seemed in an almost end-of-term mood as they all filed into the committee room. Brad wandered round to find a seat by the open windows, snatching a brief glance out across the square as he did. The blossoms were out on the trees that shaded passers-by from the warm, evening sun; lovers sat besides the fountain, or milled about outside Branco's Wine Bar. A refreshing breeze, together with faint strains of Simply Red, drifted into the room. Summer was on the way.

Finally, with all his councillors now assembled, Tom McKerrick welcomed the newly-elected ones amongst them now that Labour was firmly back in control of the Council. The party now boasted four new councillors, including an attractive, urbane young woman called Alannah James, who now sat down next to Brad. He had met her on odd occasions before, and been favourably impressed by her dedication, knowledge and enthusiasm. Her hard work had helped win Barnwood ward from the incumbent Tory. Thus, as McKerrick now addressed them, Labour held twenty-three seats to the Conservatives' eighteen, with Jane Allsop forming the sole Alliance presence on the Council. The socialists therefore possessed a healthy majority over their opponents, sufficient to enable them to commence the full agenda of programmes that their leader now outlined, notwithstanding that the Council was even so constrained by Government spending controls.

"Sounds like I've picked the right moment to arrive on the Council," whispered Alannah to Brad in a deep, haunting, almost sexual voice.

While McKerrick continued, Alannah faced away from Brad, listening eagerly to the brand new era about to dawn upon the town. This gave Brad the opportunity to cast his eye up and down her, and marvel in an unashamedly sexist manner at the way beauty and brains were so purposefully packaged together. Her dark, silky hair and the pure white skin that flowed down her slender neck made Brad feel proud to be sitting next to such potent femininity. How good it felt to be getting to know her better now, working together to build Camelot amidst the grey industrial heartland of Gunsbridge.

"...So, comrades, that's where we're heading," said McKerrick summing up. "It will be a demanding schedule, not least because the Government is shifting the goalposts all the while. But we've got to manoeuvre across all these minefields if we're to successfully implement a Labour programme for this town. So I want no histrionics," he said, looking in the direction of a sullen Derek Hooper and a grim Roz Young.

"I hear you have trouble with those two?" Alannah asked of Brad, shielding her words with a delicate hand as she watched the two Militants conferring.

"They have their moments," Brad replied casually. "Let's just say though that, for now, the drubbing their buddies in Gunsbridge South received has taught them the value of keeping their heads down!"

"Anyway," said McKerrick, quelling nascent chatter amongst his Group with the tapping of his unlit pipe, "let's get the election of chairmen out of the way. First, I'll take nominations for Education."

"I move Councillor Frank Collins." chirped someone, with someone else duly raising his hand to second the proposal. No one else volunteered any names, so the 'Poison Dwarf' was duly selected, hubris written all over his impish face as he contemplated turning the Department upside down. Maureen Tonks similarly won the Community Services chairmanship unopposed.

"Well done, Maureen. Highways?" begged McKerrick.

"I move Councillor Preston, with Councillor Rolfe as his deputy," Brad indicated.

"I move Councillor Piper," added Joe McAllister, who glared icily at Brad. The man had never liked him, and it was common knowledge that he positively despised Micky. The two of them eyeballed each other for some seconds whilst ballot slips were passed round.

"The result is Councillor Preston thirteen votes, Councillor Piper ten votes. Micky, Highways is thus your baby," the Leader congratulated him. McAllister seemed surprised at the result, as did everyone else. Everyone that was except Micky himself, who gave Brad that conniving wink that he knew so well.

"What about the Planning Committee?" McKerrick continued.

"I move Councillor Stone and Councillor Tildesley," said Micky confidently.

"I'll move Councillor Pugh and Councillor Mohammed," interjected McAllister, hot on Micky's tail. Again, Brad sensed the aggro. Walter Pugh was a grumpy old devil; but – more to the point – was as thick as two short planks! Developers like Harry Conway would run rings round him. Again, the ballot slips went out; and again McKerrick announced that Micky's choice had secured the post. The tension in the room was almost palpable. Alannah leant over to whisper in Brad's ear.

"The Deputy Leader: he seems very hostile to Micky. Who is he?" she enquired innocently.

"Micky hasn't told you?" exclaimed Brad, incredulous at such an oversight. "That's Joe McAllister. He definitely doesn't like Micky; alas, a fate I suspect Micky shares with the rest of humanity."

"Ah, now I remember. Someone said he tends to be a bit vindictive," Alannah recalled – surely the understatement of the year. Brad thought she'd be finding that out for herself soon enough anyway.

"Finally then, can we have names for Social Services," McKerrick requested of his team.

"I m-m-move C-c-c-councillor Joe M-M-McAllister," Walter Pugh declared as hastily as his stutter would permit.

"Any other challengers to the Deputy Leader?" McKerrick mumbled cheekily, not really expecting any, but hopeful perhaps nonetheless. Slowly Micky raised his tattooed arm.

"I move Councillor Bradleigh – with Councillor Miss James as vice-chair," he announced.

The silence could have been sliced with a knife. McAllister turned bright scarlet, although constraining himself: he knew such impudence must be rewarded with a sound thrashing. Ten years he'd been Labour's spokesman. He wasn't about to be thwarted by Brad and this new girl who'd not long moved into the town.

"Well, do you accept your nomination, Councillor?" the Leader asked. Brad, momentarily stunned, thought to look over towards his 'godfather' sat a few places further round the long oval table. Micky could sense his bewilderment, so offer his prodigy a discreet, telltale wink.

"Er, yes. I'm game!" Brad fired back confidently.

"And you, Alannah. Are you willing to back this young man up." McKerrick smiled, in strains of a wedding vow.

"Why, yes," she said, her eyes lighting up in anticipation. "I'll do it."

"Then let's have some ballot slips!" McKerrick demanded impatiently.

As impromptu scrutineers passed around the table, voting got underway. McAllister marked his slip, and then watched as everyone else marked theirs – one near-by councillor huddled up to his vote lest the hawk-eyed deputy discover his intentions. McKerrick waited whilst the scrutineers counted the slips, noted the result, and passed it to him. The grey-haired leader looked at the paper with surprise and ill-disguised mirth before announcing the result.

"Well, we have Councillor McAllister, ten votes and Councillor Bradleigh, thirteen votes. Robert, it's all yours!"

The seething deputy leader now changed colour again, this time to a very pale shade of white. He ground his dentures together and longed to say something outrageous. However, with undue modesty, he turned to his leader and said, "May I congratulate the young man on his elevation to the chair. I hope he will enjoy Social Services as much as I have."

Brad longed to take that as a gesture of magnanimity, but he could see McAllister would not forget such a humiliating affront in a hurry. Instead, he merely smiled an acknowledgement-of-sorts.

"I think that concludes business," McKerrick advised them all, although such a commotion now unleashed itself that few of his colleagues really cared. Several councillors, including McAllister's sworn enemies, congratulated Brad and Alannah on their triumph, while others – his silent enemies – looked on contentedly. Micky Preston was shuffling chairs (wooden variety) and colleagues out of his way in order to clear a path over to his protégés, wrapping his arms round Brad, before doing the same (only more tenderly) to Alannah.

"That was a palace coup if ever I witnessed one!" stuttered Brad in amazement. "How did you pull it off?"

"Listen," Micky humbly confessed, "I reckon I owed you one for deffin' you out in favour of Maureen a while back. So I pulled a few strings, and cashed a few favours I was owed. Whatever, you're a better councillor than he'll ever be. And you, my sweet," he continued, embracing Alannah one more time, "I know you're destined for higher things."

Alannah blushed and excused herself, motioning for the door and pleading another engagement. Brad wasn't really listening to Micky as his friend plucked a screwed-up piece of paper from the breast pocket of his T-shirt; rather he was watching Alannah drift away towards the door.

"Oy," said Micky, whacking Brad's broad chest, "take yer' eyes off her, yer' dirty little animal! Catch a look at this instead." He showed Brad his crumpled memorandum. "Isn't this just what you've been waiting for?" he beamed.

It certainly was: instructions for the conducting of interviews for the parliamentary seat of Gunsbridge South! Brad took hold of the paper himself and studied the fine print with intense excitement. "Why are you showing me this? Don't you want to have a shot at it yourself?" he asked.

"It needs a youngster, someone with the energy to smash Whitney's majority. And for my money, I'm backing you. Fasten your seat belts, our kid – the political career of Councillor Robert Bradleigh is about to take off!"

11   *YOUNG, UPWARDLY MOBILE*

It was no use. Every lane was snarled up. Craig knew it had been a mistake to attempt to make his way back to the office along the West Bromwich Road. Sinking his body back into the seat and resting his arm on the open window, he allowed the warm July sun to soak into his tired face, occasionally engaging gear to inch ever closer to the traffic lights. He also decided to take a good long look at the emerging Trescott Park Shopping City. Shimmering glass canopies shielded shoppers in an air-conditioned wonderland of high-class shops, American-style fast food stalls, and sparkling tropical water displays. The shopping centre in Gunsbridge seemed distinctly shabby and down-market by comparison. And, with thousands of free car parking places to attract shoppers wearied by the town's own vandal-ridden multi-storeys and unforgiving traffic wardens, no wonder people came from miles around to shop here; and no wonder Harry Conway was a millionaire several times over. Back to more mundane matters, Craig looked down at his watch. Reaching across, he took hold of the car phone and dialled.

"Hi, Jane. Is Geoff there? ...Thanks ...Hi, Geoff? ...Yeh, sorry. Ask MacDonald if he can stall Schumacher for half an hour... Yeh, I'm stuck at the lights at Trescott Park... okay, thanks!"

At last, Craig could accelerate swiftly across the lights and onto the wide straight dual carriageway that led up to the sprawling BEL bus plant at Berksham. It felt so good to be savouring the wind driving his blond locks about as it thundered refreshingly through the sunroof. He turned the stereo up louder to celebrate the glory of life – a life enhanced for someone of his own humble origins by all the opportunities that the liberating triumph of Thatcherism had offered him for self-advancement. Never in his wildest dreams did he ever imagine that at the age of twenty-five he'd be on a healthy salary, driving a luxurious company car, and responsible for the success or failure of a major company. Why, there was even a reserved space on the office car park that bore his name.

"Hi, Jane. Sorry I'm late," he apologised to his glamorous secretary as he finally burst through the door of the office, his briefcase and flipcharts slung under his arm.

"You're alright. MacDonald's taken him on a tour of the factory. Coffee?" she said, readying the kettle.

"Love one. What would I do without you?" he reminded her in all sincerity. Indeed, looking up from running over his presentation script once more, he mused on how easy it was to take a good secretary for granted when organising one's day and fixing life's little hiccups. She sure looked great as she bent over to dig out the cups from the cupboard, a revealing short skirt lifting gradually up her bronzed thighs. However, as she straightened herself up and the skirt advanced back down those gorgeous long legs, Craig was able to focus on revising his address once more.

"Ah, Rex. This is our marketing manager, Craig Anderson. Craig, have you've met Rex Schumacher before?"

MacDonald's sudden arrival took Craig slightly by surprise. And behold, here he was with Rex Schumacher, boss of the American parent company that controlled Bus Engineering Ltd, and who looked every inch the square-jawed, hard-hitting stereotype of a Chicago chief executive. Craig stood nervously and offered him a hand.

"Pleased to meet you, Craig," said Rex, decisively receiving and then crushing his hand. "Frank has told me a lot about you. Anyway," Schumacher asserted, turning to MacDonald. "My plane leaves at four, so why don't we crack on with our schedule."

"Good idea, Rex. We're in the room down the way. Is everything set up, Craig?" MacDonald enquired.

"Er, yes. Sure. I'll just gather up my notes."

With that he dusted off his folders, grabbed his script, and hurried off after them. Stopping, he turned about and ran back for the flipchart. Tucking it into a spare slot under his arm, he noticed Jane standing there with his coffee. Unable to find a free hand or other resting place, he managed to shrug his shoulders and grin boyishly at his ever-understanding PA.

****

Arriving home late one evening, Craig briefly leafed through his post. In amongst the bills and the junk mail, he discovered the latest list from Central Office. Tearing open the envelope, he briefly flicked through the contents: some safe seats down south, which he'd apply for even though he was unlikely to be short-listed. However, the last form made him sit up. *GUNSBRIDGE NORTH*, the pink-coloured sheet boldly proclaimed. It was certainly ideal for someone like him, being as local as local could be. He knew the area like the back of his hand, and he worked in the constituency for a company that provided employment to hundreds of its constituents. He seemed to be custom-made for their requirements. Only snag was it was hopelessly unwinnable! Craig reached for his reference book on the 1983 General Election results, which looked unpromising: Terry Johnson had a 17,189 majority – and that was in a bad year for Labour! So what it told him was that even if he was successfully selected he would still be unlikely to be sitting on those famous green benches or hearing the Queen read out a legislative agenda for the new Parliament. Still, it was a chance to cut his teeth on something – and that chance was fast slipping away as each constituency selected its man ready for the big day.

****

The train had not long pulled out of Bournemouth station, and was starting to pick up speed as it hurtled into the New Forest. Craig, who had finished reading a few pages of the bible which Nikki had bought him as a leaving present, was now trying to catch up on a copy of the *Gunsbridge Herald* that he'd brought down to the Conference and had not got round to reading. As he hauled over the first page, he discovered that Gunsbridge South Labour Party had chosen a new candidate to fight the next election: *'Robert Bradleigh is a twenty-six year old local government officer who...'*

"Brad!" he suddenly mumbled aloud, causing one or two passengers to look round.

Indifferent to this, instead he focussed his gaze on the small print. Yes, it was him alright. Gunsbridge South was difficult for Labour, but not impossible – and certainly more winnable than Gunsbridge North was for the Conservatives. It appeared his old friend could possibly win the race to enter Parliament ahead of him.

"These seats free, young man?" said a familiar voice.

"Sure! Be my guest," he said, vaguely looking up from his piece of earth-shattering news. Then he recognised the faces. "James! Eleanor!" I didn't see you on the station!"

James Whitney urged his wife into the window seat before hoisting their cases onto the overhead luggage rack. Taking off his overcoat, he tucked himself into the seat next to her and rested his arms on the table, an expensive wristwatch flashing at Craig's face as it reflected the carriage lights.

"Come to think of it, I didn't see you at the conference either," the gregarious MP noted.

"I was there. I didn't get to speak though," Craig lamented. "Anyway, what are your impressions?"

"Superb!" James assured him. "This is it – we're back in the ring now. All the dark days are behind us. I'm feeling happier than ever about facing the electors."

It had indeed been a turning point. Harvey Thomas had excelled himself, this time successfully reselling a prime minister and a party that had months earlier seemed doomed to defeat, injecting a fresh sense of purpose, unity and glamour into the Conservative cause. It had also unveiled a new programme of policies for inclusion in the next manifesto: replacing the hated domestic rating system; reform of education, local government and the health service; plus further privatisations. Furthermore, divisions had once more soiled Labour's own conference.

"You'll be facing one of my old school pals this time round," Craig enlightened his elected member smugly.

"Really. You know this Bradleigh chap then?" exclaimed Eleanor excitedly.

"We used to hang around together; chatting up the girls, listening to all sorts of weird music, that sort of thing."

"What's he like? Have I anything to fear? He's one of the local councillors, I see," said James.

"He won't be a pushover, I'll tell you that. Intelligent, cunning, hardworking; he's their ideal choice. He does have a reputation for being a bit of a left-winger, although if I know Brad he'll play that down. He's not a Militant though: far too smart for that!"

"Looks like we'll have to keep the pressure up then," James replied. "Guess I'll be calling on your skills again, Craig," he added, turning to Eleanor for concurrence.

"Except you may not have me," he advised them. "I've got an interview for Gunsbridge North tomorrow morning. So I may want to poach some of *your* workers!" the hopeful young man joked.

"Indeed," James huffed jovially, "Anyway, Terry Johnson's got his feet well under that particular table. Still, I admire your courage; good luck to you. The best you can do is to get yourself noticed, especially in the press and at Central Office. Increase the Conservative vote, then bank the experience ready for when you're chosen for a safer seat."

Craig's strategy in a nutshell! The two men talked at length as the night drew in and the train wound its way back to the Midlands. James used knowledge gleaned on the parliamentary grapevine to enlighten Craig about a few pertinent facts: Johnson was a good MP; solid, reliable and down-to-earth; and had a sizeable personal following in Gunsbridge North precisely because of this. However, he was blunt and cocky, and sometimes laid into his opponents too aggressively; which in Craig's case might prove an advantage if he could exploit it to portray himself as David facing Goliath – the underdog the British so love to align themselves with giving a spirited account of himself before a bullying foe. First, however, there was the small matter of being formally selected.

****

"Okay, yow'm' next," said a little old man who poked his head round the door of the lounge. Craig followed him out and up the stairs to the main committee room of this *anus mundi* called Berksham Conservative Club.

"Doh' yow be afraid, our kid! Yow'm' well in 'ere," the little man continued to wink reassuringly as they climbed the draughty wooden staircase. Craig then made his way to the front of the austere committee room, cutting a swathe through the lingering smoke to a table and chair set aside for him.

"Good evening, Mr Anderson," said the chairman, who sat with his secretary and treasurer at a table in front of him. "My name is David Sutton, and these are my colleagues on the executive committee chosen to select a candidate to fight Gunsbridge North," he then continued, pointing to the half-a-dozen doddery old men and women gawping and grinning at this nervous young specimen.

And so amidst the barren decor and crumbling plaster, Craig stood up, gazed across the room for inspiration to the dusty, lopsided portrait of Winston Churchill hanging on the far wall, and launched his latest bid for a parliamentary career. From the outset he threw his heart and soul into rallying the faithful in this sad, forgotten backwater of Conservatism, a task not made any easier by the presence of a rather noisy bluebottle circling the grimy lamp fitting, the bowl of which was already filled with the spider-munched corpses of more than a few of its forebears.

He'd recycled this speech many times over the past year, changing or rearranging odd paragraphs to suit his audiences, most of whom had possessed a distinctly less fossilized appearance than the geriatric selection committee mustered by Gunsbridge North. He knew the constituency had what was euphemistically described as a 'dormant party organisation' (positively moribund, it seemed, as Mrs Turridge played with her knitting, and Major Freeman dozed off, occasionally to be stirred by a low level pass by the bluebottle).

"Let us take the area of manufacturing industry, which this constituency depends on heavily. I've seen the revolution that seven years of free enterprise Conservatism has delivered. Our membership of the European Community has helped us to take..."

Craig noticed the Major wake up and frown at the mention of the abomination from Brussels, though his eyelids soon rolled and somnolence returned as Craig mollified him with some arcane Euro-statistics. David seemed impressed and nodded supportively. Outside a police car wailed past in the distance, its American-style siren whooping frantically as it sped up the high street. It's getting more like the Bronx everyday here, Craig thought (preferring the good old British 'der-der-der-der' variety himself) – which reminded him of the next theme he wished to pursue in his address.

"...This Government has vastly strengthened our police forces. If I were fortunate enough to be elected as your MP, I'd see that we give more power to our police, to keep the streets safe for young and old alike..."

"Hear, hear!" the Major roared, the bluebottle taking to the wing once more.

"Oops, sorry mate!" gasped a tattooed teenager, who had meanwhile opened the committee room door by mistake. Everyone looked round just as Craig was launching himself into his peroration. "Ah' wuz' just lookin' f' the bogs, like!" the intruder explained, and he curled his snooker cue under the doorway and promptly shut the door. It was well known that the locals frequented the Conservative Club for the snooker, the Labour Club for the darts, and the Liberal Club for the dominoes!

Grief, this is a nightmare! Craig thought, staring desperately at Churchill for some more inspiration, the indomitable figure staring back at him and oozing defiance. The bluebottle was meanwhile resting on Mrs Turridge's ridiculous woolly hat.

"...We shall fight them in the wards; and on the Council..." Craig exclaimed to Mrs Turridge, who was otherwise busy trying to fathom out where she'd dropped a stitch. "...And I want to be the man who will lead you in that fight. As our leader has said, we must... we must..."

Craig was conscious that he had lost his audience. All eyes now looked up to observe the titanic contest of the evening about to reach its climax. The bluebottle knew it was trapped. Buzzing loudly and feverishly to free itself from the web, the committee looked on in terror as the huge leggy spider edged in staccato gallops ever closer to its prey until it was almost upon it. The fly now began to regret the decision to alight on the lamp fitting.

"...Er... we must... er..."

The buzzing became more frantic as first a wing, then some legs, disappeared inside the arachnid mandibles. Crunch! Off came the other wing.

"...And... er... er..."

Still buzzing at high pitch, the bluebottle now prayed to all the insect gods for deliverance.... Oh, for crying out loud, hurry up and eat the thing! Craig meanwhile fumed to himself. Finally, the head disappeared and the buzzing stopped, the spider cocooning the remains of the abdomen for snacks later, thus permitting Craig to complete his stalling finale. As he sat down, the motley collection of party workers clapped him heartily, and David invited them to ask Craig any questions they felt relevant to the occasion.

Yes, Mrs Turridge," he said as the greying old lady put her knitting aside and stood up.

"Mr Anderson, isn't it time you MPs did something for us pensioners?" she warbled passionately.

"Hear, hear!" interjected the Major gruffly.

Craig assured her that he would, nonetheless reeling off his list of all the comprehensive measures the Government had already taken. Mrs Turridge appeared happy with the answer, so David pressed on.

"Ah, Major, I was wondering when you'd be asking the lad a question."

"Too damn right! Listen, sonny, what are you going to do about all the yobbos roaming the streets? Are you going to reintroduce National Service for the little blighters?"

Craig skilfully inched his way round the question, again quoting the *Campaign Guide* summaries on law and order. The Major was plainly not impressed with such palliatives.

"I'd flog the little devils and put them in the stocks," he said, turning to Mrs Turridge, who nodded approvingly. Craig couldn't quite bring himself to agree, although he listened politely as the Major rambled on about how the country was going to the dogs at the hands of do-gooders and foreigners.

Plus ça change, thought the candidate despairingly. Despite polite words of gratitude from the chairman, Craig pondered how his noblest ideals were out of step with his ossified listeners, his best jokes lost to interruptions by the snooker team next door, and his closing words ruined by a now deceased bluebottle. All of a sudden, he became cognisant of having flunked it.

****

"So this is it. Feels a bit like Russian roulette in reverse!" said Jonathan Forsyth, employing his infamous gallows humour. "Five clicks of the revolver and three bullets!"

An interesting analogy, Craig pondered. Out of five final short-listed candidates, two would be going forward to the final selection by the full constituency association shortly. And here were the five, sat in the dismal lounge of Berksham Conservative Club once more, looking apprehensively at each other while they waited to be called by Gunsbridge North's executive committee. Brenda Shore looked evocative in her expensive blue dress, and exuded self-confidence, even at this late stage. She turned and muttered something to Martin Radbourn, who was sandwiched stoically between the ever-fidgeting Jonathan and Neil Sharpe, who tried to look cool by smoking a slim cigar (though Craig reckoned he was just as nervous as the rest of them, and certainly didn't like the thought of such a galaxy of competition being present on his 'patch').

"Martin Radbourn?" called out the same little old man, who always seemed to end up escorting the hopefuls.

"Good luck, old boy!" Jonathan tittered. Martin smiled and rose to follow the diminutive figure out, as if he were being led out towards a firing squad.

The deathly silence returned once more, even Jonathan stuck for a humorous quip or witty anecdote. Upstairs, they could just make out David Sutton's dulcet tones introducing Martin to the committee before the lad began to outline his vision of a gentler Conservatism.

"He's been gone a long while," said Brenda ominously.

"He's probably being grilled to dry out his 'wetness'!" Jonathan chuckled.

"Why are we doing this? We must be fools!" pleaded Craig.

"Because we all want to get into Parliament so badly that we'll forsake everything to do it," replied Neil Sharpe, rather irritably pointing out the obvious. "We're all masochists with an ego problem," he then noted sagely.

The silence returned. They pondered just how far they still had to go towards achieving that monumental goal (even assuming they were successful today). Neil, in particular, had felt humiliated that he alone amongst them was not an 'approved' candidate, for though he had been tipped off in good time about this vacancy, it needled him that the seat would not be his as of right. He'd have to fight for it – and looking at Brenda, Craig and Jonathan, he knew he'd have to fight hard.

"Jonathan Forsyth?" called the usher as a wearied Martin Radbourn returned to the fold.

"Tough?" asked Craig. Martin sat down, nodding and flashing his eyebrows.

Craig knew the feeling. So much effort goes into trying to woo selection officers, from trying to study in detail all the idiosyncrasies of a particular constituency, to planning and executing a rousing call to arms that would try to please as many of the officers as possible without treading on any sensitive ideological toes. Consequently, it was difficult not to take failure personally.

"Neil Sharpe," the call came after half-an-hour of yet more punctuated conversation, Martin and Jonathan both having fled in exhaustion.

Craig desperately craved the nomination for Gunsbridge North now, despite his earlier ambivalence. Time was running out, and this could be his last opportunity. Yet he was quietly confident: Martin was always an outsider; Jonathan was bound to put his foot in it somewhere; which left just Brenda and Neil posing any real threat. His little antennae had filtered out gossip to the effect that Neil was not at all liked by his small band of colleagues in Gunsbridge North – something about him having a 'temper problem'. The chairman evidently didn't like him. Indeed, when Neil finally reappeared, his countenance could hardly be described as benign.

That left Craig alone with Brenda. She had told him that, like himself, she was the child of an NCO (in her case, a navy petty officer), who had both been the first generation of their families to enter university and succeed in high-powered careers. Now here they were – alone; waiting to see who would move closer to the prize. They were two children of the Thatcher Revolution, fighting the game of life by the rules their leader had so endeavoured to enshrine in the national psyche: work hard, be of good cheer, and never let go of your dreams.

"You look very nice in that dress... if I may say so," said Craig, hoping she'd appreciate the sincerity of his compliment. She thanked him, her usual strident tones giving way to a discernable coyness. Perhaps it had been a while since she'd enjoyed having a man compliment her undeniable femininity.

Silence descended once more. The barman collected a few remaining empty glasses, wiped over the faded burr-walnut tables, and straightened the chairs of the almost deserted lounge. The stillness of a wet Friday night in Berksham seemed a million miles from the roaring waves of sun-kissed Arabian beaches, or the esoteric idyll of university, or even fighting an election alongside the old crowd in Gunsbridge South amidst the camaraderie and excitement of victory. To these, Craig now turned his thoughts. Then again, this was a milestone on the long journey that they both hoped would span out over the next two or three decades of their lives, and which would take them from this dreary old club in an infinitely forgettable part of town to victory in a more winnable seat, ministerial careers, and.... well, who could say?

"Craig Anderson," came the summons.

"Good luck," Brenda urged him. "I don't know how we'll ever get to Westminster; yet in a funny old way I sense that somehow we will – both of us."

Craig knew what she was trying to say. Here were two ordinary people with extraordinary dreams: a man and woman who shared the same backgrounds as millions of their peers, yet who were somehow overcome with the sensation that they were set aside and destined for greater things.

****

"Ladies and gentlemen, thank you for coming today. As you will see, we have two candidates who we'll be interviewing today. Firstly, Craig Anderson, a young man from just across town; and then Miss Brenda Shore from Kent. But first, we're going enjoy the lovely buffet that the ladies have kindly arranged, during which time the candidates will be available for you to meet and talk with."

David Sutton finished his introduction and, with an arm around the shoulders of both Craig and Brenda, commended them to the small membership gathered in the lounge. This was it, they both knew: the final selection meeting. Jonathan, Martin and Neil had failed to make it, so this left just the marketing manager and the PR executive to meet the full association.

"Before you disappear, Craig, let me introduce you to my wife and daughter," David then insisted, leading Craig over to a bashful young lady, whom Craig nonetheless sensed was anticipating their introduction with ill-concealed relish. Not too tall, slim, clear-skinned and with bright, sparkling eyes, Craig felt the old charmer welling up inside as he held out his hand.

"Craig, this is Elisa, my daughter; just twenty-one a week ago. Elisa, meet Craig," David beamed, as if he'd just discovered the perfect match for his angelic-looking offspring.

"Hiya, Craig," she said with a beautiful girlish ling that almost melted him, "I've read a lot about you in the letter we had. Dad said you were young, dashing and handsome!"

"And is he right?" Craig begged, with just a hint of vanity. "Enchanted to meet you," he then bade her, milking her awe for all it was worth.

"Where's she gone? The awkward so-and-so!" David muttered. Then he took off to locate his wife, leaving the two youngsters together.

"Well, you obviously know a lot about me. So tell me then, Elisa, how do you keep yourself busy?" Craig probed his blushing host, his eyes roving round and scanning the diverse collection of old codgers, bizarre middle-aged couples and the odd spotty youth that comprised Gunsbridge North Conservative Association – that was when he wasn't inadvertently eyeing up Elisa.

"Busy? I'm always busy studying for my degree," she beamed playfully. "Still, I try to let my hair down every now and then; chat up the boys, that sort of thing."

"Lucky boys!" Craig observed, doing a little chatting-up of his own.

"Ah, here she is," David huffed in relief upon rejoining them, having successfully rounded up his beautiful wife. "Craig, this is Gemma. Gemma, this is Craig."

"How are you, Craig? I've heard all about you," she exclaimed in words drippings from one of the most haunting and sensuous voices he'd ever encountered. For a moment he froze before this stunning seductress.

"Er... I'm okay. Yes, I'm fine," he stumbled, regaining his composure. "I'd heard David had an attractive wife. Now I know it is indeed so."

Craig kissed her hand, though he sensed she almost expected it as the proper formality. She, in turn, fixed those gleaming emerald eyes upon him while he joked about something trivial to David and Elisa. Someone interrupted, and David offered to help with the problem, dragging Elisa over to meet Brenda (who had by now charmed her way through several party workers, and was grateful to be rescued from the gruff, unsmiling Major).

"I'd say it takes guts to take on a seat like this," Gemma proffered, Craig detecting that the conversation suddenly seemed to have become pitched at a different level. He began to feel a touch uneasy, the uneasiness of a child left alone on their first day at school; nervous, excited, and animated by the imposing presence of the headmistress.

"It must take courage to run such a difficult constituency," Craig rejoined. "Your husband does a superb job from what I've seen so far, Mrs Sutton."

"Call me Gemma," she insisted. "Anyway, someone has to do it. It was a shambles when he came; and it'll probably be a shambles after he departs," she noted, such cynicism seeming out of step with the tempo of the afternoon. Optimism and fighting talk were what Craig had come to try and engender.

"Oh, don't get me wrong," she continued. "There are some dedicated people in the Association. There aren't many though."

"I hope if I win today that I can reverse that state of affair," Craig asserted, trying to reaffirm his mission.

"I'm sure you will. What this constituency needs is excitement, youth and daring. You look as if you could supply all three."

"You flatter me, Mrs Sutton," Craig exclaimed, only to be corrected again and made to address her by her Christian name.

"I like excitement. I like youth. I appreciate youngsters who are daring. We shall do a lot together, I can see."

Craig felt himself becoming uncomfortable once again. He tried changing the subject. "Elisa shows promise. She would make a good YC chairwoman."

"What YCs? Oh, there's that Sharpe kid, but they don't like him though; too aggressive and cocky. He's got a nice arse though!" she joked to Craig's momentary amusement.

However, he attempted to redirect the conversation back onto the merits of Gunsbridge North's non-existent Young Conservatives instead. Gemma, seeing he was embarrassed, played along.

"Anyway, Elisa's too flighty. Doesn't really know what she wants. I suppose that's why David's taken her over to meet your colleague – give her a role model to follow after, you think?"

Just then David returned and insisted that Craig sample the buffet, grabbing his arm and hauling him into the queue for the food. Whilst the husband was nattering to him about this and that, Craig looked up and could see those evocative emerald eyes still fixed upon him. Then the wife drank her down her Bacardi and wandered off to join her daughter, who introduced her mother to Brenda.

Finally, both candidates were ushered off into a side room. David then summoned the meeting to order, introducing Craig first. Feeling a bit more at ease now he'd been introduced to so many of them, the local boy spoke eloquently about himself for about fifteen minutes in a monologue that was occasionally witty and demonstrably earnest. He sat down feeling well pleased with himself. First came the easy questions from his hosts; then came the awkward ones.

"Mr Anderson. Doh' yoh' think this Common Market thing is a bloody racket? Them French n' Germans am' really tekkin' us ferra' ride, ay' they?"

Craig stood up and paced forward towards his audience. He was a European and proud of it. He outlined his case persuasively and unapologetically, summoning a whole host of statistics to prove his point. He could nonetheless see it cut no ice in some quarters. However, he swallowed his nerves and said it anyway.

"One final question…" David advised them. "Yes, Major..."

Oh no, thought Craig, fixing his gaze upon the feisty ex-tank commander. He could see the inevitable question coming, which all constituency associations drop on their candidates: although he was amazed that the Major summoned up the self-control to ask the question without supplementing it with his own usual blood-curdling observations: will Mr Anderson vote for the return of capital punishment? Go on, sucker, tell him the worst, Craig thought, and he rose, clearing his throat, to reply.

"Whilst no one is more determined than I am to beat crime, I have to say that, no, I couldn't vote for such a measure..."

The hall rippled with consternation. The Major sat, arms folded, staring straight at Craig with a rabid gleam in his eye. Odd cliques muttered amongst themselves until David brought order to the assembly with a tap of his gavel. Craig waited before continuing,

"Once I would have said yes – without any hesitation. But I can only say that I do not believe hanging would deter hardened murderers; and that once a life is taken, it is taken for all time. I would not want to be responsible for sending a man to his death for a crime that there was always a slight possibility he did not commit. Life demands a life, Major. I know that. But I don't think we possess the wisdom or the infallibility to take that life ourselves."

Sensing the furore he had just stirred up, Craig knew he'd blown it. Why hadn't he just waffled (which Jonathan Forsyth was good at) when placed in an awkward corner? And on Europe, why hadn't he just blabbered the usual platitudes about free trade and co-operation? He retired from the room, noticing Elisa's discreet, reassuring smile as he passed beside her on his way to await judgement.

"Your turn, sister," he said to Brenda, as she readied herself to stroll out to the rostrum.

Brenda was away for ages, or so it seemed. He could vaguely hear her strident address drifting down the way, and tried to cheer himself up with the thought that Brenda's views on Europe and capital punishment were not so drastically different to his own. Both of them were superb candidates. It was to be hoped that Gunsbridge North Tories would permit them a little ideological indulgence in return for the hard work they were both prepared to bring to the constituency. Finally, Brenda returned to rejoin her rival, and wait whilst the Association sorted out who was the superior of the two. Several more minutes passed before Craig finally accepted that the decision was now completely out of his hands.

****

Friday, December 5th 1986 was going to be a glittering occasion, just as Harry Conway had intended. Anyone who was anyone in Gunsbridge had been invited, although some Labour councillors had deliberately boycotted the official opening of the tall, imposing Trescott Park International Hotel as a snub to a property magnate they both feared and despised. Brad was there though, having rejected the boycott calls as childish. After all, the retail park, the hotel, and the office complex were now established facts; bricks and mortar (or glass and steel to be more precise).

"Councillor and Mrs Robert Bradleigh, Chairman of Gunsbridge Metropolitan Borough Social Services Committee, and prospective parliamentary candidate for the constituency of Gunsbridge South."

Everyone looked round at Brad and Helen strolling in past the quaintly attired toastmaster. Then the sable-haired socialist candidate and his wife approached the millionaire tycoon for the first time.

"Councillor Bradleigh. I don't think I've had the pleasure," Conway observed, shaking first Brad's hand, then Helen's. They made some uneasy small talk before moving on.

"Councillor and Mrs Michael Preston, Chairman of Gunsbridge Metropolitan Borough Highways Committee."

"Councillor Preston. So you're the man to see about the state of the roads around this place," Conway joked.

"You'd do better seeing your friend the Prime Minister to ask her Government to stop slashing the Council's rate support grant. Then we might be able to afford to build you some new roads, Harry."

Conway was at first unsure how to take Micky's little rebuff. Then his face mellowed, and he feigned amusement, making a mental note that this particular councillor might prove to be more uncooperative than he'd hoped.

"...The Honourable Member of Parliament for Gunsbridge North, Mr and Mrs Terry Johnson MP... The Honourable Member of Parliament for Gunsbridge South, Mr and Mrs James Whitney MP..."

Micky Preston turned to Terry Johnson and pointed out the arrival of the veteran parliamentarian's new rival. All eyes followed his finger, including those of Brad and Alannah, when the toastmaster turned to announce "...Mr Craig Anderson, prospective parliamentary candidate for Gunsbridge North, and Miss Elisa Sutton..."

"So your young lad fancies his chances, does he?" Terry bellowed across to James, who was within earshot.

Gunsbridge's quick-witted Conservative MP turned to his robust, ebullient, ex-lorry driving Labour contemporary. "I'd say so!" he grinned mischievously. "Back behind the wheel after the next election, are we Terry?"

Conway had spared no expense to impress his guests with the opulence of this five-star hotel. Waiters and waitresses darted about serving huge water melons or intricate cocktails, followed by platters laced with giant salmons, ducks, and pheasants, everywhere followed by wine waiters liberally ensuring that no ones glass ever emptied. This was Craig's first official engagement in his new capacity. David Sutton was invited by virtue of being a director of one of Conway's most important contractors, Gemma loyally at his side. Craig couldn't help noticing what a cracking figure she had, adorned as it was with a fabulous dark evening dress that put all the other women to shame – and they knew it! Whether they were councillors' wives, businessmen's wives, even Conway's own immaculately attired wife, Gemma had bested them all.

Craig had fretted about having to attend on his own, but he needn't have worried. David had insisted that he permit Elisa to be his companion for the evening, and she had willingly agreed. If dressed not quite as magnificently as her mother, Craig was nonetheless proud to have her at his side. Meanwhile, there was laughter and merriment. He noticed Elizabeth Gainsborough and Peter Brereton chatting together happily, betraying that certain intimacy he'd noticed on odd occasions. Then again, the shadow chairwoman of Social Services was a very attractive lady, and any man could be forgiven for feeling privileged to be in her confidence. Indeed, the night seemed made for lovers: David and Gemma were obviously happy; Gerry Roberts (who had gate-crashed as the representative of the small businesses forum) was busy chatting up some peroxide creature in a bum-hugging mini-skirt; Brad was obviously trying to command Alannah's attention too.

"You see that man over there," Craig pointed out for Elisa's benefit, "...Yes, next to the woman with the glasses. He's the Labour candidate in Gunsbridge South. Believe it or not, I used to hang around with him in my schooldays. And that girl across the table from him – the good looking one – she used to be in one of my sparring partners in the university debating society."

With everyone coming to the end of the final courses, Harry Conway stood up from his vantage point on the top table and waited while one of his minions set up a microphone in front of him. Tapping it to ensure it was switched on he waited again until a hush descended on the gathering.

"Your Worship," he opened, turning to the Mayor at his side, "distinguished guests, colleagues, ladies and gentlemen.

"Tonight, I believe, marks an important landmark in the story of Trescott Park, our town, and its citizens. For what you see before you is a top-class international hotel set amidst a gleaming new city of shops, offices and restaurants. That's the tangible Trescott Park that thousands of visitors have discovered for themselves since this complex was first opened. But that's just one aspect of this incredible city. This hotel, I believe, symbolises the unveiling of the other aspect: namely a symbol that Gunsbridge is back in business!

"I was brought up not far from here. I remember the terraced, back-to-back houses, and the canals I used to play along that first brought the industrial revolution to the Black Country. I remember my father – a humble foundryman – coming home black as the ace of spades from a hard day's graft. Oh yes, this area was once the powerhouse of the world, and I guess the grime and the muck was the price we all paid for that success. Then, as you know, hard times came, the foundries disappeared, and it was as if a huge, gaping wound had been opened up all across this area.

"The last ten years have been tough: the men of this town without jobs, and the kids leaving school with little hope of ever finding one – all that broke my heart. That's why I was determined that this town should be at the forefront of the new revolutions in retailing, services and information technology. It hasn't been easy: to be sure, I've had a few obstacles I've had to overcome," he admitted, trying not to look at the table full of Labour councillors and their wives sat expressionless just in front of him. "But through it all, I pressed on; because what you see around you tonight is the future of this country.

"Now I'm not telling you it's been all altruism on my part," he confessed, to a ripple of amusement from those who knew him better, "I've made a few bob out of this place; yes, I'll admit that. That said though, I want this hotel to tell the world that Gunsbridge is back in business in a *big* way. No more smoking chimneys or smelly metal-bashing outfits. What this town is about is creating and marketing the goods and services of the next century.

"Let's take hi-tech operations like the Lightning Software company, which has opened a brand new R & D studio just over the way from here: fifty new jobs – and that's just the start. Or the Atlantic Finance Corporation, who'll be moving their corporate headquarters here to Trescott Park after the New Year: two hundred new jobs, all bringing spending power back into this town.

"This is my town. I grew up here. The fine buildings I've built on this once derelict site are my statement of faith in this town. I'm honoured that you've joined me tonight in celebrating the opening of this beautiful hotel, and in reaffirming our common belief that Gunsbridge can, and will prosper. We'll show that Black Country folk are still the hard-working and enterprising people who can take on the world – and win! Thank you."

It was an eloquent and moving speech. James Whitney and Peter Brereton were the first to their feet, leading the ovation that greeted Conway as he sat down.

However, Brad, Micky and Alannah contented themselves with lukewarm applause from their seats.

With the formalities out of the way, some of the guests – including Gemma and Elisa – took up Conway's offer to have the hotel manager show them round some of the superior facilities the hotel boasted, including its *ne plus ultra* – the luxurious Trescott Suite, offering commanding views of the West Midlands from its twentieth-floor vantage point. Craig, meanwhile, ambled off to the bar.

"So you really think you can topple James Whitney?" he teased his old school pal, who was queuing ahead of him waiting to be served.

"Some of us are in with a better chance than others," Brad joked, an elliptical reference to Terry Johnson's thumping great majority. "I must say I thought that Neil Sharpe would take the nomination... pint of mild, please... and what about you, what d' you fancy?" he asked, turning to Craig before the bar girl disappeared.

"So was I. Then again, sometimes it's not always an advantage being the local man. As you've no doubt discovered, you will have made enemies as well as friends," Craig replied, turning Brad's elliptical joke back upon him.

"The difference is I beat my enemies," Brad crowed.

"Was it close?"

"In the end, it came down to Sharif Khan and me. I wasn't happy it ended that way. I used to like the chap; but let's just say he fell in with a bad crowd. Anyway, Alannah was telling me she knows you from university."

"You could say that. We used to have some right ding-dongs during the university debates. You're close to both Micky and Alannah, aren't you? I mean, whenever I've seen you tonight, you've always been together: confiding, plotting, scheming."

"I suppose Micky's my political father. He's taught me all I know. I owe him a lot. And Alannah – well, she's just pure inspiration!" he confided, winking at Craig disingenuously.

Craig drank the head off his beer before replying, "I guess George Franklin was like that to me. He didn't exactly possess the intellect of Edmund Burke, but he certainly knew how to help the people he represented."

Brad felt his body rush full of guilt, knowing that Craig was blissfully ignorant of who had really broken the story of his friend's nocturnal dalliances. He fought to calm himself. What was done was done. And besides, wasn't Craig's party (if not perhaps Craig as an individual) Brad's mortal class enemy, representing everything that was anathema to him?

"Yes, it was a shame," he stuttered, "He was a lovable old chap. Perhaps he should have known that public men can never have private lives."

Wearied by the throngs, they moved away from the bar and over into a quieter corner. Craig reminded Brad that James Whitney still commanded a substantial majority, whilst Brad warned Craig that he'd need a thick skin to survive a contest with Terry Johnson. Eventually, the guided tour returned and alighted from the glass elevator that travelled up and down the side of the towering edifice. Helen looked about for Brad, spotting him alone with Craig.

"It's superb!" she enthused. "Although I don't think we'll ever be able to afford to stay here."

"Helen, I don't think you've ever been introduced properly to Craig. Craig, this is my wife, Helen."

Craig was perplexed. This bespectacled little woman looked out of place beside her tall, handsome, thrusting candidate husband. As he exchanged political gossip with Brad she seemed to switch off, taking no part in the conversation, and appearing bored and disinterested. Even some of Craig's best jokes drew no amusement; so either Craig's jokes weren't as funny as they'd been when first told to him, or this was not the sort of marriage that would survive late night sittings at the House of Commons. Love, like politics it seemed, tended to throw together some strange bedfellows!

Spotting Gemma and Elisa returning, Craig excused himself and rejoined the Sutton fold – both mother and daughter demonstrably overawed by this palace of glass, Elisa chattering excitedly about all they had seen. David, though having been given the task of marketing the development, was noticeably more blasé.

"What do you say, Craig? Fantastic place to spend a dirty weekend!" Gemma meanwhile whispered to her candidate enticingly.

"David, how are you?" Conway beamed, making the rounds to thank his guests, gripping an enormous cigar between his shabby teeth.

"I'm fine, Harry. And yourself?"

"Bostin', as we say in our part of the world! Tell me, is this the young man who will be turning Gunsbridge North blue?" he then asked, shuffling towards Craig.

"I'll be doing my utmost," Craig replied humbly.

"Well, I keep telling these Tory hopefuls, if they need a little help, just ask, just ask. 'Seek and ye shall find'," Conway reminded them all biblically, puffing on his huge Havana. "Johnson's a good bloke. But, how shall we say, he has little understanding of the needs of business!"

That was his way of saying that he despised the socialist MP. However, while Conway moved on to greet other VIPs, David dropped a few hints to Craig about not accepting too tight an embrace from the tycoon – even if he was the local Tories' most generous benefactor. Conway greeted Peter Brereton and Elizabeth Gainsborough like old friends, and then wandered over to say hello to Tom McKerrick. From a distance, Craig could see that the discourse with the Labour Leader of the Council was formal to the point of being starched, although both men just managed a gritted smile for a passing photographer.

As a finale to the evening, the hotel manager invited those guests who could still stand after so much eating and drinking to make their way to the disco that was now starting up in the hotel's glittering nightclub. The crowd had by now thinned out, but the more energetic souls amongst his guests soon loosened their ties or kicked off their shoes to swing under the battery of psychedelic lights, the house rocking to a back-to-back offering of contemporary dance singles.

"Stock, Aitken and Waterman – aren't they a solicitors' practice in Dudley?" Gemma enquired above the pounding melodies.

Actually not, Craig intimated to her, trying to educate the mother in the musical tastes of the young, upwardly mobile generation, breaking briefly from grooving shamelessly with her happy and exhilarated daughter, who was otherwise lost in the music. Gemma, meanwhile, was trying to outclass her daughter on the dance floor as well, though when she wasn't observing Elisa's steps in order to copy them she would occasionally stare up at Craig with eyes ablaze with seductive intrigue.

In the half-light Craig caught sight of Brad and Helen trying to enjoy the late-night extravaganza, although dancing was obviously not Helen's *forte*. He noticed her candidate husband later team up with Alannah James and Micky Preston, by which time Helen had presumably become bored and taken a taxi home; she was nowhere to be seen anyway. He watched Brad enjoying some slow, intimate dances with Alannah instead. Later a huge net suspended above the dance floor released a deluge of brightly-coloured balloons on the happy revellers. Elisa, manifestly a party animal (in a jolly and apolitical sense), loved every minute of it and carried on spinning to the music, her knee-length red dress swirling up amidst flickering colours racing across the dance floor.

There was no denying that Elisa was a highly desirable young lady. Her cherubic good looks, slim, elegant body, and bubbly Black Country ways endeared most of Craig's friends to her. He would have found it hard not to fall in love with her: except for the fact that she was the daughter of the man who led the constituency that he was now prospective parliamentary candidate for. And, in Craig's old-fashioned thinking, that made her somehow out-of-bounds as far as romantic affection was concerned. Perhaps more importantly, something inside just didn't click: the chemistry wasn't right. He felt it would be dishonest to pretend that, lovely as she was, he felt anything vaguely resembling love for her. And again, in Craig's old-fashioned reasoning, it had to be love or nothing!

"Gettin' old?" she chuckled, reappearing from out of the shadows and mocking Craig's attempts to keep up with her. "Come on, let's take the lift up to the top floor. There are some spectacular views from up there."

And so there was. It was a pleasant evening down below, although the breeze was quite strong up on the twentieth-floor (just as Dick Lovelace had warned them, for on the way up they had encountered the crusty old councillor, scotch and soda in hand, evidently seeking refuge from the din of the disco). Craig pulled his jacket tight around him as together they scanned the horizon for landmarks across the illuminated town. Elisa braved the chill by nestling up alongside Craig, who cast his arms around her obligingly.

"It's amazing up here, isn't it?" she exclaimed in awe. Craig, meanwhile, was transfixed by the stars gleaming in the clear night sky – or at least he was pretending to be. Elisa dug her elbow into his ribs.

"Loosen up! You're all on edge!" she teased him.

Craig blinked demonstrably. He looked down into Elisa's childlike eyes and watched as she tried to read the look of confusion written all over his face. He needed mothering, she thought, so she reached up, closed her eyes, and presented him with a lingering and totally unmotherlike kiss. Craig obliged her by following her tongue as it pierced him, towards the end adding a few twists and turns of his own.

"Somethin' worrying you?" she asked perceptively.

Craig tried to put it in intelligible form. "I guess when I look out over this town at night, it brings back memories. I never dreamed that one day I'd be staring at the prospect of becoming one of this town's MPs," he replied, though in truth he never ceased doing just that.

And did he think he'd achieve it? Not this time round. Terry Johnson was too well entrenched, his own party organisation too weak, and party workers too thin on the ground. All of which served to combine with his unease at his burgeoning relationship with the girl viewing the lights of the metropolis alongside him to induce a feeling of melancholy. And then there was his career. He was finding it ever more pressing trying to keep BEL's marketing activity on the road *and* find time to go through the motions of making himself known on the streets of Gunsbridge North. Tonight should have been a welcome chance to unwind. Now it was becoming infinitely more complicated.

"Ah, look at the young lovers," someone taunted. They both turned around to see Gemma hanging on the balcony door. Elisa seemed embarrassed and broke off the embrace. "Mind you, it is hot down there. I've left your father to do that abominable 'Agadoo' dance with Craig's friends! I have no wish to make a fool of myself."

"Come on, Craig. Let's join in!" Elisa cried, dragging him back towards the elevator. Craig had no wish to make a fool of himself either, and so resisted her appeals. Finally, she lost patience with his evasiveness, and hurried back to join the revelry, leaving Craig to fret whether he'd made the right decision. Gemma moved in closer to meet him on the windswept balcony.

"Mrs Sutton, I want you to know I respect your daughter immensely," said Craig, trying to set her mind at ease and misreading it totally.

"Don't worry. I know you're incapable of doing otherwise. And by the way, it's 'Gemma'!" she insisted. "Anyway, you'll find Elisa doesn't really know what she wants out of life. That's why I thought I should warn you not to raise your expectations. Besides, you must have girls chasing you all over town."

"I have a lot of other things on my mind right now," he assured her.

"I know, like trying to put up a good show in a naff seat like this. Still, don't let it get you down. I know you're worth better things. Just have fun and enjoy it. Ease up!"

She moved closer to him and straightened his hair and jacket in a confusion of gestures that was at once both maternal and codedly sexual.

"Look, you're all on edge. Relax! I'm not going to eat you," she said, pointedly growling like a tigress to try to inject some light-heartedness into their sexually-charged encounter.

"I hope I won't let you down. In the election, I mean," Craig said, words so starched as to sound, at worst, almost ridiculous – and at best, wholly irrelevant to the electricity flowing between them. This woman was old enough to be his mother, even though her figure, her looks, and her oozing sensuality could put most eighteen year-olds to shame. The wind blew up a gust that ruffled Craig's golden blond locks. It hurled up Gemma's beautiful dark hair across her face also, partially concealing those piercing, seductive eyes and that wilful expression.

"Craig, you're not on show now. No one's watching your performance or judging you. Anyway, I'm not interested in Craig the candidate, I'm interested in the real Craig that lurks inside," she insisted, eyes still veiled by wisps of trailing hair.

"I can see David really loves you," Craig proclaimed, "He's really fortunate to have so beautiful a wife. It's so important these days that people appreciate what a blessing a happy marriage is."

"You believe all that crap?" Gemma laughed – a remark that hurt Craig as deeply as it shocked him. "Oh, I know. You're still young; you still believe in fairy-tale romances."

"But you do love David?" he demanded of her.

"Oh, yes. I suppose I love him in a funny old way. But over the years, I've learned that excitement is worth as much as contentment. And I have that feeling that underneath that boring exterior, you've got 'excitement' written all over you. After all, don't they say it's the quiet ones you have to watch?" she marvelled, resting her long, tapering arms up onto his shoulders and curling her fingers around the back of his neck. "Craig, you're fabulously good-looking – a real stud. Women could fall for you in droves. I'm sure I could too."

The compliment sort of made up for being labelled boring. He closed his eyes while she ran her hands through his hair, along his cheeks, and down along the course of his silky blue tie, coming to rest at the belt around his waist, which she fingered teasingly.

"Mrs Sutton, I..." he burbled, opening his eyes to at least attempt a token protest.

It was no use: suddenly, he felt his mouth tentatively forming to meet her as she thrust those glistening, rose-coloured lips up towards him. Then they closed their eyes together, Craig embracing her firm and slender waist, drawing her tight unto him. Gemma ran her fingers rhythmically up and down his neck while their tongues ventured excitedly within each other for several long seconds. Then they broke apart, watching and trembling as the other drifted away.

Gemma suddenly shuddered from the suppressed inner chill that now flooded back into her as she felt for the first time how cold was the night air. She walked back slowly to the half-open balcony door, glancing back to see if Craig was following her. However, her *objêt d'amour* was sullen and nonchalant, resting his throbbing hands on the soothing cold steel of the rail running along the balustrade, and looking out across the town. She stopped at the door, partially crossing inside. Then she hung on the edge, observing at a distance that this confused and solitary figure seemed to be straining his eyes in the gusting wind to make out far more than just the tall, illuminated cross of the town's parish church that she thought he had fixed them upon.

"Coming back down?" she called across to him. Pausing some moments as if he had not heard her, he then shook his head discreetly. Waiting in case he changed his mind, she finally lifted herself off the door and stepped inside, leaving him by himself.

By now, Craig was indeed studying that beacon of faith in the night. His heart was being pulled every which way by the torrent of emotions that his excursion into adultery had unleashed. It was as if he'd allowed a freak wave to wash over him, uprooting his feet from the familiarity of the shore, and turning him upside down as he was dragged helplessly into its rip. He needed love; yet he also craved passion and carnality. Yet how could it be right? But then fear of scandal was just one component of his inner searching. He steeled himself and stared into the radiant white cross – the symbol of all that felt pure and new and liberating in his heart at that seminal moment –and whilst he did, unconsciously and uncontrollably, he uttered some obscure words made vaguely intelligible only by the tears that were by now trickling down his windswept face.

"Help me..." he felt himself weeping, "...Jesus... Lord... Help me!"

12 ECONOMICAL WITH THE TRUTH

"Okay, folks... rolling in ten seconds... nine... eight..." the producer informed them.

Brad placed the headphones on. He looked at his watch and it confirmed what the clock on the studio wall was telling him: it was 12.59 pm. Through the headphones resting idly round his neck he could hear the DJ in the other studio concluding his show. Finally, the news jingle crashed in over the dying moments of some ballad by Erasure.

"Good afternoon. It's one o'clock on Tuesday May 19th. This is the lunchtime report from Gunsbridge Sound, and I'm Alan O'Brien," the newscaster announced, waiting for the jingle to subside before summarising the day's headlines.

"In the Gulf, an American warship has been hit and set on fire by an Exocet missile... At home, it was the Alliance yesterday - today Labour and the Conservatives parties follow with their manifestoes... And here in Gunsbridge, local parents are again up in arms after the death of the third child this year crossing the busy Copthorne Road... Later on in the programme, we'll be talking to Robert Bradleigh, the Labour Party candidate in Gunsbridge South in the first of our 'Meet the Candidate' special phone-ins. The number to ring if you'd like to ask Robert a question is Gunsbridge 2-4-5-7-7-7... that's Gunsbridge 2-4-5-7-7-7!"

Brad listened patiently whilst O'Brien disgorged the news. He'd been on local radio before, so he was no stranger to the masses of buttons and dials that surrounded the casually attired newscaster. A few weeks earlier, Brad had debated the local election results with Dick Lovelace in this very same studio. Since then, the Prime Minister had dissolved Parliament and called a general election. The omens for her success were all there: not least Labour's defence policy was continuing to provide a source of ammunition for their opponents. However (and in stark contrast to 1983), this time Labour's Election Manifesto was a fairly light, desultory document, which had led Mrs Thatcher to christen it the 'iceberg manifesto' because only a fraction of its socialist policies were visible within its covers. 'Britain's crying out for Labour' was to be Neil Kinnock's rallying cry (although according to Denis Healey, so too were the Russians – one of the election's more notable gaffes so far).

After a brief resume of the weather prospects, O'Brien turned to Brad, introducing him and inviting him to tell the listeners about why he would be recommending that they vote Labour in a few weeks time. Brad responded with the usual themes he'd rehearsed over the last few months: the Tories had divided the nation, increased the wealth of the rich at the expense of the poor, and were fleecing resources from the health service to purchase horrific and unnecessary nuclear weapons.

"Right, Robert. I think we have our first caller over on line one, who I believe is Mrs Brenda Allport from Sizemere. Are you there, Brenda, my dear?"

"*Ar'. Ar'm 'ere!*" came the crackly reply from down the line.

"What's your question, Brenda?" O'Brien enquired.

"*Ar' wonna' ask if 'Labour 'am gonna' 'elp mothers wots' got young kids to get nursery places...*"

Indeed, noted Brad, supportive of such calls. Some callers also commended Labour's other action points, though others still were openly hostile. Brad was quite chuffed that he'd acquitted himself well in this opening battle of his campaign. He was quite getting into the cut-and-thrust of debate. However, eventually Alan O'Brien waded in, retaking control of his show and bringing it to a conclusion. Brad heard the DJ resume his slot, kicking off with a melody by the Happy Mondays dedicated to some obscure housewife listening in from Tower Park. O'Brien removed his headphones, which acted as a cue for Brad to do likewise. He sat back in his chair and stretched out.

"Thanks," said O'Brien, employing his more casual everyday voice. "Fancy a coffee?"

"I'd love one. But I have a meeting over at the Council House at two-thirty. I'd best be making tracks," he replied.

Brad made his way out of the studio and headed back into town. It was just as well he left when he did. Traffic was heavy and he only just made it to the Council House in time. When he arrived, Elizabeth Gainsborough was busy laughing and chatting with the director of Social Services. Alannah was by her side, although she appeared less than absorbed by whatever Elizabeth was expounding. Beside the director (a jolly bearded man with a receding hairline) sat a diminutive finance officer; and next to him, Wendy Baker; ruddy-haired and newly elevated to the post of principal social care officer in charge of all the Borough's services to children and families: at twenty-nine, the youngest principal officer within the Council.

"Right, folks. Shall we begin?" Brad opened, taking his seat and shuffling to remove his jacket.

"You were lucky. We nearly started without you!" Elizabeth quipped tongue-in-cheek.

Brad signalled the director to commence his report. He had rather hoped that the Labour candidate in Lower Henley might just have dethroned this pertinacious lady. However, Elizabeth had run a good campaign, and was now enjoying both her new four-year term of office and her reappointment as Brad's shadow. *I wonder what skeletons she has in her cupboard?* he wondered, wishing his wife possessed some titbit of information that might demolish the other Conservative councillor in his ward.

"...And so, Chairman, that's the position. I don't know whether Wendy has anything to add."

The director turned to his colleague, who replied, "Only to say, Chair, that the case managers involved are anxious that we deal with this matter as soon as possible in order to avoid further distress to the children involved."

"I think I ought to add, Chairman, that any decision to act on these proposals will have cost implications," interjected the finance officer. "There are no unallocated funds in the Social Care budget to call upon."

Bum, thought Brad! *Why does money always have to rear its ugly head?* "I take your point, but child protection work must have priority," he noted.

"I agree, Chairman," said Elizabeth, qualifying her endorsement by reminding him that, even so, "If you go ahead, you'll have to report back to the full committee for approval to vire funds from elsewhere. And are you really sure we're not jumping the gun and acting just a little hasty?"

Brad pondered the dilemma for the moment. "Move we accept the proposals; and yes, Wendy, you have my authority to set this thing in motion. God knows, there are enough abused children in this world. Let's just hope we can spare a few more from that sort of misery before it's too late."

Alannah formally seconded the resolution, and the meeting progressed to some other less controversial item. As this did not require Wendy's presence, she discreetly got up and left, clutching her notes tight to her chest like and smiling at Brad as she breezed past. He looked up at her, then at Alannah, before casting his glance back down at his minutes.

The director was droning on at length on this item, so Brad took the opportunity to daydream about how pleasant it was to be surrounded by beautiful women. He adored female attention – always had. His wife wasn't exactly a bundle of fun though. Occasionally swapping glances with Alannah, he amused himself pondering some of Helen's litany of excuses for avoiding conjugal encounters. It would be funny if it didn't hurt so much inside. Love there once was, but it seemed to disappear more and more with each ebb tide of recrimination. Meanwhile, time was moving on, and Brad was anxious to get away. Therefore he was glad that Elizabeth chose not to haggle over the second item and the Social Services (Urgent Matters) Sub-committee broke up after just under an hour.

"Still on for this evening?" he asked Alannah, gathering up his papers.

"Sure. I'll bring some helpers too. We'll paint this town red yet," she promised, winking as Elizabeth turned to offer her a discernible look of censure.

The drive back to Lower Henley caught the start of the rush hour – just as he had feared, Brad catching the mums picking their children up from school. Tuned into the news, he found himself in a line of traffic listening to Mrs Thatcher going on and on about "going on and on". Try as he might to be charitable, he abhorred the woman. She would have to go!

Helen and Mark were sat at the table eating their tea. Brad breezed past on his way into the bedroom to change suits. Finishing what was left of his meal Mark dived out of his chair and ran after his father. Brad was in a hurry, but couldn't resist those winsome eyes, picking him up and cuddling him.

"Can you call Micky?" Helen sighed, clearing away the dishes.

Putting the little lad down, he dialled his agent and spent some minutes running through the state of play so far. Already he was feeling the strain of this busier than average day – and there would be more like this before the election was over.

"That thing hasn't stopped ringing all day. Can't you get an answerphone?" Helen complained.

"Oh don't start that again!" Brad yelled impatiently.

"Well, I'm sick of it. It's like a crisis centre in this house. The calls just keep coming in, and you're never here to answer them! In fact, you're never here – period! I had a husband once. Now all I have is an occasional visitor!"

"Yes, and I had a wife. What happened to her?" he retorted indignantly.

"Oh, go on! Just sod off out! I won't be awake when you crawl in either."

"Well, that's original! Sleeping is about all you're good for!"

Helen slammed the kitchen door behind her, leaving Mark staring up at his apoplectic father. Brad looked down at him, smiled, and tried to pretend all was not really as bad as it seemed. Suddenly, he remembered someone else he had to phone. He picked up the receiver, dialled and waited.

"Hello... Donna? ...Yeh, it's Brad. Listen, meet me down at the club at six-thirty... yeh... We're doing Barnwood with Micky, Alannah and Colin... Who? Me? ...No, I'm just a bit tired, that's all... Yeh, back at your place afterwards... bye!"

****

"You're not serious? Tell me you're not serious, David!" Craig exclaimed. "How many?"

"Ten thousand," his agent replied. He could see Craig wasn't in the mood for what he was hearing. "Like I said, the guy in the despatch office left them in the wrong place, and the refuse collectors mistook them for rubbish and.... just took 'em!"

"All ten thousand?"

"The lot! I gave the manager a right bollocking. He'll try and run the batch again for next Wednesday."

"Next Wednesday! Oh, David, we'll never get them out. We've got a dozen people to deliver ten thousand leaflets in a week. If they worked round the clock they'd never do it!"

"I'm sorry, Craig," Gemma interjected, "I was there when David tore into the man. We're doing all we can."

Her soothing feminine words couldn't reach down into the depths of Craig's despair. Those leaflets were to have been a vital part of his campaign in the best Conservative areas of Gunsbridge North (and there were precious few of them). Now they were probably being cremated in some municipal incinerator. It was the cap on a disastrous campaign so far. Craig had never realised just how weak David's organisation was until the first week's canvassing, when only half-a-dozen brave souls turned up – and that included David and Gemma! All this contrasted poorly with Terry Johnson's dynamic campaign, his workers appearing to pop up on every street corner – just like his bright red posters. What's more, Craig had almost been thumped by an out-of-work skinhead who'd taken exception to something he'd broadcast about all the new jobs the Conservatives had created. And although MacDonald had been supportive, he knew that the company were less than enthusiastic about him taking a month off to indulge his love of politics. Finally, there was Gemma – still periodically eyeing him up. By the time he got to bed after midnight each night, he was ready to collapse with exhaustion, worry and despair. Yet even in his dreams, the voluptuous Mrs Sutton returned to tempt and seduce him!

****

The balloons and bunting blew about wildly as the elderly double-decker bus toured round Gunsbridge town centre. Brad enjoyed the feeling of power and self-importance that came with standing at the front of the open-top upper deck, urging his hometown to vote Labour. The bright red battle-bus had been loaned to Gunsbridge South Labour Party by their comrades in Gunsbridge North and was pretty unmistakable as it drew down the main thoroughfares of the town. Finally, the vehicle came to a halt outside Gunsbridge Town Hall. Brad spent several minutes pleading with the onlookers to prevent four more years of rampant Thatcherism. Across the other side of the square, he noticed a gaily-coloured flat-bed lorry driving past bearing James Whitney's royal blue posters. On the back of this float, Conservative supporters cheered as their incumbent candidate urged them not to strip away Britain's defences, which only the Tories could safeguard. Then the lorry moved on and left Brad in peace.

"...SO I TELL YOU, THATCHER HAS AXED YOUR LOCAL COUNCIL'S BUDGET... YOU CAN RESTORE ALL THESE CUTS ONLY BY VOTING LABOUR..."

The crowd that had gathered didn't say much, apart from Brad's own supporters, who were liberally sprinkled amongst them. He continued his harangue for a few more minutes, though he noticed some lads in collars, ties and smart jackets now mingling in with his audience. One or two carried these newfangled mobile phones and seemed to be using them to relay messages. Before long, other smartly dressed youths appeared: Gunsbridge South YCs had evidently arrived!

"...VOTE LABOUR ON THURSDAY, JUNE 11TH, AND WE WILL SPEND THE MONEY ON YOUR HEALTH SERVICE. WE WILL CANCEL THESE UNNECESSARY TRIDENT MISSILES... "

There was a short burst of staccato applause from the crowd. Then Tony Clare threw down his cigarette, stamped it into the pavement and called up to Brad, "Does that mean we'll all have to take to the hills?"

Laughter and snide heckling reinforced the salience of his question, for when pressed on Labour's defence policy, Neil Kinnock had conceded that, in the event of a Russian attack, he would not order a nuclear strike, preferring to make the country 'untenable' to any occupying force. His critics had had a field day, with Mrs Thatcher roundly denouncing such a 'Dad's Army' mentality. Meanwhile, Brad's own opponents had now scented blood, moving in for the kill.

"I hear you'll be letting Arthur Scargill loose on the factory gates again?" cried another YC, anxious that Brad should give account of his leader's other indiscretion that Labour would re-legalise secondary picketing. Slowly the gloss was washing off, and Brad knew it.

The Conservatives had costed-up Labour's public spending commitments and deduced that a sizeable increase in taxation would be necessary to pay for it all. So another young gun in the crowd yelled above Brad's reply, "What will all this cost the taxpayer? Does the councillor know?"

He didn't even deem to reply to such charges, instead taunting his opponents over their government's record. Even so, whilst he had opened his campaign in a spirit of optimism, he was not so sure now that James Whitney's majority was all that vulnerable.

****

The sleek black Jaguar roared up onto the piazza of Trescott Park's brand new business park, escorted by two police outriders. First out of the car were the shadowy personal bodyguards, ever watchful of the cheering crowd of personally-vetted onlookers waiting for a glimpse of this important visitor.

Then she was there! Stepping out of the car clutching one of her famous handbags, the Right Honourable Mrs Margaret Hilda Thatcher FRS MP was formally greeted by an adoring Harry Conway, who gently urged the Prime Minister over to meet the management team of Conway Enterprises Ltd. Lining the entrance to the reception building, each executive shook her hand until the introductions were completed, and Conway drew her over to meet more familiar company.

"Prime Minister, I think you know James Whitney from Gunsbridge South... And this young man is Craig Anderson, prospective candidate in Gunsbridge North."

"Good morning, gentlemen," she warmly greeted them. "How are you, James?"

"All set for your third term, Prime Minister!" said the MP, charming her with his superlative flattery.

"And Craig, I haven't forgotten your speech at the 1980 Conference, you know'" she continued, displaying all the concern for personal detail for which she was renowned. She turned and reminded the other senior party workers, who were anxious not to be left out of the proceedings, that "it displayed such clarity and conviction. I remember telling Denis how badly our party needed bold young men like that Craig Anderson."

"I hope I can repay your kindness with a victory in Gunsbridge North," Craig replied deferentially.

The entourage then descended upon one of the new hi-tech factories that Conway had constructed, and which he now proudly escorted this most eminent lady through. Van Hemsburg Electronics made microcircuits for the telecommunications industry. Donning white overalls, Conway led a Prime Minister raptured in wonderment around some of the remarkable machines that stamped and assembled the tiny circuit boards. Meanwhile, the Prime Minister was unable to resist a comment for the trailing press corps, who jostled amongst themselves.

"This is an example of success – *British* success," she remarked emphatically. "Let no one say the British can't take on the best in the world and win. How many new jobs have been created?" she called over to Conway.

"Eighty, Prime Minister," he replied, to the feverish scribbling of the press pack.

Next it was over to Hamilton Systems plc – Gunsbridge's world-beating manufacturer of computer-assisted design software. Staff invited the Prime Minister to sit behind one of their CAD workstations and try out the programme. At first apprehensive about what to do, a little instruction from the operator, who was somewhat bashful in the glow of flashbulbs, soon had the PM pushing buttons and racing the 'mouse' round the desk.

"This way, Prime Minister... Prime Minister, over here!" yelled the cameramen.

"This is a special programme we developed for the motor industry, Prime Minister," the managing director boasted proudly.

"Yes, it's amazing. Craig, you work in the motor industry. Does your company have one of these machines?"

"I believe we own quite a few of them, Prime Minister," he intimated, watching the screen light up.

"If you enter this command you can change the perspective," the operator advised, guiding the PM's hand. All at once, the vehicle's outline appeared, the computer filling out the contours like an invisible crayon. A few more commands and the perspective changed so that the Prime Minister could view the vehicle from above, below, at an angle, or from behind.

"Incredible! Could I borrow one of these so Denis can redesign our sitting room?" she asked, bringing great mirth to her surrounding acolytes, and making the cameras flash and the reporters scribble even faster.

After a pose for the television news teams, the Prime Minister was off with Harry Conway for a lightning visit to address a waiting crowd of well-wishers who had gathered beneath the huge glass dome of Trescott Park's main shopping mall. An odd heckler had somehow managed to dodge the intense security, and dismayed party officials by hurling garbled abuse.

"Oh, go home, you creep!" a well-heeled woman cried at him, "She's the best thing that's ever happened to this country!"

The Prime Minister was more modest, although she did take the opportunity to offer her listeners a full summary of the Government's achievements: high growth, low taxation, sound financial management, with the promise of more prosperity to come. Why let Labour destroy it all, she asked rhetorically.

"Why indeed?" muttered Conway, who was stood next to Craig, arms folded, watching the crowd lapping it all up, "And with candidates like Craig Anderson, I don't see why they should."

"You flatter me, Harry," Craig remarked casually.

"No, seriously. You're a good bloke. I'd like to see more blokes like you wandering the corridors of Westminster. You stick with me and I can make it happen."

Craig turned to Conway with only a vague appreciation of the proposition he was putting before him. Therefore, Conway elaborated further.

"Listen, lad. I know a lot of important people round this neck of the woods. They know me. They know we share, shall we say, a common desire to promote the prosperity of the West Midlands; and, most of all, keep those red bastards out. If ever you need a good word put in let me know. I'd like to help you along."

Craig could detect Conway trying to massage his words as spoke. "That's very kind, Harry, but I..."

"Don't mention it. And listen, you shouldn't be trying to hold down a full time job either. That's a mug's game. Here's my card. Just give me a bell when you're ready, and I can fix you up with a little number somewhere so that you need only show your face every now and then. The rest of the time you can devote to the real tasks of a politician. After all, I need guys like you to help me build places like this. We can do a lot together to help create jobs, attract investment and regenerate this part of the world."

David Sutton had warned Craig that Conway sailed close to the wind. Craig fully recognised Trescott Park's contribution to the Conservative economic miracle, but wasn't sure he liked the price Conway would probably demand to send yet another Midlands Tory to Westminster. Political altruism was probably not the sole motive for such generosity on behalf of Gunsbridge's wealthiest citizen.

"Well, think about it. It would be a shame to see a promising young career like yours held back," Conway concluded as the Prime Minister did likewise. There was applause, some final words of encouragement; then Mrs Thatcher was corralled back into her car to be whisked off to another engagement.

Craig watched the motorcade speed off, and then turned to search out David Sutton. Glancing about, he saw no sign of his ever-resourceful agent, though he did notice his wife standing over by the main entrance, leaning against the information board. She was dangling her car keys and grinning.

"David's very sorry, but he's been called into the office to deal with a mini-crisis. He's delegated me to look after you," she said as the puzzled candidate advanced towards her. "And the first stop is lunch back at my place. Come on, the car's over there."

The drive back to the Sutton's opulent detached house in Copthorne took about fifteen minutes in Gemma's smooth BMW. It was a well-appointed five-bedroomed dwelling, set aback a verdant lawn, with tall pines shading the property from the excesses of the midday sun. Craig followed after Gemma as she strolled up the drive, through the great oak door, and into the lovingly furnished hallway.

"Take a seat in the lounge. I'll make us something for lunch," she said, pacing off to the kitchen. "Have a look round, see if there's a book that interests you. Or switch the news on. See if they've covered the visit."

Craig did just that. Flicking the remote control, he wandered back and forth across the channels until he alighted upon coverage of Mrs Thatcher's Trescott Park visit. However, it was overshadowed by some ferocious opposition attacks on the Prime Minister over the health service. "*I pay to go into hospital on the day I want, and with the doctor I want.... I exercise my right as a free citizen to spend my own money in my own way,*" the Prime Minister retorted, justifying her patronage of private medicine. Meanwhile, Labour had wheeled out some ten-year old, who had been waiting for a heart operation on the NHS. *'FOUR TIMES THEY GOT HIM READY FOR SURGERY – FOUR TIMES THEY SENT HIM HOME!'* blazed the headlines.

Gemma returned with some snacks and joined him on the settee, watching the rest of the day's news. Later, with the meal consumed and the news finished, she took the plates out, returning to relax for a few minutes. She couldn't resist playing with Craig's mobile telephone, one of those brick-like devices that David had given him to enable them to keep in touch with each other, and which Craig had meanwhile left lying on the table in front of them.

"What are we doing this afternoon then?" she asked, kicking off her shoes. Otherwise, she lay back with her feet on the pouf and closed her eyes to meditate.

"I thought I'd go and show my face outside the new primary school in Lanes End. Press some flesh, kiss a few babies – that sort of thing."

"Will you be desiring my body?" Gemma enquired without opening her eyes, though to Craig's sudden consternation. "...To give out leaflets. Or point the mums in your direction?" she then offered by way of clarification.

"Oh…! Yes…! That would be nice, seeing that David's still tied up," Craig sighed thankfully.

"Yes, I like meeting the voters," she proffered. "You have such delightful dialects around here. One little boy came to the door, looked up at me with doleful eyes, and said "'Ers gonta' gerrim' out fer' 'is tay". Someone translated afterwards that his mother had departed to the public house to retrieve his father to partake of the evening meal!" she chuckled to herself before changing the subject.

"Tell me, do I make you feel uneasy?"

"In what way?" replied Craig – his frown belying a certain suspicion of this by now familiar line of interrogation.

"Does being with me put you on edge? Frighten you? Repel you? Come on, you tell me."

Craig thought for a moment before committing himself. "If you want an honest answer – you're a very beautiful woman, and I find you very attractive. But you're someone else's wife."

"You're so sweet, aren't you! And you're very noble too. Perhaps that's what I like about you, Craig: your most endearing quality. Tell me, Craig, are you still a virgin?" she said, getting straight to the point. Craig was dumbstruck and didn't even attempt to reply. She touched his hand, trailing her fingers back and forth across it idly.

"Maybe that's your problem," she counselled and left the matter there, sensing his embarrassment. Jumping up out of her seat, she drifted over to the door, hanging on the edge.

"I think I'll take a shower and get changed before we meet the school kiddies," she informed him. "I won't be long. Otherwise, there's a washroom upstairs on the left if you want to freshen up."

Meanwhile, Craig was busy reacquainting himself with his mobile phone, and didn't notice Gemma quietly remove her dress and skimpy black lingerie in the hallway. Taking off her panties, she then leant back against the doorpost, toying inside her pubic fur and watching in silent amusement while Craig was toying with the chunky device instead, oblivious to her presence directly behind him. Therefore she gathered up her clothes and quietly slipped upstairs.

Eventually, the candidate decided to explore his agent's substantial library. David was evidently an avid reader of history and Craig found fascinating his collection of works on the Napoleonic wars, as well as scholarly biographies of Castlereagh and Metternich – the golden age of international relations. On another shelf Craig found studies in modern European history, a subject dear to his heart. He could have spent all afternoon browsing through this literary heaven; but with time advancing he decided that he, too, better freshen up ready for the hustings. Picking up the bulky mobile phone and dropping it in his jacket pocket, he made his way up the stairs, trying to remember the directions his host had given him. Left, he recalled, but how far left? This door looked promising. Oops, the airing cupboard! How about this one...?

"Mrs Sutton, I'm sorry... I didn't realise..."

He'd never felt so embarrassed. If not totally in a state of undress, he'd still caught Gemma in the process of getting ready. A silky red dressing gown was tied tight around her and a towel was draped around her hair. Even though she didn't appear especially startled at the intrusion, Craig knew he ought to leave but found himself rooted to the spot. The thought entered his head: what could he do with her now he had her alone and vulnerable? But his conscience told him to forget it. He was inclined to agree. Besides which, it must all be a dream, a male fantasy – this sort of thing only ever happened in steamy paperback novels!

Gemma smiled and laid down the garments that she had been taking from the wardrobe when Craig had burst in, leaving them folded crisply on the bed. She straightened herself up slowly and wandered up to him. Pulling the towel from her hair, she shook her damp crown. Her moist, dark locks fell free. She paused for a long, pregnant moment. Then Craig watched as she loosened the gown. She peeled it from her shoulders and revealed the superlative naked beauty of her alabastrine figure as he gazed on in manifest disbelief. The gown now fell fully from around her, upon which she motioned to him to close the remaining distance between them.

****

Over the final weekend of the General Election campaign, both main parties held huge, star-studded rallies to mobilise the faithful for one final push to victory. Neil Kinnock reminded the nation that "in eight years Conservative policies have crushed communities and shattered families, put decent housing and regular transport beyond the reach of millions, and made school books and hospital equipment dependent on fund raising... After eight years, there is greater fear on the streets, anxiety is used as an economic weapon, prejudice is given legal force, and morality is a mixture of being economical with the truth and worshipping the gods of greed."

At her rally Mrs Thatcher retorted "I don't know about 'Dad's Army': I'm a woman, and I'd like to think that those people who believe in keeping Britain strong and free belong to Mum's Army... When people go to the polls, I believe Mum's Army will include thousands of traditional Labour supporters who just can't stomach the 'no-defence' policy of today's Labour Party. The Leader of the Labour Party talks about occupation. Occupation? Occupation of Britain? After waging two world wars without a single enemy soldier on British soil? We Conservatives will never take risks with Britain's security... Let us have lasting peace in Britain, so that you can be able to run your own life, spend your own money, and make your own choices."

****

"Brad! Brad! It's the Gunsbridge North result!" Colin called out, offering the town's other Labour candidate the headphones of his little Walkman radio to hear it for himself: Labour 31,757 votes, Conservatives 12,780 votes, Alliance 8,920 votes. Once again, Terry Johnson had sent the opposition away with a flea in their collective ears. Still, Craig at least had the satisfaction of having increased the Conservative vote. He'd surely prove a formidable opponent to whomever he decided to take on next.

Meanwhile, the counting in Gunsbridge South continued. Brad had increased the Labour vote considerably over the 1983 result; James Whitney was unlikely to have another overall majority. Even so, Brad looked at his watch: 2.33am. This had been the longest, most exhausting day of his life. Thank God it was almost over.

Suddenly, a huge cheer went up over on the far side of the Town Hall, Conservative supporters crowding around some YC, who also possessed a Walkman. What could it be? the Labour side wondered. A chuffed Dick Lovelace quickly enlightened them: the result for Barrow-in-Furness had just been announced – a Conservative 'hold' – giving the party its three hundred and twenty-sixth seat and a majority in the new Parliament. Mrs Thatcher had secured her historic third term and a place in the record books. It was hard for Labour supporters not to be disappointed. Now the time had come to hear the result for their part of the world.

"Allsop – Jane Elizabeth (Alliance), 11,996 votes."

That persistent young lady had evidently not benefited as much as she had hoped from the calls for tactical voting during her second stab at winning the seat. But she had established a solid base of residual support nonetheless...

"...Bradleigh – Robert (Labour Party), 19,959 votes."

Brad closed his eyes and felt like crying, despite the cheers of his supporters. It was a good result – but just not good enough...

"Whitney – James Jonathan Robert (Conservative Party), 27,045 votes. I therefore declare that..."

It was over: James Whitney had won again with a handsome majority. Now all that remained was the post-mortem at the microphone. As befitted the occasion, Brad was circumspect.

"My supporters have put a hell of a lot of hard work into fighting this seat," he noted. "I'd like to thank them, especially my agent, Micky Preston. Yet the time is still not right. There's lots of money sloshing about out there – for some of you, at least," he continued, partially conceding his opponents' case. "But it will not always be so. Before long, even those who think they've benefited from Thatcherism will discover the illusion they have fallen for. And when they do, we will be rid of this evil once and for all!"

The ecstatic hubris of James Whitney's supporters drowned out the frustrations of Brad's own occasionally vocal crowd. Micky thanked Brad for fighting a superb campaign, but suggested that because of the lateness of the hour, they all retire home to bed for a well-earned rest. Brad concurred, though he didn't intimate to his friend that he now had little to go home to, the campaign having driven the final nail into the coffin of his tenuous marriage. Not only had he to contemplate a future without the seat in Parliament that he so prized; but also a future without Helen and Mark either.

Driving home, he perchance passed by Joy Molson's flat and noticed the living room light was on; a television screen was obviously flickering behind the open curtains. Stopping the car on an impulse, he stepped out as if in a daze, sweeping back tears from his eyes as he mounted the steps of the hallway and rang the bell to the 'Siren's' lair.

Joy answered the door in her dressing gown. At first she seemed surprised to find a candidate finally paying her a home visit, albeit at an unearthly hour and after the votes had been cast.

"I gathered you lost," she addressed him softly, hoping he would enlighten her as to the nature of his visit. Though he was reticent, she guessed all the same.

"Has she told you it's over?" she asked. Again, no reply; but she could see he'd been crying so took his hand and led him inside.

"I've been watching the results," she elaborated as they stood in the living room observing the panels of psephologists, politicians and commentators raking over the entrails of the Conservative victory.

The Conservatives appeared to have won hands down in the south. However, the party had been massacred in Scotland, with only ten seats remaining out of seventy-two north of the border. They also lost their remaining city seats in Manchester, Liverpool, Newcastle and Glasgow; indeed, that arch-Thatcherite minister, Oliver Lyons, had thus lost his seat to Labour. Meanwhile, the Alliance had not performed well at all; the Social Democrats were reduced to just four seats in the new Parliament. Above all, despite some improvements to its share of the vote, and the capture of some twenty seats, Labour had manifestly failed to convince the electorate that it could govern better than the Conservatives. It all made very depressing viewing for the devastated ex-candidate that Joy was now trying to console. She switched the set off and stared up into his bloodshot eyes. She nursed his hot, stubbled cheeks with the back of her hand.

"Come," she beckoned him, extinguishing the living room light and loosening her gown. It was now 3.33am; Thursday, June 11th 1987 had already passed into history.

Part III

1987-1992

13 *THE LONELIEST ROAD*

The vicar had said his piece. The coffin was solemnly lowered into the grave excavated to bear the mortal remains of Albert Charles Ferriday. Brad looked on while his mother and several other relatives wept at the graveside on this warm, sunny day – sunshine and death seeming terribly incongruous together. His grandfather had enjoyed a long life. Despite the fact that he'd not been able to visit the old man in later years as much as he'd liked, Brad had still enjoyed the rare opportunities they'd shared together to discuss politics, philosophy and the meaning of life. Now he was gone, following his dear wife to the silence of the grave.

All his life Brad had been forced to be emotionally independent, circumstances fashioning him into a solitary, occasionally abrupt (and almost certainly selfish) character in so many areas of his life. He had always valued his grandfather however – one of the few constants in his life. As the earth was restored over the coffin even he could not resist a rare show of emotion now and he pushed a tear away. Mark stood shielded by his father's arms, unappreciative of the terrible finality of it all as he observed the macabre spectacle through the eyes of innocence. Of all the things Brad wanted to be in his life, nothing else mattered more to him than that he should prove to be a solid and reliable father to his beloved son. Yet somehow, like so many things, the reality had fallen sadly short of the intentions. His marriage to Helen was now finished. As they walked away from the plot he tried to get straight in his mind just what part his political ambitions had played in the expiring of his marriage. Maybe it had placed unbearable pressures on Helen. However, he came to the conclusion that it was not central to what had transpired. There was somehow a terrible inevitability about this moment.

The car was waiting outside the cemetery. Sat in the front seat was one of Helen's old friends; and next to her, Helen herself – looking on wearied and without emotion. She could finally be free of an unhappy marriage, although for Brad it would mean he would be seeing less and less of Mark just when, paradoxically, he now had more time to himself in the aftermath of the election. The door opened and beckoned for the infant, who looked up at his father longingly, almost as if he seemed to understand at last that his father would not be coming with him. Brad lifted his son into his arms and placed them tight around him, feeling the tenderness of those fragile infant limbs. How the sins of the father were now being visited on the son. As he placed the boy into the car and the door was closed, his own heart was cut to ribbons. And so he took his final look at the son who would no longer be there at the end of the long days to come.

****

The closing months of 1987 would prove to be the halcyon days of the Thatcher decade. The election success seemed to infuse new life into the Conservative Party. The Prime Minister seemed to have a spring in her step as she proclaimed her intention to pursue the policy offensive once more. Her command of Parliament was not in doubt. The new House of Commons would comprise 376 Conservative members, 229 Labour, 22 Alliance, and 23 others, giving her a 102-seat majority over the other parties. Furthermore, the party conference that autumn had given the leadership a mandate to press ahead with the introduction of the Community Charge, a new system of local government finance based on a flat rate personal tax, rather than property-based domestic rates. The fact that it was perfectly feasible for a duke to pay the same charge as a dustman was not lost on the few brave souls who decried it as unfair and unworkable, including former environment minister Michael Heseltine, who saw at last a clear-cut policy difference upon which to articulate his opposition to the Prime Minister.

The election confirmed to Neil Kinnock that Labour had failed in its bid for power not because it had ditched some of its more bizarre policies, but rather because it had not ditched enough of them – including the two sacred cows of nationalisation and unilateral nuclear disarmament. So, while the Conservatives basked in their eighth glorious year of office, the Labour Party quietly sat down to begin the long, tortuous job of hammering out acceptable policies to present to the electorate for whenever the euphoria of Thatcherism wore off.

During that autumn, other post-mortems were being carried out. The SDP-Liberal Alliance had been disappointed at its poor performance in the election, and activists were especially critical of its dual-leadership. Moves were afoot to merge the two parties and present the voters with a more united front. However, David Owen simply could not contemplate the dissolution of the party he had so come to personify, and his tiny rump of Social Democrat MPs would soldier on for a while longer. Even so, he knew his hopes of ever holding high office again had come to an end – a brilliant political career drawing to a close amidst charges of arrogance and personal vanity from those who had once been his friends.

Above all, 1987 was to be the year of the 'Yuppie' – those bright young things who had realised their fortunes on the back of a bullish stock market which, with the coming of the 'Big Bang' reforms the previous year, had liberated the City to compete in the truly global financial system created by the advent of computerised trading. Alas, like all good parties, it had to come to an end: on 'Black Monday', October 19th, the value of shares worldwide plummeted when the markets were suddenly gripped by a confidence crisis. Careers ended and those vast fortunes vanished, with central banks desperately intervening to prevent a crash turning into a recession. In Britain, the Chancellor, Nigel Lawson, slashed interest rates to try and buoy up demand in a move that seemed eminently sensible at the time, but which would soon return to haunt him with a vengeance.

****

The lights of the town flickered enchantingly as the wind rushed through the swaying trees that shaded this promontory overlooking the town of his birth. Coming up onto the town's favourite beauty spot was the only way Brad could find of contemplating his predicament with anything vaguely resembling detachment.

Although he had performed well during the election, he could not take reselection for his council seat in Lower Henley for granted. The hard left, in particular, were in a mood for revenge. Micky and Brad, as prime instigators of their humiliation last year, had to be prepared for a stormy ride. Had his marriage not broken down, Brad had idly toyed with standing down now that his turn for re-election was fast approaching. Except now there was no point! There was nothing to go home to except an empty house. Besides, he had no intention of letting his seat go to the likes of Sharif Khan without a fight. Meanwhile, the wind cut into the tears running down his face.

****

The two most powerful men on Earth strolled into the room as the Marine band struck up their national anthems and the cameramen moved in to capture the historic moment for posterity. Where once he had icily chided the faceless old men who ran the 'evil empire', now President Ronald Reagan shared some of his legendary bonhomie with the General Secretary of the CPSU, Mikhail Gorbachev, whose smile concealed a slight wince as he listened to the president crack his 'trust but verify' joke for the umpteenth time in his most unfluent Russian.

The signing ceremony complete, a new era in superpower relations was ushered in amidst an array of flashbulbs and excited questions from the irrepressible Washington press corps. Forty years of Cold War had at last given way to a thaw, the Soviet leader finally conceding that an entire category of nuclear weapons should be scrapped. Soon those fearsome missiles which had once brought hundreds of thousands of people onto the streets of Europe in protest would be cut up to make ploughshares (or perhaps, more probably, knives and forks).

Brad watched expressionless as this great turning point unfolded on the television screen. He sat back in his seat, feet on the coffee table in front of him, which was now littered with the empties of a partially consumed six-pack. Important as this moment was, he wasn't really concentrating on the news coverage, but rather on the photograph of Mark that sat atop the set. How he missed him on lonely nights like these!

Finally bored with events on the other side of the Atlantic, he crushed an empty can in his hand and then cracked open another, fumbling with the remote control. Head swirling, he tried to forget about these things. As the video engaged, lusty and well-endowed girls began to cup their ample breasts for him to view. If nothing else, Helen's infamous list had proved a valuable reference point when acquiring a good film to watch!

****

"...That's why I believe the chairman of Highways must be prepared to face the electors of this Borough for the way he has shamelessly played politics with our highway system."

Peter Brereton sat down to Labour members crying 'rubbish', the Mayor becoming increasingly angry at the heckling and sniping that was coming from both benches. As Micky Preston rose to answer the Conservative charges, he had to wait several seconds before the Mayor had calmed down the more excitable councillors sufficiently for proceedings to resume.

"Thank you, Mr Mayor," Micky acknowledged before commencing. "I suppose I ought to treat Councillor Brereton's remarks with the contempt they deserve. Far from neglecting this town's road network, we are actually putting more resources in. As usual, this Government isn't helping the matter by cutting back..."

Micky's riposte brought groans of derision from the Conservative benches. "Mrmayorhispartynevercomplained aboutthegrantwhenhisownpartysgovernmentwasinpoweritsjustanexcuseforpoormanagementinthehighwaysdirect labourorganisation!" gulped Spencer 'Fitzgibbcrish' indignantly, the Mayor ordering him to sit down and shut up.

Micky continued. "More to the point, I am not willing to accept the proposition that certain developers in this locality can bulldoze aside this council's planning decisions, construct a gaudy great shopping mall that destroys our local town centre, and then expect this council to direct funds from other priority areas like education and social services to pick up the tab for their uncontrolled commercialism. It's just not on!"

"You didn't say that when you were waltzing round the dance floor of his hotel!" snapped Neil Sharpe.

The debate rumbled on. Harry Conway desperately wanted new roads to ease the notorious congestion around Trescott Park. The Conservatives had tabled a vote of 'no confidence' in the Labour Group for refusing to commit resources to mitigate the problem. Labour were fuming that the Secretary of State had overturned their planning refusal for much of Trescott Park on appeal, and did not see why they should now be made to pick up the bill for development they hadn't wanted in the first place. Sufficient Labour members were present to defeat the motion by just one vote, Jane Allsop joining their ranks. Tom McKerrick could breathe again.

Brad had no further contribution to make now the main business was out of the way, so felt at liberty to slip away. Wandering down the stairs into the foyer, he bumped into Wendy Baker, who was strolling down the hallway loaded up with reports.

"Bedtime reading?" he joked, holding the door open for her.

"Hardly! Drafts of the report on the setting up of the Abuse Action Team. Look at this. This is just one lad we came across on our files," she said, pulling a slice of paper out of her folder. "He suffered terrible abuse at the hands of his stepfather. We were almost in tears when we were writing this report. It's our intention to ensure that we can react fast enough in future to prevent this sort of thing taking place again. We're almost ready to bring a report to the full committee."

"But that won't be for another month or more. We need to get cracking on this as soon as possible. Call an urgent matters sub-committee. I'll sanction whatever action needs to be taken to stamp this out," he insisted, wincing at what he was reading in the file.

Outside it was raining in torrents, so they both ran down to their respective cars. Brad started up the engine and backed out of his parking spot. Straightening up, he noticed that – try as she might – Wendy was unable to start her car. He pulled up alongside her and wound down the window.

"You okay?" he yelled above the beating of the rain.

She shook her head. "It's been on-and-off like this all week. Now it looks as if it's died altogether. I suppose I'll just have to call the breakdown people out," she sighed, looking at her watch resignedly.

"Hop in mine. I'll take you home," he offered, upon which Wendy abandoned her vehicle and took off in Brad's car on this most miserable of nights.

"So how come you decided to specialise in children's work? Do you like kids?" he asked her casually.

"Only other peoples'," she chuckled. "Anyway, how's your wife and little boy?" she then enquired innocently.

"Mark? Oh, he's okay. And Helen? Well... I'm on my own now. I guess I'm just one more fool who sacrificed the ones he loved for some abstract ideal he'll probably never realise."

"I'm sorry. I guess I'm lucky being single; not knowing the pressures that you must face."

"Pressure? I'm under pressure alright," he groaned. "I've got a reselection battle on for my council seat, my parliamentary ambitions are stalled, and my mother's joined some weird Christian church and keeps telling me that I need to give my life to Jesus. What more pressure do I need?"

"How about me dropping my massive report on your desk soon!" joked Wendy, trying to make him see the funny side of it all. "Seriously though, don't give up. I've been watching your career progress. There are an awful lot of people throughout the Council who respect you and the sincerity of what you are trying to do."

Brad grinned, but looked otherwise unconvinced.

"I can see you're bottling up an awful lot of hurt inside," Wendy noted. "I know it's hard, but keep on in there. You're the finest your party has."

Brad was more modest. "Sometimes I wish I hadn't started out in politics, you know. Why couldn't I have had normal ambitions – like other kids? To be a truck driver; or a fireman; or a striker for the Wolves?"

"I can't imagine you racing round the Molineux somehow! No, cling to your vision. Thatcher won't last forever."

Brad still wasn't convinced. She had lasted nearly nine years: through an economic holocaust; a war for which her government was at least partly culpable; the bitterest strike in living memory; and the division of the nation into two unequal hemispheres. And that was before the 'Lawson Boom' had heralded the arrival of the good times!

Leaving the motorway, they finally arrived at Wendy's flat, located in one of Gunsbridge's more up-market suburbs. Grateful to this white knight in a blue Austin Maestro, she invited him in for coffee, a sleek black cat greeting them as Wendy opened the front door. The flat itself was nicely furnished, but not excessive. The obligatory hi-fi and video systems shared the room with wicker armchairs, a bookshelf stocked with studies in social administration, a double settee, and a dramatic mural of Steve Biko.

"Sugar?" she called from the small kitchen at the end of the hall.

"Two, please," he replied. "Can I have a browse through your record collection?"

"Sure. Be my guest."

Flicking through the albums, tapes and CDs, he could see she certainly had eclectic musical taste spanning names like Wet Wet Wet, Level 42, The Smiths through to the Communards and T'Pau. Indeed, he was pleased that she also boasted a collection from the likes of Joe Jackson to prove she too was a product of his own generation. Returning with two mugs in her hands and the biscuit tin wedged under her arm, she laid them on a low table before placing a record on the turntable. Then, as she sat down, Brad probed her further.

"Tell me, your sympathies definitely lie to the left of centre," he noted, a thought prompted by the provocative cover of one of her albums.

"I used to be into radical politics once. Now I don't really have the time. Shame really, because like you, I'm not happy with the way things are. I'd like to feel in some way I could contribute to the building of a better world, or at least help someone else who is," she said, staring at him over the top of her mug. Did it imply what Brad thought it implied? Probably not, he pondered resignedly, mindful of the proprieties of officer-councillor relationships. There was a long interlude while Brad ran his fingers back and forth along the cat's fur, Wendy meditating on the brash, haunting reggae dub drifting from the stereo. Finally she broke her silence.

"Reminds me of my youth, this... Do you remember the Anti-Nazi League and 'Rock Against Racism'?" Brad replied that he did.

"That, I suppose, was the high-point of my politically-active years. Somehow it all fell away after that. Maybe one day someone will rekindle that flame, and make me feel I'm doing something worthwhile for the cause once more."

"You mean like the Handsome Prince waking Sleeping Beauty with a kiss?" he teased her.

"Mmmm. Maybe," she sighed wistfully.

As time moved on, Brad could sense that, willing as she was to continue reminiscing with him on years past, her eyelids were slowly growing heavier. It was time to leave and to let this overworked officer catch up on her beauty sleep. Wendy agreed and escorted him down the hall to the door.

"And remember," she admonished him as he headed out for the cold and the rain. "Don't give it all up. You're the future of this country. If at any time you feel like putting your head in the oven, call me."

Then she popped her head back round the door and returned a few seconds later with a piece of paper torn from a notepad. "Here's my number. After all, I am a trained social worker!"

Brad was touched by her kind words. How many times over the last year had he longed for a sympathetic human voice and a cheerful smile to convince him of the righteousness of his cause.

"Thanks," was all he could say, though he said it in earnest. He disappeared down the stairs and out into the storm, mindful that here, at last, on the lonely road to his dreams, he had found a friend.

****

"Well, comrades, there's not much more to do other than vote, although I have to say this has been one of the most acrimonious meetings I can remember."

The Chairman's words were no exaggeration! Brad often marvelled how one of the more farcical quirks of the Labour movement seemed to be that their hatred of the Tories was only surpassed by their hatred of each other. Perhaps it was the same in the Conservative Party, he wondered. Either way, he hadn't expected an easy ride at the reselection meeting. Eric Sims, the tough, no-nonsense chairman of the branch, had fought valiantly to keep the warring tribes apart. Brad, supported by Colin, Jimmy Dearn and some of the older membership, was opposed by Sharif Khan and his hard left followers, boosted by a posse of Militants, who'd this time taken the precaution of making sure that their bed-sit addresses or trades union affiliations were all above suspicion.

Brad and Khan eyeballed each other malevolently from across opposite sides of the room. The man who'd once introduced Brad to the local Labour organisation now had no time for his fallen protégé. Brad, in turn, despised the bull-necked Kashmiri. How dare he accuse Brad of not doing enough for the area as a councillor, or of not attending enough branch meetings, when Brad had sacrificed a marriage for the cause of socialism.

"Comrades, the result is Councillor Bradleigh, twenty-four votes; Mr Khan, twenty-three votes. Councillor Bradleigh's name will therefore be forwarded to the general committee as Lower Henley's prospective candidate this May. That, comrades, is the end of the matter, I trust," Eric asserted.

Neither camp said anything, although menace pierced the air. As the chairs were pushed under the tables, mutterings and grumbling could be discerned amidst the clinking of beer glasses as the bar tender cleared up.

"Just watch your back, Councillor," someone warned Brad as he drifted down the stairs with Colin. Brad turned round and tried to identify who had issued the threat. Then he saw Ricky Serrano, a swarthy, bearded fellow who sported a long college scarf. Brad had often seen him about and had tracked him down to the staff room of one of the town's big comprehensive schools. He'd also discovered that he was a pal of Gary Bennett's. Serrano broke into a nervous grin, aware that he'd shown his colours for all to see.

"I see another one has crawled out of the woodwork, Col!" Brad commented to his fellow councillor.

"Like I said, just watch your back," Serrano repeated, and marched down through the middle of them to depart without elaborating further.

"Whazzee' on about?" Colin quizzed him, the two councillors walking into the smoke-filled bar.

"He's just mouthing off," Brad chuntered nervously. "One thing you learn about creeps like him, Colin; they're ninety-nine percent mouth."

****

The Council van pulled up alongside the information board erected outside Lower Henley public library. Opening the rear doors, the driver took out his pasting bucket, his brush, and a roll of posters. Cleaning odd bits of paper left from previous bulletins, he then pasted up the vacant space and unrolled the notice he intended to apply.

Just then, unnoticed by the workman, a long, sleek Mercedes drew up into the bus lay-by on the opposite side of the road. The powered windows eased open, and Harry Conway emerged from behind the smoked glass, lighting up a cigar as the engine idled. Gradually, the workman smoothed out the air bubbles, and the tycoon was able to make out the contents.

THE METROPOLITAN BOROUGH OF GUNSBRIDGE
Notice of Election in the Municipal Ward of Lower Henley
Thursday, May 5th 1988

There were some finely printed legal niceties which he could not make out from that distance, but then the larger type caught his eye…

1. Bradleigh, Robert   *THE LABOUR PARTY CANDIDATE*
2. Clare, Antony Gerald   *THE CONSERVATIVE PARTY CANDIDATE*
3 Rawlings, Candy Helena Judith   SOCIAL & LIBERAL DEMOCRATS

…And finally – that name that he was really looking for. His face lit up as he made his way down to…

4. Taylor, Stanley William   *INDEPENDENT LABOUR CANDIDATE*

The workman stood back, admired his handiwork, then slung his bucket and brush in the back of the van and drove off. Conway was pleased with his handiwork too, and powered his window back up, that cunning grin disappearing behind the tinted glass of his purring machine.

****

The television was flickering back and forth between scenes of the gunning down of two IRA terrorists in Gibraltar and the horrific lynching of two off-duty soldiers in Belfast. However, the viewers in this particular Barnwood residence didn't seem particularly interested. Sprawled out on a rug in front of the sofa, Brad and Donna Tromans were too busy rediscovering the joys of each other's bodies as they clasped and kissed with abandon. There was no doubting that, his council seat apart, Donna's attention was the best thing he'd acquired from his local branch of the Party. He watched with ill-concealed delight as she removed her sweater, unclipped her bra, and then pushed him back down onto the rug. There their tongues searched out the desire, Brad's hands trailing through her long, dark hair as it dropped down over his rugged chest. Slowly and teasingly, her tender lips made a passage down to his loins.

Halfway through their love games, the soft bleeping of the telephone began, Brad at first trying to ignore it. Gradually, he levered himself up and reached out somewhere in the direction of the sound, his roving hand finally alighting upon the receiver. Donna broke free herself and permitted him to answer it, playing with the hairs on his chest while she waited for him to get rid of the caller.

"Who? ...Ah, Jim... no, it's okay... Yeh, what do you think?" he asked. Meanwhile, he began to run his free hand over Donna's breasts while he settled into a lengthy explanation. He toyed with each aroused papilla, watching her absorb each spasm of excitement.

"...I told Wendy it was okay... No, go ahead and fix an Urgent Matters 'Sub'... Let's see..." he said, reaching over for his diary whilst Donna began removing his trousers. "...How about Wednesday? ... Four o'clock? ...Sure... No problem... Bye."

He replaced the receiver and returned to his playmate. "Who was it?" Donna asked him.

"Only my director of social services. Now, where were we?" he said, pushing her back down onto the rug, where she welcomed his warm, sensuous mouth biting at her. And so the foreplay resumed.

****

"Brad! Brad!" Colin called out, waving a piece of paper above his head.

Not only Brad, but Micky Preston, Alannah, Donna, and what seemed like most of Gunsbridge's Labour fraternity hurried back down the garden paths of the run-down council properties that each one had been canvassing. There was excitement and anger that, at last, they had caught up with one of the illusive election addresses. They gathered round as Colin paraded his find.

"What's he got to say for himself, the little jerk?" Frank Collins snarled, the others placing a thumb and finger on vacant edges of the pink gestetnered copy to catch a glimpse of this act of treason. Micky read it out aloud.

"Vote for Stan Taylor, your Independant Labour Candidate.... I worked for the Labour Party for years, and was one of their leading councillors..."

"That's a lie!" Jimmy Dearn swore incredulously. "That pillock day' do a thing f' this bleedin' ward!"

"And he's spelt 'independent' wrong!" Donna charged, pointing to the error.

"Look, what's he telling them?" Brad insisted impatiently. Micky continued.

"...That was before I saw the activities of the Militants, and decided it was no longer the party I once knew. Nowadays, it's full of extremists and all manner of evil people. The sitting Labour councillor for this ward is himself an extreme left-winger, having started a punch-up in the Council House during the Miners' Strike. He voted down attempts to improve the local road network in order to fritter away your money on other wasteful left-wing projects. So next time you fall over a broken curb stone, or you're stuck in a traffic snarl-up, think of your militant councillor and remember his extremism. Vote for a REAL Black Country Labour candidate, who talks the language you understand. Vote TAYLOR on Thursday, May 5th".

"How dare he call us 'evil'!" Maureen Tonks fumed indignantly.

"How dare he call you of all people a 'Militant'," Alannah riposted, placing her hand on Brad's shoulder, fearing he was incensed enough to take off in search of Taylor and break his face for him there and then.

Micky read the candidate's thoughts perfectly, counselling "Come on, mate. Don't let it get to you. Best thing we can do is put the message about. Let's go to it!"

The team swarmed off once more, emphasising to those residents who cared to listen that, whatever they might have heard, Brad was the *only* Labour candidate they should consider voting for. Eventually, with dusk fast approaching, everyone called it a day and drifted back to their cars.

"Same time tomorrow?" Micky suggested.

"Yeh, thanks," Brad replied. "You want a lift?"

"No, ta'. I'm going back to the club with Donna in her boyfriend's car."

"Guess that leaves just you and me," Alannah noted as she drew up to the passenger door of Brad's battered old Maestro. It was not a situation Brad found at all disagreeable

"Fancy going somewhere classy?" he asked.

"You mean you're not going back to the club as well?"

"I'd rather not. I seem to be spending half my life there lately. What about that new wine bar up town? No disrespect to this town's working class, but let's go somewhere with no pool tables, no dartboards and no old men supping ale!"

The journey into town took about ten minutes. By this time, with the commuters all gone home for the evening, Brad was able to join the Porsches parked on the street outside the cosy little bar. This most unproletarian of hang-outs wasn't too packed either, though a group of 'hooray henries' were posing and guffawing noisily at the bar whilst supping exotic cocktails with funny names.

"Look like estate agents," suggested Alannah, "celebrating yet another hefty hike in house prices."

"How come you never went into a money-making profession?" Brad asked her, half in jest. "I look at you and sometimes think you'd make a better stockbroker than a revolutionary! In fact, how come a girl of your background ever acquired socialist convictions to start with?"

"Tradition, I suppose. My parents were active in the upheavals of the sixties. I remember being carried on my father's shoulders at all those demos against the Vietnam War. You could say I grew up into radical politics."

"They still sent you to a private school though," Brad observed poignantly.

"So that proscribes me from wanting better state schools for other peoples' children?" she countered rhetorically.

Quite so, he acknowledged; though her accent and mannerisms belied the truth that Alannah's socialist pedigree was vastly different to Brad's own rugged brand of high-rise proletarianism. He watched as her slim, painted fingers were splayed backwards while she waved her hands about to emphasise her point, her large, crafted ear-rings dancing about and sparkling in the lights that washed the tables with hints of crimson and azure. Ten-out-of-ten for ideological soundness – but how good was she beneath the sheets? he pondered to himself flippantly.

"So is Gunsbridge Council the pinnacle of it all?"

"Probably not," Alannah opined. "Why settle for being a big fish in a small pond when there's an ocean out there." Then she paused before turning the question around. "Have you still got your eyes trained on higher things?"

Brad's dour mien told her exactly what she needed to know long before he spoke. "Success in this party, I've learned, depends on who amongst your enemies lives in, or has trades union affiliations with, your constituency. Or if he's smart, he'll have his cronies in the Fabian and Co-op branches too."

"So in other words, your gaze has been lowered. Maybe you should be looking to other seats. You still have a reputation as a good councillor. But a word of advice as a friend, Brad: you'll do yourself no favours playing fast and loose with that reputation."

She paused and gazed at him achingly, knowing instinctively that his brusqueness was borne of a deep hurting inside.

"Brad, I know it's been tough since Helen left you. But don't turn a setback into a disaster by throwing away everything you've achieved so far. That would just hand your opponents victory on a plate. They want you to quit and throw it all away. I like to think that you're made of tougher stuff."

She looked into his eyes and tried to convince him of her sincerity. She thought she'd possibly won him round, so changed the subject. "Anyway, who is this Taylor chap?"

"Oh, he used to be the councillor for this ward. Of late though, he's become one of Conway's stooges. That's why we deselected him. Now I'm told he has a sinecure with Conway Enterprises as their press officer. More to the point, only two seats separate the Tories from control of the Council. If they retake Gunsbridge Conway knows he'll have an easier time on the planning committee; save him the time and expense of keep running back to the Secretary of State on appeal. So what better service could he do for his golfing pal Brereton than to put up an 'independent' candidate and split the Labour vote in the most marginal seat on the Council. And that's why Tom McKerrick has ordered every available party worker into this ward."

****

The wearied expressions on the faces of the people drafted in to count the votes told each of the candidates that three recounts was past a joke. Jane Allsop was also now pacing back and forth behind them impatiently, for all the other results had long since been announced. It was thus apparent that she would have the casting vote in the Council now. On the outcome of the Lower Henley result would turn the question of whether she would have the casting vote over a minority Labour administration or a minority Conservative one.

Each of the candidates watched the counting to see what was transpiring. Candy Rawlings had put up a good show, as had Stan Taylor, who stood there and just sensed his former socialist colleagues bristling at him hatefully. Yet from the previous three counts it was obvious that it was a contest between Tony Clare, the unsmiling and oleaginous Conservative candidate, and Brad – who was looking more depressed by the minute.

He had resigned himself to being ejected off the Council. The first count had given him a victory by one vote, the second a victory to Tony Clare by one vote. Now the returning officer huddled together with candidates and agents to break the news about this third and final recount. Satisfied they now knew where they stood, he invited them to mount the stage.

"Bradleigh, Robert, 1442 votes... Clare, Antony Gerald, also 1442 votes... Rawlings, Candy Helena Judith, 1189 votes... Taylor, Stanley William, 605 votes."

Taylor had certainly done his stuff: six hundred votes, of which the bulk would have belonged to Labour in any other year. A sitting councillor usually has an edge on his rivals; more so, for Tony Clare's right-wing election address had been blunt, unimaginative and (in places) plain silly. So what now? The supporters of both men waited anxiously as a deathly hush descended upon the hall.

"Will Mr Clare and Councillor Bradleigh therefore step forward. I will toss a coin to decide who will be duly elected as the councillor for Lower Henley."

There was some considerable excitement in the hall. Nothing like this had ever happened in Gunsbridge before, although the returning officer assured everyone that it *was* constitutional. It was not without moments of drama either, with the returning officer in the centre, Tony Clare to his right (appropriately enough!) and Brad to his left, sizing each other up at close range like old-style duellists.

"Whatever happens, don't let it roll under the stage," the officer joked, taking the shiny coin from his pocket. "I don't get paid until Monday!"

Each candidate managed a wince at this attempt at gallows humour. The game they were now playing was deadly serious though, especially for the wearied Labour candidate, who watched the returning officer lay the little gold coin on the nail of his thumb. He knew that, within the space of a year, he could suffer the multiple ignominy of losing Gunsbridge South for the party, losing his marriage, losing custody of his son, and losing his council seat – and with it, losing his party control of the Council too. All eyes watched as the coin was briefly flung into the air, spinning rapidly until the officer slammed his hand down on it, clasping it tight between the back of one hand and the palm of the other. Brad looked at Tony Clare, who stared back at him in return. Both looked at the returning officer, who held their fates in his hands – literally!

"Incumbent's prerogative..." he said, turning to face Brad. "Heads or tails?"

Brad looked down at the veins bulging on the back of that rugged hand, sensing the tenseness of the occasion and the lateness of the hour ticking away on the officer's gold watch. Which way should he declare? He looked down at his supporters. Micky Preston whispered 'tails' – his judgement in such matters was usually infallible! Alannah, however, gave him a coy glance before flashing those big beaming eyes and whispering 'heads'.

"Heads!" he said, revealing a weakness for pretty women.

The returning officer looked down at his hand, slowly drawing it back to reveal the coin once more. Inscribed upon it were the words D.G.REG.F.D.1984... ELIZABETH II'! Never had Her Majesty looked so radiant to this closet republican, and Brad's face lit up, announcing the momentous news. The Labour crowd let out one almighty cheer. Then the comrades broke into the *Red Flag*, directing their crowing at the glum-looking Stan Taylor.

Meanwhile, Brad was back in the Council House for four more years. Casting his eyes about the hall, he found himself gazing up into the balcony at the rear of the auditorium as the jubilation subsided. There, standing at the balcony's edge, was the dapper and unmistakable figure of Harry Conway, watching Brad move up to the microphone from this vantage point. Their eyes locked onto one another for several long, tense moments until Conway grinned just a little to mask his disappointment. Then he lit up another cigar before turning to walk away.

14 THE GOLDEN AGE THAT NEVER WAS

"IT'S TWELVE MINUTES TO THE BIG ONE-TWO HERE BY THE BAY ON FRIDAY JULY 1ST. IT'S 'CANADA DAY' AND YOU'RE TUNED TO WKVRT 'METRO TORONTO', GIVING YOU THE SOUNDS AS THEY BREAK... OUTSIDE, IT'S SET TO REMAIN FINE ALL DAY, WITH TEMPERATURES IN THE HIGH EIGHTIES, AND EVERYONE LOOKING FORWARD TO THAT LO-O-N-N-N-G-G W-E-E-E-K-K-E-E-N-D-D. ALL THE MAJOR FREEWAYS ARE CLEAR; THE 401 IS MOVING, AND THE 'QEW' IS SMOOTH. MEANWHILE, CHECK OUT A YOUNG MAN FROM ENGLAND WHO'S DOING JUST GREAT OVER HERE... CHECK OUT RICK ASTLEY ON WKVRT... THE STATION THAT NEVER STOPS ROCKING...!"

As the warm, lakeside breeze ran through his hair, and the sun bore down brashly from the clear blue heavens, Craig knew what feeling great was all about. There was an indescribable feeling of liberty and life about cruising down a twelve-lane North American freeway in his luxurious Mercury hire car. Was it the incredible sense of space and vastness all about him? Or was it the all-pervasive frontier spirit that still drove this young continent remorselessly out to build a gleaming civilisation in the midst of a wilderness? Or was it just that by leaving the pettiness and introversion of the Old World behind men somehow rediscovered the excitement of the human experience in all its richness and diversity?

He cast his eyes heavenwards briefly at a glittering airliner that edged up into the cloudless sky. Over the last few months he'd travelled the length and breadth of North America, working on Rex Schumacher's personal staff. How fortunate he'd been to catch his eye that day back in England. Offered the chance to work with North American Bus & Truck Inc, his secondment had taken him across the continent. While most of his sojourn had been spent in boardrooms, seminars and (inevitably) an awful lot of hotel rooms, he had still found time to see the sights and spend invaluable hours taking the pulse of this vibrant, irrepressible continent. He felt like de Tocqueville, discovering for himself the wondrous, ethereal dynamism that had made this continent the most prosperous and exciting place on Earth. He wouldn't have missed it for the world.

Leaving the freeway, he arrived beneath the gaudy neon sign that welcomed him to some motel by the bay. Booking himself in, he wandered through the complex until he located his room number, depositing his belongings on the bed and opening the sliding glass door that led onto the balcony overlooking the swimming pool. In the distance, out across Lake Ontario, he could see the glittering skyscrapers of downtown Toronto, the tall spire of the CN Tower rising up out of the haze. He could get used to this life! It was at times like these that he was tempted to take up the offer Rex Schumacher had made of a secure and prosperous future working Stateside for him. What was there to keep him from emigrating permanently to Canada or the United States and creating an exciting new life for himself? Show me a reason to go back home, he begged the Almighty as he wandered back into his room.

That reminded Craig, where had he put his bible? Ah, there it was – his greatest treasure. In one of his last acts before leaving for America, he'd finally confirmed his new-found commitment to Christ by walking into Gunsbridge Elim Church and telling the world how it had bestowed upon him such a sense of liberation, purpose and inner peace, such as he'd never known before. His American sojourn had given him a useful period of reflection and meditation on his future, away from the hustle and bustle of British politics. He had until the end of the summer to give Rex Schumacher an answer either way. Show me a reason, he prayed.

****

He couldn't help feeling like an exile as he stood there huddled amongst the multi-ethnic commuters lining up on the sidewalk. Canadian politics seemed to revolve almost entirely around endless debates in Ottawa about the nature of the federation. How lucky a country must be if that's all they can find to argue about, he mused. Eventually, the *Don't Walk* sign flashed *Walk*, and he crossed the street to commence a voyage of discovery in downtown Toronto, starting with that famous CN Tower that seemed to reach defiantly into Heaven itself.

Upon ascending to the upper viewing deck, Craig spent what seemed like hours staring out in all directions at the fabulous views across the metropolis that this vantage point afforded. He thought he could just make out the southern shoreline of Lake Ontario that was the United States. And for those who didn't suffer queasiness at such extreme heights – which included a group of noisy, camera-wielding Japanese tourists, who jabbered excitedly at such panoramic thrills – there was the brand new Skydome Stadium and Union Station almost directly below them, the cars on the elevated Gardiner Expressway racing along like tiny insects as they traversed the city. Gripping the handrail, he was almost in a world of his own. Finally, he stepped back, accidentally bumping into a young woman as he did so, knocking her against the glass panel that was all that then separated her from the street – over two thousand terrifying feet below!

"I do apologise!" he cried, steadying her as she edged back from the precipice.

"I'm alright. I think," she said, nervously glancing back down at the distant city below her.

The English accent didn't register with him at first. Then he looked up at her, suddenly noticing something familiar about her hair, and those dark eyes. He sensed a jolt of sudden shock run through her as she looked him up and down also. Slowly, in disbelief, their faces both began to glow as she shook her head imperceptibly. He blinked to make sure it wasn't some sort of dream.

"Is it? ...It can't be..."

"It is... Craig?"

"Nikki?"

Just then, the party of Japanese tourists turned about and fell silent, absorbed in this most extraordinary sight – two English people locked in an embrace, kissing and crying, not quite sure how Providence had led them to trip over each other two thousand feet up above some North American city. Nikki ran her hands up and down through Craig's blond hair and wept, Craig holding her so tight that she was lifted off the ground. Finally looking into each other's eyes, they both began to weep great tears of joy at their rediscovery. The Japanese were unsure precisely what to make of it all; did Westerners always greet each other so demonstrably? Finally, one little old man called out and motioned to them to look his way, poking his eye through the viewfinder of his camera. Suddenly, the other two dozen or so squawking Orientals joined in, waving and calling frantically as they bathed Craig and Nikki in the flashes of their cameras.

"Well, it looks like we've made someone else's day as well!" Craig riposted to her, and the two of them broke into fits of uncontrollable laughter, little Nikon's clicking ever faster at these inscrutable Occidentals.

****

The long 'Queen Elizabeth Way' stretched right up to the horizon, which was shimmering at its edge as the Mercury cruised onwards. Only this time Craig was not travelling alone: sat to his right was the girl he'd always dreamed of, hair tied back the way he always loved it to be as it fluttered gently in the warm summer breeze. Through the sunglasses they both sported they glanced at each other across the divide, Craig resting his hand on the transmission shift, Nikki's gentle hand joining it there as they smiled the smile of two people rediscovering what was once lost, and was now found – the glimmering shoreline of Lake Ontario their constant companion. The important thing was that they were together. And, this time, they both sensed that they had stumbled upon a permanence that neither of them had known before.

Eventually, the Mercury entered town, past all the neon motels and souvenir shops until suddenly their quest was over and a sound like distant thunder drifted all around them. A mist rolled in isolated cloudlets, providing a wonderful sensation of coolness in the humid midday sun. Parking the car, they were both drawn obediently to the cliff's edge until such an awesome sight greeted them as neither had ever witnessed before. There before their very eyes millions of gallons of Niagara River crashed over the twin precipices, swirling down under the Rainbow Bridge on its remorseless journey to the Atlantic Ocean.

"I told you it was a sight to behold," said Craig, resting his arm gently around her shoulder.

Nikki enjoyed the feeling of protection that he offered as she stood there captivated by such an amazing natural wonder.

"Come on!" Craig suggested, pointing to the little boat bobbing about in the seething currents below. "I'm told it looks even better from down there!"

And so it did. They stood in awe at the front of the *Maid of the Mist*, dwarfed by the raw power of the waters that had honed these superlative falls. Casting off the hoods of their oilskins, they preferred instead to feel the spray hurrying through their hair, standing there captivated by the God of all Creation, who had moulded something before them that was beyond human scale – just as His Son had liberated both of them from their pasts in an act of sacrificial mercy upon the Cross that was also beyond human comprehension. Such mercy gave meaning to carefree hours spent in each other's company, each moment conveying a purpose and oneness – the sound of those timeless waters always present. At the end of the day – as the sun set and the riverside neons commenced their evening vigil – they made their way back along the rolling 'QEW', knowing that – far from being the end – this was only just the beginning of a joyous new chapter in their lives.

"You know, I still can't believe this is happening. I know why I'm here: I'm Rex Schumacher's personal trouble-shooter. But what's your excuse?"

Nikki was reclined back in her seat, eyes closed, her face painted intermittently by the glow of advancing headlights. She broached no response for some moments, prompting Craig to break his gaze on the road ahead and look down briefly at her contented smile.

"Like I said, we had a long-standing invitation from one of our sponsoring churches in Toronto to come up and share news of what our organisation was doing in Mexico. They suggested we spend a week up here. So here I am!"

"And you just happened to be sightseeing on the day I decided to journey into town?" Craig asked a trifle rhetorically.

"Why not? A God that can raise a man from the dead shouldn't have too much difficulty fixing up a date for two people living on opposite sides of an ocean! He must have heard my prayers when I was on furlough in Britain, and found out you were out of the country on business. I had so hoped to see you again."

"How did you know I'd become a Christian? I don't remember saying anything about it in my last letter."

"When you wrote your last letter I seem to recall you mentioning that Mrs Thatcher had just won herself a third general election," Nikki reminded him, with just a hint of sarcasm. Craig felt a twinge of guilt that he had been less than diligent in replying to her letters. "And wasn't your MP, what's his name...?"

"James Whitney."

"...That's the fellow. Wasn't his wife expecting a baby?"

"She's probably had it by now," he said, noting just how out of touch with events he'd become.

"It's a good job Elaine still tells me what's going on in Gunsbridge. I thought you'd forgotten about me."

"Not at all. I guess I just needed to sort out where I was going," he confessed, pausing to construct a statement of intent. "I've been thinking about giving up politics – losing elections can have that effect on you! Since I've been in America I've been tempted to jack it all in and come and make my fortune out here. Yet something deep down in the very heart of me still keeps telling me I'm a politician. So how do I square the circle?"

Nikki frowned. "I've always had no doubt about you. When Elaine told me you'd given your life to Christ, I asked myself what opportunities this opened up now that I was coming to the end of my three year mission to Mexico. As it happened, she also sent me that article that the *Gunsbridge Herald* ran on you, remember?"

"I do indeed! '*A Day In The Life Of A Tory Candidate*' – complete with a photo of me alongside the Prime Minister," Craig recalled with a sentimental grin.

"Well, I read that and just knew that you were called to be 'a fisher of men's votes', as it were; and a good one at that! The more I prayed about it, the more I felt I had to get back together with you again. The only question was: was it me wanting that, or was it God? So, again, I prayed that if it was His will then he'd rearrange our getting back together in such a way that would leave no doubt about the rightness of it all. And so, I guess He has!"

Craig guessed that he had also found the answer he was searching for. He turned and offered a warming smile. "You are the most beautiful woman I've ever been blessed to meet. Please open the glove compartment," he bade her. "...Go on, open it up!"

She was puzzled, but followed his instructions faithfully, picking up a small black box from amongst the maps, and drawing it out as he had gestured her to. As she lifted the lid, a tiny diamond twinkled in the light of passing headlights. Awestruck, she lifted the ring out with her dainty fingers.

"I don't intend to let go of you this time. So I'd be honoured if you'd accept this ring as a token of my love for you. And promise me that when your service is complete you'll come back to England and be my wife."

Nikki stared down once more at the beautiful gem. She slowly slid it onto her finger until it rode over the knuckle and gripped the upper part of the digit snugly. Her expression changed from one of awe to one of self-satisfaction, a similar countenance apparent now on her fiancé's face as he looked down approvingly on the shining band of gold.

****

"PASSENGERS FOR AMERICAN AIRLINES FLIGHT AA7450 TO DALLAS-FORT WORTH ARE REMINDED TO PROCEED TO GATE 20 WITHOUT DELAY, WHERE YOUR FLIGHT IS BOARDING. LAST CALL FOR FLIGHT AA7450 TO DALLAS-FORT WORTH."

Craig watched from the observation lounge while the destination blind flickered and the monitor returned to a blank screen. Soon the gleaming silver bird was cast free from the umbilical of the terminal walkway, and began to taxi slowly out onto the shimmering tarmac. Then the sun caught the huge silver wing, a blinding flash obscuring it as it turned tail towards him and made off out of sight behind the terminal building

He felt the overbearing clouds of uncertainty, loneliness and self-doubt breaking up, and the sun bursting through in all its warmth and newness. At last, he knew where he was going; and, equally importantly, he knew who would be accompanying him there. He felt the powerful arms of destiny fold around him, casting out doubt and urging him on. Now, at last, he could give Rex Schumacher an answer.

Nikki had written him a beautiful letter pledging herself to him when she returned. She reminded him not to trust feelings alone, but rather to look to the God who was greater than himself, who alone could sustain the vision through the dark valleys of despair and temptation. He now pulled it from his pocket and read down her promises, noticing that the most potent words were not her own, but words inspired by the One who had later sealed them with the blood of His own precious Son; words which she had attached to the foot of her letter.

> *"Though the fig tree does not bud, and there are no grapes on the vine; though the olive crop fails, and the fields produce no food;*

though there are no sheep in the pen, and no cattle in the stalls; yet I will rejoice in the Lord. I will be joyful in God, my Saviour. The Sovereign Lord is my strength. He makes my feet like the feet of a deer. He enables me to go onto the heights."

Habbakkuk Chapter 3, Verses 17-19

The words seemed inappropriate at such a moment as this, when he felt he could almost reach out and make everything he'd ever dreamed of happen. But he knew what she meant. Trials and tribulations would almost certainly come; for the road he had chosen was not, and never could be an easy one. He folded the letter back into his pocket and stored up the words in his heart.

Just then a roar like thunder caused him to gaze up at the thrusting silver machine taking off into a clear blue sky, ascending steeply into the distance and banking sharply round over the baked and dusty plains of Ontario. Up, up and up it soared, until it disappeared into the fiery sphere suspended beneficently above the bright blue firmament, carrying away his Beloved as it did so.

****

As Craig stared out of the big wide window of the speeding train, the familiar verdant, rolling Downs hurtled past, recalling that first journey to his *alma mater* all those years ago. And so, here he was – back on the arduous road to Westminster once again. So much had changed since he'd been away. The centre parties had chosen former marine commando Paddy Ashdown to be the man charged with lifting them from their dismal poll-ratings to somewhere closer to the heights they had enjoyed during the SDP-Liberal revival of the early eighties – now sadly all but a distant memory. Meanwhile, a Labour leadership bid by Tony Benn had been resoundingly crushed. How distant the glorious days of the early eighties must have seemed to the Labour left as well!

The dilemma for Craig's own party was that, from its position of unrivalled supremacy, the only way they could go was down. Like many Tories, he recognised that the very prosperity they had delivered had only served to place an increasing premium on so-called 'quality of life' issues: health, education and, lately, the environment. And then there was Europe! After languishing for so long amidst rows over butter mountains and budget contributions, under the assiduous Commission presidency of French socialist, Jacques Delors, the European Community heads had begun to catch a visionary fire for the further harmonisation of trade, foreign and economic policies – and even for a common European currency.

One woman had watched all these developments with growing suspicion. The Prime Minister increasingly viewed the Delors manifesto as a dangerous and unwanted intrusion into areas where decision-making belonged at Westminster.

So, on September 20th 1988, she had issued a counter-manifesto of her own in Bruges, where she had given notice that "we have not successfully rolled back the frontiers of the state in Britain only to see them re-imposed at a European level, with a European super-state exercising a new dominance from Brussels." From now on, the Conservative Party seemed to become increasingly polarised between advocates of a *Europe des Patries* and those who favoured a deeper Community (and who numbered amongst their ranks the exiled Michael Heseltine, who had discovered yet another policy difference with which to articulate his claim to Mrs Thatcher's crown whenever he chose to assert it).

Craig blinked upon awaking from his ruminations. As the train began to slow, he recognised the familiar arched roof of the station, and that impressive viaduct that carried the little electric trains over the rooftops of the tenements nestling in the streets below. Then the brakes ululated and the train drew to a halt. He was back in the town where he had first cut his political teeth in those heady days of varsity debates with Alannah James. He'd come a long way since then, and thinking back on it all gave him the confidence to press ahead down the uncertain road that still lay before him. He stepped down from the train and wandered out onto the concourse. There, along with the bustle of the street and a lungful of stiff sea air, he noticed a large billboard bidding him greetings – *BRIGHTON WELCOMES THE 105TH CONSERVATIVE PARTY CONFERENCE.*

****

Craig shuffled his feet out of the way to let some fellow delegates out. Meanwhile, the chairman asked for those in favour of the self-congratulatory motion on further state sell-offs to raise their little ballot papers. A sea of pink cards thus appeared round the hall. Even so, voting was a mere formality. Most people preferred to stream towards the exits and the refreshment areas. Was anyone against the motion? Oh, only some brave soul up in the back of the conference hall who probably didn't think the motion was congratulatory enough!

Craig often wished it could be more like a Labour conference, where the platform luminaries lived in constant fear of revolts from the floor. But then the Conservative Party valued its image of unity too much to risk having the cameras zoom in on some rabble-rousing rebel. Still, the final debate of the morning was on law and order, where angry firebrands from the shires were once again about to bark for the restoration of the 'rope'. The Home Secretary sat on the platform looking less than smitten with the thrill of winding up this particular debate.

Craig chose instead to browse through the *Gunsbridge Herald*. Folding it in half to fit into his lap, he amused himself with a little piece on Tom McKerrick having to share power with that remarkable Councillor Miss Jane Allsop. It had apparently grieved the Leader of the Council that the price this twenty-seven year old journalist had exacted for co-operation voting through the bulk of the Labour programme was the chairmanship of the Community Services committee. Indeed, this Allsop girl was no fool, Craig pondered: with the gravy train of grants to voluntary bodies and community organisations under her belt, she could certainly make a name for herself – and buy a few more influential votes. Elsewhere, Harry Conway had unveiled plans for 'Fun City' – his brand new, multi-million pound leisure centre-cum-theme park adjoining the Trescott Park development. Was there no end to this man's ambitions? Craig asked himself. And, on page four, more abused children were being made wards of court by Gunsbridge Social Services after raids by social workers and police on the homes of startled parents – a sad indictment of the times, he noted.

"This seat taken, young man?" said a stern, military voice from behind him. Craig glanced around.

"Dick! No, be my guest," he said, and Dick Lovelace, the crusty old councillor from Amblehurst, squeezed past, coat folded over his arm. He sat down, brushing back his brylcreemed white hair and twitching his moustache as he made himself comfortable.

"I wanted to speak in this debate," he informed Craig gruffly. "But I guess they know me. I'd soon tell the Home Secretary where to put his namby-pamby civil servants! I'd have the little blighters in stocks, where they belong. Flog the bastards, I say!"

"Who? The criminals or the civil servants?" Craig enquired light-heartedly. To Dick Lovelace though, crime and punishment was a serious matter and he neither laughed nor commented on Craig's pun. Therefore Craig changed the subject. "I was hoping I might see James. He's down in Brighton this week."

"Ah!" Lovelace muttered gravely. "He's a man with a lot on his mind lately. You've heard that his new son has been diagnosed with a terrible disability. Eleanor was absolutely devastated! I've had James in tears at my place," he said, reminding Craig that he was this year's constituency chairman, with responsibility for liaising between members of Parliament and constituency workers.

Craig had heard the dreadful news already, but hearing it again didn't lessen the hurt that he felt within for the tragedy that had befallen his friend, the Honourable Member for Gunsbridge South. For years (or so Dick now told him), they had been trying for a family; with Eleanor over forty they had all but given up hope. Then the joy of pregnancy and the unspeakable delights of parenthood had been cruelly dashed by a crushing diagnosis. Life could not have been crueller to ones whose hopes had been raised so high.

"I tell you, it's affected every area of his life. He doesn't seem to be able to concentrate on anything. Terrible thing to happen; makes you want to fall down on your knees and give thanks for the beauty of life, doesn't it?" he asserted, before standing and cheering one speaker who'd cheekily asked for a show of hands for hanging before the chairman could censor him.

Needless to say, the floor was overwhelmingly receptive to such an audacious interpretation of the democratic process. The Home Secretary didn't appear very amused though. In a debate on law and order it seemed that the Conservative Party conference was as adept as their socialist contemporaries in occasionally asserting a smidgen of independence from the platform!

****

The nightingales almost did sing in Berkeley Square when the pianist played mellow wartime memories for the delegates gathering in the luxurious hotel lounge. The soft, relaxing ambience was further enhanced by the chatter of constituency officers fraternising with ministers, and members of Parliament spinning entertaining yarns to enthral humble party workers. For one week each year, the psychological divisions of Westminster, Smith Square and constituency associations became blurred and all and sundry could chat together. Mrs *A* from Tonbridge could discuss this new tunnel under the English Channel with a minister from the Department of Transport over a vodka and tonic; and Councillor *B* from Formby could prop up the bar and debate the more arcane aspects of standard spending assessments with some spotty graduate seconded to the party's local government research staff. Craig stood about idly watching all the conviviality.

"Ah, here's the man I want as my home secretary!" someone called out jovially, causing him to turn around. "Melissa, I don't think you've met Craig."

It could only be Jonathan Forsyth, neat and resplendent in his lounge suit and black tie, urging forward a patrician young lady in a flowing dress to meet him.

"Jonathan'sth' told me what a sthuper' chap you are. I'm fwightfully honoured to meet you," she lisped, offering him a delicate white paw.

"So what's been the highlight of your week, Craig, old boy? I hear Martin's been hobnobbing with Heseltine again," Jonathan guffawed incredulously. "Me, of course, I'm not into lost causes! Anyway, I say old boy, I've secured a nice little number up in the Lakes: eighteen thousand majority; mountains; sheep in the meadows – fantastic! So you won't have me to plague you at selection finals in future. Have you got your feet under anyone's table yet?"

Craig was relieved that his old university chum had broken from this one-sided conversation to come up for air, although he regretted having nothing positive to advise him of – except that he'd met, and would soon be married to, an exceptional young lady he'd once met at university.

"Oh, yes. Not that lass from the God Squad I remember you being bowled over with, eh?" Jonathan teased him, unaware of the accuracy of his waggish first guess. Craig smiled, but didn't get the chance to enlighten him further. Hauling Melissa away, the prospective Cumbrian had meantime spotted the Foreign Secretary arrive and just had to say hello!

"He doesn't change, does he?" a soft female voice chuckled in Craig's ear.

Turning round once again, Craig was pleased to see Brenda Shore standing there, glittering in some fabulously expensive gown. Beside her stood a tall, bronze figure with a neatly trimmed moustache.

"This is my husband, Gerry Primero. Gerry, this is an old friend, Craig Anderson," she said, introducing him.

"Hi, pleased to meet you," he said, sporting a rich Californian accent.

"Gerry's from San Diego," Brenda interjected. "We met last year when I was over there on business."

Craig was pleased that he could now lay claim to being a transatlantic high-flier too and spent some moments in small talk with Brenda and her fiancé. Inevitably, the conversation returned to the pet subject of all parliamentary hopefuls.

"No," she said, "not yet. I've got an interviews coming up; and I keep rising higher in the play-offs. I'll crack it eventually," she confidently predicted even so.

"Looks like it'll be down to just you and me soon," Craig predicted.

"And him!" said Brenda, pointing out Craig's arch-inquisitor, the ex-MP and former Home Office minister, Oliver Lyons, who was listening politely to some old lady drone on, and who was also known to be on the look-out for an opportunity to re-enter Parliament.

****

'*LEADING BRITAIN INTO THE 1990s*' proclaimed the bold Conference motto. "Ladies and gentlemen, the Prime Minister, the Right Honourable Mrs Margaret Thatcher FRS MP," proclaimed the chairman.

The hall was packed to overflowing as eager delegates applauded before waiting on the Prime Minister's every word. In the media enclosure, the cameras hastily zoomed in on the woman who, more than any other post-war prime minister, had left her mark upon the nation; for Margaret Thatcher stood erect at the rostrum at the very peak of her power, her party supreme in shaping the destiny of the British people. Not for nothing did she boast "it is still the Conservatives who set the pace, generate the ideas, and have the vision."

Craig was sitting next to Brenda – both listening intently to the record the Prime Minister now recounted for them: the record of nine-and-a-half years of Conservative administration. Meanwhile, Mrs Thatcher remained confident that her party's policies would carry them safely into the new century. And so on such a note ended a triumphant conference, with the delegates rising to a man to cheer the personification of their three election victories, and who now wandered down onto the floor of the Brighton Centre. As she passed by, ordinary party workers from all over the country stretched out hands to greet her, as if, by some mystical power, touching the very garments she wore might infuse newness into their distant constituencies.

The ovation, like the Government she led, seemed as if it might just go on forever. Still they kept cheering and applauding; still she kept acknowledging them, touring the aisles while organisers cleared a path for her through the adoring throng. Craig smiled down, even so sure in the back of his mind that there were clouds on the horizon that had still to cast their full shadow over this raptured party: difficult policies that might rouse the party faithful on occasions such as these, but would take considerably more explaining on the doorsteps of suburban Britain. How this moment would all too soon prove to have been the high point of some "golden age that never was".

****

The dim bedside lamp was extinguished, leaving just the silvery shimmer of a tropical moon with which to make out the glow in each other's eyes. His hand slowly pushed her hair back away from her face and they stared intently and expectantly at each other, captivated by a brief moment's reflection on the wonder of first intimacy. Their noses cautiously brushed against each other before their lips were pressed together, and the first exploratory kisses began.

She held her breath as his assiduous lips purposefully trailed over each soft area of her supernal body, closing her eyes while he animated and quickened his beloved. She panted at first imperceptibly, but then with ever-greater frequency and vigour as he began to explore her secret places, generating yearnings that now burst forth from her innermost depths. Then, at last, she cried aloud upon the consummation of their union. Finally, compulsion gave way to reflection, the moon still glowing. The room fell silent, except for the distant lassitude of a fricative sea.

Looking out from the veranda, Craig could make out the white of the water as the waves beat upon the warm tropical beach. Further along the front the occasional lights of the little line of hotels twinkled in the darkness. In the distance, African rhythms drifted across on the gentle offshore breeze. He could make out the little fishing boats, just visible by moonlight as they bobbed up and down on the tide. Indeed, the sea seemed to capture perfectly the profundity of the human experience; and there could be no more profound experience than the union of a man with a woman.

Behind him, he heard movement; then Nikki was there at his side. He put his arm around her, and together they savoured the calm and stillness of the deserted beach for what seemed like an age. Finally, she cast her arms up around his shoulders and enjoyed the tenderness of a long, intimate kiss before they both returned to gazing out to sea. Then Craig felt moved to share a little candour with his bride.

"Did I ever tell you about the day I nearly caused a scandal?" he smirked.

"No. Tell me more," she teased him playfully, awaiting this sensational revelation.

"Well, it was during the General Election. I was having lunch at my agent's place when I accidentally burst into his wife's bedroom..."

"Yes, we know, and she was wearing next to nothing!" Nikki laughed in disbelief.

"Well, actually, yes. No, don't laugh – this is true! She actually asked me there and then if I wanted to make mad passionate love to her!"

"And, let me guess, you struggled to free yourself from her amorous advances!"

"Well, yes. Sort of. You see, I had this mobile phone in my jacket pocket – all the PPCs had one. And all of a sudden, it went off! ...no, straight up! So I answered it. And, blow me down, if it wasn't her husband telling me he was on his way back to the house to pick me up for some engagement. Man, I tell you it was that close! Can you imagine the furore...?"

"Craig Anderson, you do tell some whoppers!" Nikki mocked, imagining the kind of headline one might come across in the *News of the World*. "Product of an overactive imagination and a bloated ego. No wonder you want to be a politician!"

Craig could see Nikki didn't believe him; and if she didn't, who else would? Still, all that was behind him now. This was the beginning of a new dawn, and he was confident that he would soon be in Parliament where he knew he really belonged

15 *SCAPEGOAT*

She hadn't quite planned it the way it was about to happen. Yet now that he was spreading his powerful hands upon her she felt no reason to resist. He was strong and he was handsome, and it was as if he could overcome any misgivings she might have harboured and impose his will upon her solely by virtue of the desire he was capable of arousing within her. Thus he slowly slid his hand inside her loose-fitting blouse and grasped at her determinedly.

She was a very attractive and highly intelligent woman: the kind that would make other men turn their heads in the street, or sit up and listen when in polite conversation. He was appreciative of this; and yet somehow that very sophistication intimidated him – even now that he had her partially undressed and at his mercy. He wanted her, but felt himself driven by a desire perversely devoid of any emotion. Thus he opened her blouse more fully, the culmination of a long and increasingly ignoble obsession with her body.

She watched the outline of his face reflect the lights of a passing car. She had no doubt he was going to enjoy the experience of making love to her. Perhaps it would deepen the nascent relationship that they had come to share over the last few months. Yet he seemed not to appreciate the beauty and tenderness of the moment. Instead, he just leaned over from his seat, clumsily negotiating the console of the car until he was on top of her and the real passion could begin. She readied herself to receive him, abrupt and demanding though he was. It was vigorous, it was sordid, and she was silently apprehensive; but it was evidently what turned him on.

Thereafter, the journey back passed off with little or no conversation between them. Brad watched the built-up outskirts of the town begin to reappear over the horizon, the dull orange glow of civilisation visible long before the archipelago of lights came up over brow of the hill. Alannah, meanwhile, tried to reapply some make-up to her face.

"You're quiet, aren't you?" she observed, unruffling her skirt.

Brad shrugged his shoulders. "Not much to say, is there?"

"How about 'did the Earth move'?"

He looked at her with a mild air of disinterest. "Well, did it?"

She could sense he found this line of conversation both tedious and perhaps embarrassing. The frown on her face as she looked away must have told him that she still found her mercurial lover very difficult to fathom out. He seemed such a dark and often contradictory character: kind, yet often abrupt and defensive; a superb romancer, yet often blunt and insensitive; a profoundly high-minded visionary, yet she'd often encountered a cynical, and even callous, streak in him, both as a politician and as a person. Truly a tormented figure!

Brad had been captivated by Alannah's charm, and respected her immensely. Or at least he had until about fifteen minutes ago! Perhaps he hadn't expected such a smart woman to be quite such a pushover; perhaps he hadn't intended to push quite so hard! Even so, he still felt uneasy in her presence: intimidated and humiliated, as if her degrees in law and economics and her bourgeois pedigree made this a terribly unbalanced and morganatic affair. Finally, he drew up outside her Amblehurst flat, the engine idling restlessly as she searched in her bag for her keys.

"I'll see you at Education tomorrow, no doubt," she said. "I take it you'll be raising hell over the item on staffing ratios." she assumed, expecting a fire to thus be kindled within him at the opportunity of a lively debate in committee. Instead, he just flashed his eyebrows and looked down impatiently at the instruments on the facia. Turning to open the door, she paused, looked back and offered him a kiss, which he dutifully intercepted.

"Thanks," he muttered timidly. "I'd like to see you again. I'll try and call over during the weekend."

"I'll look forward to that," she smiled. She opened the door and stepped out. Then she waved and disappeared inside, leaving him to ponder the evening's events.

It had felt good; and it had been worth waiting for; and, yes, he did look forward to seeing her again. Yet would he ever be able to overcome these negative feelings he'd been plagued by since Helen had done the dirty on him? Women were all the same and seemed to him to be good for only two things – and one of those wasn't politics! He was determined that, unlike his grandfather, no woman would ever stop him from realising his political destiny.

****

It was a good speech, full of stirring calls to the party faithful. Yet Brad left the room to only polite applause from the membership, sensing that perhaps Alannah had been right, and that he had seriously misjudged the situation.

There were by now several candidates waiting in the otherwise deserted lounge of Tower Park Labour Club, all eager to present their credentials to the General Committee of Gunsbridge North Labour Party – the people charged with the penultimate stages of deciding who would be the new parliamentary candidate for the working-class constituency now that Terry Johnson had officially announced that he would not be standing again. Dedicated socialists from all over the country had descended upon Gunsbridge North to compete for the job of representing one of the safest Labour seats in the Midlands.

Whilst putting his coat on to leave, Brad found himself staring over at Clive Bell, the handsome young councillor busy talking shop to some bearded colleague. Brad had watched Bell's career progress, noting especially how, even under fire from the other side, he was always smart, always reasonable, and always superbly self-controlled. He had thus built up a reputation as a smooth operator, recently elevated to vice chair of Education. As his rival pushed his steel-framed glasses further up onto the bridge of his nose, folded his arms, and made effortless and intelligent conversation, Brad felt himself overcome with a heady sensation of envy and hatred. Of course, he thought, it helped that he had Joe McAllister's patronage. How unfair it was that one malevolent old man should possess such inordinate power to make or break a career.

On the way back he stopped off at Alannah's place, knowing she'd be concerned to hear how he'd fared. As the door opened, there was a welcoming smile and an affectionate kiss. She had even refilled the kettle in anticipation of his return.

"So how did it go?" she called anxiously from the kitchen.

"I gave them my very best. Now all that remains is to wait on the postman," he replied glumly.

Alannah said no more until she had returned from the kitchen with two mugs of tea. The intermission gave Brad the opportunity to reacquaint himself with her delightful little flat. Pretty furnishings gave it a distinctly feminine touch. There was a large framed photograph of Alannah with her parents on her graduation day which sat atop the large bookcase, home to works by J K Galbraith, Noam Chomsky and other left-leaning thinkers. On the coffee table in front of him rested a folded copy of the *Guardian*, which Brad now opened out to browse through.

"I still say you shouldn't have attempted the nomination," Alannah said before diverting to fetch the biscuit tin. She elaborated further upon her return. "It looks bad, especially when Gunsbridge South have still formally to decide on your reselection. Your opponents will say you're chickening out of a fight you know you can't win; and your supporters will be left thinking you've abandoned them – hardly something designed to encourage them to fight for you.

"Anyway," she continued, "I know a vacancy for a safe seat like that only comes round once in a blue moon. I can understand you wanting to grab it with both hands. But you must have known that Clive Bell was fated to win that nomination: he's one of their local councillors; Joe McAllister thinks the sun shines out of him; *and* he's a happily married family man."

That last quality stung Brad, throwing him into ever-gloomier fits of envy and self-pity. Alannah sensed that she had hit a raw nerve. She wandered around the back of his chair, leaned forward and draped her long, smooth arms around him, running her soft cheek up and down his hard, stubbled face.

"Listen, don't despair. Play your cards right and there's more than enough support in the local party to secure you another stab at Gunsbridge South. You did well in 'eighty-seven, and there's no reason why you can't win it next time. The only obstacle in the way is your own impetuousness. Let me tell you this: I wouldn't have minded having a go at North myself; but I held off when I knew you were trying it. And I'll hold off from South if you want this job, because I believe in you."

She smiled and pulled his body closer to hers. Something seemed to be weighing heavily on his mind, and she couldn't coax him to tell her quite what it was, even though it made him unresponsive to her advances. What was it with this guy that made him so broody, so melancholy, and so wrapped up in his own self-centred preoccupations? Here she was, prepared to surrender her own ambitions (and to offer him her body as a supplement), yet he seemed neither to care nor to reciprocate by allowing her to be a party to his innermost thoughts.

****

"Councillor, we're from ITN News, can we have a statement from you?"

"Councillor Bradleigh, I'm from the *Daily Mail*; what do you say to the parents' charges that you have...?"

The battery of questions came thick and fast as the curator tried to force a path through the clambering crowd of journalists and newsmen now besieging the Council House, thrusting cameras into the faces of both Brad and Alannah as they jostled each other for a story. Brad could take no more, so mounted the steps and waved his hands about. A silence slowly descended, broken only by the whirring of camera motors.

"Gentlemen, we will be consulting with the officers of the Social Services Department shortly, and a full statement will be issued later today. That's all I have to say for now," he said, moving off again. However, the commotion broke once more as pressmen pushed and shoved, anxious to hear more.

"Councillor Bradleigh, what do you say to charges that your officers have grossly overstepped their powers?"

"Councillor, BBC *Midlands Today*, what is your answer to...?"

Once inside the Council House, both councillors let out a collective sigh of relief, marching up the marble staircase and down the long corridor that echoed to the clicking of Alannah's heels. They made their way to the Chief Executive's office, where the enquiry team had already begun to assemble. At the head of the table was Tom McKerrick, chewing at his pipe in the manner he was accustomed to whenever he was in no mood for messing about. The Chief Executive was sat to his right, leaning over to brief his leader informally, while opposite was sat the ashen-faced director of Social Services, flanked by Wendy Baker, the trauma of the last week making her pale complexion appear even more ghostly and unreal. The legal officers were huddled in like a team of eager courthouse attorneys. Meanwhile, Joe McAllister was also sat there, sternly eyeing Brad and Alannah as they entered. Micky Preston, Frank Collins, Clive Bell and Maureen Tonks were also present.

"Right, folks," said McKerrick gravely, "take it from the beginning – the whole sorry story." Meanwhile, the director of Social Services looked to his colleagues before deciding that it was incumbent upon him to bat first.

"Leader," he opened, "the current concern is the result of a decision taken by the Social Care division to look further into evidence that, vigilant as we liked to think the Department was, it was somehow apparent that we were only really scratching the surface of the problem of child abuse in the Borough. Therefore, two year ago we decided to establish a special investigative unit, which Wendy in her role as PSCO agreed to lead, to take a more in-depth study of the scale of the problem; and to recommend a response that would target resources at those children we believed at serious risk. The report came back to the committee in last February..."

"Which committee, may I ask?" McKerrick interjected bluntly.

"The Urgent Matters Sub-Committee. In view of the need to act swiftly, it was agreed that the team proceed quickly to secure 'place of safety' orders, which were effected between April and October of last year. So far twenty children have been made wards of court. Criminal investigations are advanced in fifteen of those cases."

When the director had finished there was a brief silence before Wendy continued, "The evidence of systematic abuse, both sexual and physical, in those fifteen cases is overwhelming. We believe we have broken a major ring of abuse and that juries will have no hesitation in returning guilty verdicts on the perpetrators. Here are just some of the horror stories we've unearthed," she said, passing a folder to McKerrick.

The Leader spent a few seconds in desultory reading of the document. Then the grey-haired chief looked up and noted, "Of course, the problem is not these fifteen, is it? It's the five who we seem to be in some doubt over." He passed the folder back across to Wendy.

"Leader, the best evidence we have at the time indicated..." Wendy tried to emphasise.

"...Yes, I know, it's not the full evidence we have before us now," McKerrick intercepted her. "And now we've got the police surgeon disputing that evidence, James Whitney jumping up and down in Parliament, half of Fleet Street on our backs, to say nothing of the Ombudsman breathing down our necks." He paused briefly to stare sombrely at each of his colleagues seated around the table before telling them straight. "We're in it deep, real deep. Make no mistake about it. What I want to know is what went wrong?" He turned to Brad specifically, charging "And why wasn't this brought to the full committee until the orders had already been issued and the children dragged screaming from their parents? Why didn't you cover your arse, Councillor?"

"Leader, I was thinking of the urgency of the problem. We had to act," Brad insisted.

"And over the course of next two years you never thought to once bring a report to the full Social Services Committee?" McKerrick gasped in disbelief. "You're aware of the charge that you conspired? Come on, Robert, where have you been lately? Haven't you ever heard of Cleveland?"

"Good grief! You've read some of the stories in that report, Leader. I'm a father; I acted as a father to protect those kids. I'm sorry if I forgot about protocol in my self-righteous indignation, but I challenge anyone who's read Wendy's report to say they wouldn't have done the same!"

"Let's cut out sentiment. Politically, we've got the media and an outraged public out there. We know the score," Joe McAllister reminded them.

"Sentiment! Politics! Bullshit! We grabbed fifteen kids out of this evil that might otherwise have gone unnoticed. My officers acted with my sanction, doing the job they are trained to do, and I stand by them!" Brad insisted.

The Chief Executive tried his hand at reasoning. "I think we have to remember that this was a very sincere attempt to deal with a very real problem. The best we can do for now is to bring a full report back to the Council and to try to salvage some kudos for the prosecutions that will stand up in court."

"That the best suggestion I've heard so far," McKerrick sighed resignedly. "Joe, we'll sit down with the PR people afterwards and draft a statement that will get the press off our backs – at least until the dust has settled."

"We should never have let it come to this," McAllister scowled pessimistically. "In my day, everything controversial like this came back to full committee."

Brad could sense eyes burning into him as the deputy leader fumed aloud. The director said nothing; neither did Wendy. Alannah was itching to say something, but seemed uncharacteristically reticent. And so it was left to Brad to offer a final plea in defence of the decision they had each been party to.

"We saw a problem. We knew we had a duty to take steps to tackle it. I admit that at the time we were faced with the difficult decision of whether to act on imperfect evidence or hold back, possibly risking a child's life. But if there's one thing I've learned about social work it's that you really are damned if you do and damned if you don't! Remember that story about that little girl down in London whose stepfather beat her to death? How would you all feel today if my officers had permitted that sort of crisis to explode across the front pages of the tabloids? The PSCO was faced with an invidious dilemma of acting or doing nothing. She acted in good faith on the best evidence she had at the time. And whatever comes out of this wise-after-the-event inquisition, I'm not going to say I condemn my officers' decisions. I stand by the professional judgement they exercised – even if nobody else on this council has the guts to!"

****

Brad sat lost and dispirited amidst a coffee table full of empty bottles. Summoning the mental energy, he scanned through the front page story of the *Gunsbridge Herald*, pouring himself another stiff one with which to wash the stories down.

"'FACTS WERE WITHHELD FROM ME', CLAIMS OPPOSITION SPOKESWOMAN'. The story then quoted Elizabeth Gainsborough at some length as she charged, *"I warned at the start of this process of the dangers of delegating these sorts of powers to officers. Councillor Bradleigh must therefore bear some of the responsibility for the loss of invaluable goodwill his secretive decision-making has resulted in."*

Elsewhere, Jane Allsop had put in her few column inches, saying *"This scandal is a classic example of the obsessive secrecy of two-party politics in this town. The Tories did exactly the same when they privatised the bin men - concocting secret deals in smoke-filled rooms. If nothing else, I hope the presence of a Social & Liberal Democrat councillor on this council will help bring a little openness to this stuffy and uncaring bureaucracy."*

Meanwhile, '*PARENTS MAY GO TO HIGH COURT'* warned the headline on page four. *"Councillor Bradleigh has devastated our lives",* claimed an unnamed mother of a ward of court from the Scotts Estate. *"My marriage has broken up, and my daughter lives in constant fear of the doorbell ringing. I just wish he knew the misery his social services people have caused us all."*

Brad looked up at the dusted portrait of his own dear son. He certainly knew the misery of a broken home. And, interrogating his conscience mercilessly, he knew the Social Care team had acted only with the best intentions – not that good intentions meant much amidst the fury that was now enveloping Gunsbridge. One must act, often on imperfect evidence; but either way, one must act. His eyes ached as he drank himself silly pondering it all.

****

Lisa Stansfield's silky voice faded and *Gunsbridge Sound's* familiar news jingle burst out of Alannah's car stereo, the headlines majoring on yet more revelations from Gunsbridge Council House.

"Gunsbridge Conservative councillors are calling for an inquiry by the town's Labour administration into how five serious errors came to be made during investigations into child abuse... Shadow spokeswoman, Elizabeth Gainsborough, has openly called for the chairman of Social Services, Councillor Robert Bradleigh, to resign... Meanwhile, it has been announced that Miss Wendy Baker, the Council's principal social care officer responsible for the abuse investigations, has been suspended pending a review of the Department's handling of the affair..."

Alannah could bear to hear of the humiliation of her friends and colleagues no longer, and switched the radio off, just wishing she'd had the courage to swallow her indecision and stand up for her fellow councillor a bit more forcefully. She recalled the terrible mauling Brad had received at a recent Labour Group meeting, when Joe McAllister had accused him of incompetence. Meanwhile, McKerrick had done nothing to restrain the venom. Only Micky made any conciliatory noises in Brad's favour. Of course, the Group presented a united front in public, issuing bland platitudes to waiting journalists. Perhaps it was the hypocrisy of it all that now infuriated her most. She cursed herself for her inexplicable reticence in defending her lover.

Pulling up outside Brad's flat, she took out the bag of provisions she'd just bought and lumbered up the stairs to the door. Finding herself unable to balance the weighty bag, she placed it on the floor, rung the bell, and waited. There was no reply. She tried again, this time squatting down, her flowing dress fanning out across her legs as she lifted the lid of the letter box, peering inside lest she find the pressure of the last few weeks had led him to hang himself from the light fitting!

Then she saw him wander naked past the door of the bedroom; then wander back again, having gained a pair of trousers. Then her faced dropped. The supple frame of a young woman also darted across the doorway, also completely naked. Then Brad reappeared, shut the bedroom door and headed her way, unbolting the front door as Alannah rose to her feet.

"Allie! What are you...?" he frowned, half asleep.

"Don't you dare 'Allie' me!" Alannah screeched, pushing her way in and bursting into his bedroom just in time to catch Donna Tromans hauling a sweater over her head, her pendulous breasts swinging freely as she worked it down over her body.

"What is she doing here!?!" Alannah screeched. Meanwhile, Donna hurriedly squeezed into her denims and rushed out past them.

Alannah drew up to Brad, breathing out her censure upon him. "I thought you'd just forgotten that I was coming round tonight to prepare a supper together to try to take your mind off some of your worries. But – silly old me – I ought to have known dear old, selfish, self-absorbed Robert Bradleigh has his own recipe for working off tension – screwing cheap little tarts like her!"

"Allie, let me..." he bleated in front of an incandescent Alannah.

"No," she insisted, "Let me tell you what *I* think *you* ought to hear. I've tried to understand you for far too long. But you know what? Every time someone tries to offer you a helping hand, you just snap at it! Face it, Brad, you have eyes for no one except yourself. You think we all exist solely to serve your purposes. Well, as from now, I've had it with your pathetic little ego. I used to think you just had an appalling attitude towards women; and, given what you've been through with Helen, I tried to make allowances for that. But, no, you've just got an appalling attitude to people – period. Well, stuff you! I'm damned if I'm going to carry on being one of your many pieces of flash while my own career goes sailing by!"

"Alannah!" Brad cried remorsefully as she stormed out, tears now streaming from those beautiful eyes, and causing her lovingly crafted make-up to run as she turned and picked up the groceries she'd left outside.

"Here, you two-timing bastard! Choke on them!" she screamed, thrusting the bag at him.

Her high heels clattered as she scurried down the hall stairs and out of the block. Brad rushed up to the corridor window, only to see her jump into her sporty little hatchback and rev up the engine, slamming the car into reverse before pouring all her hurt and her fury upon the tyres, which squealed painfully as she spun the wheels and the car shot off at speed out of the car park.

****

"...So, Mr Mayor, this whole unfortunate episode needs to be wrapped up now, and the guilty parties censured. They have done irreparable damage to the reputation of this council, damage which will take years to put right."

"Leader of the Council to reply," the Mayor requested, and Jane Allsop sat down, her righteous indignation giving way to Tom McKerricks' purposely flat and lacklustre summing up.

He had managed to buy the councillor's continuing support only at the expense of humiliating his chair of Social Services. Brad knew that much would be inevitable. What he had not expected was that his leader would take so public an opportunity as the special council meeting called to discuss the finding of the report into the child abuse investigations to publicly distance the Labour Group from him. Clive Bell would be the new chair with immediate effect. If it wasn't bad enough suffering the indignity of having that cocky little toe-rag win the Gunsbridge North parliamentary selection, he now had to witness the snub of having Bell assume the chair of the committee he loved and had tried diligently to lead. Bell was sitting next to Alannah, whispering something witty in her ear. So Brad also experienced the nausea of seeing Bell now flirt with the girl who had once been his own. Indeed, Alannah had been the only one to come out of this whole affair unscathed; party to all the deliberations, and yet not bearing any of the scars of the vicious recriminations McKerrick had set in train. She briefly broke from chatting with Bell to offer Brad an icy glare. Meanwhile, the Leader's pedantic words bored the Chamber into letting the affair rest – Labour had survived to fight another day. If only poor Wendy had been so fortunate, Brad mused angrily, aware of the pressure she been put under to resign.

With formalities over, the Mayor dismissed them all while the sun was still shining outside. Slowly and noisily, everyone filed out into the foyer until Brad was left alone by himself, doodling on his agenda papers and staring into space. Alone that was except for one bearded colleague, who was packing his own papers away in his battered old briefcase. Seeing his one-time protégé, Micky couldn't resist wandering up to him in dismay.

"You're a fool, Brad," Micky insisted, shaking his head despairingly. Brad said nothing, just carrying on staring down with indifference at the pretty shapes he'd drawn on the reports. "You had everything going for you. Forget this social services lark; that'll pass. You may even have been right; we'll have to wait and see. But while everyone else has been bending over backwards to help you, you had to be running round like a dog with two dicks, trying to make everyone else a part of your obsession with yourself. And you know what I can't forgive – that you've made a fool of Alannah. God, if you knew how you've cut her up! Well, I've got news for you, pal: the world doesn't begin and end with Robert Bradleigh.

This is a movement about people; for people – ordinary people – who don't have your talent and ability; and who look up to people like you to secure for themselves all the things that the rich and powerful geezers of this world would deny them. Most of all, pal, this movement is a team. We can't afford to worry about the likes of *prima donnas*. There is a party for puffed.up, ambitious, self-seekers like you. But, I tell you – it ain't the Labour Party!"

Still Brad said nothing. Micky left him to his artwork and wandered out of the cavernous and deserted chamber. His favourite son had now betrayed him. Brad knew it must grieve him. He, himself, shed a quiet tear as he heard his political father descend the marble staircase that led down into the foyer and out of Brad's life.

****

GUNSBRIDGE SOUTH LABOUR PARTY
Press Statement
Friday, June 2ⁿᵈ 1989

Gunsbridge South Labour Party today announced Alannah James has been chosen as prospective candidate for the constituency. Twenty-eight year-old Alannah, a legal officer for a welfare rights charity, is currently a councillor for the Barnwood ward of Gunsbridge Borough. In her spare time, she enjoys reading biographies, cooking exotic cuisine, and helping out at the Gunsbridge Women's Refuge. Local chair of the party, Councillor Micky Preston says, "I am overjoyed that Alannah has been selected. She possesses great warmth and dedication, qualities that will make her a superb MP. We will make sure she is returned as our Member of Parliament at the next election."

****

21 Swallows Court,
Lawnsmere,
Gunsbridge.

June 12ᵗʰ 1989

Dear Councillor Bradleigh,
*   Just a little note to say how grateful I am to you for your brave and selfless defence of both myself and my former colleagues at Gunsbridge Social Services throughout the traumatic events of the last few weeks. Words cannot express my sadness that it has all*

ended the way it has. I am sorry that you have paid a very high price personally for steadfastly supporting us as you did.

Throughout it all, I want you to know that my estimation of you, both as a politician and as an individual, stands higher than ever. Whatever comes out of this unfortunate chapter in your career, I know that you will pick yourself up; and, in time, prove to all those who have let you down so badly that it takes more than the barbs of the media and a handful of second-rate councillors to keep you from realising your destiny. Above all, I want you to know that because of the tremendous support you have offered me during the last few weeks - even when everyone else appeared to be against me - I'd like you always to consider me a friend.

Thank you, and I'm sorry I let you down.

Yours

Wendy Baker.

16 *WALLS COME TUMBLING DOWN*

Gunsbridge South Conservative & Unionist Association
Press Release
Friday, July 7th 1989

It is with deepest sadness that James Whitney MP has today officially informed his colleagues that he will not be seeking to contest the Gunsbridge South parliamentary seat at the next election. James felt it was only right and proper that, as his disabled son reaches school age, he should spend more time with his wife, Eleanor, in caring for him.

Constituency chairman, Councillor Dick Lovelace said "The whole party has been saddened that James has felt his decision necessary, but we fully appreciate and endorse his courageous decision to put his family first. He has proved to be an exceptional, hard-working and caring MP, and will certainly prove a hard act to follow."

****

It was precisely the sort of get-together with ordinary party workers that the former defence secretary used to assiduously cultivate friends and spread his vision. To be sure, Michael Heseltine was a politician down to the very last nerve-ending in his tall, elegant frame, and fashioned his words carefully as he addressed the businessmen's lunch organised by Gunsbridge South Conservatives; ever mindful that in his audience were also many who regarded his talk of "greater European co-operation" with suspicion, if not outright hostility. Then, following questions, the Right Honourable Member for Henley was ushered downstairs to say a few words to the waiting press before being chauffeured off to another engagement.

"Still don't trust him!" muttered Elizabeth Gainsborough discreetly.

Craig said nothing, though he'd always retained a soft spot for the one-time conference darling of the Conservative Party. Instead, he readied himself for the drive back to the office, his insides still reeling from the three-course feast he'd just partaken of. He was hunting around in his jacket pocket for his car keys when he suddenly felt a hand alight upon his shoulder.

"So this is it," enthused a familiar voice, "your big shot at the prize."

He turned round to find Harry Conway grinning at him, a huge cigar swivelling about between his teeth. Craig feigned surprise, though he knew exactly what Conway was about to say.

"I must admit I didn't think it would be up quite so soon. Mind you, James has done the right thing," Conway sighed, removing the cigar in order to lecture Craig with it. "A piece of advice, son: politics and families don't mix. Anyway, tell me, you put your name down for this patch?"

"I might have," Craig teased him.

"You'd be a fool not to. You're well liked around here – and rightly so. You'd win the nomination hands down."

"Thank you for your confidence in me," Craig replied, still wary of what the tycoon was building up to.

"Listen, I look upon you as a favourite son. I think to myself that if I had a son, you're the sort of lad I'd like him to grow up into: good-looking, upright, clever – and successful too."

"I see you had some objections to 'Fun City' yesterday," Craig noted, referring to a peaceful demonstration in the shopping mall of Trescott Park by environmentalists and local residents angry at Conway's proposals to press on with his ambitious and controversial project.

Conway puffed on the cigar and poured out his thoughts. "Oh, I can see their concern; very admirable. But sometimes one has to sacrifice a little of what one loves for the greater good of progress. A field full of buttercups and bunny rabbits might look nice, but it won't provide jobs and prosperity for the people of Gunsbridge, will it."

"It's a risky proposition though, what with the economy slowing and the cost of borrowing money so high."

"Long term investment," Conway boasted philosophically. "Leisure is the growth industry of the future, you'll see. And this one will make money for this town, unlike the Council's own leisure facilities, which are invariably over-budget political showcases. Besides, if McKerrick's rabble were ever to build something like this you know yourself that they would inevitably appoint a gaggle of 'equal opportunities' advisors on thirty grand a year just to count how many dykes and darkies are using the bloody thing!"

Such pejorative banter made Craig visibly wince. Nonetheless, he listened politely while Conway rambled on, assuring his young listener that "My vision won't cost the people of Gunsbridge a penny. There'll be a sports stadium, concert halls, a water world, a ten-screen cinema, bowling alleys, plus a Disney-style theme park – complete with the biggest roller-coaster this side of the Atlantic. There will be a museum of Black Country history complete with trams and trolleybuses, a real old-fashioned blacksmith... and a good old-fashioned Black Country brewery just so that Dad doesn't feel left out. It'll really put our town back on the map."

"But the roads you're proposing to link it to the motorway will cut straight across the countryside on the other side of the Wolverhampton Road – which is very special to the people of the town," Craig reminded him.

"Quite so. But this is wealth creation; regenerating the inner cities – what our Prime Minister wants us to do. And I'd like to think you'd want to be a part of that regeneration process. After all, there are plenty of fields around here – half-hour's drive and you're almost in Wales!" Conway joked with a touch of exaggeration. "You support me and I can make things happen for you. Come on, son, what do you say?"

"I say 'Fun City' is a brave concept, Harry, and deserves to succeed," Craig replied. "But not at the expense of losing all that green land."

Conway wasn't used to rebuffs from people he courted. He sucked his cigar, thought for a moment, then grinned diplomatically. "I see," he said. "Well, it's a free country... Ah, Ian!" he continued, spotting some smart young entrepreneur who could serve as a convenient means of retreat, "Ian, meet Craig. Listen, Craig was telling me that he's gone all environmentally-friendly. Why don't you tell him about the new recycling facility at your factory..."

****

"Labour has abandoned unilateral nuclear disarmament, or so they tell us; although, for once, I find myself in agreement with Tony Benn when he says that Labour's policies are nowadays written by Dr Gallup!"

Craig's witty little observation did at last bring a smile to the faces of the Executive Committee as he began to wind-up his presentation. He had stood before them convinced of an almost divine sense of mission. This was his moment to assume the throne of prospective Conservative parliamentary candidate for Gunsbridge South, and he had planned and prayed for hours over these deliberations. Yet there was something strange, if intangible in the air as he spoke. The committee seemed polite, yet not especially enthusiastic, which Craig could only put down to the sheer fatigue his colleagues must be succumbing to after weeks of having to interview all the most promising candidates. Elizabeth Gainsborough fidgeted with her pen, not looking at him directly as he spoke. Spencer Fitzgibbon, Mrs Lambert and Dick Lovelace all seemed preoccupied.

Gerry Roberts listened politely but, even so, would occasionally look round at his colleagues as if something present in the room was casting a malign and oppressive influence upon them all.

Craig concluded his address and sat down to await the inevitable battery of questions. Spencer Fitzgibbon volunteered to be first, and the white-haired Ulsterman leaned forward to interrogate the local boy.

"MrandersonmayIaskyouifyousubscribetotheviewthatweshouldplacesterlingwithin theERMandthenmovetoasingle europeancurrencyordoyouthinklikesiralanwaltersthattheexchangeratemechanismis halfbakedandunworkable?"

Craig took a few seconds to decipher the councillor's 'gibberish' (under the guise of composing his thoughts) before offering an in-depth defence of Mr Lawson against his doom-saying economist critic. Spencer Fitzgibbon was probably none the wiser, but was evidently content just to have thought he'd put Craig on the spot with his little display of pseudo-erudition. Several others asked him routine questions on law and order, capital punishment and bias in the BBC, Craig seeing off these grassroots gripes eloquently and proficiently. Yet whatever he said, and however well he said it, there was some kind of invisible barrier between Craig and his audience that was preventing them from enthusing over what their favourite son was telling them. There really was a malign spirit abroad in the room. Even the chairman, Dick Lovelace, seemed to take impartiality to the very bounds of starched formality when he thanked Craig and summed up. Craig guessed that he just had to accept that with Oliver Lyons, Martin Radbourn and a newlywed Brenda Primero also being interviewed this weekend, he faced some rigorous competition. On his way out, Gerry Roberts smiled at him. However it was an ambiguous smile – not wholly reassuring to his young friend.

****

'*LAWSON QUITS!*' screamed the headlines on the morning of October 27th, and all at once a crisis had befallen the Conservative Party. "For our system of cabinet government to work effectively," the Chancellor had asserted in his resignation speech four days later, "the prime minister of the day must appoint ministers whom he or she trusts, and then leave them to carry out the policy." The strain for Nigel Lawson of having to spend the last few months not seeming to enjoy the Prime Minister's unreserved confidence had by now become intolerable, and so he had resigned. In his place, Mrs Thatcher appointed a bright, young Treasury minister called John Major to 11 Downing Street, charged with the task of reining in an economy increasingly in distress.

There is a mechanism available to Tory MPs to challenge the leadership of the party should discontent prove in need of the gravest expression. The last time such expression had been made had been the fateful challenge to Edward Heath by Mrs Thatcher herself in 1975. Her standing in the party since had been such that no one had ever contemplated challenging her as leader, even during the dark days of the 1981 Budget and the Westland Affair. Yet suddenly a maverick backbencher now put his name forward as the stalking horse in the hope that a more robust challenger might enter the fray.

For a whole tense week, the Prime Minister's supporters watched to see if her arch-rival, Michael Heseltine, would avail himself of this window of opportunity to transform the contest into something a little less one-sided. Heseltine declined, however, sensing that his hour had not yet come. Yet there was now clearly a body of opinion amongst Conservative members that the premiership of Margaret Hilda Thatcher was now inexorably slipping from her grasp.

****

"So that, gentlemen, is the challenge. With our British order book emptying in the wake of bus de-regulation I can't stress how important it is that we secure the Singapore deal."

As he sat on the edge of his desk addressing his most senior sales managers, Frank MacDonald's words had a deadly earnestness about them. Behind him, a flipchart stood laced with scribbled statistics and charts explaining how, unless these Asian exports could be secured, several hundred men risked being laid off next year.

"Craig will lead the team and provide the necessary liaison and back-up support. We know we'll be facing stiff competition. But let us have faith in our product and faith in ourselves. So good luck, chaps."

"Ah well," someone quipped as the meeting broke up and they all wandered back into the office. "Bang go my hopes of getting the decorating done next year! Hey, Craig, you're still on the lookout for an MP's job, aren't you? This is going to bugger you about a bit, isn't it?"

It certainly would. He was still waiting to hear for sure that he was through to the finals of the Gunsbridge South selection, though if all went well and he was adopted, being on the other side of the globe for most of next year wouldn't exactly give him much of a start in defending the seat against the formidable challenge that Alannah James was preparing to mount for Labour.

It weighed heavily on his mind on the journey back through the evening traffic. The pressures of trying to hold down a demanding job, be a hundred places at once for the party, and be a good husband to the wife he loved were becoming very difficult to juggle. He was partial to finally branching out on his own, perhaps into consultancy work: something that might permit him to fit his daily timetable together a bit more sympathetically.

Arriving home, he cruised up onto the drive of his opulent new redbrick home. Once through the front door, he found Nikki in the lounge with Pastor Scott Eversley and Elaine from the Elim Church. Something on the television had plainly captivated them as they watched with incredulity the drama unfolding on the screen – so much so that they only casually glanced his way, acknowledging his arrival.

"Amazing!" the boyish pastor gasped, entranced by someone taking a pickaxe to the ghastly grey concrete.

They were all astounded at the speed with which the whole system had been toppled. Poland and Hungary had quietly abandoned communism some months earlier. Now the world had similarly witnessed nightly demonstrations in East German cities too. The communist authorities had tried to pacify the people with meaningless titbits of reform. Yet it had availed them nothing. The Berlin Wall had been the very embodiment of the division of Europe into capitalist and communist, pro-American and pro-Soviet, the free and the enslaved, and (lately, and all-too-obviously) the affluent and the impoverished. Now, as the world's television cameras looked on, angry Germans were busily demolishing this evil edifice.

"I never thought I'd ever live to see this," Elaine wept, still trying to take in the enormity of events bubbling beneath the Brandenburg Gate.

"Oh, by the way. There's a letter for you in the rack," said Nikki, looking up at her husband momentarily.

Craig eased himself away from the television and strolled into the kitchen. A pine letter rack hung above the refrigerator. He dug out a white, typed envelope bearing a Gunsbridge postmark. Tearing it open, he pulled out the letter and began to read down the contents.

> *Dear Mr Anderson,*
>   *After considering all the interviewees for the Gunsbridge South parliamentary constituency, we regret to inform you that we shall not be recommending your name to go forward for consideration by the full membership of the Association. We thank you for the time and effort involved in acquainting us with yourself, and wish you all the best in pursuing your political ambitions further.*
>   *Yours sincerely*
>   *Cllr R E V*
> *Lovelace MBE, Chairman*

It was as if he'd just been doused in cold water. For a moment he just could not believe it. To have not at least made the final selection was a painful snub.

"Did you get it? Are you through?" Nikki tried to ascertain as he marched back into the living room.

"Evidently not!" Craig hissed, trying not to let his emotions show.

"You're not serious?"

"Deadly serious!" he said, tossing her the letter.

She read it for herself, still unconvinced. "What will you do now?"

"What can I do? I'd didn't get it. I'll just have to carry on looking elsewhere."

"So you're not going to be our next MP after all?" Scott enquired.

"Doesn't look like it!" Craig huffed, all his confident assurance of victory having been shattered. He shook his head.

"It's Conway. I can smell his fingers all over this. Why else is it that people who I have worked with for ten years can't even look me in the face? Just because I told him the truth? He's taking it all too far now. He's trying to buy up the whole town – including its politicians."

"Don't give up. The One who is within you is bigger and stronger than some mere man, no matter how rich and powerful," Nikki reminded him.

The television cameras closed in to show the final triumphant scenes of Berlin becoming one city once more. Scott took it as his cue, drawing up to Craig to cast a reassuring hand upon his shoulder.

"Remember Joshua and the city of Jericho: a city with walls as imposing as anything the communists could put up. Just as you now see this impregnable wall broken, so the walls that prevent you from realising your dream will also come tumbling down," he said, pointing to the graffiti-covered obscenity now being pulled apart before the watching world. "Anyway, Elaine, I think we ought to leave these good people to enjoy their evening."

The visitors drifted outside into the chill November evening, leaving Craig to absorb their words of comfort. Otherwise, he folded up and binned the Association's letter. He was sure that Scott was right. It's just that at moments of great disappointment, it was difficult to place one's trust in a god one could neither see nor touch. But then such was the essence of faith. His God had brought him this far; surely he would lead him on to victory; if not in Gunsbridge South then surely in any one of the safe Conservative seats that were looking out for a talented young man to be their voice in Westminster. Nikki closed the door and drew back up to him; faith was really all he had to sustain him now. He tried to draw strength from her comforting presence as she threw her arms around him and waited upon him, his forehead gently falling on her shoulder.

****

The gathering was not a happy one. Dick Lovelace smoothed the way through the evening's business in the knowledge that something sinister was brewing. Every muttering of the membership and every whisper behind shielding hands caught his anxious eye. His bushy moustache twitched like a little antennae desperate to pick up the first warning of trouble.

The candidates had given the membership of Gunsbridge South Conservative Association their very finest performances. Martin Radbourn had fought a difficult corner well, even if it wasn't entirely orthodox Thatcherism. Brenda Primero had delivered her finest oration, which must surely have dispelled any doubts about the capability of women in politics that might have lingered amongst the stuffy old 'squires' of the 'Maywood Heath Mafia'. She would certainly have been Craig's choice had he been present tonight. Protocol dictated that he should not be though; this left his friends anxious and concerned about the pretensions of the third choice before them tonight: Oliver Lyons had all the assurance and self-confidence borne of his eight years in the House of Commons. His impatience to return to that illustrious chamber had been all too evident in his mannerisms. Meanwhile, Dick Lovelace was consulting with the agent from Area Office before taking the vote and so didn't notice Gerry Roberts rise from his seat and wait patiently while the hall fell silent and the chairman chose to look his way.

"Mr Chairman," he began, coughing nervously to re-pitch his voice. "There is a feeling amongst the membership that there is one candidate that the Executive Committee has not permitted us to interview tonight – despite the fact that it had already been made clear beforehand that there was a preference for a proven local candidate. I believe we have been deliberately denied that preference tonight."

Lovelace looked him up and down dismissively. "Are you referring to Craig Anderson, perchance?"

"I am indeed referring to Craig Anderson."

"Well, Mr Roberts," he replied, wagging his finger impatiently, "Craig Anderson was interviewed along with all the other short-listed candidates. The Executive Committee was delegated the power to decide who is and who is not suitable for presenting before you at this meeting. This it has now done. It was all above board."

Gerry wasn't convinced, so pressed on. "Mr Chairman, with respect, I was a member of that committee, and I was not entirely happy with the proceedings – in particular with the composition of the Committee, and how it was that certain wards seemed to possess a disproportionate number of places."

The insinuation brought howls of derision from some corners of the room. Gerry tried to elaborate further, but the Chairman banged his fist on the table and trained his fiery tongue on the lone figure who had dared to question the integrity of the proceedings.

"Again, Mr Roberts, the constitution of the Committee was all above board. If you had reservations about the Committee in that respect, why did you not speak up at the time?"

"Mr Chairman, maybe that is so. Yet I know that certain committee members were being lobbied by higher authorities to vote for a particular candidate..."

"That's a disgraceful charge!" someone screamed.

"Yes, make him withdraw it!" another feisty old member insisted.

"And that... and that..." Gerry tried to continue, "...and that since the meeting, I have heard from a reliable source that intense pressure has been put upon officers of this association by those higher authorities to make sure this meeting does the same."

Pandemonium broke out amongst the membership, Lovelace anxiously seeking the advice of the area agent. He then turned and savaged his critic once more.

"You, sir, are way out of order. I advise you to sit down unless you can substantiate your accusation."

"Yes, go on. Tell us who this 'source' is!" Gerry's opponents jeered.

And that was the point at which Gerry ran out of steam, insisting vainly that his source was nonetheless 'reliable'. It was generally known that the big money was on Oliver Lyons. He was, after all, desperate to restart his parliamentary career; and the party were desperate to once again be able to employ his skills against the Labour frontbench. To cap it all, Harry Conway had been favourably impressed with Lyons's commitment to 'the needs of business'. However, without evidence Gerry could press Dick Lovelace no further and so he sat down.

Then up jumped Des Billingham, observing that, "Some of us have read the allegations made in this morning's *Observer* concerning the City dealings of one of the candidates before us..."

"I have been advised," the Chairman snapped back, "that those allegations are currently the subject of a libel action. So you, sir, would do well not to pursue your question any further!"

"Nice try, Des," someone muttered to him, but the chairman had killed any hope of tackling Oliver Lyons' business dealings stone dead.

Gerry returned to his feet once more. "Mr Chairman, the Committee has treated our views with contempt...."

"Mr Roberts, you are out of order. Sit down!"

"Let him speak!" someone called back at Lovelace, who was growing ever more agitated.

"Mr Chairman," Gerry continued, referring Lovelace to some obscure rule of the Association that permitted the membership to overturn the decisions of the Committee. "...So I propose that this association has no confidence in the Executive Committee, and demands that the whole selection process be run again."

"Have you taken leave of your senses, man?" Peter Brereton exclaimed, the two opposing camps hurling accusations at each other.

"Maywood Heath had five members on the Committee to everyone else's two!" Jean Taylor retorted back at him amidst the sudden uproar.

"...And that Lyons fellow is definitely hiding something!" someone else heckled.

"I don't care what they say. Someone at Central Office has set this up for him all along," Joan Knight muttered. "I dare say the Chairman can look forward to a knighthood to add to his MBE – that's if he does as they say!"

"Can we have order!" Lovelace roared angrily. "We will have a show of hands. All those in favour of Mr Roberts' motion, please show."

The hands of the rebels went up, the Area Office agent counting them methodically. The mass of arms seemed to encompass the ordinary party faithful from Lower Henley, Foxcotes and Barnwood, Elizabeth Gainsborough being conspicuous by her failure to support her fellow ward members.

Her action prompted Gerry to note to those huddled around that "The thing that really bugs me is the way Elizabeth has stabbed Craig in the back – and after all that Craig has done to help her over the years! I just hope we all remember that next time she's up for re-adoption."

"I count ninety votes," the agent announced, the chairman concurring.

"And those against."

Up went the hands of the 'squirearchy', which included all the party's wealthy patrons from the 'Maywood Heath Mafia', plus the *nouveaux riches* of Amblehurst and Little Worcester – the three wards with an unequal influence on the course of Conservative politics in Gunsbridge South.

"Ninety-seven votes against the Motion, Chairman."

Dick Lovelace's voice had an awesome finality about it as he boomed, "Mr Roberts' motion is therefore defeated. I will take no more debate on this matter. We will proceed to elect one of our three candidates."

Gerry looked devastated. He dragged his car keys out of his jacket pocket and shook his head in disbelief.

"Where are you going?" asked Mrs Lambert in her delightfully genteel tones.

"This is a complete farce!" he snapped, standing up to leave as the ballot slips were being issued. "I want no part of this travesty of democracy!"

"Don't be a fool!" the sweet little old lady lectured him. "We need every vote we can muster to stop that horrible Oliver Lyons from taking the nomination. Stay and vote for Brenda Primero. Craig told me she is a lovely girl; and now I have seen that he's right. If Craig can't have the nomination, at least secure it for her. I know it's what he would have wanted."

Gerry slowly slipped back into his seat after succumbing to the old lady's logic. Voting got underway. Then the counting took place. Finally, Dick Lovelace broke the news: Oliver Lyons eighty-two votes, Brenda Primero sixty-five votes, and Martin Radbourn forty votes. A majority for the arrogant former Home Office minister, though he was not home and dry just yet. Martin Radbourn's name was eliminated and a second ballot took place to decide between Lyons and the woman who had now assumed the mantle of champion for those mourning Craig's premature removal from the contest.

"If this guy wins, he's lost the support of half the party at a stroke," Gerry warned those who cared to listen.

The vote was counted. Everyone waited with baited breath while Dick Lovelace studied the result through his bifocals for a moment that seemed to last forever. Then he removed them, looked up at the membership, and broke the news, noting solemnly, "You have cast ninety-five votes for Oliver Lyons and ninety-two votes for Mrs Brenda Primero. I therefore declare Mr Oliver Lyons to be duly selected..."

A whole swathe of people all around him sighed with dismay at the result. But that was that. Sure, Gerry insisted, someone ought to set up an enquiry into the conduct of the selection process. But it would do little good, and Des Billingham told him so. What was done was done, although it would be hard to heal the divisions that had been opened up. Gerry caught Elizabeth Gainsborough's eye momentarily, but she turned away as soon as she realised. Some things would never be the same again.

****

7a Patens Court,
Bromley,
Kent.

December 15th 1989

Dear Craig,
    This is just a short note to let you know how sorry I am that you were not selected for your own seat the other week. I must admit I was surprised that my name was selected in preference to your own. Then a 'little bird' told me about some of the goings-on behind the scenes; all the dedicated service you have given over the years to people who then passed you over.
    Then again, that's politics! We must both put it all behind us and continue the search. If I'm honest, your tremendous sense of your own personal calling must be rubbing off on me too, because more and more I have come to believe that as we tread the long winding road we have set out upon, I just know that we will both reach that journey's end somehow. And what is that journey's end? To serve our party and our country at the very highest levels. Don't apologise for that ambition; rather persevere, despite all obstacles and all the hurts, and never be discouraged by setbacks.
    See you in Westminster one day!

Brenda

****

No one seemed capable of eating anything else. Craig sat back in his chair and rested his hands contentedly on his stomach, Nikki glancing across at his bloated expression with eyes that told him he would soon be forced onto a post-Christmas diet. In the meantime, she offered to help his mother with the washing up, the two women collecting up the remains of the Christmas dinner and hauling them off to the kitchen, leaving just Craig and his father alone at the dining table; both slightly somnolent from the meal; and both sporting the sort of silly paper hats that fall out of cheap Christmas crackers. Neither one said a word for several minutes. Craig couldn't help thinking about the change in his father he had observed lately; as if no longer having his son around the house had cleared the miasma that had traditionally hung over their often tenuous relationship. Nikki had helped, Len Anderson suddenly appearing to manifest a touching paternalism towards her – as if she was the daughter he'd always wanted. The old man had visibly mellowed since she'd been around.

"I'm sorry," his father muttered laconically, "...About what happened the other week."

"Oh, you mean...."

"Yeh... I wanted you to win the nomination. You deserved it. You were the local man, after all."

Craig was humbled. It was the first real effort he'd known on his father's part to express support for his political aspirations. He was so surprised that a shrug of the shoulder was momentarily all he could summon up in response.

"Yes, she's been a good 'un has Maggie," Len sighed after another long pause, running his fingers lazily up and down the side of an empty wine bottle.

"Who? ...Oh, Maggie," Craig realised, again a shocking revelation of a sea change in his father's attitudes, even if he did disapprove of this thing called the 'Poll Tax'.

Craig itched to set him right on one or two things, but appreciated the genuine *rapprochement* that this other, backhanded compliment symbolised. Perhaps not being together all that often now had enabled them each to view the other more objectively. Craig loved his father; and he guessed now – if ever he had had any doubts – that his father loved him also. If nothing else, at least this one seemingly insurmountable 'wall' in his life had been brought tumbling down.

After a brief silence, Len Anderson bounced out of his chair and beckoned his son to follow. Craig was intrigued, so trailed his father out through the kitchen, past Pat and Nikki gossiping over the dishes, and down into the garage. Switching on the light, he folded his arms proudly and turned to Craig.

"What d'ya think, son?" he said exclaimed, "A 1965 'E' Type. The finest Jaguar they ever made!"

That wasn't immediately obvious from the appearance of the dusty old car that sat jacked up on house bricks, adorned in red oxide primer, and with bits of the engine stripped down and scattered across the workbench.

"A mate at work had stored it in his backyard for years on end. He'd lost interest in it, so I slipped him something for it and towed it back."

"Will you ever be able to put it back on the road again?" Craig asked him excitedly, stepping into the driver's seat and lining up the gears. The very smell of the faded leather upholstery and the varnished wooden dashboard evoked a golden era of the British motor industry that had long since passed.

"I hope to. I tinker about with it at weekends and during the odd evening; whenever your mother's not about. I thought it would keep me busy now that I've taken early retirement: something to put my mind to – something a bit more practical than a train set or a stamp collection! I guess everybody has to have a goal in life, something to work towards. I think that was my trouble: the best years of my life were in the past; so I was always looking back, never actually addressing myself to what I wanted to look forward to in my life. After all, it's no good thinking of what might have been; you must always be positive. The only obstacle to your ambitions is you yourself."

Craig concurred. It seemed that Anderson father and son had more in common than they'd ever realised.

17 *THIS EVIL TAX!*

1990 started badly for the Government. The economy was slowing, and inflation was heading for double figures. However, the real storm about to break over the Government's head concerned the imminent abolition of domestic rates and their replacement by the Community Charge, or 'Poll Tax'. The principle was simple: unlike the property-based domestic rates, under the new system everyone would now pay something towards the cost of local government, thus restoring a measure of accountability, the absence of which had permitted a roll-call of left-wing councils to indulge in all manner of bizarre and extraneous activities at their ratepayers' expense. The Government believed that by making the level of community charge closely related to the performance of local councils, these profligates would have to answer to the voters for huge bills and poor and inefficient service delivery. Or so the theory went. However, the outcome was that even some Conservative-controlled councils were setting high community charge bills per head. In a household made up of several adults this meant a shared rates bill of a few hundred pounds overnight becoming a combined poll tax of several thousand pounds.

Suddenly, all those new working class voters so painfully won over to Thatcherism were up in arms. In all the major British cities there were demonstrations against the tax. Even some Conservative councillors resigned in disbelief at the effects the Poll Tax. Throughout March – the traditional budget-setting time of British local authorities – the "sound and the fury" of councillors debating the most controversial measure of the whole of Mrs Thatcher's eleven years in office grew deafening. The month finished with a violent demonstration against the Poll Tax in central London. And so was launched this 'flagship' of the Conservative's third term of office?

****

Shopping at the giant hypermarket at Trescott Park did have the advantages of everything being under one roof – and the parking was free! Even so, it was a pleasureless excursion on a damp Monday night, and Brad was glad to be able to depart the frozen meats counter and arrive for a linger on the line displaying magazines and periodicals, everywhere the headlines proclaiming '*NELSON MANDELA IS FREE'*.

"Cause for celebration?" asked a familiar voice from behind. Brad turned around. There, leaning on a half-full shopping trolley, was the girl with a flame-coloured crown that he recognised straight away.

"Wendy! How are you? They told me you'd moved out of the area," he exclaimed excitedly.

"Sort of. I work for a children's charity in Birmingham now. Anyway, how are you? And how are things in the old place?" the erstwhile social worker replied.

"Same as always," Brad shrugged his shoulders as they commenced a slow pacing up and down of the aisles of the cavernous food palace. "After the publicity that surrounded the trial of that step-father from Tower Park some of my comrades realised that perhaps we were right after all about the Abuse Action Team. Which reminds me, I never did thank you for your letter, did I."

"It's okay. I appreciate that you had a lot on your mind back then."

"You didn't exactly have an easy ride yourself," Brad noted regretfully.

"Maybe. But it's all turned out for the better," she replied stoically, lifting a bottle of 'own-brand' washing up liquid off the shelf. "It's just a shame no one listened to us at the time."

Changing the subject, Brad continued, "I took your advice; you know, about getting out of the claustrophobic world of local politics. I've applied for parliamentary seats elsewhere. Also, I work full-time for the union now too. It's useful because they're much more supportive of my political activities. I suppose it's a bit like your situation. Sometimes it takes a jolt to knock the jagged edges off you and prepare you for the next phase of your journey. I guess I was going through a bad patch. It was all the pent-up anger and frustration at my wife walking out on me. I had a bad case of the misogynist's blues!"

"Yes, I gathered that you had something going with Councillor Miss James," she hinted mischievously.

"You could say that. Alannah was a nice girl. But because of all the confusion I felt within, I guess I just poured all my anguish out on her, although it was not my intention. Looking back, I was real selfish."

Wendy paid for her provisions at the checkout, and waited while the conveyor hauled Brad's own purchases along to be scanned. Pushing their respective trolleys out through the sliding doors and onto the huge floodlit car park, the journey over to their cars gave him the opportunity to dwell upon precisely what his feelings were towards Wendy, who carried on chatting merrily about herself, the light drizzle forming tiny droplets on her hair as it drifted in the breeze. He certainly felt a deep respect for her – always had. But he had that sensation familiar to all men at some point; that here was a girl who he had placed on a pedestal, above the mostly erotic feelings he felt towards so many other women he knew. Finally, he decided to put an end to his rambling and got to the point.

"Listen," he said, halting his trolley, "I'd really like the pleasure of meeting you somewhere more conducive to entertaining a young lady? How about dinner at my place sometime – with a bottle of something?"

She carried on pushing her trolley. Opening up her car, Brad waited until she had teasingly loaded her things inside and shut it back down. Then, at last, she replied, "Yes, I'd look forward to that very much."

****

"All be upstanding for the Worshipful Mayor of Gunsbridge," the Mayor's attendant announced. The entire chamber dutifully rose to its feet as the mayoral train proceeded up to the chair, and the Mayor bade them all be seated.

Indeed, each of the councillors seemed to be psychologically readying themselves for what lay ahead, altering odd sentences in their notes or fidgeting with their pens while the Mayor dealt with notices of deceased ex-dignitaries and petitions about broken paving slabs. Outside they could hear the distant chanting of hundreds of demonstrators outside the civic complex. Meanwhile, up in the crowded public gallery, several police officers sat at strategic points along the aisles to watch over strange spectators, most of whom sported weird garments and even weirder hairstyles. Eventually, the time arrived to transact the real business on the agenda, the Labour finance chairman, Tim Eaves, rising to his feet. Broad, mid-thirties, and with the robust composure of a proletarian, he sorted out his notes and looked sternly across at the Conservative benches.

"Mr Mayor," he opened gravely, "tonight is a very sad night for this town. For tonight we have gathered here not to levy a rate to pay for our municipal services, but to set a POLL TAX!"

He almost choked on those two pejorative words before diving into the facts and figures of why he was proposing to levy a personal community charge on each of the two hundred thousand inhabitants of Gunsbridge, exemptions and rebates not withstanding. Occasionally someone from the Opposition benches would throw out a disputation on some point of his budget, but Eaves kept up the pace, condemning the loathsome deed he had been obliged to partake of.

"Finally, I say shame on the Tories, who have emasculated town halls at every turn. Far from this tax being a 'flagship', their Poll Tax will prove to be the final torpedo in any hopes we may have entertained of improving services in our boroughs. Mr Mayor, this tax is unjust, it is wrong, and there can be only one remedy to its imposition. Scrap it! Scrap it!" he said, his voice rising in an agonising crescendo while his colleagues began to cheer, "Scrap it! Labour will do just that!"

"Shadow Chairman to reply," said the Mayor, a semblance of order returning to the tense proceedings.

"Thankyoumrmayor," said Spencer 'Fitzgibberish' excitedly."Thisbudgetisacynicalattemptbythelabourgrouptoburden uswiththeconsequencesoftheirfouryearextravangzaoffiniancialfollyandculpablemis management."

Following such verbal somersaults was a taxing experience itself, more so when the white-haired old councillor drifted on to the precise financial details of his group's alternative budget. Brad used this interlude to size up the force arrayed against them on this memorable night. Peter Brereton and Mike Rotherwood looked set to train their tongues like turrets on Eaves, who was trying to scribble down what he could decipher from his shadow's rapid monologue. And then there was Neil Sharpe, the steely-eyed young councillor having amassed in front of him a pile of scribbled notes and a collection of briefing papers from Smith Square, which he now anxiously digested. Furthermore, he had at last gained the nomination of his party for the parliamentary seat of Gunsbridge North and seemed eager to prove himself to the journalists watching the debate progress from the gallery above.

Several councillors stood up and breathed fire at each other before the Mayor finally called Alannah James to speak, everyone anxious to hear what Labour's new girl in Gunsbridge South had to say. Brad watched her eyes blaze with passionate intensity as she tore into the whole legacy of the Conservative Party on local government.

"Every action of this Tory government has been purposely designed to undermine local councils," she charged, the Conservative side groaning mockingly as she continued, "First there came the Government's 'right-to-buy' legislation; the enforced sale by councils of their municipal housing stock. So what have we now? A rising tide of homelessness, where our stock of houses has been decreased, and the Government prevents us from spending the money to build new properties to meet the demand.

"From then on our ability to meet local needs has been progressively squeezed by further spending controls imposed upon us. In 1986, the metropolitan county councils were abolished – another butchering of local democracy. Since 1988, they have saddled us with the Education Reform Act, urban development corporations, and the Local Government and Housing Act – all further drastically usurping the proper role of local government in providing comprehensive essential services like housing, planning and decent schools, as well as cutting the grants we need to pay for them.

"Now we have the Poll Tax: an iniquitous tax that has burdened councils with colossal bills for collection and the probability that a sizeable proportion will go uncollected anyway. You will see; the next step will be that the Government starts taking whole tracts of local services out of our hands, removing local choice and local participation. History books will not only record the Poll Tax as an obscene and unworkable tax, but also the final assault on local democracy, which this Government lacks any real understanding of, or commitment to!"

A rousing cheer greeted her as she sat down from her stunning oratory, her colleagues clapping and stamping their feet. The Conservative side were impressed too, but kept quiet, preferring to see how ably their prospective candidate for Gunsbridge North would defend the Government's record.

"Mr Mayor," Neil Sharpe began calmly, "Councillor Miss James has wearied us all once again with her usual histrionics. I shall content myself only to correctly and objectively state the facts."

Labour councillors weren't impressed, hissing and groaning in anticipation of some of the councillor's own highly charged rhetoric. However, the Mayor intervened, and Councillor Sharpe was permitted to continue.

"Mr Mayor, she mentioned the sale of council house; and indeed, why shouldn't council tenants enjoy the right to own the home they occupy. Of course, the policy has proved wildly popular, despite the shameful efforts of this council to drag out applications from its tenants. Indeed, certain Labour councillors present tonight have even availed themselves of the opportunity to buy *their own* council houses. And you can bet their applications have been processed with a bit more haste!"

His allegations of hypocrisy on the Labour benches brought fearsome cries of indignation before the Mayor, as well as hysterical counterattacks – precisely as the cunning and controversial young councillor had hoped they might. He waited smugly while the Mayor restored order to the debate.

"Mr Mayor, the metropolitan counties were abolished because they were expensive and bloated talking shops. They served no useful purpose other than to act as propaganda platforms for the Labour Party!" Braving the jeers, he continued. "The Education Reform Act rightly takes power out of the hands of town hall bureaucrats and puts it back in the hands of governors, parents and individual schools. 'Tenant's Choice' meant plainly and simply what it said: that if the Housing Department offers botched repairs and poor maintenance then those tenants can choose another landlord to do the job properly. And remember all those pieces of derelict land that councils sat on for years and years? Urban development corporations are now able to sell them speedily for regeneration to create homes and jobs. And the Government quite rightly intervened to cap local government spending because local government spending is out of control – of which this socialist borough is a wonderful example!"

"Mr Mayor, no longer are our citizens prepared to be fleeced on the rates for an inefficient and wasteful service. Gone will be the days of council offices filling up with expensive and unnecessary staff like rabbits in a warren; gone will be the 'freebies' and the profusion of unnecessary sub-committees stuffed up with councillors all debating nothing of any consequence whilst claiming extra attendance allowances; and gone will be the corresponding rates rises offloaded onto the relatively few who ever paid them. Now everyone will pay something; and you can bet that they will be watching like hawks to see if the Labour Group is indulging in some ideological silliness at their expense. Mr Mayor, I say that that is what worries Councillor Miss James most, never mind her flatulent prose about unfairness. The Community Charge is only unfair to high-spending Labour councils like Gunsbridge Metropolitan Borough Council!"

All hell broke loose. The Labour benches vented their full fury on the Tories sat opposite, who cheered on their own man wildly. Finally, it came to the vote, which was set to be a perilously close thing. Labour had won an extra seat in the Lanes End by-election only a few weeks before, but left-wingers Roz Young and Derek Hooper were adamant that they would abstain, being joined by that vocal Liberal Democrat councillor, Jane Allsop; as well as by Colin Tyler, who was no less vocal in insisting he would not be a party to such an iniquitous deed ("It bay' fair, it bay' right and Ar' bay' gunna pay it!" he had reminded the chamber).

The illuminated voting panel above the Mayor flashed to show who was for, against or abstaining. He duly counted eighteen lights for, eighteen lights against, and four abstentions. A Conservative councillor had defied the best endeavours of the Group whips to drag him out of his hospital bed, yet still the Opposition looked set to embarrass Tom McKerrick by rejecting his budget. However, light number fifteen wasn't showing. 'Who was light number fifteen?' everyone muttered frantically.

Brad sat impassively watching the seconds flashing away towards the voting deadline – his finger hovering over the button for vote number fifteen, which was his own. Tom McKerrick looked down the line at him. So did Joe McAllister. Micky Preston also stared at the man he'd once trained to be a politician, knowing that the fate of the Council's budget now hung on his vote. If he abstained, or even voted against it, they'd probably have to sit into the small hours working out a compromise with the other side. And failing that, they all risked being surcharged if they failed to set one at all!

"I hate this evil tax!" Brad cried. Then he pressed one of the little buttons on his voting console. Everyone turned to the illuminated panel above them that registered Brad's vote just as the countdown marker hit zero.

"Mr Mayor, members of the Council," the Chief Executive noted as it did so, "The budget is carried: nineteen votes for, eighteen votes against, and four abstentions."

Just then, as McKerrick sat back in his seats and breathed a sigh of relief, Derek Hooper sprang to his feet.

"This is wrong! This will not do!" he cried, his face red with fury. He then cast his eyes up into the gallery. "A Labour council screwing the workers; doing the Tories' dirty work for them; implementing their abominable Poll Tax! I say don't screw the poor – screw the law, SCREW THE TORY LAW! Can't pay – won't pay! Can't pay – won't pay...!"

His demagoguery appeared to act as some kind of signal to the crowd in the public gallery, who cheered him on. Within seconds, the whole gallery seemed to explode in an orgy of protest, missiles raining down and angry expletives hurled at the councillors. An egg hit the Mayor, splattering all over his fine civic garments, the Chief Executive pulling him out of the way as several other salvoes came raining down.

"WE WON'T PAY THE POLL TAX, WE WON'T PAY THE POLL TAX, NA-NA-NA-NA, NA-NA-NA-NA..." came the chant. A boyish-looking police constable tried to restrain a shaven-headed young woman in torn jeans as she tossed a flour bomb down into the chamber, councillors scurrying for cover when she followed it up with some more eggs. By now, swarms of officers had burst into the gallery and quickly restored order. Thus had Gunsbridge Metropolitan Borough Council has set its first community charge.

****

The Easter Sunday traffic was considerably lighter that afternoon as it splashed past. The inclement weather was probably the main reason, although it made for a quieter stroll through St James Park, the tourists only occasionally in evidence and the ducks on the lake suitably indifferent to the monotonous rain that shrouded the capital on this otherwise dismal bank holiday.

Along the lakeside promenades Brad and Wendy strolled arm-in-arm, sheltering under the wide and colourful canopy of a huge golfing umbrella, content just to be passing the time of day in the company of the other. Wendy was appreciative of the new spirit of optimism that had infected him since she'd met him again. He seemed to possess a new reason for getting out of bed each morning, and she liked to flatter herself that it was all her doing. She could see he was now yearning to be back at the centre of events, propitiating that other great desire in his life – politics. Crablike, she employed her feminine subtlety to probe him further.

"I see Oliver Lyons in the papers again talking about local events," she noted pejoratively. "Looks like your friend Craig Anderson has sunk without trace."

"Who, Craig? Yeh. Shame. But his trouble was he was too nice for the rough and tumble of politics. I think he's realised that now. I have it on good authority that he's left for the Far East to make his fortune out there," Brad scoffed.

Then he changed the subject, saying "Hey, did I tell you, Micky Preston bought me a drink after the budget-setting meeting the other day? I do believe the old guy's sort of half-forgiven me. I was quite shocked. All I need to do now is work on some forgiveness from Alannah."

Wendy couldn't help feeling a twinge of jealously within her at the mention of such longed-for reconciliation. "Does she still mean anything to you?" she murmured softly.

Brad could sense the motive behind the question and stopped to reassure her. "Once, maybe. But that's all over now. It was a phase in my life that was full of mistakes and regrets. No, she doesn't mean anything to me now – at least not in that sense. Perhaps it still stings that she came out of all that trouble unscathed; but that's all."

They spent a brief moment in a gentle and loving embrace, their mouths locked in a tender kiss. Then they wandered out into the environs that backed onto Whitehall, the fine offices of state deserted and silent as the two of them strolled along the damp streets.

"You mean a lot to me, you know," Brad confessed with humility that she found deeply touching. "In a special kind of way too. I guess I like being with you."

Gradually the sound of the traffic drew closer and they found themselves in Parliament Square, the chimes of Big Ben ringing out across the city. They lingered for a short while in the rain, staring up at the impressive Palace of Westminster before continuing their Sunday stroll up into Whitehall itself, pausing under their umbrella to gaze up into Downing Street and the solitary policeman standing on the steps of the seat of Her Majesty's Government.

"Dreaming again?" suggested Wendy, observing how her lover's eyes appeared to glaze over. "What you need is a good holiday. Listen, my brother lives in the South of France. I visit him most summers. Why don't you come with me? We could take Mark with us too. He'd like a holiday, I'm sure."

"Hmmm," Brad mused aloud, still daydreaming. "That would be nice."

****

Local elections rarely stir the blood of the average British voter. Indeed, it was a trusted maxim of British politics that a councillor could be as active as the day was long, fighting hard for local amenities, and yet still be ejected at the polls if his party was going through a bad patch at Westminster – so irrelevant were they viewed by the electors at large. However, the local elections of 1990 were different, and helped to dispel some of this traditional apathy in that, by virtue of the Poll Tax, local government itself was the theme of the campaign.

At the outset, Conservatives had watched their fourteen thousand majority in Mid-Staffordshire transformed into a nine thousand Labour majority in a parliamentary by-election there. Now the local elections produced a similar stark message of anger against the Poll Tax, leaving many Tories were increasingly sceptical about its selling qualities.

****

All of a sudden it all seemed so peaceful. The fast train to Paris had slid effortlessly out of Calais-Maritime station and only the seabirds now disturbed the pleasant sunset. Brad ran his fingers through his son's fine dark hair and savoured this precious moment as they sat together on the footplate of the carriage. This was the first time he had ever been on a proper holiday with Mark, both of them exhilarated by the prospect of the long voyage to the sun. For now though, tranquillity and restfulness descended upon father and son, together in unspoken communion with each other. It was the first time Brad could remember sharing moments such as these, ones that would often pass unnoticed amidst the rush of everyday life back home: pointing out a huge ferry as it swung out into the harbour; or crudely translating the advertisement hoarding into English. He tried to point out on the map the winding route they would take to their destination: little things of priceless value to a small boy.

From a distance they could pick out the slender figure of Wendy weaving her way across the station and up the platform towards them, her summer dress blowing in the pleasant evening breeze and her gorgeous hair dancing across her face. Brad sensed a smile breaking out as she approached. Mark also looked up in anticipation. She saw his happy grin and tossed the six-year old a chocolate bar before offering Brad one too. Then the three of them stood about enjoying a quiet moment in the fast fading light before their train departed.

Finally they climbed aboard, Mark over the moon at his first experience of sleeping on a moving train. His father bade him sleep tight, the sun and the sand and the *joie-de-vivre* only a dream away – all two weeks of it. Then he drifted back out into the corridor to rejoin Wendy by an open window, wind rushing through their hair as the powerful locomotive worked up to full traction and began to haul the long, snaking train out across the Pas de Calais and into the advancing night, siren wailing and lights ablaze like a beacon of civilisation in a dark and alien land. He clung to her possessively and pondered what new discoveries they would make together on this new departure, the sun finally going down on a previous life forever.

****

"Right. From now on I want no more talk of politics. For the next three weeks it's no more newspapers, no more television, and no more worrying about the state of the world. Clear?"

Brad lay back in his bunk resignedly. "Yes, Miss. Three bags full, Miss," he sighed, determined to heed Wendy's advice. After all, they were on holiday.

"Are we there yet, Dad?" came a voice from under the sheets of the bottom bunk. Wendy searched for the owner and dug her fingers into his ribs, causing the little lad to giggle impishly. Then she rolled up the blind and gazed out of the speeding train across the dusty landscape. Overnight the surroundings had changed and the verdant meadows and lush orchards of northern France had given way to the arid coastal plains of the far south.

Almost at once the journey took on a new and wondrous feeling. The clattering train began to hug the coast, with clear blue skies above and tempting glimpses of the Mediterranean below as it trundled inexorably through charming old citadels and out over the marshy *étang* before drawing into Perpignan.

Stepping down from the train, Brad ended up being the porter for everyone's belongings, Mark hurrying along with an oversize die-cast model car and sporting an '*ENGLAND*' sunhat, and Wendy a shoulder bag and conspicuously large sunglasses. Together they passed through the station foyer and out into the car park, where Brad noticed a young man in shirt sleeves leaning against a quintessentially Gallic Citrôen estate car, the white paintwork still just able to gleam in the powerful sun, despite a liberal coating of dust. Wendy began to quicken the pace, racing into the arms of this man, holding him tight as they exchanged greetings.

"Paul, this is Robert, who I told you about, and his son Mark," she enthused to her brother.

"Hi!" he said, squeezing Brad's hand and ruffling the boy's unruly mane.

"Everyone calls him Brad though," Wendy qualified her remark.

"Well, might as well start off as we mean to go on! Welcome to the South of France, Brad."

Brad soon warmed to Wendy's charming brother, who nattered away merrily above the noise of the refreshing breeze rushing in through the car's open windows.

"Look, Dad! Palm trees!" Mark exclaimed.

"Oh, yes, we've got plenty of those here. A bit different to England, eh?" Paul surmised.

It certainly was. The countryside that flashed past now was beyond Brad's experience: vineyards and olive groves; little farmsteads and rustic villas. It made him painfully aware of just how parochial he'd allowed himself to become. Even so, at least now he felt he had left behind the small-town politics of Gunsbridge. He felt himself coming alive to something else: certainly a different culture and a vastly different ambience. It felt every bit as illuminating as anything he'd ever learned from Micky Preston.

Finally, the car turned off up a dusty driveway and pulled up outside a diamond white villa with a charming red tiled roof, where a beautiful sun-kissed young woman was waiting upon their arrival. Wendy stepped out first and threw her arms around her whilst Paul unloaded the luggage. Chatting away in fluent French, Wendy exchanged girlish gossip. Finally she turned and drew her English boyfriend up to meet her.

"Brad. This is my sister-in-law, Isabelle."

Brad was quite bowled over at his first encounter with a real live Frenchwoman; and such an attractive one at that! Stuttering nervously, he cleared his throat. "Bonjour, Isabelle. Je suis très enchanté. Comment ça va?"

"I'm just fine, thank you. How's your little boy? Wendy's told me so much about you."

Ah well, he thought as Isabelle bent down to dote on the little lad. So much for all the weeks he'd spent swatting up the old 'parlez-vous francais'! Wendy evidently found it highly amusing though and curled her fingers into his waist as she drew alongside him.

"L'homme qui veut s'exprimer et communiquer dans la langue extrangéré toujours trouvera une femme très bonne qui parle anglais... heureusement!" she noted to general amusement.

****

The meal was truly delightful. Cooked exquisitely by both Paul and Isabelle, they joined their two adult guests to enjoy the tranquil evening on the patio, with the soft lights and the cicadas lulling them into relaxing to jovial banter and much trading of backgrounds. Now Brad understood why there was such a phenomenon as a 'Mediterranean' way of life. After all, with the sun's warmth still lingering into late evening, who worried about work? Work was something only far-off Parisians did for a living!

"You see, the whole reason why I stayed down here was because I fell in love with the place," Paul insisted. "The people are great. The climate is superb. It's just an incredibly agreeable place to live!"

"Someone has to stay behind and look after Old Blighty," Wendy exclaimed, pouring everyone some more wine.

"I thought I'd be homesick when I left London; but no, not a bit of it. I hear a lot has changed though."

Brad and Wendy looked at each other briefly to see who might venture a response. Brad took the lead.

"I'd say you wouldn't even recognise the place now, Paul. It's changed in so many ways. As to whether it's changed for the better or for the worst, well... I'm biased, perhaps."

"Oh, yes. Of course. You're a politician, aren't you? Il est un conseiller socialiste d'un arrondissement anglais," Paul explained to Isabelle.

"Very interesting. Paul works in advertising." Isabelle informed him in her lush Gallic tones, delightfully misplacing the emphasis in 'advertising'.

"Everything seems so much more...outward-facing here," Brad mused. "I mean..."

"You mean European. Yes, well, I often think that that English Channel is less of a channel and more of a moat – a chasm even," Paul asserted to his English visitor, who was mindful of his own party's peregrinations on the issue of Europe.

"And how's my beloved little sister these days. Grown out of demos and sit-ins?" Paul joked.

"I think I've discovered a different channel for my political energies," she replied, staring at Brad possessively.

"Yes, you always were the rebel of the family," Paul continued. "I remember you used to get into all manner of ding-dongs with Mom and Dad. And me too! Wendy used to charge that I was insufficiently dedicated to the revolution just because I preferred to spend my spare moments playing bass guitar in a punk band!"

The lazy discourse continued well into the night until, with the wine finished and the moon attending to its lonely vigil in the heavens, they all retired. However, Brad found it difficult to settle down on his first night. He wasn't sure whether it was the humidity or the cicadas, or just the novelty of sleeping in a strange bed. Perhaps Wendy was right: he was still carrying Gunsbridge round on his shoulders. He rolled over and resolved once more to shed the burden for the duration of his stay.

"Dad," came a tiny voice from the other side of the room.

"What?" Brad enquired, half snoozing.

"When will you be a famous politician?"

Brad was taken aback by his question, even though he was almost dozing off. "I don't know," he grunted.

"Mummy says one day you'll be famous... even prime minister, like Mrs Thatcher."

Again, Brad was touched. Evidently, despite all the hurt and the bitterness, Helen had still found it within her to salute her ex-husband's aspirations, even if she no longer considered herself to be a part of them. Time has its way of healing.

"Dad!"

"What?"

"I don't want you to be like Mrs Thatcher."

"Why not?" Brad burbled somnolently, thinking that perhaps his precocious seed might offer him his considered purview of why the Conservative administration that bore her imprint had been such a blight upon the nation. Instead he just sighed and noted wistfully.

"Mrs Thatcher's always busy doing things. I don't want you to be always being busy. I love you and always want to be with you; cuz' you're my dad!"

Brad smiled to himself and drifted peacefully off to sleep. Perhaps he wasn't such a bad dad after all.

****

The sea broke in lithe rhythms upon the glowing, gilded sands, and the unforgiving fireball beat down on them mercilessly. Despite having dolloped on sun cream with a factor rating akin to that of axle grease, Wendy's skin had already turned a colourful shade of pink, and she wisely covered up as she lay there; supine, relaxing to the sound of the plangent waves crashing on the beach. Brad was meanwhile absorbed in a travelogue, hungry to learn about all sorts of faraway places. Indeed, his antipodean paperback was only just wetting his appetite for the experience of other cultures that he'd missed having locked himself away in Gunsbridge for so long. Everyone should travel, he agreed.

"I hope that book's not political!" Wendy warned him, still lying motionless on the towel.

"No. It's about Australia actually. You haven't got a long-lost relative living in Alice Springs, have you?" he asked.

"Sorry," she sighed, dashing any hopes he might have entertained of piggy-backing a cheap holiday down under as well. "Have you enjoyed your holiday so far?"

"Yes. Have you enjoyed having Mark and I gatecrash yours?" he replied, grabbing a handful of sand and slowly squeezing it out along her outstretched arm.

He felt drawn ever closer to Wendy. She seemed so perfectly tuned into his wavelength; and she, too, seemed to discover the true Brad she knew always existed inside the hard, defensive carapace that he preferred to offer to outsiders. The loner had a secret door into his inner places and Wendy, alone amongst those who had known him, seemed to possess that elusive key that granted access into his phlegmatic, mercurial character.

"I wouldn't have had it any other way. I've enjoyed being with Mark too. It's nice to be able to treat a child as a child instead of a case number." She smiled. Then she raised her head and shielded her eyes from the sun. "Where is Mark?" she wondered aloud.

"Oh, he's down there," said Brad, pointing out his son expertly instructing two French boys and their little sister on how the British build sandcastles that could survive the ravages of the advancing tide. "He looks like he's enjoying himself."

"Time to head back soon," Wendy reminded him, fumbling in the beach bag for her watch. Even so, dallying on the beach a little while longer needed no great exertion on either of their parts, and they relaxed for a further half-hour – at least until even British civil engineering prowess had been confounded by the remorseless sea.

Strolling back along the esplanade, they idly drifted past the beachside stores, Mark taking a fancy to some juicy peaches and Wendy exchanging a few French francs and a few French banalities with the girl serving inside the shop. This gave Brad the opportunity to browse the magazine stands in the neighbouring *tabac*, anxious to search out a little World Cup coverage. As he did so, his eyes alighted on the headline on the front of one of the English newspapers.

"FORMER MINISTER INDICTED ON FRAUD CHARGES...
Former Home Office minister, Oliver Lyons, today appeared at the Old Bailey indicted along with several other leading City figures on charges of unlawfully conspiring to gain from a huge 'insider dealing' ploy. It is alleged that the former Home Office minister and Tory candidate for Gunsbridge South knowingly acted to acquire stocks in companies whose share prices subsequently soared. Lyons, 43, claimed he had never knowingly acted unlawfully or improperly in conducting his business affairs. Bail of £50,000 was granted. The chairman of the Gunsbridge constituency party was unavailable for comment.'

"What is that thing in your hands?" bellowed Wendy, advancing his way with Mark at her side.

He turned around to find her rubicund face even redder than the sun had otherwise fried it, an expression of censure only partially concealed by those ruddy locks, which the stiff sea breeze tossed across it.

"Er, er, er... I was only looking at the sport," he exclaimed, waving the back page at her to emphasise that only desperation for news of Bobby Robson's lads could have led him to break his promise to her.

"I believe you," the suspicious virago grudgingly mumbled. "...thousands wouldn't. Here! Have a peach!" she said, tossing him a succulent fruit after he had hastily replaced the paper back in the rack.

****

The flags fluttered spiritedly in the breeze, the strong winds whipping up the sea so that today only the very bravest windsurfers dared to battle against the gusts to enjoy the thrill of racing across the bay at speed on their gaily-coloured craft.

Onshore, Brad and Wendy strolled together across the grassy dunes, holding each other by the fingertips. They both enjoyed the simple romantic pleasure of feeling the warm sand running through the gaps between their toes and the wind in their hair. Soon they would be back home; for all good things must come to an end, and Brad was anxious to be back in the arena where he belonged. He pondered this and gripped her soft, tender hand. He squeezed it gently, causing her to look up at him and smile benignly. She moved in closer to him, gathering her arms around his waist and huddling up under his shoulder as he cast his sun-bronzed arm around her and they carried on walking.

He was grateful that she was there. He'd behaved himself impeccably, just as he had promised, never mentioning politics once. Such an exemplary performance had been rewarded the previous night when, relaxing together on the veranda in the cool of the evening, she had bared her soul to him, outlining where she saw her life heading. To Brad's delight, she noted how important his political ambitions were to him and how she, too, wanted to be a vital part of those ambitions; supporting him and uplifting him because she loved him deeply.

Brad for his part had never wanted any girl before like he now wanted Wendy. No one had ever moved him so profoundly, inspiring such trust and devotion and banishing all those dark fears that lurked inside him. All the striving was over. He'd loved Helen; but she had never considered herself a part of his world. He'd loved Alannah; but, for whatever reason, had never been able to satisfactorily convince himself that she was not, somewhere or somehow, in competition with him. No, Wendy was different. She'd turned his whole life around. It was almost a religious experience, of the kind his mother was always rambling on about. Indeed, even Brad's spiritual outlook no longer seemed to be haunted by that bleak nihilistic abyss of the previous year. The dark skies were clearing, and loving Wendy had helped him to see the sun breaking through on the other shore.

Wendy detected the spring in his step and knew well enough the processes now going on inside his head. He was a curious fellow. Right from the moment when she'd first witnessed him in action on Gunsbridge Council, she knew he was one of those 'special' people; called for higher things. All the while they had worked together on the Social Services Committee she had had to maintain a proper officer-councillor relationship when she had instead ached inside to befriend him and to love him. Now, at last, her chance had arrived. She had told him the previous evening of all those awesome things on her mind, unsure of exactly how this enigmatic individual would react towards her foolish preoccupations. Yet patience and faith had now revealed its own reward.

They halted on the dunes; for the sun had begun to rest inexorably on the far side of the *étang* and the evening sky was fast transforming itself into a haunting shade of crimson. He took her in his embrace and stared into her eyes right up until the final moment when their lips touched and they were both overcome with that sense of oneness and purpose: a man and woman starting out on the first stage of life's most exciting voyage – together.

18   *A STORM IN THE DESERT*

"Hullo... Frank...?" he cried upon hearing a voice at the other end of the telephone, "Yes, it's me, Craig... WE DID IT! We finally got a signature out of them this afternoon! We've won the Singapore contract! By the way, you received my letter?" he enquired anxiously.

"*Yes,*" came the voice from the other end. "*I wish I could change your mind about leaving. But, it's your choice, and I understand. But before you do clear your desk, hang around because we're planning a little party for you and your team. Rex might even be flying over especially.*"

Craig was flattered. Cutting himself adrift from BEL had not been an easy decision to make, but he knew he had to do it. He was just glad that his eight years with the company had witnessed such a phenomenal transformation of its fortunes, and that perhaps just a small part of that turn-around had been thanks to his own hard work. He was happy too that his time there was ending on a high note, and told MacDonald so. Finally, he signed off and rested the receiver for a moment before redialling the long string of numbers necessary to connect up with someone far more important than his boss.

"Hello... Nikki? ...Yes, you guessed.... How are you? ...Listen, we've cracked it! The whole contract! A thousand beautiful new double-deck buses!"

Nikki sounded less than exhilarated with such corporate titbits, and Craig gradually sensed that she was somehow more than just lonely.

"*I miss you,*" the faint feminine voice whistled down the line. "*It seems such a long time since we've been together. I mean really together: just you and I – no overseas trips, no overnight drives up to distant constituencies here, there and everywhere. When will you be back?*"

"We've still got some loose ends to attend to. I'll try and be away for Monday or Tuesday if I can. Anyway, you know I love you. I will be back before you can blink. Look, I must go..." he said, spotting one of his colleagues tapping his watch at him. "Bye! And Nikki... I miss you!" he said, unsure whether she'd caught his closing remark.

****

The music droned on in the hotel lounge, the suite filling with an occasional cheer from the lads when someone cracked an ace joke. Craig was happy to see his team with their hair down and engaged in some harmless schoolboy fun, ties loosened and singing along to the tunes, a multitude of bottles and cans scattered about the table. They had endured the demanding rigours of long days, hard, thrusting negotiations, and a fair measure of disappointments along the way. They deserved a final fling on their last night in Singapore. It now looked unlikely that Craig, himself, would be able to get away before Wednesday though.

He wandered over to the window of the suite, which offered a commanding night-time view of this fabulous island city. It had certainly come a long way since Raffles had founded it on a tropical swamp one hundred-and-seventy years earlier. The lights of the city reached out into the distance, with the river that gave the city its name visible like a dark snake carving up the prosperous entrepôt. He thought of Nikki sitting there at home; waiting, brooding, praying that this would be his last great expedition to distant lands. Perhaps his branching out into marketing consultancy work would grant her that wish. It would certainly be a challenge to be working freelance. It might also permit him the opportunity to concentrate on finding one of the dwindling numbers of parliamentary seats still up for grabs. Time was running out, the clock ticking away inexorably towards the day when Mrs Thatcher would once again have to go to the country for another mandate to govern.

****

He must have slept well because he couldn't remember a thing after taking off from Singapore. Craig rubbed his eyes, rolled up the blind and stared out at the sunrise that had caught up with the huge Boeing.

"Where are we?" he asked, turning to address a smart, middle-aged Chinese lady sat across the aisle from him. She looked up from fanning herself with the paperback novel she had been reading and peered over the top of a pair of forbidding, matronly spectacles.

"I'm not sure. Someone said it's Kuwait," she replied with a tense expression. "We've been here three hours already. Surely it doesn't take this long to refuel an aeroplane."

Craig lifted himself up in his seat, staring out of the window again. He ran his hand over the stubble now sprouting on his weary face and tried to pick out the terrain outside. The terminal building shone in the sun some way off across the shimmering tarmac. The place seemed deserted, only the soft humming of the plane's generators breaking the eerie morning silence. All of which made him grow more impatient. He had work to do, a political career to pursue, and a wife who he'd hadn't seen since in weeks; none of which he was partial to having disrupted by either an airline or a sleepy Bedouin kingdom that couldn't get their acts together.

"Miss, when are we going to..." the Chinese lady anxiously beseeched a passing stewardess, who in turn just smiled emolliently if unconvincingly, not really informing them of much they hadn't already discerned.

The Chinese lady mumbled something before settling back into her novel. Craig fumbled in his jacket stowed above his head, taking out his bible to pass the tedious hours in like manner.

"LADIES AND GENTLEMAN, THIS IS YOUR CAPTAIN SPEAKING. MAY I APOLOGISE FOR THE DELAY IN GETTING AIRBORNE AGAIN, BUT WE HAVE BEEN UNABLE TO OBTAIN FURTHER CONTACT WITH AIR TRAFFIC CONTROL. WE BELIEVE IT MAY HAVE SOMETHING TO DO WITH SOME CIVIL DISTURBANCE IN THE COUNTRY AT THE MOMENT. WE WILL INFORM YOU FURTHER WHEN WE HAVE A BETTER PICTURE OF PRECISELY WHAT'S HAPPENING. THANK YOU."

The passengers all slumped back in their seats angrily. Craig shared their frustration. His early days in Arabia had taught him, even as a young lad, that Arabs are volatile enough to become roused over the most trivial of matters; the local rulers had probably banged up some opposition agitator in jail! He dozed off periodically, largely oblivious to the mounting tension brewing inside the plane. The Chinese lady had stormed off in the direction of the cockpit umpteen times, and must have been returning from giving the crew yet another piece of her punctilious oriental mind when Craig stirred himself once more. He looked out of the window and noticed movement at last: there were vehicles heading towards the plane.

"LADIES AND GENTLEMAN, THIS IS THE CAPTAIN SPEAKING. CAN I HAVE YOUR ATTENTION FOR A MOMENT. I HAVE A STATEMENT I HAVE BEEN ASKED TO READ OUT..."

Craig sensed that something was definitely not right. The other passengers began to sense this too – especially once heavily armed soldiers in combat dress began to board the plane.

"...OVER THE PAST WEEKS, A CRISIS HAS DEVELOPED BETWEEN THE PEOPLE OF IRAQ AND THE DEBAUCHED AND LICENTIOUS REGIME OF THE EMIR OF KUWAIT. THE MASSES OF KUWAIT HAVE NOW RISEN UP, AND HAVE SHAKEN OFF THE CORRUPT YOKE OF THE OPPRESSORS. THEREFORE, THE PRESIDENT OF IRAQ, OUR BELOVED LEADER SADDAM HUSSEIN, HAS LAUNCHED A DECISIVE STRIKE TO ROOT OUT THEIR SCHEMING. HOWEVER, IN ORDER TO PROTECT THE LIVES OF FOREIGN NON-COMBATANTS, ALL PASSENGERS WILL BE EVACUATED TO A PLACE OF SAFETY FROM WHERE THEY CAN BE REPATRIATED. YOUR CO-OPERATION IS REQUESTED SO THAT YOU MAY BE ESCORTED FROM THE

FIGHTING STILL BEING WAGED BY THE GLORIOUS ARMED FORCES OF IRAQ..."

"ALLAHA AKBAR!" one of the soldiers cried, his fellows holding their weapons aloft and cheering as they strutted menacingly down the length of the stranded plane.

****

It had been yet another fine day during this most gorgeous of summers. The birds were singing their virtuoso tunes from the big tall conifers that shaded the estate and the distant whirring of someone's lawnmower drifted over from a few gardens away. Nikki sat quietly on the sun lounger, which she rocked lazily with the one foot she had dangled on the lawn, relieved at last that Craig would soon be back by her side.

She gathered up her things and drifted back inside the house, reappearing briefly to retrieve some odd items of washing from the line and to survey the skies to see if there was a remote possibility of rain tomorrow. Then she closed the patio door and switched on the nightly news, perchance to see what all this kerfuffle in Kuwait was about.

****

They had been warned to keep away from the windows of the hotel. However, as he peered out from behind the blind, Craig could see that all the fine boulevards and squares that led into the Kuwait City had become littered with the debris of occupation. Burnt-out cars stood at every intersection, as did the armoured vehicles of the Iraqi invaders. Shops had either been looted or torched; neon signs hanging by their wiring. Official buildings stood ransacked, documents scattered about inside. Some hapless Kuwaiti had driven up to an Iraqi checkpoint only to find his Mercedes summarily commandeered. He, himself, was bundled into the back of an APC.

Looking out across the seafront to the blue Gulf waters that fronted those expensive apartment blocks, Craig was tempted to recall all those happy memories of Aden and Bahrain where he had grown up; only this time he was not travelling courtesy of the Royal Air Force, but was rather a 'guest' of the gruesome Iraqi dictator. Along that same wide expressway that looked out to sea, he noticed an American-style school bus motoring along, escorted by a covered truck full of soldiers. Manoeuvring around the square, the convoy halted on the forecourt of the hotel and the soldiers leapt out, ordering the group of bewildered Europeans civilians to do likewise. They were then shepherded inside the hotel.

Craig moved away from the window and decided to drift downstairs in the hope of obtaining further news on what was going on. As he descended the stairs into the hotel reception, his hands stuffed wearily in his trousers pockets and his shirt undone at the collar, he was greeted by the sort of traumatic *ensemble* one might find at a strike-bound airport on a bank holiday. Scores of frightened civilians were huddled about in the foyer, distraught and tired, the failed air-conditioning making the building hot and oppressive. Mothers with screaming babies sat on the stairs comforting their infants while the men stood about aimlessly, trying to make sense of the sudden disaster that had befallen them.

"What's going on?" Craig asked one of the young men arriving inside the hotel from the bus parked outside.

"This is the price you pay for listening to the advice of the Foreign Office!" the guy cursed in a lush Belfast accent as he deposited himself and his assortment of photographic equipment against the shutters of the locked-up perfumery. He took a few pictures of the scenes of chaos and confusion he witnessed in the foyer. Then he slid his short, muscular body to the floor before sighing with exhaustion. He looked up at Craig, forcing a chunky hand through his wiry, rust-coloured hair to shake the dust out.

"'Catch the special embassy bus', they said. 'Congregate at the hotel', they said. Bullshit, I say! No, we should have all got out across the desert. Now we're stuck here – pawns in Saddam Hussein's little game of brinkmanship."

Just then an Iraqi NCO noticed the man's sophisticated-looking camera as he stepped over the assortment of bodies. He pointed to it and mumbled something in Arabic. To Craig's surprise, the stocky little Irishman rose to his feet and began answering back in equally fluent Arabic. Craig had learned the odd phrase or two during his schooldays in Bahrain, but couldn't hope to understand what was transpiring, the sergeant pulling the camera out of the man's hands and inspecting it in his own. All the argument in the world didn't seem to impress the burly guard, who called over a few of his subordinates bearing Kalashnikovs to make his point. He tapped the film out of the back of the camera and muttered something further. The Irish arrival turned away in despair as the soldier pocketed the film and offered him his camera back, shrugging his shoulders and handing it to Craig instead when he realised that its owner was less than amused. Then the NCO and his men moved on.

"You with the press, by any chance?" Craig asked.

"You guessed. The name's Ben – Ben Anderson," he said, offering Craig that firm, chunky hand.

"Ah, a namesake!" Craig joked. "I'm Craig Anderson. Pleased to meet you."

It did not take long for the two captives to strike up a friendship, trading on each other's backgrounds and ruminating on the less than enviable predicament they were in. During the day, the foyer of the hotel continued to fill up with foreigners rounded up from various parts of town, the ever-present cries of infants and the intolerable heat making even the most phlegmatic of Englishmen as impatient and agitated as the other assorted nationalities thrown together in this cauldron.

"So what's your excuse for being here?" Ben asked him. "Business? Construction? Ex-pat?"

Craig joined him as he slid back down to the floor. "No, I was on a flight stopping off from Singapore. Unfortunately, we never quite got airborne again," Craig continued, trying to see the funny side of his predicament, which was not easy in the one hundred-and-ten degree heat. Repeating something he'd picked up on the BBC World Service, he further proffered that "It's rumoured that President Bush has ordered a task force into the Gulf."

The two men continued to talk at length to while away the hours of boredom. In passing, Ben intimated to Craig that he had 'contacts' amongst the locals. Later on, they were joined by some of the other male 'guests', who added stories of their own, everybody conscious that the rounding-up of Western nationals and the herding together of them in the major hotels did not bode well for any of them.

****

THE GUNSBRIDGE HERALD
Saturday, August 11th 1990
Evening Edition - Still only 22p

TRIAL OPENS ON 'INSIDER DEALING' FORMER MINISTER
The prospective Conservative parliamentary candidate for Gunsbridge South, Oliver Lyons, is due to appear at the Old Bailey this week to face charges of illegally supporting shares during the flotation of...
CRAIG ANDERSON TRAPPED BY SADDAM
It is now known that the man responsible for successfully negotiating the huge contract that has saved hundreds of jobs at the giant BEL bus manufacturer is amongst several thousand British civilians trapped inside Iraq...
LABOUR CONDEMNS 'SELF-INFLICTED RECESSION'
Prospective Labour candidate for Gunsbridge South, Alannah James, has accused the Government of pushing Britain into a 'self-inflicted recession'. Miss James was commenting on warnings from the local CBI about the harmful effects of high interest rates...
FUN CITY IN CRISIS
Controversial property developer Harry Conway is believed to attempting an eleventh-hour bid to secure desperately needed finance to restart his multi-million pound 'Fun City' project. It is thought likely that the sale of the Trescott Park Shopping Centre may be the price that heavily-indebted Conway Enterprises will

have to pay to prevent insolvency after being adversely affected by the slump in property prices...

****

'Bring one case and be ready to leave by nightfall', the Iraqis had told them all. It was obvious it meant just one thing. Ben Anderson wasn't planning on staying around to find out and had persuaded Craig to steal away with him by means of a service yard they had reconnoitred. Sure enough, the Iraqis rounded up their captives – men, women, children and babies – and herded them onto buses and trucks, the miserable convoy setting out into the night to join the highway north to Baghdad.

Meanwhile, the two escapees were about to steal into the back streets when they heard footsteps approach. Ducking, they peeped through the gap in the gate to watch some Arabs youths check to see if anyone was about before one of them took out an aerosol spray and began to daub some slogan on the wall of the wall opposite.

"What's he doing?" Craig whispered.

Ben strained his eyes in the half-light to translate before deciding that it was distinctly uncomplimentary of their new Iraqi masters. Taking a chance, he beckoned Craig to lift him up onto the wall, where he called over to the teenagers. After a few brief exchanges, he lifted himself up onto the ledge and hauled Craig up too.

They were soon in the labyrinth of alleyways that led away from the plush hotels along the seafront. Following the boys, who crept along hugging the shadows, Craig asked himself just how his triumphant business trip had ended up with him skulking round the side streets of some hot, fearful Middle Eastern city, behaving like a fugitive. It all had a terrible feeling of unreality about it, like the worst of bad dreams. The leader of the gang suddenly spotted headlights and beckoned to his clan to scatter. Ben grabbed Craig, and they dived into a doorway.

The sound of a labouring diesel engine grew louder and louder until an armoured vehicle appeared across the end of the street, a powerful searchlight beam flooding up the little passageway as the terrified group pressed itself tightly into any available shadow. The vehicle stopped and the beam shone further up the street. Suddenly, a burst of machine gun fire tore out into the night, ricocheting wildly off the overhanging apartments. It was one terrifying moment. As bits of masonry bounced all around him, Craig closed his eyes and prepared to be welcomed into the radiant-white arms of his Saviour. Meanwhile, a troop of feral cats bolted away in terror, abandoning the jumble of boxes and refuse that now lay riddled with bullets and scattered about the street.

It was all good fun; so much so that the crew of the tank laughed heartily and encouraged their gunner to fire off some more volleys to see the feline scavengers on their way. Having emptied the magazine, the driver clanked the vehicle into gear and rolled off around the block to enforce the curfew elsewhere. Meanwhile, Craig was trembling nervously. He'd never been machine-gunned before!

****

It was a superb opportunity to pause and reflect on the meaning of life, if only because there was nothing else to do. Craig sat perspiring heavily in the corner of the small room, the sunlight barely filtering through the closed shutters of the solitary window.

Ben sat opposite, depressed and alone with his increasingly desperate thoughts. Two escape plans had been drawn up and both had failed ignominiously: the first when an Iraqi patrol had foiled a rendezvous with the resistance, the second when the car of their Kuwaiti hosts had packed up on the outskirts of town. Fortunately they had made it back. Yet their two weeks confinement in the dingy, dusty little attic had not done much for their sanity ever since.

"Hey, what day is it today?" Craig wondered aloud, drawing his hand over his rough and fatigued face.

Ben gazed down at his cumbersome wristwatch. "Monday, September 10th."

A further silence ensued before Craig noted without emotion, "It's my thirtieth birthday today."

"Many happy returns," said Ben, lifting the bottle of warm, stale water he kept at his side and toasting his friend.

Shortly thereafter Ben's ears began to twitch. Then suddenly, he leapt to his feet and dashed across to the shutter, peering through the narrow slits as best he could. The sound of engines revving up could be heard in the street below. Furthermore, he could just make out the sinister silhouettes of soldiers.

"Hell! It's the Iraqis. Get down!"

They both hit the floor, Craig listening through the floorboards as the master of the house in the room below desperately explained himself to whoever had summoned him to the door.

"Someone's betrayed us. They know we're here!" Ben whispered with alarm, piecing together the dialogue.

All of a sudden, the sound of boots marching up the stairs drove the two men to their feet again, just in time to witness the door of the room being kicked open and a posse of soldiers bursting in. Their commanding officer strode forward and signalled to his men to grab Ben and Craig, who did not resist, even when the soldiers shoved them forcefully down the stairs and out into the street, where's Ben's friend and his family were already standing, hands in the air, against the wall of the house opposite. Ben tried to plead with the officer, but his cries went unheard. Instead their hands were tied behind their backs and the two men were pushed to their knees, the rifles of the guards aimed menacingly at their heads. A further conversation ensued, the officer demanding details of who they were and what they were doing. Ben answered as best he could before the officer strolled round to Craig and grunted some question in Arabic.

"CIA?" he tried to suggest with his crude command of English. Meanwhile, Ben struggled to put the record straight, but this infuriated the commander, who pulverised the journalist in the stomach with a cracking blow from his boot.

"We're not spies!" Craig pleaded pathetically. Never had he experienced the terror of death so intimately before. He began to weep, imploring the officer, "Businessman! Businessman!"

"No, spies! You spies! CIA!" the officer taunted him, curling the barrel of his pistol through Craig's curious blond locks. "Iraqi soldiers kill CIA!"

Ben's friend himself tried to intervene on behalf of the Westerners, interceding with the officer, who turned and yelled at him. Then he took his pistol and holed the man through the forehead, the wall against which he had been standing suddenly splashed with scarlet as he was catapulted backwards and slumped to the ground.

By now, Craig was almost fainting with fear. Ben was still doubled up in the street, so that the Iraqi officer's attention turned to the wife and her three petrified children, wailing and crying as they beheld the lifeless body of their father. Craig didn't dare look round as he felt the barrel of one of the soldier's rifles digging into his scalp, an itchy finger on the trigger the other end. There was a struggle, some pleas in Arabic, and Craig guessed he knew what was happening – hearing two of the soldiers hurry over to hold the woman down. For several minutes, there was grunting and heaving, the woman's demented screams gradually growing less urgent as she settled into her humiliation. The children continued to cry pitifully. Finally, when primal urges had been satisfied, Craig heard the officer readjust his clothing. Then there was a solid click and shot number two echoed down the street. The children's cries grew agonisingly desperate. Shot three and shot four terminated all cries, except those of the tiniest infant, who carried wailing until shot five – when all fell silent.

Craig knew this was the end; he should never have listened to his companion's daring schemes. The only words of comfort he could summon to mind he now issued, his lips trembling, his voice stuttering, his innards churning up as he watched the officer approach out of the corner of his eye.

"The LORD is my shepherd, I shall not want. He makes me lie down in green pastures, he leads me beside quiet waters..." he quivered prayerfully.

****

"...Surely goodness and mercy will follow me, and I will dwell in the house of the Lord forever."

Scott Eversley finished reading and stared down solemnly at the weighty pulpit bible that he now closed, pausing for reflection before he looked up at his congregation.

"The Psalmist David wrote those words at that point in his life when all seemed lost. In the mountains of Judea, where he dwelled, there are crevasses in the rocks that are so dark, so narrow and so forbidding that for a shepherd boy like David to have to steal inside to rescue a lost sheep is almost to walk "through the valley of the shadow of death". And I believe tonight that one of our number is also walking through that same dark, narrow, forbidding valley," he said, emphasising each grim adjective.

It was obvious to whom he was alluding. Nikki listened anxiously from a few rows back, trying to hide any sign of self-consciousness as a terrible hush blanketed the packed church. Elaine Joyner cast her eyes sideways, laying a reassuring hand on that of her friend.

"We have no idea why God permits some Christians to suffer," the pastor admitted. "But we are sure of this: they are never called on to bear such suffering alone. No, He is there in the midst of it all to encourage, to strengthen, and to reveal the full measure of His power and majesty and love. And nobody, least of all some mortal man, some evil dictator, can ever come between a Christian and his God. *"Who shall separate us from the love of God? Shall trouble or hardship or persecution or famine or nakedness or danger or sword? No, in all these things we are more than conquerors through him who loved us.*

"For I am convinced," Scott thundered as he gripped his pulpit and quoted from Paul's epistle to the Romans, *"that neither death nor life, neither angels nor demons, neither present nor the future, neither height nor depth nor anything else in creation will be able to separate us from the love of God that is in Christ Jesus our Lord!"*

****

"Where are we?" Craig asked from the bunk on which he was spread out, staring up at the ceiling from which a solitary light bulb was dangling – as if to symbolise the bleakness of the tiny storeroom in which they were being held.

"I don't know," Ben replied, peering past the bars of the tiny window to behold the mountainous backdrop to the little cluster of plain-looking building that nestled in the valley to form their prison. "It appears to be some sort of factory. It must possess some strategic significance to the Iraqis; or else why would they have spared us and transported us hundreds of miles up into the mountains."

"It'll be my wedding anniversary soon," Craig proffered.

Ben, meanwhile, returned from his survey of their surroundings and sat back down on his own bunk, tempted to try the mush on his feeding tray, only to decide that today's offering (probably yesterday's offering warmed up) wasn't particularly appetising.

"How much longer, Lord?" Craig meanwhile found himself muttering under his breath.

He felt the coarseness of his face, and that seemed to remind him that there was always the possibility that he might never see England again. He leant against the wall, the plaster flaking as he slid himself down to the bare stone floor.

****

"NO! NO! NO!"

The response could hardly have been more emphatic. It now seemed certain that whatever her other European partners decided to do, Britain would definitely not be 'catching the train now departing the station', as one senior cabinet minister had described the Delors plan. Meanwhile, as Mrs Thatcher was now cheered on by Bruges Group Euro-sceptics on her own backbenches for having offered the House of Commons this concise summary of her own thoughts on 'ever-closer union', that same senior cabinet minister finally decided that he could no longer go on onerously supporting a line of argument he considered both fatuous and self-defeating. And so, on Thursday, November 1st, Sir Geoffrey Howe resigned as Leader of the House of Commons.

****

They both entered the room with just a little trepidation, unsure of exactly what to expect of the party they'd been invited to. The large hall was bursting with all kinds of different people: gentlemen in expensive suits; the Mayor resplendent in his insignia of office; a group of Sikhs in turbans; the local police superintendent;

a Rastafarian illuminated by his shining eyes and milk-white teeth; and an assortment of clergymen.

"Hello, can I help you?" a young lady asked as they passed through the doors.

"Yes. We've come to say goodbye to Sam Fletcher... there, that's us," said one of the visitors pointing down to the list of names on the table in front of her.

"Ah, yes. Pastor Scott Eversley... And Miss Nicola Anderson."

"It's 'Mrs', actually," Nikki blushed.

The woman stared up at her; in Gunsbridge of late, the name Anderson plainly meant something. She smiled sympathetically and altered Nikki's badge accordingly. Then she pointed them into the hall.

"Just help yourself to the wine and feel free to mingle. Sam's on his way round to say farewell to everyone."

The two evangelicals felt slightly self-conscious as they lifted their glasses of grapefruit juice from the table and located a corner of the room from where to watch the guests chatting merrily away. Just then, Scott noticed someone he knew and flashed his eyebrows in acknowledgement, prompting a slim, bespectacled clergyman to start snaking a path through the other guests towards them.

"Dave! How are you?" Scott enthused. "Nikki, I don't think you know the Reverend Dave Grey, do you?"

"Er, let me see... the face is familiar. Yes, the *Gunsbridge Alive '85* crusade!" she smiled.

"That's right," Dave replied. "By the way, you're the wife of that businessman trapped in Iraq, aren't you?"

Nikki knew it was inevitable that someone would bring up the fate of her husband. She tried to mask the pain as best she could, offering her smile and a few platitudes to ease them onto the next subject.

"Yes," Dave sighed, "I've worked with Sam for years now. He's always taken an interest in our pastoral work."

"Yes. There are a lot of people here that I've never seen before," Scott confided, casting his eyes over Sam's motley collection of well-wishers.

"Oh, you probably have," Dave joked. "Over there, that's Terry Johnson, MP for Gunsbridge North, together with Clive Bell, their new prospective candidate. I hear they did invite James Whitney, the town's other MP, but he's away on a parliamentary delegation to Australia at the moment. And, of course, *his* replacement is now serving time in Wormwood Scrubs!" Dave tittered in an irreverent reference to Oliver Lyons final denouement amidst the anger and recriminations of his constituency party.

"Then over there, that's Jane Allsop. She used to be chairwoman of the Community Services Committee until Labour regained overall control of the Council. Then they appointed Robert Bradleigh – well, I say Robert Bradleigh, but everyone calls him 'Brad'. His mother attends our church."

Brad was accompanying a bearded gentleman around the room. As they edged past some people to greet Dave and Scott, Nikki suddenly caught sight of the tall, sable-haired councillor, who in turn caught sight of her. Without removing his gaze from upon her, he listened as Dave introduced them all. Brad broke away briefly to shake the pastor's hand before returning to smile at the pretty female guest.

"Delighted to meet you," he said, captivated by her smile. Then he continued, "Aren't you...?"

"Yes, I am!" she beamed, quite taken by the superlative charmer.

"Well, well! I always knew Craig had an eye for a good-looking girl. You see, I used to hang around with him at school. I always used to be envious because all the best-looking girls used to hover around him. Now I can see that he has chosen *the* best-looking girl to be his wife!"

Such flattery was plainly working on Nikki. She found herself not really listening to Brad as he introduced Sam Fletcher, who grinned through his grey beard at her, preferring instead to look Brad up and down and wonder why such a fine, strapping young man had not himself been able to rival her husband in attracting the attention of women. He must be understating matters, she decided. Gradually, Scott, Dave and Sam Fletcher began sharing gossip together, enabling Brad to return to addressing Nikki.

"Tell me," he frowned, "have you heard any news about how he is?"

"The Foreign Office reckon he's probably being held somewhere in the north of the country; on an air base or a weapons factory. But that's all they can say at the moment."

"I'm sorry. I hope they get him out; indeed get them all out! One thing is certain though: he'll never be able to walk down the street again. He's almost a hero in this town, what with all the media coverage his plight has been receiving."

"I didn't realise that you were chairman of Community Services," Nikki confessed, even though Craig had told her quite a bit about his old school pal.

"Yes, since June. There was another round of left-right in-fighting going on in Gunsbridge Labour circles. I think Tom McKerrick's was trying to ensure that I stayed on his side of the fence. Politics can be a topsy-turvy world, as I'm sure Craig would tell you. You know, it was wicked what they did to him; the selection I mean. I just hope they've learned their lesson after that Lyons bloke was sent down."

Nikki wasn't a political animal to the extent that she could identify with the cut-and-thrust world of policy differences within Gunsbridge Labour Party, or the wheeling-and-dealings of their Tory rivals that Brad now ruminated on. Slowly he began to sense this, and so subtly manoeuvred the conversation back onto territory that was of more mutual concern.

"So what's Craig told you about me, eh?" he teased her.

"He told me how much he admires your sincerity. In fact, he's often told me that if he wasn't a Conservative, he'd vote for you," she smiled. Though flattered, Brad struggled to control a sudden flush of guilt about whether he really deserved such an accolade. Nikki knew nothing of this, and so continued "...unlike Jane Allsop, who he's always been very suspicious of."

"Yes. 'Goldilocks'. She's over there," Brad huffed, pointing across the room with his empty wine glass to the vivacious young blonde girl who both he and Craig had come to fear and distrust.

Meanwhile, Sam began to drift away from them. Brad sensed it was time to catch up lest he lose sight of the jolly little man in the throngs of people anxious to shake his hand and bid him farewell. He excused himself to Nikki, who smiled understandingly, idly reflecting on what might have been if, instead of evangelising Craig on that fateful night, she'd called on his handsome rival instead!

"Excuse me," a genteel voice echoed in her ear. She turned about to find an attractive, dark-haired woman about to offer her a hand. "Are you Craig Anderson's wife, by any chance?"

"I am indeed," said Nikki, slipping her own hand inside it, certain that she recognised the face to which it belonged.

"I thought you were. I'm Alannah James. For my sins, I'm prospective Labour candidate in your constituency; but more to the point, I also went to the same university as Craig. In fact, we used to argue politics together in the student union debates."

"Oh yes. Craig often recalls those days. How you used to run rings around him in debate."

The two girls shared amusement at such distant memories and began to feel a little more relaxed in each other's company. Alannah put her slender hand to her lips and tried to recall where she'd seen Nikki before. "Hold on, you were there too! Weren't you one of the Christian Union people?" she asked.

"That's right. Nowadays, I'm the youth leader at Gunsbridge Elim Church. I guess that's why I'm here. I've always been grateful to Sam for the support of the Community Services people in helping us with grants towards our sports and recreational activities."

Just then, the Mayor mounted the stage and began to test the microphone, waiting for silence to descend on the gathering before addressing them.

"Anyway, good luck with the youth work, and I hope he'll be back with you soon. Tell him I often think about him," Alannah hurriedly concluded.

Meanwhile, in the to-ing-and-fro-ing Scott and Nikki somehow found themselves washed up again in the centre of the room. As they did so, the Mayor, who this year was Walter Pugh, stuttered some platitudes before eventually handing over to the Chairman of the Community Services, who edged up to the microphone.

"Thank you, ladies and gentlemen," Brad opened, looking and sounding every inch like the statesman Nikki thought he deserved to be. She listened to him with interest as he continued.

"The Mayor has rightly explained why we're all here this evening. It's a farewell party; but it's also a celebration. Tonight, we're saying goodbye to Sam Fletcher and good luck in his retirement. And we're also celebrating the twenty-five years he's been with Gunsbridge Borough Council..."

Brad spoke eloquently of the part this dapper, unassuming man had played in helping youth groups, community associations and the arts. Nikki was glad she'd come after all, despite the fact that during the speech, her eyes happened to meet up with those of the shadow chairman of Community Services. Dick Lovelace looked at her uncomfortably for a split second before turning away, consciously trying not to look her way again.

"...And it only remains for me to say what a superb and visionary public servant we have been privileged to have at the helm of the CSD. Thank you, Sam; and all the best during a long and happy retirement."

The applause was warm and genuine, and Sam was overcome by the gratitude of his friends and acquaintances. Then, unexpectedly, Brad returned to the microphone and waited until the cheers had abated.

"Mr Mayor, there is one final thing I'd like to say before I hand over to Sam to say a few words of his own. Community Services has always been about helping to get the best out of the human beings this town is blessed to possess. To that end, I know that his successor will want to continue to build on Sam's good work, and will be eager to work with the town's various community groups. Together I hope we can all help create that sense of community and civic pride in our town, even though we're living through difficult times in local government.

"But, you know, we also owe a tremendous debt of gratitude to the local business community in this town, who often sponsor the various youth and community activities that help to foster that sense of civic pride. And I, personally, would like to pay tribute to one special businessman to whom I believe this whole town owes an enormous debt of gratitude; and who, even had we invited him, unfortunately could not have joined us tonight.

"I've known Craig Anderson ever since we were at school together. And I guess that we sensed even then that we both harboured a secret longing to become active in the politics of this town – he on one side of the divide, me on the other. Yet tonight, I think we local politicians should all lay aside our party differences and pray in earnest for the release of Craig Anderson from the cruel captivity that has befallen him."

A cheer went up and applause broke out while Brad paused to find an appropriate conclusion for his touching message. He continued, "For whatever we have done for the people of Gunsbridge as councillors or community leaders; or whatever Sam has done as a dedicated servant of this Council; Craig Anderson, by his long periods away on behalf of this town's biggest employer, has done just as much, if not more. That is why I say to you, Nicola," he explained, looking down at her with all the sincerity he could muster, "we're all with you. We're all with Craig, wherever he may be tonight. We all pray that he will be back at your side before too long."

Nikki felt a twinge inside her. Tears began to swell in those sparkling brown eyes as the whole gathering turned to reinforce Brad's good wishes with their own. She didn't know how to respond, and so Scott offered her a handkerchief. She tried to smile and thank them whilst dabbing away the tears. Alannah moved in from behind to cast an arm around her shoulder, hugging her gently.

Brad was meanwhile gazing down at Dick Lovelace, who sensed what he was being told. As Nikki smiled once more, wiping away the tears streaming down her face, she also caught sight of the crusty old councillor as he glanced about to observe the emotional scenes for himself. She unleashed a gracious smile for him personally. He seemed to long to be able to smile back in return. Yet something within him would not permit him to. Caught between the Scylla of Brad's glare and the Charybdis of Nikki's forgiving smile, he could bear it no longer, and shuffled out of the room without waiting to hear Sam thank his guests for their kind words.

****

"I must be the first minister in history to have resigned because he was *in agreement* with Government policy!"

So joked Sir Geoffrey Howe, who rose to address a House of Commons positively intoxicated with the anticipation that, on this afternoon of November 13th 1990, history was somehow in the making.

He seemed such an odd vessel to instil such expectation in this august chamber. Calm, monotone, polite and gracious, his style was a world removed from the acid wit of Lloyd George, the Olympian oratory of Churchill, or even the abrasive self-righteousness of the woman whose fortunes he had done so much to shape. 'Like being savaged by a dead sheep' was how someone had once cuttingly described an encounter with the downbeat former chancellor. Now, without even raising his voice to express the indignation that had fermented within him, Sir Geoffrey was about to prove that he was more than capable of mauling the carnivorous leader of the Tory pack.

It was a flawless performance. Before her own very eyes the Prime Minister had been ridiculed as wanting to "retreat into a ghetto of sentimentality about our past", to use Sir Geoffrey's damning phrase. Suffice to say, 'Bruges' backbenchers were furious at an attack on someone who they saw as the very last bulwark left defending the British people from the insidious and all-pervasive cancer of a European super-state. Yet they sensed it was not for them that he saved his closing words as a reminder that "the time has come for others to consider their own response to the tragic conflict of loyalties with which I have, myself, wrestled for perhaps far too long."

****

Craig paced about the cell restlessly, occasionally glancing out of the window, clinging to the bars to see what constellations the black night sky might have thrown together. It wasn't that he felt like screaming or banging his head against the wall of the bare room – although he did. It wasn't that he had driven himself silly trying to envisage what combination of circumstances might one day lead to his release from this soul-destroying confinement – although he had. It wasn't even that he desperately missed Nikki; and that he yearned to feel her soft, gentle fingers against his face, or admire the sweetness of her smile and the glow of those gorgeous brown eyes just one more time – although it ached to just think about her. No, he just felt it in his bones that back home something big, something dramatic, something of cardinal significance, was about to happen. Yet here he was – thousands of miles from home, imprisoned and alone.

****

He stood erect and purposeful as he strode onto the steps of his London home, the newsmen gathered round in a throng lapping up those fateful words that he now read out from a prepared statement.

"I am persuaded that I now have a better prospect than Mrs Thatcher of leading the Conservatives to a fourth electoral victory..."

And so Michael Heseltine had thrown down the gauntlet, confident that his appointment with destiny had finally arrived. To be sure, the odds facing him would be tough. In his favour was his reputation as a vivacious performer in the House and on the hustings. His downside was that, despite his long and assiduous cultivation of the party grassroots, he was anathema to the many activists on the right wing of the Conservative Party. He would inevitably pay a high price for humiliating someone who had not only delivered them three historic election victories, but also made them feel proud again to call themselves Conservatives. "I fight, and I fight to win," the Lady reminded the Pretender defiantly.

****

It was already dark by the time the big green Boeing 747 gently touched down. Everyone held their breaths, standing at the windows transfixed by the plane as it came to a halt on the perimeter of the airport and began to taxi slowly back to the terminal building.

To one young onlooker, this was a very precious moment. It was as if the modern-day 'Pharaoh' in Baghdad had been ordered from above to release the 'Israelites'; and here they were, the final plane-load of the remaining 'human shields' about to step down on British soil for the first time in almost five months.

Suddenly, he was there! He looked tired and slightly bewildered, but was smiling even so. Then he saw her! For a moment, it was as if there was no one else there in the concourse; no relatives waving gladly, no cameramen clicking frantically, no policemen patrolling discreetly. In that tender moment, their eyes locked. Then they rushed headlong into each other's arms and let the tears burst forth like a torrent. He squeezed her so tight that she was hauled up off her feet.

Eventually Craig and Nikki made their way out past the journalists rushing forward upon the freed hostages. Before long, it was Craig's turn to express what was on his heart: yes, it was good to be back; yes, he had missed his wife; yes, he had witnessed atrocities; yes, his faith had seen him through it all.

They were about to continue down the escalator when a sudden urge gripped Craig. The politician in him (which had lay dormant during his incarceration) suddenly bubbled up when the realisation hit him that the eyes of the world were upon him. He rose to the occasion instinctively.

"...And three cheers for our prime minister, Margaret Thatcher," he cried, "one of the greatest prime ministers in our history. Long may she remain leader of this great country of ours!"

The journalists looked at one another slightly perplexed; but none of them ventured to enlighten him. Instead they moved on to accost the remaining exhausted passengers.

"I love you, Nikki. I don't ever want to leave you again," Craig wept quietly, arm-in-arm with the girl he adored.

She nestled under his shoulder, squeezing him possessively. "I love you too, Craig... By the way," she then ventured cautiously, "about Mrs Thatcher: there's something I think I ought to tell you..."

19 SCANDAL

"Ladies and gentlemen," said Sarah Packington, upon assuming the chair, "before I introduce the final item on the agenda of our AGM, I would like to thank everyone who supported my nomination for the chairmanship of this constituency association. I would also like to thank my predecessor, Dick Lovelace, for the sterling work he has put in during an extraordinarily challenging three years of office. I know that my debt of gratitude to him will be shared by all the members gathered here tonight."

Well, not quite. As the slim, attractive physician smiled and led the applause for the humbled ex-marine, a sizeable body of the assembly gave only half-hearted applause, if that. Undeterred, she pressed on, saying, "I will now call upon our brand new prospective candidate, a man who needs no introduction. Ladies and gentlemen, I give you the next member of Parliament for Gunsbridge South – Mr Craig Anderson!"

There was general applause for Craig, who rose and toyed with his jacket pockets in the manner of political orators the world over. The applause came especially from the otherwise reticent anti-Lovelace faction. For Craig though, it was a proud moment, one he'd yearned for ever since he'd first wandered into a YC meeting in this very same opulently-appointed function room twelve years earlier. Nikki sat at his side at the head table, gazing up at him, knowing that this was where he was destined to be. How silly of either of them to have ever doubted it.

"Ladies and gentlemen, friends, colleagues, fellow Conservatives," he opened confidently. "It says somewhere in the Good Book '*behold all things are become new!*' And I guess that just about describes where we find our party and our country at this point in time. The world has changed beyond recognition since I last had an opportunity to attend an AGM two years ago: revolutions have swept socialism from Eastern Europe; we now have a new prime minister; and, of course, we've had our own 'little local difficulties' here in Gunsbridge South."

It was a painful episode, yet Craig felt it only right to exorcise it right at the very start of his first official address as their candidate. His triumphant return from the Middle East, complete with a deluge of media coverage and interviews, had confirmed his status as a local celebrity and made his selection for the seat that had been so cruelly denied him upon an earlier occasion virtually assured. Little opposition had in the end materialised from the 'Maywood Heath Mafia', who were humiliated and chastened by the ignominious 'Lyons' debacle.

A few places to his right sat Dick Lovelace, arms folded. Craig now turned to him and graciously complimented him on his leadership of the Association. The new candidate hoped he had captured the mood of the evening. He smiled graciously at members of the 'Mafia', as well as at Gerry Roberts – a man not smitten by Craig's unnatural propensity for Christian charity, who had warned him that he had effortlessly captured the nomination because of his media popularity and not as a result of any sudden 'Damascus Road' conversion on the part of Councillors Brereton, Lovelace and Gainsborough.

That aside, Craig was doing that which he loved best of all: rallying the faithful with some good old-fashioned political rhetoric. And they seemed to be enjoying it, enthusing and cheering as he commended to them John Major and his new cabinet. James Whitney sat there well pleased, cognisant that he would be bequeathing his seat to a fine pair of hands. Maybe the candidate had momentarily dispelled the doubts with his witticisms and *tour-de-horizons*. Yet while he spoke these words of encouragement, he became all too aware of the magnitude of the task facing him. He looked around the room one final time whilst summing up. Some of the faces that stared back at him encouraged him to believe that they would go to the ends of the Earth to see him elected: Gerry Roberts, Des Billingham, sweet little Lucy Lambert; as well as the voluble new councillor for Lower Henley, Julie King (who had captured the seat from that neanderthal Labour councillor, Colin Tyler, the previous year, after his campaign against paying his poll tax had backfired upon him). Then there were those whose synthetic expressions probably concealed all manner of antagonisms and resentments: Dick Lovelace – cold, unsmiling and bitter; Peter Brereton – cold, supercilious and scheming; as well as Elizabeth Gainsborough – cold, enigmatic and ashamed. Why exactly did they harbour such animosity towards him? he agonised to himself.

****

"I therefore declare that the result for the Lower Henley ward is as follows... Brevitt – Keith Andrew (Labour Party), 1089 votes..."

The customary cheers went up from the phalanx of Labour supporters, though they knew their man hadn't made it. Up on the stage behind the returning officer, Brad felt aggrieved that their candidate had failed to make inroads into the vote of that vexatious Elizabeth Gainsborough. Yet looking across the stage, he noted that neither she, nor her agent – none other than Craig Anderson himself – took any great delight in Labour's humiliation.

"...Gainsborough – Elizabeth Alexandra (Conservative Party), 1405 votes...."

She'd thrashed her socialist tormentors by a sound margin. However, with the Tory applause subsiding, Elizabeth's eyes glazed over. Craig swallowed hard. Brad watched the returning officer stare out into the cavernous civic auditorium.

"...Rawlings – Candy Helena Judith (Liberal Democrats), 1422 votes."

The small huddle of Liberal Democrats were overcome with joy, Jane Allsop lifting her candidate's arm aloft, presenting a generous photo opportunity for the press snapping and scribbling away down below them.

Craig wasn't really listening to the youthful victrix thanking her supporters. He had offered himself as Elizabeth's agent in the hope that such an act of magnanimity, tied in with the vote-pulling power of his own name, might have proved a timely prophylactic to the insidious march of Gunsbridge South Liberal Democrats, who had long been targeting Lower Henley as a prize. The result had proved to be a fatal haemorrhaging of Elizabeth's once-formidable personal vote. Of course, the known divisions within the local Tory Party hadn't helped much, Craig painfully recalling how difficult it had been to motivate party workers – even with him at the helm. Gerry Roberts, in particular, had been unwilling to offer much by way of his usual resourcefulness. And of course, neither had they been helped by the supreme ignominy of their new prime minister having to abandon the 'flagship' they called the Community Charge (and which everyone else had universally dubbed the Poll Tax!) just one year into its maiden voyage as a panacea for the woes of local government. All told, Craig had little to celebrate, aware that his party would be reduced to just sixteen seats on the new council. Inevitably, therefore, the local press now descended upon him.

"Mr Anderson, what are your thoughts on tonight's unfavourable results?" one of them quizzed him bluntly.

"It's disappointing," he pondered grimly, "But we're a fighting party, and we'll be back to reverse our losses."

"And losing Councillor Mrs Gainsborough; was that a shock?" asked another.

"Of course. She's a good councillor," he riposted defiantly. Personally though, it did at least eliminate a known antagonist from her power base, such as was left of it.

"Mr Anderson, I'm Sally Robinson from the *Gunsbridge Herald*," a bright young girl called out to him, "Do you think that her failure to be re-elected has damaged your own credibility, given that you've put your own name so visibly behind her campaign?"

He stopped and looked her up and down for a moment while she gripped her biro between her diamond white teeth, ready to note down his response.

"No, not in the least! I have every confidence that John Major will lead our party to its fourth election triumph," he insisted, conveniently sidestepping the question.

Yes, remember the one about the Poll Tax being fairer than the rates? Brad grinned to himself, seeing the eager young newshound looking less than convinced. Seeing the Labour councillor approach, she turned to descend upon him instead, eagerly joined by several other journalist colleagues. However, Brad seemed to listen to their questions only vaguely, his gaze panning out instead to survey the intriguing within his own party. There, gathered over by the final recount for Foxcotes ward, were all his old rivals: Sharif Khan, Gary Bennett, Ricky Serrano and Frances Graham; joined by the latest convert to the cause of uncompromising socialism, Colin Tyler – newly-elected once more, this time for the rock-solid Labour ward of Gunsbridge Central. Perhaps it galled Brad that his one-time protégé had been poached by a bunch of Militant rowdies, all laughing and joking together, occasionally looking his way as if to emphasise their plotting, scheming and vilifying. To look away was only for his eyes to alight instead upon Alannah James and her fiancé, busy cosying up to fellow party workers – a vista equally as galling to the tall, unsmiling councillor for Lower Henley.

"Councillor Bradleigh... Councillor Bradleigh..."

Finally, Brad drew his eyes away and returned to his media pursuers. "I'm sorry," he apologised.

"I said, are you still confident that you can return Alannah James for Gunsbridge South when a general election is called?" the *Herald's* petite little reporter asked him, repeating her question.

Brad swung back into action. "Watch us! Just watch us!" he sung, frowning to emphasise his grit. "We'll make her our next Member of Parliament alright, you'll see!"

His protestations failed to convince young Sally Robinson either, though she pressed him no further. Perhaps she'd followed the trajectory of his eyes as he cast an ambiguous glance over at his candidate, sensing that inwardly he loathed the bitch! Alannah had received extensive media coverage of late with her campaign to prevent Gunsbridge General Hospital from 'opting out' of NHS control. The party was obviously targeting this seat as a winnable one, and he couldn't help feeling bitter that somehow the Gunsbridge South that Alannah James now had within her grasp was by rights his own. As the press pack melted away, her brooding ex-lover decided to rejoin his wife instead, the couple bumping into Craig Anderson and his wife in the foyer.

"Bad luck, Craig," Brad commiserated him, employing all the sincerity he could muster at the end of an exhausting day campaigning.

Craig's decided to make no bones about his predicament, saying, "We knew it had to happen. Allsop and her band have been crawling all over our estates. Any other time we could have faced down their challenge."

"But not with a divided party, eh?" Brad suggested. Craig didn't deem to reply to what he guessed wasn't intended to be a snide remark, but one that stung nonetheless.

Brad took the hint, turning to his partner. "By the way, folks, I don't think you've met Wendy, my fiancée, before."

"Enchanted!" Craig smiled, shaking her hand and momentarily abandoning the evening's melancholy. He was in half a mind to kiss that tender white paw, but glanced at Nikki and thought better of it. Wendy was certainly a very beautiful woman; but – more to the point – those dark and determined blue eyes seemed to radiate a steely purposefulness. "I bet you keep him on his toes," he opined mischievously.

"Best place for him," Wendy grinned, intrigued that the Conservative PPC for her constituency was every bit the tall, handsome charmer she had been led to believe he was. Shame he hadn't been into left-wing politics when she had been twenty-one and single, she pondered wistfully.

Brad reclaimed his fiancée and, after exchanging a few more idle words, Craig led Nikki off down the corridor ahead of them. Brad couldn't resist concluding, "All the best, Craig. I'm counting on someone like you to bring Councillor Miss James down a peg or two."

His closing remark brought the wrath of his partner down upon him, Wendy digging him hard in the ribs, appalled at this verbalising of the atavistic loathing that reflected his true feelings towards his candidate. Donning a fierce mien, she dragged him off into a side recess off the main corridor to remonstrate with him. However, she had scarcely had time to raise her voice in anger before they were interrupted by a gruff, slurring voice from behind.

"Always rely on the youngsters, that's what I say!"

Turning, they noticed Dick Lovelace staring into space as he lounged in one of the low chairs that lined the alcove. He seemed slightly the worse for drink, Brad thought; though who could blame him. If anyone would be having his 'ass' kicked after tonight's fiasco, then the crusty old councillor for Amblehurst was probably first in line!

"Then it's a shame you never trusted your maxim, Dick," Brad chided him caustically. "Craig Anderson was destined for Gunsbridge South, and you knew it. So what if he does hold the 'wrong' views on the Europe."

Lovelace visibly gasped and sat up, all lethargy cast aside. "Europe! Europe! Oh, don't think I fought his nomination because he's into this 'monetary union' business," he snapped. "Oh no! And don't think I turned him down just because he fell out with Conway either. Oh no," he repeated adamantly, "Harry and I often exchanged words, especially over that 'Fun City' monstrosity," he insisted.

"So why the antagonism, eh, Dick?" Brad persisted indignantly. "Did the kid's opposition to hanging bug you?"

Lovelace shook his head slowly, conveying a certain reticence. "Oh no, sonny," the ex-commando continued, Brad becoming ever more impatient with each twitch of his albino moustache. Then Lovelace looked into his eyes once more, albeit gravely.

"You think the sun shines out of him, don't you?" he charged. "I can see he's pulled the old 'loving Christian couple' guise on you too!"

Brad looked at Wendy in utter puzzlement. What did the old man mean? Okay, Craig was a Christian; everybody knew that! Big deal!

"Let me tell you a secret, son," Lovelace confided, something he would never have done minus the whisky and dries. "He ain't what he seems. No way! You recall all those jokes in the council chamber about Neil Sharpe?"

"What? That he's knocking his constituency chairman's wife off on the side?" Brad sniggered.

"That's the one! Well, that's just a rumour. But I can tell you that the rumour originated with Anderson. Remember that night they opened the Trescott Park International Hotel? Well, he was at it then – all over her!" he staggered. "Of course, he was going around with her daughter for a time as well. And to think; there was the husband and father working himself into an early grave to get Anderson elected – hope against hope. He's such a nice bloke, David Sutton. Have you ever met him?"

Lovelace's casual enquiry enabled Brad to say that he hadn't, as well as to enquire "Is this general knowledge?"

"The people who matter know alright," he replied, implying principally Craig's detractors amongst the 'Maywood Heath Mafia', prompting Brad to ask why they had not gone public.

"He's a marvellous guy, David Sutton. Do anything for anybody. I wish we had him in South. Believe you me, I wanted to go public. You know me, Brad – I call a spade a bloody shovel! But we couldn't crucify David in the press. And anyway, we've had enough adverse publicity to last us a political lifetime recently."

There was a pause while Lovelace stared vacantly at the surrounding murals, time enough for Brad to digest the revelations he'd just heard and put together some semblance of a defence for his old school friend.

"Not Craig," he shook his head in disbelief, "Not the way you make it sound. I've known him for years. He's just not the adulterous type. I doubt if he even knew what sex was until Nikki showed him!"

Still Lovelace was not pacified. "No, I despise a man like that. You might not think highly of my generation, son, but at least we had some principles."

Brad had run out of things to say, utterly shocked and devastated by such scandalous goings-on. Lovelace had said all he intended to say, probably more. He stood up, a little unsteady, then turned and headed out into the night.

"If only they knew!" he sighed wistfully.

****

The billows crashed noisily against the sea wall, whipped up by the stiff sea breeze blowing onshore. Marvelling at the pounding of the leaden swell, Brad lingered along the promenade, his morning paper rolled up and protruding conspicuously from his back pocket. There he watched the sun's outline attempting to break open the morning from behind an ominous mass of dark clouds, symbolic perhaps of how, out of the gloom of past failures, he had fashioned one Miss Wendy Baker into a new Mrs Wendy Bradleigh. This time he was older, wiser and more certain he had discovered a conducive match, not just for himself but also for those precious political ambitions too.

The spray seared his face while he gazed out to sea. When the honeymoon was over, he would recommence his search for a parliamentary seat, an endeavour that had still yet to bear fruit. Yet he was convinced that his chairmanship of Community Services was the key to those ambitions being realised. During her brief chairmanship, Jane Allsop had transformed an otherwise mundane, low priority committee into a high profile and influential platform for wooing important sections of the community. Brad was now setting about using this power base for his own ends. No doubt 'Goldilocks' had not intended that he should be the beneficiary of such a bounty, but he was. His face was becoming increasingly well-known across town by virtue of the youth festivals, street carnivals and grants to voluntary bodies that now bore his name – almost as well-known as those of Craig Anderson and Alannah James in fact.

He drifted back over the footbridge to the little hotel that nestled under the cliff tops, wandered past the pubescent waiters serving breakfast in the dining room, climbed the stairs to the top floor, and entered into his room. There he cast his eyes upon Wendy, sat up in bed and reading a paperback thriller. She turned to him and shook her hair, thrusting her fingers through that wild, ruddy mane.

"You don't *have* to get up early, you know. This is your honeymoon too," she chirped.

"Force of habit," was Brad's excuse. "Besides, you were fast asleep!" he continued, shedding his jacket onto a convenient coat hook. Then he sat down on the bed beside her and opened out his slightly moist newspaper, absorbing the simple pleasure of his new wife trailing her fingers through his hair whilst he scanned down the print. She observed him pensively, trying to fathom out which gears and cogs were crunching and grinding beneath his furrowed brow.

"Anything interesting in there?" she smiled, perching her hands on his firm right shoulder and alighting her chin upon them. There she remained until he suddenly answered her, voice animated with excitement.

"'*THE LEADER, HIS LOVER AND THE YACHT,*'" he commenced in disbelief, reading aloud the headline. "'*Local Tories in Gunsbridge in the West Midlands were today stunned to discover that the leader of the Conservative opposition on the local council, Peter Brereton, has been engaged in a longstanding affair with former councillor and fellow party worker Mrs Elizabeth Gainsborough. Brereton, aged fifty-two, was photographed above with his lover on a yacht in Marbella, the culmination of a two-month investigation by the local* Gunsbridge Herald *newspaper into the secret life of the wealthy industrialist...*' then it goes on to mention the infighting over Craig's nomination and the fraud conviction of Oliver Lyons."

Wendy grabbed a corner of the page and began to compete for a view, especially when Brad pointed out a picture of her former chair of Social Services sunbathing topless beside Brereton on the foredeck of some expensive-looking vessel.

Brad tried to take in the magnitude of Brereton's misfortunes, which, by implication, were also those of his hapless candidate, Craig Anderson. Wendy had meanwhile risen from the nuptial bed and had wandered into the bathroom. Still scanning the fine print, from the corner of his eye Brad noticed her peel off her top and begin to test the water of the shower. Reluctantly laying the newspaper down, he began to make his way towards the sound, leaning against the door and observing the outline of his wife's fabulous little figure through the shower curtain.

"You coming in?" Wendy asked.

He rapidly divested and then thrust open the curtain. Inside, Wendy had her back to him, her delightful rear end exposed as she allowed the vaporous torrent to gush over her. She realised he was there and turned about slowly, her rubicund crown saturated with a multitude of tiny droplets that cascaded down her soft, pink body, and over and around her full, rotund breasts. She looked him in the eye with seductive defiance. Then, excitedly, she watched while he advanced under the powerful spray and took her in his arms.

****

THE GUNSBRIDGE HERALD
Thursday, August 22nd 1991
Evening Edition - Still only 26p

YACHT LINKS TRAIL OF CORRUPTION
The 'Herald' has discovered today that the yacht in Marbella that served as an exclusive retreat for Conservative leader of Gunsbridge Council, Peter Brereton, and his lover, former councillor Elizabeth Gainsborough, was owned and provided by recently bankrupted millionaire property developer Harry Conway. Furthermore, Brereton had substantial investment links with the local tycoon that were not disclosed when controversial planning applications were discussed for both the Trescott Park retail park and the abandoned 'Fun City' project...
FULL ENQUIRY ESSENTIAL, SAYS LABOUR
Prospective Labour candidate for Gunsbridge South, Alannah James, has called for a full investigation into the 'Trescott Park Scandal', and how developer Harry Conway used secret Masonic connections, as well as outright bribery, to influence vital planning decisions. Meanwhile, Liberal Democrat spokesperson Jane Allsop has warned that both main parties will be tarred by this scandal unless they come clean over the extent of their members' involvement in these murky dealings...
COUP OVER: RUSSIA DUMPS COMMUNISM
Hard on the heels of the victory of the democratic forces, led by Russian president Boris Yeltsin, the statue of Felix Dzerzhinsky - founder of the Soviet secret police - has been toppled from outside the KGB headquarters in Moscow by excited crowds celebrating the smashing of the coup against Mikhail Gorbachev...

****

They all shook hands across the big round table that filled the compact little studio, and were invited to don their respective headphones to take the sound check. Alannah slipped the device careful onto her head, eyes cast heavenward as she eased it into a comfortable position before smiling at her interviewer and assuring her all was fine. Jane Allsop shook her golden mane free before pulling the phones apart and allowing them to spring back into place. She, too, smiled confidently.

"I'm sorry, Craig, but it looks like you're the thorn between three roses," the interviewer joked.

The Conservative candidate smiled back, but didn't let on that he wasn't exactly sorry to be the sole man sealed in a room with three such attractive young ladies. Each one waited patiently while some reflective ballad from Deacon Blue gave way to the familiar *Gunsbridge Sound* news jingle. Craig took the opportunity to look up from his preoccupations and break the air of expectation.

"By the way," he opened, glancing earnestly to each of them in turn, "I want it understood that on no account am I venturing any comment on what has happened regarding Peter Brereton and all that. It is an unfortunate local scandal that I, personally, am not a party to. I've come here tonight to debate national issues and expound my party's national policies. Is that clear?"

The pretty interviewer looked slightly taken aback by the bluntness of his demand and so turned instead to his opponents. Alannah rested her elbows on the table and rubbed her hands together slowly before propping her chin up on the apex she had formed with her bunched-up fingers.

"Suits me," she said crisply, shrugging her shoulders at the same time.

"No problem, Craig," Jane Allsop grinned mischievously. "That still leaves us plenty of rope to hang you with!"

Glad that that little matter was resolved, Craig waited while the weather report was read out. He could take heart that his opponents were backing off slightly as revelations emerged that some Labour councillors were not entirely above suspicion. Masonic influence – probably another reason why the 'Maywood Heath Mafia' had never liked him, this unclubbable Christian mused to himself quietly.

"Ten seconds to go..." the producer called to them all. They each sat up to attention and began to comport themselves in the demeanour they thought becoming to the next Member of Parliament for Gunsbridge South. "...Okay, folks, we're rolling!"

"Good evening," the presenter chirped into her microphone, launching straight into her introduction, "Welcome to this week's edition of *Gunsbridge Matters*. I'm Melanie Brindle; and tonight, with election fever increasingly in the air, we've invited Gunsbridge South's three prospective parliamentary candidates into the studio to talk about why you should be catching that fever too. Craig Anderson is the Conservative Party's choice; never a stranger to controversy," she noted tongue-in-cheek, casting a cheeky glance his way, "he's probably better known on account of his five-month captivity during the Gulf War." She turned away, continuing, "Jane Allsop is Liberal Democrat councillor for Foxcotes ward; and a tireless practitioner of what she calls 'grassroots politics'. And finally, Alannah James is Labour councillor for Barnwood; who has made a name for herself with her outspoken opposition to NHS 'opting out'. The number to call if you want to put a question to any of our guests is Gunsbridge 2-4-5-7-7-7, that's Gunsbridge 2-4-5-7-7-7. Our lines are now open to take your calls."

Melanie then ran through a summary of key issues for the benefit of the listeners, which gave Craig the opportunity to survey his opponents for the first time at close quarters. Jane Allsop was busy scribbling away some final additions to her notes when the presenter asked her to briefly outline the themes the Liberal Democrats would be pursuing.

"Thank you, Melanie. Of course, the real appeal of the Liberal Democrats rests on our still being the only real opposition to the Conservative Party..."

...Which was truly astounding news to her Labour opponent, who couldn't resist a discernable grin. Yes, Craig thought; the very audacity and determination of this bubbling young councillor was her greatest asset. And he had to accept that, this time round, the once-dismissible 'Goldilocks' was in serious danger of repeating the Democrats' triumph in Lower Henley at constituency level. He watched as she swiftly damned both main parties and pressed home her record of action in Gunsbridge, impressing upon her listeners that it was her full intention to carry on repeating this at national level if they would only lend her their votes. Alannah, meanwhile, was casting an astute and calculating glance at Craig.

"I think by now, Melanie," she calmly opened after being invited to follow on with the case for Labour, "that nobody in this country today can be in any doubt at all about the damage caused by twelve years of Tory rule..."

Craig was suddenly struck by a terrible feeling of *déjà-vu* as he watched her eloquently pick holes in his party's government, deploying a fearsome cocktail of charm, semantic precision and passion that carried him back to a sunny evening in June 1980 when they had last sparred together like this. To be sure, she'd matured physically, seeming ever more beautiful and graceful as the years had progressed. Yet she had also refined her debating style, perfecting the technique that now permitted that deep, haunting voice to deliver her message like an ineluctable song with such force and gusto. How God determines the seeming trivialities of life that ultimately shape one's perceptions of reality, Craig pondered philosophically, observing her oratory in full flow once more. What profound event in her childhood, or what sudden dawning insight, had set her upon the path she now trod? Had that seminal event or insight set her upon his own path, she could well have been a close colleague, or a friend, or even his lover – a fate he would not have been averse to accepting! Yet here she was; neither his companion, nor a close colleague nor, sadly, his lover; though true to the spirit of their varsity days, they remained on genuine, respectful terms. Rather, she was his rival – what really stood between him and the prize he had spent the intervening years coveting so intensely.

"Well, Melanie," he confided, commencing his own opening remarks, "contrary to what has been said, the Conservative Party is fully committed to..."

He was fighting for his political life and he felt the adrenalin surge inside him, compelling him to refute the arguments of his tormentors, and to go on the offensive with some powerful arguments of his own. Tonight was just one more battle in a war he was obsessed with not losing. He was determined that, however much he feared Jane Allsop's beguiling sophistry or Alannah's devastating logic, he would prevail – both tonight, and whenever the election campaign would commence in earnest.

"Right, I believe we have our first caller on Line Five," Melanie announced.

This particular voter was agitated and concerned about the state of the economy and she proved to be just one of many voters who sought to pit the three candidates against each other mercilessly. Maybe at home, or to those listening in on their car stereo as they cruised across town, this was just one more tedious barrage of the pre-election offensive. Yet, in the studio, the anxious young presenter could sense only too well that more was at stake to the belligerents than just a few intellectual 'brownie points'.

"...No, Alannah, I beg to differ. The Prime Minister never said that, it's just a..."

"...Look, the Labour Party has made its position crystal clear over..."

"...And, of course, it just proves that neither main party has the guts to..."

Finally, a Mr Matthew Watson – a college student from Amblehurst – brought up the question of the reform of the National Health Service, pitting Alannah and Craig together in a desperate attempt to win the evening.

"...Nonsense, Craig! And you know it!" she scoffed indignantly, increasingly irritated and scornful of her rival.

"No, it's not, Alannah. You opposed it on purely ideological ground!" he riposted sarcastically.

Determined not to have her convictions so trivialised by him, Alannah hit back hard, saying, "Listen, what the Tories are doing is a sham; yes, a sham! They're creating the illusion of action when what is needed desperately is more money – money that Labour will direct..."

"...On the contrary, we've given the NHS more money than ever before."

"No, you haven't!" Alannah maintained. "Craig, somehow I don't think the voters are able to square your statistics up with the evidence they see around them of cuts and closures."

Jane Allsop and Mr Watson concurred. All at once, Craig felt himself hemmed in like a cornered beast. Sensing impending humiliation, he knew he had to break out fast. Winning this debate obsessed Alannah too; she stared at him intently, hoping she had thus delivered one more deadly blow to her rival. Craig had other intentions though, and sprang back on his wits.

"No, Mr Watson, permit me to warn you about trusting the promises of Councillor Miss James' party. You see, they've been down this road before of promising to spend on public services just like they did in..."

"Can you be brief, Craig?" Melanie interrupted him sharply. "We're almost out of time now."

"...You see, as a young man of your age," he noted, feeling terribly old as he did so, "I remember how Labour was forced to go cap-in-hand to bail Britain out of this sort of folly..."

"Be quick, Craig!" Melanie fretted again, watching the clock. Alannah fretted also, though for a different reason. She was visibly witnessing her prey escape the net and just knew he was about to deliver a devastating blow of his own in the ten or so seconds of the programme that remained. Her facial expression turned dire as he fought off her attempts at interrupting him.

"...But, of course, they chose instead to cut investment in public services. Remember, Mr Watson, Labour will promise you the Earth, but in the end they will deliver nothing because a Labour government will always run out of someone else's money to spend!"

He'd just made it in time, leaving Melanie to race through her concluding remarks before the nine o'clock news jingle burst in and brought her phone-into an abrupt end. She gasped excitedly and cast off her headphones, thanking them all for joining her. Then they all stood up and shook hands across the table once more.

"I almost had you then," Alannah noted as she presented her slim feminine paw for his acknowledgement.

Craig appreciated that fact only too well, and was relieved that he'd outflanked her so masterfully. "Almost," he concurred. "Almost, but not quite!" he then smiled gleefully at his tormentor.

Alannah paused before motioning to exit the claustrophobic intensity of the studio. "*Touché*, Mr Anderson," she tutted regretfully, collecting up her papers, "*Touché!*"

****

It was to be the keynote speech to the Labour Party Conference that would propel Neil Kinnock on course for that illusive abode in Downing Street. The Leader of the Labour Party looked confident and relaxed as he strode up to the rostrum to offer the delegates his thoughts.

Alannah and her fiancé, Philip, together with Clive Bell and his wife, were huddled up towards the back of the cavernous Brighton Centre. Already their hopes, as well as those of their impatient leader, had been dashed – albeit temporarily – by cryptic leaks from Downing Street that there would be no election now until next spring. Even so, they took heart that their appointment with destiny had only been deferred. That said, Alannah was still annoyed with herself for having allowed Craig Anderson to wriggle off the hook during debate. Still, his days, like those of his government, were now well and truly numbered: there would soon be no place in the sun for the Conservative Party, despite Mrs Thatcher's fateful departure and the quiet jettisoning of some of her most cherished policies

Sometime during her idle musings, Alannah spotted Brad (along with the unmistakable ruddy mane of his new wife) somewhere down in the forward rows, and she pointed him out to Philip. Thereafter, she found herself glancing down at him occasionally. She deeply regretted how things had worked out between them. For all the hurt that he had occasioned upon her she still loved him in a funny old way. Though she'd never let on, it was she who had privately commended him to Tom McKerrick for the Community Services chair, of which she knew he would make a roaring success. Maybe one day she would pluck up the courage to tell him to his face that, for her part at least, their bitter feud was over. Meanwhile, Philip edged up alongside her and gently kissed her cheek reassuringly. She was at peace with herself now, for she possessed the love that she wanted most.

20 THE LAST HURRAH

With the frost draped cold and hoary all around them, the mourners stood impassively at the graveside while the coffin was slowly lowered into the ground. Craig pulled the collar of his sombre black overcoat tight around him, observing the proceedings from the background. It had been a long time since he'd last seen George Franklin; yet he'd felt compelled to come and witness this final farewell to his old friend and political mentor, who had died a broken man. Even so, there remained nothing else to do now but withdraw and maybe give thanks for the remembrance of the friends he'd known. Craig ambled back to his car, the silvery sleek Rover glistening with a thick coating of frost that had settled upon it. Driving back towards town, the fog began to disperse, a resplendent sun melting the heart of an otherwise cold and unforgiving day.

"You're listening to Gunsbridge Sound *on 94.8 FM. I'm Rajveen Dhillon; and this is the 'Midday Report' on Thursday, December 5th 1991... The headlines at midday so far... the trial has opened today of the defendants in the so-called 'Trescott Park Scandal'... Leader of Gunsbridge Council, Tom McKerrick, is to quit his job for health reasons... and an administrator has been appointed to run the companies once owned by disgraced newspaper publisher Robert Maxwell..."*

"Good afternoon," poured forth the news from his car stereo, *"Millionaire property developer Harry Conway and former Gunsbridge councillors Peter Brereton and Elizabeth Gainsborough today went on trial at Gunsbridge Crown Court accused of serious breaches of the Local Government Act. It is alleged that..."*

Craig could only sigh wearily. Elizabeth was another dear friend he'd 'lost' along the way. It still hurt to think of the circumstances in which their friendship had ended – she stabbing him in the back in order to propitiate her lover and his business cohort. Gerry had been right about her all along, and it offended the innocent sense of trust that had constituted one of Craig's more endearing, if at times tragic-comic, personality traits. He hoped that when the trial finished in a week or two (almost certainly in convictions), the whole sorry business would be quickly forgotten. Then again, maybe like all his other high hopes for Gunsbridge South, it would all just be bulldozed under more terrible headlines and tales of trust betrayed.

"Tom McKerrick is to step down as the leader of Gunsbridge Council's controlling Labour Group following several months of deteriorating health, exacerbated by the recent controversy over the 'Trescott Park Scandal'. It is widely expected that either the present deputy leader, Councillor Micky Preston, or the colourful chairman of Community Services, Councillor Robert Bradleigh,

will emerge as the new leader when the Labour Group reassembles after Christmas..."

Well, well, Craig thought. How far they'd both come since those distant days of debating politics at Gunsbridge College. Maybe they were both now within sight of their dreams. The vacant grin on his face as he guided the car back along the Worcester Road belied a few idle moments spent in carefree daydreaming of the metaphoric road that they had travelled so far along. Outside, a gentle breeze once more swept effortlessly through the long, tall trees that lined the roadside like a whispering phalanx.

Up on the horizon his eyes alighted upon another familiar milestone of his youth, of which he had opportunity to observe in more detail when the line of traffic ground to a halt at some road works. Drumming his fingers in time on the steering wheel while the oncoming vehicles streamed past, the memories all returned: for the battered old neon sign still read *Tropicana* (albeit minus the letter 'p'). His thoughts swept back to a warm, late summer evening in 1978; of cars screaming out of the darkness; of densely-packed bodies swaying to music on mezzanine balconies; of boys and girls and swirling lights; of crisp night air and quick romances. Noticing the lights change to green ahead, he acted upon a sudden impulse, and swung out of the line of traffic and up onto the car park of the faded old nightclub, halting over in a shaded corner and extinguishing the engine. Through the rear-view mirror he could see a group of people inspecting the sad, forgotten building, guided by an officious-looking figure in a hard hat. Craig decided to step outside and inspect the edifice for himself to see what remained of the boarded-up property, keeping a discreet distance from the others. Then he noticed someone familiar amongst the gathering. Brad also caught sight of his old friend; at the earliest opportunity, he broke free from his colleagues to wander over.

"What brings you here?" he muttered informally.

Craig shrugged his shoulders. "Just passing through. And you?"

"Site visit: to inspect progress on the new M44 motorway, and see how the plans to widen the Worcester Road will affect our own section of the route," Brad replied.

Craig stared up at the *Tropicana*, his mirror sunglasses catching the glare of the midday sun. "Ah, so that's why they closed this place down."

"Sure is: compulsory purchase order. Work commences next year; soon there'll be a six-lane motorway whistling through where once we used to spend all those carefree evenings."

Craig smiled, noting how Brad seemed already to be exhibiting the euphoria of being feted as the future leader of the Council. "Ah well," he couldn't resist sighing mischievously, "Let it never be said that the Government never spends any money on roads in Gunsbridge!"

Brad bore the aside with a grin. Not wishing to muddy such a moment smitten with nostalgia by talking mere politics, he asked his friend casually, "You doing anything right now? Fancy a pint for old times' sake."

"Sure. I tell you what. Make it a game of snooker too. There's a place I know the other side of town."

Brad's eyes lit up, remembering how he always used to thrash Craig at the game back in the old days. He bade his old friend wait while he sprinted off to take leave of his colleagues.

Craig returned to the car and waited, watching the activity in his rear-view mirror. Then, with Brad aboard and fastened into his seat, the big air-conditioned Rover glided off the car park and back onto the busy Worcester Road. Soon the familiar sign that read '*Welcome to Gunsbridge Metropolitan Borough - the Black Country*' greeted them, their hometown appearing over the horizon in all its raw urban splendour.

"Nice motor this," Brad noted, admiring the plethora of gadgets at Craig's fingertips. "You've certainly done well for yourself."

"I work for myself now. This morning I've been to a funeral though. You remember George Franklin?"

Brad did indeed. Guilt rushed back in, and all he could do was burble a few banalities to skate over this awkward subject. Meanwhile, the car cruised up the Wolverhampton Road, past the ghostlike structures of Harry Conway's 'Fun City' project, which now lay derelict. The huge swinging cranes stood motionless and deserted as Craig stared up at them, his dark glasses reflecting blinding glimpses of that pale yellow sun hanging low in the sky, which flashed rhythmically between the huge flanking towers that would have supported Europe's biggest roller-coaster had Conway ever completed his scheme. But that was history now also, Craig pondered as he stared at the road ahead.

"Many years ago," he recalled aloud, "we both reached a turning point in our lives, if you remember. We had to decide whether we wanted to go on as we were, going nowhere in particular; or we had to decide whether to follow that arduous road to realising our dreams. I don't know about you, but I sense that I'm almost in sight of my prize. I believe I've certainly come within reach of my dream. And you?" he paused, "...The next leader of Gunsbridge Borough Council?"

Brad was mildly amused. "Who? Me?" he gaped.

"You're widely tipped. You're certainly the most dynamic and appealing personality they've got. Everyone in town knows who Robert Bradleigh is. Your face is in the papers at least once a week."

Brad was flattered. "I haven't given up all hope yet of joining you at Westminster. I've got one last shot at the nomination for the safe Labour seat of Walsall West in the New Year. I'm quietly confident. Anyway, do you really think you can reverse Alannah's lead in the polls, despite stunning performances on the radio? You certainly gave her a good rogering!" he roared, somewhat pruriently in Craig's opinion, though he said nothing more until they arrived at their destination.

There these two unlikely friends soon settled into a quiet game of snooker. Characteristically of their somewhat esoteric relationship, many shots and many moments passed by with neither player saying anything, both of them locked in their own contemplations and preoccupations. Then finally, Brad missed a shot, prompting Craig to break the silence.

"I guess you owe me one then for bringing Alannah down a peg or two," he mumbled, sizing up the opening his opponent had handed to him. "You did want me to even up the race, didn't you?" he then asked, missing the shot and handing the game back to Brad. "Anyway, I thought you liked her. After all, she's the 'likeable sort'!" he grinned in a wry *double entendre*, the nearest thing to prurience that Brad sensed Craig felt comfortable with.

In return, Brad came as close as he dared to baring his soul, saying, "She's also the infuriating sort. Let's just say her feminine charm masks an icy determination to brush aside all those who stand in her way."

Craig understood perfectly. Once such sparring had been part of the fun and games of student life; now he felt locked in a duel to the finish with the girl he'd once crossed in idle debate. Yet he was intrigued by the intensity of the bitterness that Brad's words seemed to convey. People might think him naive, but he guessed that the councillor for Lower Henley had probably crossed Alannah's path on matters other than pure politics – much to his cost, it seemed. Brad sensed this, and took the decision to match his friend's reputation for candour.

"Okay," he admitted, "I'm bitter sometimes. We had something going. I blew it. She got even. That's why she's PPC for Gunsbridge South and I'm not."

Craig tried to sympathise. "Sounds like your path has been as stony as mine," he grinned.

Brad potted the final red ball and halted play. "You always seem to smile through. What's your secret?" he asked, knowing that his friend possessed the kind of self-assuring faith that he also secretly longed to possess.

Craig sat down and tried to verbalise his thoughts. "I just trust in God and tell myself that He knows what He's doing. Does that sound trite?"

Brad shrugged his shoulders. "I wish I could believe in this Jesus fellow. I'm not good enough to be religious though."

"You don't have to be good," Craig assured him, "just trusting. After all, no one's perfect," he sighed, knowing just how greatly the traumas of the last few years had pitted his own faith against frustration and resentment.

We certainly aren't perfect, Brad thought to himself. Craig undoubtedly had his skeletons in the proverbial cupboard, although he doubted whether Lovelace was right about him screwing Gemma Sutton. It was all too far-fetched – not Craig; not someone else's wife! Brad could imagine himself doing that though. Yes, he'd made a pretty ghoulish mess of his life: tormented by guilt about losing Helen and losing Alannah; and now, looking up and down at Craig once more, sartorially sombre from George Franklin's funeral, he felt guilty again about destroying the reputation of one of Craig's close personal friends. Maybe Jesus might just stoop to forgive him for that, he thought. Maybe the time had arrived to be purged of at least some of his ghosts from the past. Meanwhile, he continued with the game, his concentration ruined though. Soon Craig was picking up the shots and regaining the momentum over his opponent, until he had triumphantly holed the black and stood back from the table proudly. Perhaps this pious Tory had a way with miracles after all!

Brad could see his friend was quite chuffed at having won the game. Taking advantage of both Craig's good cheer and his placid Christian temperament, he began to edge crablike towards what he felt unnervingly compelled to share.

"I guess I'm not perfect. The whole world has discovered that by now. I had a seedy, mendacious streak in me once. I think Wendy has slowly drained that out of me now. Sort of like your faith in Jesus has. I try to forgive too, even though it's hard."

"Can you forgive Alannah?" Craig asked, leaning on his cue.

"I think so," Brad replied, doing likewise.

"Can you forgive yourself though? That's often the most difficult part."

"I don't know. You Christians have to confess your sins, don't you?" he asked, though more by way of prevarication than enlightenment.

Then Brad felt something virtuous cry out from within him. Maybe this was this 'holy spirit' that his mother was always lecturing him about, for it urged him to finally plunge into the cleansing stream; to confess his needs and his misdeeds to this, his sincere friend. Craig was a Christian; he would understand. And so he swallowed hard and heaved the burden from his heart.

"It was me..." he felt his tongue confess, "I was the one who went to the press."

"You? Told the press what?" Craig puzzled, at that moment somehow perversely insensitive to his friend's inner turmoil.

"About... about George Franklin..."

"You?"

"Like you said, Craig, we all make mistakes," he mumbled, suddenly beginning to sense that his gamble on Christian forgiveness might not pay off after all. Why had he done it? "I wanted to tell you because I've hated myself for it ever since. Like you said, he was a really nice guy."

Craig was dumbstruck. A strange and irrational feeling of outrage gripped him and made him in turn grip his cue, unsure whether or not to bend it around the head of this pathetic figure. Christian charity prevailed though – after a fashion! Casting the cue down on the bright green baize, he looked the supplicant in the eye. Brad had never before felt the rare fury of Craig Anderson unleashed upon him.

"I thought better of you, I really did. Okay, I know the press like rooting these things out; and I had a pretty good idea that it was one of your lot who told them. But you – you, whom I respected? You, whom I considered a friend...?"

Brad held his breath and meekly awaited the concluding damnation.

"...It appears that you're as slimy and despicable as the rest of them. No wonder your party deselected you! I thought it was because you weren't mean enough. It now appears that you must have been too mean even for them!"

With that, Craig left. He hurried down the stairs into his car and raced off the car park, leaving Brad shell-shocked as he (as well as the hushed clientele of the snooker club) watched while his furious friend disappeared into the afternoon traffic, disabused of yet one more cherished illusion of that tragic-comic trust in others.

****

"Councillor Bradleigh, can you tell us...?"

"Councillor Bradleigh, if you're chosen as Leader, will you...?"

Then a sudden camera flash momentarily caught the tall, dark figure bearing a rare smile of self-confidence.

"You're being slightly presumptuous, aren't you?" he replied, turning about on those same entrance steps to Gunsbridge Council House where he had once been so mercilessly pursued by some of those same correspondents. Yet it felt good to be being pursued once more, this time for all the right reasons. He felt sufficiently buoyant to engage himself in some jovial banter with them, though without giving anything away.

Finally, he broke free and emerged into that familiar grand foyer, up the long, elegant marble staircase and into the main committee room for the most critical gathering he'd ever attended. He sat down amongst his colleagues, laid out his papers, and waited for Tim Eaves to open the meeting.

"Right, comrades, you all know why we're here. Tom's still poorly and can't be with us, though he sends his good wishes. And you've all heard about Joe, no doubt," Eaves continued, interrupted by a certain merriment that rippled around the table. "I visited him in hospital yesterday and fortunately..."

The merriment resumed, with councillors breaking into umpteen inevitable jokes. "Prostrate trouble was it?" Phil Rolfe divulged, "Or was it a hernia?"

"Put it this way. He won't be riding the missus' for a while yet!" Frank Collins grinned impishly.

"...Fortunately," Eaves attempted to continue, "there's life in the old bugger yet. Anyway, let's not waste any more time. We're looking for a new leader of the Council in the difficult days to come." He folded his arms on the table in front of him, leant on them purposefully, and asked them, "Have I any nominations?"

For a moment the air was still. Brad looked up expectantly when Phil Rolfe broke the silence to say, "I move Councillor Micky Preston."

There were mumblings of approval before Eaves looked at them all again. "Can I have a seconder then?"

Brad swallowed hard and began to speak, immediately attracting the attention of his anxious group. "I'll second Councillor Preston's nomination, Tim."

He watched while anxiety turned to relief, the Group issuing another communal mutter of approval. Brad had said his piece and bade farewell to another high hope. How unfair is the game of politics, he thought, knowing that he had little choice but to accept the inevitable. Micky was by far the most popular and respected figure in the Labour Group; this was the supreme accolade of a career spent battling tirelessly for his vision of caring socialist local government. Brad knew it would be inappropriate (indeed foolhardy) to kick against it.

"No other nominations?" Eaves asked. Derek Hooper, Roz Young and Colin Tyler said nothing, not even bothering to mount a token protest. There truly was no realistic alternative.

Micky was jubilant, if restrained. The joy of achieving his supreme political ambition was instead easily discernable under his grey beard, and he gratefully accepted the handshakes of his colleagues, smiling at Alannah as she congratulated him from across the table.

"Of course," Eaves continued above the excitement, "Micky's elevation now means that the position of deputy leader is also up for grabs. So, again, I'm looking for nominations, comrades."

"I move Councillor Bradleigh," a familiar voice opined while Brad was otherwise absorbed in doodling on his papers. He looked up when he belated realised his name had been called. He suddenly felt very humbled, smiling to himself for a second in disbelief. Micky was sat opposite, and gazed at him longingly now that he had his attention, the gaze giving way to that familiar wink.

"I would very much like Brad to work alongside me; if, of course, the Group are amenable to that," Micky continued, intimating that he was now ready to formally welcome his favourite son back under his wing.

There was some mumbled discussion within the Group, Clive Bell muttering something to Frank Collins that Brad's suspicious mind interpreted as highly uncomplimentary of the new Leader's choice. Colin Tyler also mumbled something to his Militant pals.

"Are you proposing someone else for the nomination, Councillor Tyler?" Eaves enquired impatiently.

"What? Me? No, Chair. Ar' bay'!" he grunted, a little taken aback at being put on the spot.

"And you, Clive?" Eaves begged, clearly irritated that Bell's voluble grumbles were still interrupting proceedings.

"No, Tim, not at all. If Micky's happy to have Councillor Bradleigh as his 'Man Friday', then who am I to disagree," he replied, his arrogant articulation contrasting sharply with Tyler's blunt denial. Brad despised both of them, but he especially loathed the ill-disguised conceit of the prospective candidate for Gunsbridge North. Their eyes locked briefly in an icy exchange of glances.

Alannah could sense her colleague's brusqueness was agitating Brad intensely. He deserved the deputy leadership, and she wondered if now was not the time to make some gesture of reconciliation towards her former lover. Formally seconding him would seem a divinely appropriate instrument with which to make her peace, and she took a long deep breath.

"Tim, I...."

"May I s-s-s-second Councillor B-b-b-bradleigh as Deputy, T-t-t-t-tim," stuttered Walter Pugh magnanimously. Meanwhile, his booming stutter drowned out Alannah's nascent syllables of contrition.

"Great. No other nominations? Were you going to say something, Alannah?" Eaves asked her.

Brad stared straight at her – frozen as she was in mid-sentence. She promptly sealed her lips, looking away from him in embarrassment. "No, Tim. I just... no, it doesn't matter."

"Good. Well, congratulations on becoming Deputy Leader, Brad."

In the intervening moments while Micky and Tim swapped places at the head of the table and Brad moved up alongside him, the new deputy leader could barely disguise his contempt for Alannah. What had the bitch got against him? Could she not let bygones be bygones even now?

"Right," said Micky, assuming his throne, "we now know that we've got some painful choices to make with regard to the budget for next year. In fact, we are in serious danger of being 'capped'..."

Brad wasn't listening to the town's poll tax woes. His eyes focussed in on Alannah for a few moments more. Even Walter Pugh had found it within him to concur in Brad's nomination; and yet all she could manage was a brief, pathetic smile that told him nothing. Wait until I get Walsall West, he silently spat at her; then she'd see who was going to crap on who, just like that hypocrite Anderson would.

Alannah's train of thought was broken by Clive Bell whispering something further in her ear. She nodded before glancing up at Brad for the final time. Then she buried herself in her briefing papers, ashamed that that peculiar and inexplicable reticence had gripped her once again, just when her comrade from Lower Henley had once more been in need of her outstretched hand.

****

It was past midnight when he cruised up onto the drive. All was as still as the crisp night air enveloped the sleeping estate, and he stepped out of the car exhausted, hauling his briefcase with him.

He must be mad, he thought – as well he might after another acrimonious party meeting! The rump of the 'Maywood Heath Mafia' was still arguing with the rest of the association, with Craig trying invidiously to defend his support for that controversial Maastricht Treaty on European union. Business was proving tougher than he'd anticipated too. The recession had forced him to work all hours just to stand still, not helped by customers who failed to pay up on time, or inquisitive tax inspectors.

Once inside the house, he deposited his jacket on the back of a kitchen chair and made for the fridge, swinging the door open before delving inside and emerging with a carton of fruit juice and the somewhat depleted skeleton of Sunday's oven-ready chicken. He glanced at the notes Nikki had left him, picking at the corpse with his fingers: '*Sarah Packington called*' – yes, I've seen her tonight; '*the man from the Inland Revenue rang you*' – bollocks to the Inland Revenue! He strolled off to toss the note into the bin.

Shovelling in the last mortal remains of the chicken, he washed it down with the final drops of juice, and dropped both carcass and carton into the bin as well. Then he extinguished the light and made his way up to bed, digressing only to brush his teeth and empty his bladder, the flushing of the lavatory vaguely stirring his wife, who turned around to witness his shadow enter the room.

"Zat' you, Craig?" she murmured dozily

"Sure is," he replied, rapidly divesting, then sliding under the quilt, his cold, greasy hands undulating like a snake up onto the submerged promontory of one of her feminine hips before slithering swiftly under her nightie, over the smooth, supple skin of her belly, and attempting a sneaky, serpentine entrance into her clitoral redoubt.

"No, Craig," she sighed, recoiling at the sensation, "come on, it's late." She then wriggled, squirmed and turned herself over once more. Meanwhile, the snake retreated, another attempt at arousal aborted.

Whatever happened to the girl who used to wait up loyally for him? Whatever happened to the wife who couldn't wait to snuggle up to him under the bedclothes? What was happening to their marriage? He depended on Nikki's emotional support, far more than he was loath to admit; and it was hard to accept that she wasn't always going to be there at the end of a tiring day on the road.

Lying there, feeling unloved by his wife, his local party and the tax inspector, all kinds of demons seemed to emerge from under the furniture to torment his restless mind. As well as the customary flashbacks he'd been prey to lately of dead Kuwaiti kids, he was further tormented by the notion that the campaign was all going wrong; and that he just couldn't handle it. Everything and everybody was now out to trip him up – even his old friend, Brad! That miserable little shit had proved every bit as devious as all his other detractors. What else had he done to derail the campaign? Had he tipped off the *Herald* about Brereton and Gainsborough? Why was Dick Lovelace proving so unhelpful still? Meanwhile, while the demons played, he flitted between thoughts of older women – of Sarah Packington and Gemma Sutton – finally stumbling on the release he sought.

Bradleigh had certainly fallen on his feet, he noted, now trying to get to sleep. He recalled the *Herald* photograph of the newly elected Deputy Leader of Gunsbridge Borough Council posing on the steps of the Council House. Yes, Bradleigh would be providing far more vigorous and pro-active support to Alannah's candidacy than he'd first realised, using every device of the Council, every photo opportunity, every conceivable 'pork barrel' tactic to build up Alannah and paint down himself. Maybe he should take a leaf out of Bradleigh's book; dig up the dirt; plant malicious stories; remind them of the Abuse Action Team scandal. Indeed, hadn't Brad's wife been that incompetent social worker who'd cobbled the whole thing together!

"Oh, what's the use," he cursed, angrily demanding that the demons depart him. "I'm just not devious enough to make a politician... I'm not up being what You want me to be, Lord... Then why have You called me to walk this road, eh? ...Answer me that! ...Jesus... please..."

Crying out the name of Jesus seemed to banish the demons, who melted away under the wardrobe and the dressing table from whence they came, leaving Craig to drift off to sleep, vaguely aware that he had been talking to himself. Not that it mattered at that late hour. Nikki wasn't listening anyway.

****

Hugh Dalton House,
Lineham Street,
Walsall,

March 2nd 1992

Dear Cllr Bradleigh,

I regret to inform you that the committee has decided not to forward your name to the membership for consideration as our prospective parliamentary candidate. May I thank you for the time and trouble you've taken to acquaint us with yourself.

I should point out that the committee are highly impressed by the work of Gunsbridge Borough's Community Services Department, of which you are chair. They have asked me to relay these sentiments to you, and to advise you that the decision to eliminate you at this stage in no way detracts from the example that Gunsbridge offers to other local councils seeking to enhance the effectiveness of their youth and community programmes in these difficult times.

Yours sincerely,

Diana Cushman,
Chair, Walsall

West Labour Party

****

The guests and their spouses filed into the grand old banqueting suite and bounded up to the long lines of tables, ready for a sumptuous feast. Centre stage amongst them was Joe McAllister, this year's outgoing mayor, who was being congratulated by his Labour colleagues, as well by those Conservative councillors magnanimous enough to forget all his old tricks. He would not be standing for election again, so even some of his many enemies were disposed to permit him this last hurrah before he retired from a lifetime of often vicious political intriguing.

The annual Mayoral Ball itself was something of a last hurrah. It was Friday, March 6th. A general election was now imminent, and all the politicians were anxious to step down into the arena – none more so than the ebullient Labour councillors. After all, for one or two this was the eve of a sparkling new career: for Clive Bell, almost certainly; for Alannah, probably; and for Neil Sharpe, possibly, if unlikely. Brad had noticed that, of late, the normally buoyant Tory candidate for Gunsbridge North had something heavy weighing on his mind, something that left him less than attentive when in conversation with his Conservative colleagues. Also a man with much weighing on his mind was Craig Anderson, accompanied tonight by his charming and elegant wife. Who could say what the next few weeks held in store for them all.

Conversely, Clive Bell seemed to ooze conceit and impatience as he chatted to his fellows, knowing his appointment with destiny could only be a few weeks routine campaigning away. Alannah sat in the midst of a neighbouring clique, making polite conversation with Tom McKerrick and some other civic worthies. She looked immaculate in her beautiful red dress, her bright smile and expensive jewellery glittering beneath the ornate chandelier suspended above her. Meanwhile, a five-piece ensemble provided easy listening for the diners.

All of which, of course, begged the question of Brad's own destiny; for his chance to fight the election had now disappeared. Wendy couldn't help but notice the gloomy melancholy that had descended upon him in the past few weeks, despite his elevation to deputy leader, and despite being on target to retain his Lower Henley seat in the coming local elections. He could appear cheerful enough, laughing and joking with his colleagues. Yet she knew that something malign had gotten the better of him; and that, in reality, he was bitter and close to despair, withdrawing into the fearful insularity that she thought she'd cured him of. She looked at him as the dance floor was thrown open to those who wished to enjoy the remainder of the evening, just knowing his mind was febrile with resentment.

"Next stop Westminster!" someone cried out. All of a sudden, Alannah was the focus of a tremendous cheer when she returned with Micky from the opening waltz, beaming self-confidently and feeling slightly humbled by the enthusiastic applause of Phil Rolfe, Frank Collins and the others – end-of-term antics that brought not a little trepidation to the Conservative councillors and their wives dotted around the room.

"It's not over yet!" their heroine reminded them, offering an alabastrine cheek to Phil Rolfe, who kissed and hugged his champion unselfconsciously. "The real fight is only just beginning. Your contribution will make the *real* difference in this race. So let's go for it!"

The Bradleighs also returned from a sortie on the polished floor to join in the spirit of expectation abroad in the Labour camp. Yet somehow Brad could only grit his teeth in a poor semblance of a smile, trying to conceal the visceral hatred welling up inside for the lauded Councillor Miss James. Wendy sensed this instinctively, and gripped his trembling hand lovingly.

"His crowd are finished," Frank Collins assured Alannah whilst pointing conspicuously at Craig Anderson and his colleagues. "Shame. I'm told he's quite a nice lad really!" he laughed, the nearest thing the impish little man could summon that might conceivably pass for sympathy for the hated Tories.

"Don't count yer' chickens, pal," Dick Lovelace muttered aloud as he passed by on his way to the bar.

"Like I said, no complacency," Alannah reiterated to her loyal fellows. Then she saw Brad and Wendy looking on and turned to make her way over to them.

"I also need the help of the Deputy Leader of Gunsbridge Council. Your face on the hustings is worth several thousand votes at least," she declared, beaming at him.

The compliment was delivered from the heart; or at least Wendy thought it was. She watched for her husband's reaction, squeezing his hand a little tighter to ease of out him something equally conciliatory. He looked down at her briefly before addressing his former lover.

"Then the Deputy Leader will be delivering his 'several thousand votes' for Alannah James, the next Member of Parliament for Gunsbridge South. You have my full support," Brad assured her.

"Thank you," Alannah smiled; a soft smile that brought all the happy memories of their time together flooding back to him. Brad tried to smile too, Wendy using her grip on him to ease out some more conciliation.

"You're a very lucky woman," Alannah continued to her, "because, in Brad, I know you have a fine, fighting politician – and also a very loving husband, I'm sure."

"Thank you," Wendy replied, the wilful eyes of these two determined women locking onto each other briefly.

"And you, Brad," Alannah noted, turning to address him once more, "never let go of either Wendy or your dreams. I knew you were both right when you went ahead with the Abuse Action Team. Now events have proved you right – it was just the tip of the iceberg. Your time will come. Not this time perhaps; but one day. The world is waiting for Robert and Wendy Bradleigh!"

Alannah spoke the words as a heartfelt assurance and intended no malice, though Brad began to seethe inside. If the cow had thought he was right at the time, why had she not spoken up when half the town had been after his scrotum on a platter? Alannah went to shake his hand before deciding to dispense with such starched formalities. Instead, she placed a silky soft hand against his neck and kissed his cheek, turning to Wendy to do the same. There was obviously nothing sexual in it, though Brad didn't see it that way. It was the first time they had touched since that fateful day when she had stormed out of his flat. He was convulsed with the notion that somehow it *was* a subtle sexual gesture – a typical piece of female prick teasing! Indeed, had Wendy not been there (as well as some of the most prominent politicians and business leaders in Gunsbridge!) he was in the frame of mind to have floored the little tart there and then!

Finally, Alannah and Clive Bell were guided off to meet some other worthies, leaving their friends to debate the forthcoming election – and Brad to fume at his humiliation at the hands of that hated woman. Wendy thought she had the lid back on his emotions, and thus felt confident enough to excuse herself to visit the phone booth in the foyer and answer the little telecom bleeper that she carried around in her bag.

"Sitting out the General, eh, Councillor?" sprang a jaunty voice approaching him from behind. Never had Brad ever assaulted a member of the fairer sex. Yet, for a second time, such homicidal thoughts entered his head. He might have finally exploded had not Jane Allsop followed up with an uncanny remark that helped assuage his other obsession. "But for what it's worth, your friend Councillor Miss James might find herself coming a cropper."

"You must be joking!" he hissed, instinctively rallying to his candidate's banner, if not to her. "She's ten points ahead in the polls, and we're putting all we've got into this campaign. You can only hope to dent Anderson's already depleted vote, not ours."

The golden-haired minx joined him in observing the Andersons dancing cheek-to-cheek across the floor to one of the band's more intimate melodies. "No, I reckon you're all in for a surprise. The Liberal Democrats may not have the muscle of the big parties, but we do our homework – and we can sense the ground moving. You're right – he's blown this one; but voters aren't necessarily drifting to your candidate either," she informed him.

"So it's a contest between a jumped-up, middle class brunette and a jumped-up, middle class blonde, is it?" Brad observed cynically.

"Ooooh! Come, come, Deputy Leader! How does that square with your Council's policy of anti-sexism?" Jane tutted playfully, ignoring the slight and instead baiting her opponent to justify his chauvinist remark. He turned and looked down at the diminutive Liberal Democrat candidate.

"Let's just say that had the people that mattered known then what is now common knowledge about child abuse in this town, then you might have been facing me and not 'glamour girl' over there. In fact, I seem to recall you playing no small part in the casting of aspersions."

"Ah well, Councillor, that's politics! Anyway, don't be too harsh on your candidate. She's got where she has because she's smart, rather than because she's a 'glamour girl'. A bit like me, really!" she chirped provocatively.

Such feminine solicitude seemed only to fuel Brad's mounting paranoia. Why should she complain? He couldn't help but despise her assertiveness, for she was every inch as aggressively monomaniacal as Alannah. This affront to his male pride was compounded by the fact that she was every inch as attractive as Alannah too, attired as she was in a short, slinky white dress, which only served to emphasise more the appeal of her gorgeous bronzed legs. He was by now experiencing great difficulty in his disentangling his sexual and his political thoughts, the skittish Councillor Miss Allsop looking eminently screwable in that pretty little outfit.

"Anyway," she concluded, looking up at him with a stare that could have been interpreted one of two ways, "don't give up. An energetic, up-and-coming politician like you – something'll turn up, I'm sure."

And with that she drifted away, each lingering movement of her high heels fuelling Brad's pitiful misogyny as she wandered off, only to be reunited with her boyfriend requesting her hand for a dance. Her fine, blonde hair shone in the light as she swung it across her shoulder, smiled and answered him in the affirmative, embracing him.

"I'm afraid I'll have to desert you," fumed Wendy, rushing back in. She kissed her husband and fumbled in her bag for her car keys. "Something's cropped up over at the hostel. They need me to go sort it out. Tonight of all nights!"

"Here. Take mine," said Brad, offering her his own set. "As I recall, at least mine's got some juice in it!"

After swapping keys, Wendy was also gone, leaving Brad by himself. He lingered about idly in a corner, not really a part of the evening's celebrations, despite the admonitions of his friend Phil Rolfe to 'loosen up'. Joe McAllister came over and fleetingly shook his hand: another gesture of 'no hard feelings' by someone else who'd expended much time and energy trying to do him down. Meanwhile, Anderson was wooing those 'captains of industry' present, accompanied by a beautiful wife, who looked truly resplendent in her expensive blue gown. But, most of all, it was seeing Alannah continually being feted by local VIPs that made even his ascent to deputy leader and chairman of Community Services seem like second best. He vowed to finish his drink and retire to the seclusion of his bed.

Then Alannah made an unintentionally noisy exit, her supporters cheering her and singing the *Red Flag* before she was permitted to reach the door. The Labour Group were in such a fighting mood that they could ill-disguise their anticipation of the Tories' impending trouncing, just as the smaller Conservative Group could ill-disguise their annoyance at such unseemly tomfoolery.

"You'll do it, Alannah... *WE'LL KEEP THE RED FLAG FLYING HERE...!*" chanted Frank Collins, his tie loosened and his shirt-tail hanging out.

"I noticed you haven't got your car with you," Micky Preston pointed out to Alannah above the commotion. "Can I offer you a lift?"

"No, it's okay," she smiled. "Philip's borrowed it. He's had to stay over at the college working late. I said I'd stroll across and meet him there."

"You sure?" he repeated paternally. Alannah nodded and tried to free herself from her fans. Micky kissed her farewell and then watched his 'treasure' depart, thankful that her big moment had arrived at last.

She left a happy Labour crowd to contemplate their coming victory – and Brad to contemplate a wasted opportunity. Somewhere in his heart, a part of him still loved Alannah and ached that things could not have turned out differently. But what the hell! He knew that cunning bitch would always upstage him with her degrees, her mellisonant accent, her disarming smile and that devious female mind. It was in the nature of things for women like her to always render men like him superfluous. Wasn't the whole *raison d'être* of the feminist movement to psychologically emasculate men? he brooded. Okay, so this time she'd won a battle. However, depressed and frustrated as he was, the anger and resentment welling up within him made him determined that he'd win the war that was still raging between them – she'd see! Acting on a furious impulse, he downed his drink and raced off out of the room to plan on how he might one day get even.

21 TOMORROW IS ANOTHER DAY

THE GUNSBRIDGE HERALD
Wednesday, March 11th 1992
Evening Edition - Still only 29p

ELECTION LATEST – PARLIAMENT DISSOLVED
Following on from Chancellor Norman Lamont's give-away budget yesterday, Prime Minister John Major today formally petitioned the Queen to dissolve Parliament. Polling Day has been fixed as Thursday, April 9th...
ELECTION LATEST – ALANNAH IS DROPPED
Gunsbridge South Labour Party today reluctantly announced that, in view of her critical condition in the town's General Hospital, they will not be formally nominating Alannah James as their parliamentary candidate at their adoption meeting tomorrow. Cllr Miss James, 31, is still unconscious after being struck by a 'hit-and-run' driver a week ago shortly after leaving the annual Mayor's Ball, and not far from the College where she was heading to meet her fiancé. Meanwhile, Gunsbridge CID are anxious to hear from anyone who may have observed a dark-coloured Vauxhall hatchback seen speeding through the town at about the time of the attack...
"SHE WAS THE BEST SORT", SAYS RIVAL
Conservative candidate and former fellow student, Craig Anderson, described Alannah James as being "the best sort", and slammed her attacker as "cowardly and sick". Tying his remarks to a call for stiffer sentences for violent criminals, Mr Anderson called both her fiancé and her local party to express his regret at the necessity of their decision...
I'M NOT 'TOYBOY', SAYS TORY CANDIDATE
Gunsbridge North Conservative candidate, Neil Sharpe, has furiously denied rumours that he is to be named in divorce proceedings between local constituency chairman David Sutton and his wife, Gemma, describing them as "a vicious Labour Party smear"...

****

No one seemed more shocked than Craig. The Conservative candidate stared vacantly into space, perhaps still trying to rework in his head a whole new election strategy in the light of the events of the last week.

"Good evening, I'm Melanie Brindle; and welcome to the first of our special election *Gunsbridge Matters*..." chirped the vivacious presenter, hard on the heels of the hourly news summary. She, too, seemed slightly disbelieving that she was running an edition of her current affairs programme minus the personable presence of Alannah James, who she reminded listeners was still on a life-support machine after receiving terrible injuries: truly the whole town had been devastated by such a mindless piece of thuggery against a life so full of promise. ".... And we're therefore pleased that the new Labour candidate for Gunsbridge South, Councillor Robert Bradleigh, has agreed to join us here in the studio to debate the issues in this election. You, too, can call in and talk to our candidates... our lines are now open."

Craig cast an indifferent glance in the direction of his new rival for this most critical of target seats. A quaint thought ran through his head; this would be the first time he'd ever really debated directly with his one-time friend. Indeed, when their relationship had not been so fraught with personal animosity, there had been little reason to talk 'shop' except to exchange amusing anecdotes drawn from their respective experiences. Now Craig sensed that mutual self-restraint had been left hanging by some very tender threads; there was little love to be lost between the two erstwhile companions, who had been thrown together now into the unforgiving arena of what promised to be the dirtiest, most hard-fought contest of a hard-fought general election. Spasms of excitement tinged with trepidation even seemed to emanate from Jane Allsop as she also waited for this first battle to be joined, perhaps marvelling at the fantastic new opportunities the entrance of the controversial councillor into this campaign had opened up.

Melanie rambled on until Craig opened the debate with the case for the Conservatives. Meanwhile, Brad submerged himself in his own preoccupations, surfacing occasionally to note a point and scribble down little asides. He pondered the fateful selection meeting a few days previously that had so suddenly propelled him here tonight, recalling how the awful revelation of Alannah's incapacity had visibly broken Micky Preston. Sitting at the front of the room, next to local chairman Eric Sims, Brad had watched from the floor while he had drawn out a crumpled white handkerchief to mop away a stray tear, devastated that his shining prodigy had been so cruelly cut down in this way. Meanwhile, Sims had swallowed his own anguish and collected his composure, driving himself to plough on with the meeting.

"...That is why the heartbreaking decision of this committee," he had informed the local party, "is that we find another candidate to fight the election that is now only a few weeks away. In view of the obvious urgency of the matter, and in view of the need to pick a known candidate with the widest possible support in both the party and the constituency at large, the Committee have taken soundings and decided to present just one candidate to you.

"It will be someone we are confident can match the tremendous hard work that Alannah has put into this fight; someone who possesses all the popular appeal, vitality and commitment that Alannah also possessed; someone who can retain and capitalise on the lead she has held in the polls in this critical target seat. That is why, after much reflection and a lot of consultation, the recommendation of the

General Committee – supported by the trades union, Co-op and ward branches – is that you vote to accept Councillor Robert Bradleigh as the Labour Party candidate for this constituency."

The decision had not met with universal approval. Sharif Khan, Ricky Serrano and Gary Bennett, clinging on for dear life against expulsion from the party for their Militant activities, had vented their full fury upon Brad and his nomination. Indeed, he knew now (if ever he had any doubts) that they regarded him as the antithesis of all that they stood for – a man whose socialism had 'matured' in order to win this most crucial of elections, in contrast to the steadfastness of their own atrophied and irrelevant beliefs. It was an investment in realism that Brad hoped would pay handsomely now; a hope made all the more earnest by the fact that, because of the complicated and overlapping timetables of both the general and local elections, he would not be able to realistically seek re-election as a councillor. Thus he had taken the painful decision to stake everything – his council seat, the chair of Community Services and the deputy leadership he so treasured – on winning this highly marginal parliamentary seat at such short notice. But, oh the prize that beckoned if he were to win!

"Melanie, I believe that the sad experiment in greed and selfishness that we now call Thatcherism is finally coming to an end..." he insisted, commencing his own *tour-de-horizon* of the election. That he did so in a style of rhetoric so brash, redolent and assertive visibly irritated his Conservative opponent, who did not look at him directly as he spoke, but who, in his agitation, also scribbled down odd stratagems to use later on.

It was obvious now that something had happened to them both on that day they'd last exchanged idle words. Since then, Craig had lost whatever sense of admiration he had once possessed towards his contemporary. Meanwhile, his eyes and ears in Gunsbridge South Labour Party had furnished him with a pretty clear picture of the events that had led to him having to face this patently ambitious councillor.

"Are you saying you disagree with the Committee's decision?" the question had been put to one of Brad's opponents within the party called Ricky Serrano – according to the version of events that the loose-tongued Councillor Colin Tyler had proffered to one of Craig's campaign aides. It had put the dishevelled arts teacher slightly on the spot, aware of the surrounding battery of eyes staring at him censoriously. He had twitched and looked first to his right, then to his left, before continuing. "He is not the choice of the Young Socialists."

"Trotsky himself wouldn't satisfy that bunch of weirdos," someone at the back had called out cynically.

"He was chosen before and subsequently deselected. He is not acceptable," Serrano had said pressing on, his lips curling up contemptuously. Brad had been sitting impassively at the front next to his wife, saying nothing, rather leaving his defence in the capable hands of the chairman.

"Then precisely who is acceptable?" Sims had bellowed sarcastically.

"I propose Sharif Khan," Serrano had replied, to isolated applause from some of his cohorts, "A bloke who has worked hard to establish a Young Socialist presence in this town; a true, red-blooded activist."

"Yeh, an' 'e doh' sleep around with every scrubber in town neither!" Tyler had admitted yelling in support.

There had then followed pandemonium, with calls from the floor for the chairman to censor him. Brad had turned about and poured all his anger into a livid, contemptuous stare. Wisely, Wendy had swallowed her hurt and had turned his head back again to face the front, the only one who had probably prevented him from blowing his top and blowing his chances by digging his throbbing knuckles into Tyler's face.

Sims had banged the table again. "Mr Khan, I take it then that you are putting your name forward against the Committee's nominee?"

The dark, bulky figure of the Kashmiri had then risen ominously out of his seat. "Yes, Chair. On the basis of my belief in real socialism – and the councillor's minimal commitment to the cause – on behalf of the Young Socialists, I challenge him to the nomination."

Tyler had recounted to Craig's 'source' how Khan had grinned at his opponent, who had cast his head about briefly to behold the man who had apparently once taught him all there was to know about Labour Party activism. Then Brad had cast his glance back again to observe Sims lean back in his chair and fold his arms behind his head for support.

"How old are you, Mr Khan?" he had wanted to know as a matter of interest, donning a lawyer's demeanour to wheedle information out of him. Khan had seemed unable to respond for a moment, appearing somewhat puzzled.

"I'm thirty-three," he had eventually muttered, somewhat indignantly.

"He's thirty-seven, Chair," said the secretary, one Donna Tromans, who had been sitting next to Sims consulting her bulky membership file, presumably in order to unearth just such a timely snippet of information.

"Then, at thirty-seven, aren't you a little old to still be hanging around with the Young Socialists?" Sims had enquired wryly. Khan was finished, and he knew it. Yet Sims had continued to string him along, conscious that a little exercise in 'rank-and-file' democracy might be just what he needed to see him on his way. "But," he had noted derisively, "so that everything is done in a right and proper fashion, we shall vote on it."

Craig recalled how it had been intimated to him that Tyler had been as unimpressed by this blundering oversight on the part of his revolutionary cohorts as he had by the decision of the membership to subsequently vote 132-41 to select Brad to face the electorate on their behalf. Still, Craig could pick out the useful bits of this conversation from the dross of the uncouth Tyler's wounded pride: deselected once before; sleeping around with a local Labour Party floozy called Donna Tromans. Interesting, he thought, as the new candidate for the Labour Party finished his monologue and looked across the table at him, all smug and self-assured.

Jane Allsop's remarks studiously avoided any hint that she might be prepared to dabble in a little personality politics; although, knowing her as he did, Brad could not entirely dismiss such concerns. While the switchboard began to feed the questions to Melanie and she, in turn, unleashed them upon the three young candidates, Craig also sensed this undercurrent of inclemency pervading their responses. The stakes were too high now for any of them to be forgiving.

"I know Craig is anxious that his party be seen to be concerned about investing in education; but it sits unsurely with the record of his party in government..." Brad chortled sarcastically.

"John Major – the man with more 'charters' than Dan-Air!" Jane Allsop observed wittily.

Craig tried to take it all in his stride, concentrating on homing in on what he saw as the inconsistencies in his opponents' policies. He was not going to descend to the kind of cheap jibes that littered Bradleigh's comments.

"He has a point." Melanie insisted, turning to the councillor, determined that Brad should clarify his response to an issue Craig had raised.

"It's nonsense!" Brad riposted, craning forward across the table in a display of earnestness. "Let's take homelessness. In 1992, homelessness on the scale that we are witnessing in Mr Major's Britain is a crime. It's immoral." Then Melanie noticed a malicious sparkle appear in his eyes as he continued. "It makes a mockery of my Conservative opponent's pious and oft-repeated claims to be a Christian when he is unashamedly a member of a party that seems to express such indifference to this tragedy. Indeed, the acts of his party's government have knowingly engineered the present crisis."

That was below the belt! All at once, something inside Craig fused and any pretence of him being 'above the personality fray' evaporated. He interjected; and, despite Brad's plea to be permitted to finish his sentence, he interjected again. The gloves were off!

"How can the councillor talk about 'homelessness' and 'indifference to the tragedy' when his own council's housing department is such a bastion of waste and inertia!" he charged, Brad momentarily taken aback. He was being offered a reminder of the rare fury of Craig Anderson. "Yes, Councillor, I'm talking about the colossal backlog of empty council houses that Gunsbridge Council has amassed, despite the number of families on the waiting list..."

"If we could spend the capital receipts from the council house sales your party encouraged, then we could..." Brad tried to protest.

"Oh no! You have the resources; you just can't manage them. How about the subsidies given to the Caribbean Women's Co-operative? Or the fifty thousand pounds squandered on the Gunsbridge Community Arts Festival – over budget, over hyped and under attended? Or the mismanagement of the grants to voluntary bodies?" Craig interrogated him mercilessly. "All of which you, as chairman of the Community Services Committee, must answer for. And is it any coincidence that the venue for this year's Community Arts Festival has been moved to a site in Councillor Bradleigh's ward...?"

"...But, of course, Mr Anderson didn't complain too loudly when the church youth club that his wife runs received a grant towards..." Brad scoffed when he could get a word in edgeways.

"Gentlemen! gentlemen! I think we're losing sight of the wider issues here," Melanie waded in, separating her two male guests with a rare display of authority. "Jane, I believe you wanted to come in on a point?"

"Thank you, Melanie. I believe that the voters are heartily sick of the kind of two-party 'ping-pong' that my opponents have just indulged in. The Liberal Democrats want to rise above this sort of silly politicking and..."

Plainly irritated, Craig sat up and was about to interject again when Melanie gesticulated to him to hold fire until his attractive, golden-haired rival had stated her case. When she had finally finished, Jane Allsop was also made to feel the rare fury of Craig Anderson – both barrels of it!

"...It would be endearing to think that Councillor Miss 'Calamity Jane' here, alone amongst us, is so pure, noble and above this so-called 'ping-pong'. But let me, if I may, Melanie, remind people that, in the past, she and her party have not been above deliberately misleading the voters..."

"I beg your pardon!" Jane retorted indignantly. Meanwhile, Brad was mentally kicking himself. 'Calamity Jane', he smirked: why didn't I think of that one!

"...And, of course, we can't blame Councillor Bradleigh for *all* the muddle at Community Services," Craig conceded, ploughing on. "For he has only inherited such a profligate and wasteful committee from Councillor Miss Allsop, who, as the price for her support for a minority Labour administration four years ago, demanded the chairmanship of Community Services, together with a bloated budget to match her political ambitions. Indeed, the Labour Group meekly submitted to this outrageous request because – let's face it, Melanie – they yearn for power at any price almost as much as Neil Kinnock does. I will conclude by also reminding the voters of Gunsbridge that in ninety percent of the votes taken on the Council Councillor Miss Allsop has sided with the Labour Group. I will leave them to decide for themselves what to make of her sanctimonious claim that the Liberal Democrats represent some kind of rational 'third force'!"

Melanie finally halted Craig; but the damage was done. Jane Allsop had lost her halo (though having gained a new epithet in return!), and no amount of protest by her to the contrary seemed to alter that. Brad had meanwhile been treated to some uncomfortable home truths about his department's activities. And Craig had been rattled into throwing off his carefully cultivated coolness under fire. Eventually, the other phone-in guests moved the debate on, but the die was now cast. And when the nine o'clock news jingle finally brought this furious opening barrage to a close, and the three rival candidates stood up and grudgingly shook hands, their exhausted and somewhat traumatised host sensed that, unlike on an earlier occasion, this time the hearts of the three main candidates were distinctly not present in the hollow and grudging words they exchanged.

****

Amidst scenes that were growing uglier by the minute, the grave expressions on the faces of the Special Branch officers told Craig that somebody must be on the verge of announcing a tactical retreat back to the safety of campaign headquarters. But, no; on they pressed defiantly. Craig had ended up some way behind the main body of the entourage, but a sudden surge by the crowd now lifted him bodily and deposited him back alongside his leader.

"Shove off, Major!" someone yelled.

"Yeh, on yer' bike, mate! And take your fascist policies with you!"

Craig turned about to behold the clumps of revolutionary banners juxtaposed amidst curious shoppers, doting campaign workers, police officers and assorted ne'er-do-wells that hemmed the PM in on all sides.

"Hullo. I'm John Major, pleased to meet you," the PM smiled to some little old ladies – seemingly oblivious to the chaos his visit had created.

"Oh, isn't he a lovely man," one of them chimed to her friends excitedly.

"Bollocks to the Poll Tax!" someone else yelled, and an egg whizzed by unnoticed.

"Hullo. Do you shop here often?" the Prime Minister grinned again to another bystander.

Craig had experienced some brushes with rent-a-mob in his time, but this was something else! A burly police sergeant ordered the pursuing cameramen to make room before conferring briefly with the PM and his minders. Gunsbridge must be proving livelier than any of them had imagined. Suddenly, the sergeant grabbed a large wooden crate handed to him over the heads of his colleagues. An ideal weapon, Craig thought, watching the officer use it to shoo away some of the trailing press corp. Then, at the behest of the Prime Minister himself, he placed it down in the centre of the gap he had created and helped the premier up onto its rugged lid.

"Can you hear me?" Major cried out through cupped hands.

Evidently not! So some resourceful party dogsbody passed him a megaphone. Meanwhile, some more eggs flew past in formation.

"*IS THAT BETTER?*" the oscillating prime minister chuckled, causing a roar of approval from his supporters which momentarily drowned out all contrary cries.

"This is incredible!" Craig gasped as Sarah Packington, his agent, and Neil Sharpe, his fellow candidate, were at last heaved alongside him. "No prime minister has dared do this in years."

The crowd seemed to appreciate the novelty of it all as much as the Prime Minister did, the multifarious mixture of revolutionary thugs, true-blue Tories and incredulous bystanders cheering or heckling as the mood took them, all swirling wildly about the makeshift soapbox.

"End the Tories' politics of greed!" a shaven-headed lass yelled in righteous indignation.

"*DON'T LET THEM FOOL YOU.*" Major barked, his gravel voice echoing back off the corners of the Town Square. "*PEOPLE ALL OVER EUROPE HAVE BEEN CONSIGNING SOCIALISM TO THE DUSTBIN OF HISTORY.*"

Another flight of eggs buzzed the PM, who was still too consumed in debating to bother to notice them. Craig and Sarah ducked. Neil Sharpe didn't – and the sleeve of his overcoat was splattered by an incoming volley.

****

Expectation gave way to high drama when the lights dimmed and grave strains of Purcell filled the makeshift auditorium, ably assisted by some hagiographic montage on the huge video monitors that surrounded them all. Frivolities over, on strode John Major himself, waving to the invited audience.

"I know socialism. Britain does not want it; doesn't need it; can't afford it. It spreads envy; creates division; nourishes spite. It makes people feel uneasy about the things they've achieved for themselves. Are you successful?" Major cried rhetorically. "Then feel guilty! But you shouldn't feel guilty about being successful. You should be proud, and that's what we want you to be."

Craig wasn't prone to feeling guilty about success, just anxious for a little of it in Gunsbridge South. However, the Prime Minister's visit had seemed to jolt his campaign up a gear, and he was only too grateful for his encouragement. At the end of the televised indoor rally, the Prime Minister invited all the PPCs up onto the stage and held their arms high in triumph before the television cameras. Craig noticed that even Dick Lovelace was nodding in approval. Things must really be looking up at last, he consoled himself.

"Don't worry, Craig. Your offensive – plus the PM's visit – means we should hold on to this seat. I knew you wouldn't let us down," Sarah reiterated to him as the Gunsbridge South crowd raced back to the car park, Nikki glad to see her husband in a more relaxed and jovial mood, as befitted the occasion.

"Yep!" said Gerry, pulling his mackintosh tight around him to expel the damp night air. "It's official: even the *Herald* admits that you're ahead now."

"Crikey!" said Des Billingham with disbelief. "We must be on top if the *Herald* thinks we're winning."

"Yes, they've caused us some anguish," Craig noted. "We won't forget that in a hurry. Anyway, I don't like the way Allsop's support is holding up. Sarah, we'll have to watch her," he continued, his eyes darkening anxiously.

"We'll have another rummage through their manifesto and put out a press release," she insisted, soothing her candidate with her firm, motherly touch, the psycho-sexual connotations of which Nikki was not always happy with (though she never said so).

"I say carry on hammering the 'reds'," Julie King chortled in her flat, Brummie accent. She nestled in closer to Craig as if to emphasise her chosen vocation as his most loyal of lieutenants, something that Nikki was even less happy about – especially when the podgy little councillor nudged her way in hover a little closer to her idol.

Upon reaching Gerry's car, Craig, Nikki and Sarah hurried to scamper inside before another downpour arrived overhead. It was definitely not election weather. Then, all of a sudden, just as Craig and Nikki had satisfactorily apportioned themselves a piece of the rear seat, a fifth passenger shoved them back together on the nearside.

"Room for a little one?" Julie enquired, squeezing onto the back seat alongside them.

"I thought you'd come with Des," Gerry noted, observing in his mirror the sudden discomfort being inflicted upon the Anderson couple, for the girth of their new passenger could not even charitably be described as being 'little'.

"Well, I did. But you know me – I like to be close to the action," she said, smiling angelically at Craig, who was now sat invidiously between his number one admirer and his wearied and agitated wife.

Either way, Des had now sealed their fate by racing off ahead of them. How thoughtful of him, Nikki sighed. Craig indeed tried to be charitable towards his unsubtle colleague, although he had occasionally confessed to moments of mild despair concerning the crush she plainly had on him. They cruised back along the motorway through the swirling spray, only the dull pounding of Gerry's wiper blades breaking the silence. Then, out of the blue, Julie stared up at Craig's blond locks and tapped his knee suggestively.

"Listen," she urged him conspiratorially, "You remember what I told you about Colin Tyler the other night – yer' know," she continued, enlightening the others too, "that leftie councillor for Gunsbridge Central. Well, he's been telling me some more secrets about their candidate. I bet you didn't know that he once had an affair with Alannah James. Apparently they hate each other's guts now – especially after she caught him in bed with that other bird."

"And why would Colin Tyler want to tell you that?" Craig wondered aloud with just a hint of impatience, though he was vaguely aware (as was probably half of Gunsbridge Council) that Brad and Alannah had once been close

.
"I told you," she nudged him playfully, "the Left are dead against him. They see him as a typical Kinnockite: abandoning his socialist roots for flash ideas and media popularity. They're just itching to nobble him!"

"Then why haven't they gone to the press themselves with these revelations?" Gerry enquired pertinently, to which Julie was at a loss to explain.

"Well, Oy' dunno', do Oy'!" she shrugged her shoulders in umbrage.

There was sighing and groaning. "Use your noddle, Julie!" Sarah wailed, "They know there's no mileage for them in being seen to be attacking their candidate publicly. So they're pumping you so that our side will take the blame for trying to play dirty tricks."

"I was only trying to be helpful. You said we needed all the votes we could find," she replied dolefully, looking to Craig to rescue her from the derision of the others. His earlier dismay blunted by those puppy-dog eyes, he therefore risked Nikki's further irritation, and indulged his hapless assistant with some tender words of encouragement.

"Listen, Julie," he smiled, "I appreciate the things you told me the other day. But I've been thinking. I want dirty tricks to play no part in this campaign. No," he insisted emphatically, "I have to nail the socialists on issues, not personalities. You can help me by helping Sarah dig up some facts on the Liberal Democrats – they're our other major headache."

Julie seemed relieved to be back in her candidate's confidence. She leaned forward and grinned at Nikki – not something calculated to restore her worth in the eyes of the candidate's longsuffering wife!

Halting briefly at a service area in order to down a coffee and a few late snacks, they all had time for some last banter about the day's events: the rowdy walkabout; the soapbox stunt; the rally and the keynote speech. Then it was time to go home, Julie indiscreetly signalling her need of the ladies' room first.

Craig halted Nikki in the corridor and laid his hand gently against her face. "You okay?" he whispered.

She nodded dutifully. "Yes, it's just that bimbo – the way she keeps hanging around you. I'm sorry, but she annoys me intensely."

"I know. But at least she's enthusiastic," he said, kissing her forehead tenderly.

"I wish she wouldn't keep dreaming up all these silly schemes either."

"She's only trying to impress me. I don't really think there's too much mileage in what she says anyway – especially not if it involves badmouthing the local Labour Party's poster girl, who is now lying critically ill in a hospital bed! Besides, I have no intention of sinking to unseemly personality fights," he assured her.

Just then, unnoticed by either of them, Julie emerged from the ladies' toilet, fumbling up inside her black velvet skirt to straighten her underwear, wriggling a few times to free whatever was uncomfortable before pulling the skirt back down – all while overhearing the couple talking a few yards away.

"Of course," Craig continued, unaware of her presence, "it still leaves me the problem of what to do about Bradleigh's campaign. I must find another weak point on which he's vulnerable, perhaps continuing to attack his record on the Council."

Who will rid me of this turbulent priest, did Julie catch him saying? Perhaps he did want to exploit his opponent's blatant Achilles heel after all, despite his wife's reluctance to so do. Her hero was not out of trouble yet, despite the *Herald's* latest poll prediction. The others might be too squeamish to attack Bradleigh head on, but she wasn't going to let such niceties stand in the way of Craig's victory. She peered from behind a vending machine to observe Craig and Nikki stroll out together back towards the car. She had never much liked Craig's wife: she was a bad influence upon him, rendering him too placid and insufficiently aggressive and ruthless. It needed someone close to him to counter her forbearance – someone to make him swallow his inhibitions and go after his opponent's jugular.

****

"Neil, I'd like you to meet the next Member of Parliament for Gunsbridge South – Councillor Robert Bradleigh." Thus did the excited Leader of Gunsbridge Council introduce the Leader of the Labour Party to their favourite son.

"Only ten days to go till I take my seat," Brad remarked in humour, taking the Welshman by the hand.

"Just you believe it, boyo!" the Leader grinned, piling another hand upon their grip as if to emphasise the point.

Further introductions were made, Brad dutifully offering his hand until it alighted in the soft, petite palm of a sable-haired girl in a business suit.

"...And this is Gillian Warley from Campaign HQ," someone enlightened him, a most delightful piece of news. Her looks and the purposeful manner of her comportment certainly made her stand out in the crowd.

"Pleased to meet you, Gillian," the old charmer in him smiled.

"Likewise," she replied, not wholly oblivious to or disinterested in the attention being lavished upon her. "I've heard a lot about you, Councillor."

"Anyway, shall we proceed into the mall?" said another minder, shepherding them all towards the sound of the waiting crowds. Toss in those ubiquitous television cameras and a few hundred cheering supporters and the effect was complete: a stunning *coup de théatre*.

"Hi there, how you doing? Great to see you!" beamed Neil Kinnock as he boldly waded into the sea of hands that stretched from behind every balcony to greet him. The roar of the crowd was deafening, and Brad was stunned that the party managers had been able to rustle up so many well-wishers at such short notice.

"Almost there, Neil," someone cried.

"No more Tory cuts," some other strident housewife assured him.

"Left to your councillors this place would never have been built! Tell that to the bloody cameras!" a lone pensioner fumed, prodding the breast of the Leader's crisp blue suit with a crooked finger. However, Kinnock preferred instead to salute his admirers and offer the kind of banal felicitations of politicians the world over.

"Gillian, this is a beautiful sight to behold. A vindication of thirteen years of struggle," Brad beamed to the ever-watchful campaign aide. "Only a few years ago this place symbolised locally the kind of devil-take-the-hindmost capitalism that held sway nationally," he enlightened her as she looked his way momentarily, having removed a walkie-talkie from beside her ear to ask why.

"It was the brainchild of Harry Conway, wasn't it?" she said.

"Yep! Bulldozed his way through planning regulations, bribed his way into favour with the local politicians, and turned his stooges on people like me who tried to stand up to him. All told, he turned one half of this town against the other; and I'm not sorry that he had his comeuppance when the property boom ran out of steam."

"Happily, the new owners of Trescott Park, like a lot of business leaders, realise that a Labour government is now inevitable. They're doing what any wise businessman would do; they're hedging their bets and building bridges. How else do you think we got an 'invite' to a place like this?"

They watched Kinnock take a microphone and offer up a few thoughts to the crowd to send them home with a warm feeling inside. It certainly gave Brad one. And maybe soon his bright, ambitious and patently attractive young graduate friend would be experiencing a wholly different role for herself as a policy advisor to the new Labour Cabinet, forsaking that buzzing walkie-talkie for an office in Downing Street and the ear of the Prime Minister himself – something that had for far too long been the exclusive preserve of the 'best and the brightest' from Smith Square. He had only a few brief moments to eye her up and down as she stood there relaying instructions to her colleagues before the Labour leader bade his audience farewell, and hauled Brad and Clive Bell from the sidelines to thrust their clenched fists high above him in a final pose for the television crews.

"I say, he's good is old Neil," Phil Rolfe grinned approvingly.

"I'm sure. But how good's your candidate?" Gillian enquired, thinking aloud whilst listening in to more periodic instructions on her radio.

"Who? Brad? He's very good: one of our best local councillors. If there are votes out there then he'll find 'em."

"It wasn't all that long ago he was out on a limb," she noted poignantly. "Some crisis in your Social Services Department, I believe."

"Overblown by the media," Rolfe corrected her. "That said, you could say Brad was offered up as the fall-guy."

"Okay, Steve, the Leader's moving out towards the business park," she noted, speaking into her walkie-talkie before returning to the conversation. "So explain his phoenix-like rise back to popularity," she begged, both of them following after the campaign entourage.

"Consider the events of that summer. Over-zealous child abuse specialists up and down the land had suddenly become the *bête-noirs* of Fleet Street. But to err is human; his big mistake was to cling on when all around him were letting go. But Brad always was a fighter. He was convinced his department had acted correctly. I think now his party realise that. Some of us never doubted him. We knew he'd be vindicated in the end."

"And Councillor Preston never doubted either?" Gillian quizzed him, displaying a remarkably acute nose for what had transpired in the corridors of Gunsbridge Town Hall. Someone in Walworth Road evidently made it their duty to dig such things up.

"I think Micky realised early on how premature he had been in writing his colleague off. I'm sure he was the principal voice who buttered up McKerrick in order to have him rehabilitated. That said, I'm sure he didn't do all the persuading."

"I'm sure you're right," she affirmed, teasing him by not letting on who else she had in mind. "His past doesn't worry you though?"

Rolfe assumed she must know the answer to her own question. "He's a first-class candidate," he grinned instead. "Anyway, we all have our skeletons in the cupboard – even some high-flying Tories in this town."

"Yes," she winked coyly before moving off to escort her leader over to his final photo-call, "so I'm told!"

****

Arriving back from work, Wendy nonetheless knew where to find them, and parked her dark blue Astra on the car park of Gunsbridge Central Labour Club before wandering inside and locating her husband and his *côterie* tucked away in the main committee room upstairs. As she laid her briefcase and handbag down on the table, she noticed Eric Sims ploughing through the *Gunsbridge Herald*, a discomforting expression on his face. She was tempted to ask what had so vexed him. However, the perceptive chairman pre-empted her, folding down the page and handing it to her. The candidate's wife glanced down the story, her countenance darkening as her eyes hit the bottom of the page and she looked up, noticing Brad's face ablaze with fury.

"Bastards! Bastards! I'll sue the little jerk!" he yelled, grabbing the paper off her and tossing it away in anger. Wendy rescued it from the floor to reacquaint herself with the frightful allegations.

"They're true though, aren't they?" she gasped. Brad nodded and tried to comfort her as she shed a tear. Then he looked up at Eric and Micky.

"Okay, if you want me to resign, I'll do it!" he said, calming himself down by rubbing his wife's shoulders to dissipate both his anger and her hurt feelings.

"A bit hasty that," Eric chirped. "We've already lost one candidate. There's no time to lose another. You've made 'mistakes' in the past – we knew that before we alighted on you. But that was more than offset by the tremendous hard work you've brought to this campaign. Anyway, my guess is that by dragging in Alannah's name, Julie King's allegations will backfire on them."

"Yes, they've quoted her, the dumb Tory bitch! She's one of Anderson's cronies – thinks the sun shines out of his slick Tory arse. In fact, he's probably put her up to this."

"Well," Eric continued, easing himself off the desk he'd been seated upon, "if her accusations are true then there's little point in going to law. You might as well tackle this one head on: 'Yes, I had a drink problem – but at the time my marriage was breaking up'; 'yes, I once had a relationship with Alannah – but that's all in the past now'. That sort of thing."

Brad was partially consoled. What his chairman had told him had a ring of plausibility about it – making the best of a bad job. But then he snapped back, "...And what about Wendy. Look!" he demanded of him, snatching the story back off Wendy a second time and reading it verbatim, "*'Councillor Bradleigh is not fit to run...'*, blah, blah, blah, '*...his inept handling of the child abuse scandal in 1988... His wife, the principal social care officer responsible at the time, and who* *was later sacked for incompetence...'* Listen," he said, beseeching his campaign managers, "no one accuses my wife of malice and incompetence – certainly not that hypocrite Anderson; for all this is his doing!"

"Forget it," Eric smiled dismissively. "You'll have to face far worse smears in Parliament. It's a politician's lot!"

"Eric's right, Brad," Wendy pleaded, "Forget it. If anyone ought to be angry it should be me. But you can ride this one out. Keep on attacking Anderson on his government's dismal record in office; that's where the mileage is."

The matter weighed heavily on his mind all through the evening. He neither spoke to her, nor looked directly at her during the journey home after the evening's campaigning. All she could do was trust that Eric's common sense had dispelled any thoughts of doing something hasty. She retired to bed with that hope in mind.

However, Brad decided to remain up to watch the late night campaign coverage on TV instead, observing Neil Kinnock flatulently addressing a star-studded rally in Sheffield. "We're alright!" the Labour leader harrumphed, to the ecstatic delight of his expectant followers. However, slowly Brad's attention waned and that gloomy miasma of foreboding visited him once more. This secretive and enigmatic character had tried in all sincerity to confess his sinful past to Craig Anderson – someone he'd once considered a friend. Yet what had he discovered of Christian forgiveness? That Anderson had vengefully instructed his minions to blacken not only the name of Brad himself, but also to savage the reputation of his wife – something wholly unforgivable to the brooding councillor. Wendy was his wife, his friend, a most precious treasure.

No, he fumed. Anderson would have to pay dearly for the insouciance of his campaign. The more he pondered it, the more it got to him. Finally, he picked up the phone by the side of the settee.

"Hello, Phil? ...Yeah, you've read the stories... Bastards! ...Yeah, Anderson..." Then there was a long, pregnant pause before he sat up, cracked open another beer and grinned, "Yeah, why not. My sentiments exactly…"

****

The candidate emerged into the press briefing for what should have been his biggest attack on Labour policies so far. Yet, as he clutched his notes, his wife loyally at his side, and wandered up to the seat reserved for him, he knew that all that was off the agenda – at least for today. The press and television crews wanted answers to far more grave matters than just the candidate's views on matters political.

"Mr Anderson... Mr Anderson..." they screamed. "Can you tell us...? Is it true that...?"

Craig held out his hands to urge the excited newshounds to be still. "Ladies, gentlemen, please..."

The room fell silent except for the whining of camera motors, while occasional flashes bathed Craig, Nikki and Sarah Packington in their sudden glows. Nikki raised a delicate finger to chase away a stray tear for those who cared to notice, though most eyes were trained on her tired and frustrated husband.

"Gentlemen, I wish to make the following statement in relation to stories that appeared over the weekend pertaining to aspects of my private life. Afterwards, I will answer briefly any questions that you may have. And then, as far as I'm concerned, this matter is closed." He then settled into his prepared script, clearing his throat while, all around him, the media stood ready to analyse his words.

"Accusations have been made in the *Gunsbridge Herald* by unnamed parties that during the 1987 General Election, whilst I was a candidate for Gunsbridge North, that I had an affair with Mrs Gemma Sutton, wife of the chairman of Gunsbridge North Conservative Association, at a time when I was dating her daughter, Elisa. I confirm that during the previous year, I did share a romantic relationship with Miss Elisa Sutton, although we subsequently parted amicably."

The photographers clicked faster as his voice began to rise and state emphatically "However, never did I have then, neither have I had since, a sexual relationship of any description with Mrs Sutton. These allegations are therefore wholly without foundation, and have been fed to the *Herald* with a view to destroying my campaign, the unhappy consequences of which have been to also cause distress to my wife, my friends, and, of course, to the Sutton family – people who I respect immensely for the genuine friendship they offered me during that campaign."

Placing the script down on the table, he sat back and waited for the furious scramble of questions – a haunting and debilitating spectacle for him. For Nikki, the trauma was almost too much to bear, every last drop of faith being summoned forth to sustain her through the merciless tirade. She gripped Craig's hand discreetly under the table. Finally, his roving finger alighted upon one of the more persistent members of the press corps.

"Yes... yes, you... third row back."

"John Nizello, *Birmingham Evening Mail*. Mr Anderson, do you intend to sue the *Herald* over these allegations, and thus clear your name?"

"At this stage, I hope it won't come to that. But if this situation is not resolved satisfactorily, then that option may be pursued. In particular, I would like to know who these 'senior local Tories' are that the *Herald* quotes throughout the story." he replied, knowing damn well that it was not necessarily in his interests that these shadowy accusers (who he guessed resided in Maywood Heath) reveal even more than they had already intimated. To complicate matters further, Gemma's divorce lawyer had instructed her to refuse to comment at all.

"Someone else," he continued, "yes... you."

"Germaine Adams, BBC *Midlands Today*. Mr Anderson, what do you say to the allegation that you were plainly observed kissing and embracing Mrs Sutton during the opening of the Trescott Park International Hotel?"

Craig knew that one might cause problems. "Who are these accusers? Let them tell us openly what they know," he snapped in desperation, angrily defying the logic of his own predicament nonetheless.

"But you don't deny the charge?" the journalist riposted doggedly.

"Listen, it was a night of celebration – a milestone in our town's economic regeneration. I probably kissed a lot of lovely ladies that night. I don't deny that I may have kissed Mrs Sutton in a moment of... purely... well, you know," he fumbled, the watching press keen that he spell it out properly, "...a moment of high spirits – nothing more, you understand!"

The answer caused a ripple of amusement to race around the room, Craig sensing another dent appearing in his credibility. He plodded on, pointing his finger once more, though studiously avoiding the *Herald* reporter who'd been gesticulating patiently throughout.

"Lindsay Roebuck, the *Independent*. Mrs Anderson, how do you react to these allegations of a bizarre *ménàge-a-trois* between your husband and the Suttons?" the reporter enquired, pointing to a copy of the *Herald's* glaring headlines.

Nikki had lived in dread of this moment. The lifeblood almost visibly drained out of her when she tipped her ghostly white face forward to speak into the clutch of microphones taped together on the table in front of them, stuttering and groping for words, despite the best endeavours of Sarah Packington and Eleanor Whitney to counsel her in anticipation of this agonising moment.

"Er... I... I stand by my husband. I love him and, er... I believe he... that he... he is not, I mean, was not... in any way involved. It's all a horrible smear."

"Mr Anderson, do you think you can possibly close the gap on your opponent now?" someone else interjected.

"You mean can he close the gap on me!" Craig fired back boldly, causing some stirring amongst the excited journalists. He clarified, saying, "We are still ahead, and we will stay ahead. Our canvass returns and feedback from the doorsteps all tell us we can safely hold this seat. I believe the voters will treat this whole smear as just that: a last-ditch dirty tricks campaign with no basis in truth whatsoever. No, my friends, John Major will be our next prime minister, and I intend to be there when the Queen opens the new Parliament!"

Despite the manifest scepticism of his interrogators, such bombast was not entirely without foundation, though the campaign was still locked into an uneasy stalemate. Paddy Ashdown, the Liberal Democrat leader, was expected in town today to join Jane Allsop for a walkabout in the shopping centre, and Craig knew his visit would only bolster the campaign of the indefatigable little councillor, reinforcing locally the painful squeezing of the Tory vote by their party.

"One final question... yes... back row, greyish hair..."

"Mr Anderson, some people are saying that these allegations are retaliation for a highly personal attack upon your Labour opponent recently by one of your own campaign staff. Is that a fair comment?"

Craig sighed regretfully. "Unfortunately, the remarks in question were not authorised by either me or my agent. Councillor Miss King was speaking on her own behalf, and I profoundly apologise for the distress this may have caused Councillor Bradleigh and his wife. I intend to fight my campaign on policies and issues, and not personalities. I therefore unreservedly disassociate myself from those allegations. All this muck racking on both sides is highly distasteful. For my own part, I think it's sad that the *Herald* – not satisfied with having failed to pin this sort of 'toy-boy' scandal on my colleague in Gunsbridge North – seems to think it can now try and pin it on me instead. I'm appalled at such poor journalistic standards from our town's main newspaper."

Time was ticking away, and Craig had to be moving on to his next engagement. He disentangled himself from the press and was herded out to Gerry Robert's waiting car, only to find Sarah, Nikki and himself still being pursued at close quarters by insatiable journalists, all anxious to know more about his 'torrid past', despite Craig's insistence that the matter was now closed.

"Mr Anderson... Is it true what they say? That you prefer older women...?" they were still screaming after him as Gerry's car sped off the car park.

"I told you we should never have brought that stupid girl onto the campaign team. She's been a liability right from the start!" Nikki wept. Craig couldn't disagree, so Nikki tearfully hurled one final painful lament in his direction, saying,

"I just hope we never have to face this torture again, Craig. Or you will be facing it on your own!"

"Do you think I enjoy it?" he shouted back at her impatiently. "I'm about to witness months of hard work unravel before my very eyes. All because some evil swine amongst the 'Mafia' thought he saw what he didn't see. I never slept with Gemma Sutton! Never! You must believe me! You believe me, don't you, Gerry?" he said, leaning forward to interrogate his driver, as well as Sarah Packington sat next to him.

Gerry looked in his rear-view mirror at Nikki, who was listing sullenly against the window of the vehicle, watching while her adopted town sped past. He sensed to the full her sudden feelings of rage towards her anguished husband.

"Believe him," he consoled her, "believe in each other. I admire your faith, even though I'm not very religious myself. Cling to it, and cling to each other. You'll need both if you're to last out the final week of this campaign, that's for sure."

****

The little green line of the monitor blipped and jumped with monotonous regularity inside the darkened room. It was just as well, announcing that the woman who had once worn his crown was still alive, albeit silent and still.

Brad had decided to come of his own volition, for the doctors had said that it was likely that she would soon rouse from her comatose state. And so he clung to the hope that he might just be the one who would awaken her from her involuntary slumber, slim though that hope was. He stood peering through the glass at her limp and bandaged body. Then he gently eased the door open and wandered inside.

"Alannah... Alannah... Allie..." he whispered remorsefully, for he knew he had wronged her. He drew his fingers along her pale white arms, but she did not respond. So many times he had despised and reviled her with as much passion as he had once loved her; but he had never dreamed it would ever come to this. Where now was the bubbly, vivacious campaigner? Where now the caring, charming companion? Where now the fighting, spirited woman who had come so far, only to be robbed of her prize so close to the finishing line? He didn't know and she didn't say.

He stared down at the floor for what seemed like hours, pondering the meaning of it all. How vile the human race is, how steeped in evil is each mortal soul, hope of redemption only seeming to vanish like a mirage each time one tried in vain to find it. Yet one had to have faith in something. He took out a crumpled note from his pocket and began to pour over it once more...

All the time, I never lost faith in you; either of you. You are the finest of your generation. I still believe in you both now, and even though one of you is lying there motionless in that hospital bed, I have faith that the other will keep the dream alive. He has hurt me and disappointed me so often, but I had to forgive him, and I had to sacrifice everything once more to put him back in the fight.

Don't fail me, Brad. Think of me, and think of Alannah; and go out and win. Win for us! Win for the Party! Win for all the people we've known who've never had a chance in life because of an accident of birth, or the colour of their skin, or because of the side of town on which they grew up. Let that be your faith and let it be your goal!

                    Comrades always,

Micky

Tomorrow would decide whether he could fulfil Micky's dream – he'd certainly done his very best. For tomorrow surely the voters would decide. For now though, all he could do was cry, gushing soft tears onto the crumpled bed linen, the 'son' resting his heavy brow upon her helpless body and pondering the 'father's' words, each staccato sob gathering up momentum for further lamentation. At this final hour, the 'father' and the 'son' were reunited once more; and tomorrow, Thursday April 9th 1992, the 'son' would go out and try to offer up the symbolic sacrifice that might just atone for the failings of the past. Maybe he might also redeem Gunsbridge South for his party.

****

"There is a redeemer - Jesus, God's own Son.
Precious Lamb of God - Messiah, Holy One."

How treasured the words of the soloist were to him as he listened on, eyes closed and heart slowly sailing away in adoration of the Saviour. He reflected back on his life when the guitars and the keyboards ceased, leaving the lone voice to pierce the stillness with the haunting chorus. So many times in the past he had failed to live up to the expectations of those who'd loved and trusted him. So many times he'd cursed himself for the presence within him of inner fears and dark longings. So many times he'd lost hope of ever arriving at this moment where dreams and reality were almost converging. Yet "never will I leave you, never will I forsake you", his heavenly Father had assured him. And so it had been. Anew, he wept a solitary tear and grasped hold of that awesome promise, the 'precious Lamb of God' unfailingly washing away and atoning for all those past failings.

He fumbled in his jacket pocket and discreetly unfolded that letter that he had often glanced at over the years, and that now nestled crisply and neatly inside the torn envelope. He quickly read over the promises once more.

> *"Though the fig tree does not bud, and there are no grapes on the vine; though the olive crop fails, and the fields produce no food; though there are no sheep in the pen, and no cattle in the stalls; yet I will rejoice in the Lord. I will be joyful in God my Saviour. The Sovereign Lord is my strength. He makes my feet like the feet of a deer. He enables me to go on to the heights."*

Nikki looked down into his lap at the letter, recognising her handwriting. Then she gently slipped her hand inside his. Together they both prayerfully closed their eyes and heeded the words of life that were still embossed, now as then, on that same whitewashed wall that provided the backdrop to that same grand oak pulpit: *JESUS CHRIST IS LORD*. There in essence was the inner strength that had brought them this far, that had enabled them both to 'go on to the heights' – to fight on to almost within sight of the prize. They recalled all these things; and, all at once, that inner strength came flooding back into them, lifting their hearts on 'wings of eagles' and casting aside all the doubts, all the anguish and resentment, all the things that had no place in the hearts of a man and woman who would aspire to do the will of God in their lives. Tomorrow, Thursday April 9th 1992, Craig William Anderson would be taking hold of that faith once again. And if God willed, maybe he might also buck the polls and win Gunsbridge South for his party.

****

The tension was becoming overbearing inside the familiar cavernous interior of Gunsbridge Town Hall. No one knew what to make of it all, least of all those three anxious candidates who had stood in this same auditorium on so many previous occasions, and who were now within an ace of making it to Westminster. All day long, the British people, in the privacy of polling booths throughout the nation, had delivered or denied the hand of government to someone – soon they would all know for sure. And surely they had also now delivered or denied that imperceptible hand of opportunity to these, the next generation of players in the tempestuous game of British politics.

Jane Allsop stood alongside Candy Rawlings discussing the state of play in hushed tones, her vote having rallied better than expected, on occasions the batched-up ballot papers in the counting tray overtaking those of her other two rivals. Craig and Sarah watched over the counting of the final table full of votes, his vote having also held up well given the unfortunate circumstances that had dogged his campaign. Maybe Sarah was right; maybe his tireless campaigning, the visit of the Prime Minister, and his youthful enthusiasm had made the difference, although the pessimist in him could see that the publicity surrounding the *ménage a trois* affair had taken its toll on the slender lead he'd briefly enjoyed. Brad and Micky certainly weren't grateful for him making any kind of difference: Labour might just conceivably snatch this seat, though not by the kind of margins their more exuberant supporters had hoped.

The candidates couldn't help but notice the reappearance of the television cameras in the Town Hall for the first time since the by-election ten years earlier. And with good reason: party officials would be watching very closely for the first signs of movement in seats like this, a swing either way in which could determine the careers not only of Craig Anderson and Robert Bradleigh, but also of their party leaders also. Nationally, Labour was still in the lead by a whisker, the Conservatives close behind, and the Liberal Democrats confident of holding the balance in a new Parliament. "Don't sleepwalk into this election," John Major had warned the electorate bluntly, and Conservative campaign chiefs had undoubtedly prayed that a salient gaffe by the Labour leader would rouse any undecided voters somnambulantly partial to Labour's remorseless 'It's Time For Change' campaign theme. Yet while Labour had undoubtedly fought the better campaign, it was still too close for Neil Kinnock to boast of victory without at least one set of fingers crossed behind his back.

While counting continued into the small hours, Nikki and Wendy strolled about watching events unfold. Occasionally, their eyes would meet across the expanse of polished floor that divided them, encounters that seemed the only contact of any sort during the evening between the Anderson and the Bradleigh campaign teams. Relations between the two men, once so open and easy-going, had frozen over completely. Neither one spoke to the other, whether by a deliberate act of indifference or whatever, their long friendship broken by the pressure to win one of the most hotly-contested seats of a hotly-contested General Election.

Finally, the last ballot papers were collated and the counting staff rested their arms lazily on the tables, their job apparently over. The returning officer performed his sums and gathered the candidates and their agents together for a *tête-a-tête*.

"Right," he sighed, perching his pencil back behind his ear, "this is how it looks: Allsop 20640, Anderson 20754, Bradleigh 20875... There are twenty-eight spoiled ballot papers."

Micky rested his weathered hand on Brad's shoulder reassuringly, though it was not over yet – one formality remained. "I'll go through these with you, if I may. These votes may make someone's day, after all," they heard the officer mutter.

"Right, this one?" he said, holding out a slip with a cross slightly wide of the 'Anderson' box.

"That's ours!" Sarah insisted. None of the others demurred, and the Conservative vote leapt up by one.

"And this?" he enquired, fishing out another.

Someone had written a 'yes' instead of a cross in the 'Bradleigh' box – the Labour vote leapt up by one. Another tick was awarded to Craig, Jane Allsop failing to acquire one with half a tail in the 'Anderson' box – paper spoilt. Another slip fell to the Tories, another to Labour. The remainder were all judged to be too equivocal, too obscene or too vague (no cross at all!). And so the returning officer drew his pencil out from its auricular scabbard and briefly reworked his figures.

"20640, 20757, 20877...." he noted to Jane and Candy, Craig and Sarah, and Brad and Micky respectively. "Speak now or forever be condemned to opposition!" he chortled, not entirely oblivious to the electricity buzzing back and forth between the three main contenders. A quick consultation took place.

"I think it's..." Craig and Jane both rushed to announce together.

"Ladies before gentlemen," Craig offered his pretty, young rival.

"Age before beauty," she insisted. Maybe the fun hadn't entirely vanished from this contest after all.

"Recount?" the returning officer sighed wearily, if sympathetically.

"There could well be a hundred of our votes in there!" Sarah insisted, pointing a long, bejewelled finger at the elastic-bound batches of Labour votes, adamant that Election Day having been the first sunny day of a rain-sodden campaign it must augur well for a Conservative victory.

"There could well be a hundred more of our votes in amongst yours," Micky countered, mocking her self-assurance.

"And there could well be a hundred of my votes in each of your piles!" Jane grinned, still determined not to concede to her two unhealthily self-absorbed male opponents. Then she turned and withdrew to converse with her anxious party workers.

All the assembled supporters had gathered by now that there was to be no Sistine smoke this side of one o'clock and so were not wholly surprised to find the batched-up slips being returned to the counting staff for another try at king (or queen) making. Nikki looked up at her husband's drained appearance. Though still optimistic, where and for whom were the illusive hundred votes? she wondered, if indeed they existed. She smiled at Craig and watched Sarah offer him a motherly hug, a gesture of encouragement before they all settled into the tedious recounting of some seventy thousand ballot slips.

"*Well, we thought we had a result just there from Gunsbridge South,*" David Dimbleby informed his nocturnal audience disappointedly, "*but it looks like they're going to a recount. Of course, John, this is one of Neil Kinnock's most prized target seats...*"

"*That's right, David,*" veteran political commentator John Cole concurred in his dulcet Ulster tones, "*he can be sure that if he's won in Gunsbridge South, then he's probably won the election as well...*"

Brad could have continued watching the little portable television set resting on the returning officer's desk for the rest of the recount had he not had so personal a stake in the result that the studio *cogniscenti* were busily trying to second guess. Instead, he strolled back over to cast his glance across the counting table.

Meanwhile, Wendy's stamina was clearly flagging. She felt like sleeping for a thousand years, but reasoned that she might just miss her husband's big moment. Eventually, she settled for a short voyage to the ladies' room. After justifying her visit, she rinsed her hands, stared into the mirror that ran the length of the one wall, and forced open her bright blue eyes to see if there was still intelligent life inside her weary head. She was just about to commence running her hands up into her fiery red mane to put some bounce back into it when a door opened, and a by-now familiar face emerged to join her in the act of preening.

"Hi," came the tentative greeting from an equally exhausted candidate's wife.

"Hi," Wendy replied, continuing to perk up her crown.

There was a silence that lasted for some moments before Nikki tried again.

"I just want a hot bath and a nice, warm bed," she pined longingly, racing a brush through her own dark, silky mane.

Wendy glanced across at Nikki's reflection in the mirror, joking "I'd be content to settle for the nice, warm bed!"

The two women shared a moment of light amusement before each began to reflect quietly again upon the fateful catalogue of events that had brought them both together on this night. They each knew enough about the other to appreciate the bizarreness of it all: the missionary's daughter with the girlish good looks, and the wild child with the bushy red mane; the born-again Christian who prayed in Spanish, and the anti-*apartheid* activist with the mild Cockney ling. Unlikely companions; yet tonight, while they quietly brushed their hair and put on their faces, they were suddenly overcome with a strange and mutual affinity with each other; for they both shared a common belief in the destiny of their men. They each sensed and understood the traumas and disappointments that doggedly clinging to that belief had visited upon them in the name of politics. For all the regrettable animosity that had flared up between their husbands, they were both somehow at peace with each other now – at this final stage of an often circuitous and tormented journey to the rainbow's end.

"Not long now, eh?" Wendy smiled.

"No, soon be over... until the next time," Nikki grinned.

Had they known more they could have talked for hours: how they'd both proved the catalysts that had swung their otherwise fearful and faint-hearted lovers around and locked them determinedly onto the course that had brought them both side-by-side in Gunsbridge Town Hall tonight.

"You know, Craig was appalled by Julie King's comments in the press – about Brad and his... well, you know," Nikki fumbled tentatively, closing up her bag as she did. "He really blew his top when he found out what she's done."

Wendy paused for a moment. "Forget it, sister," she sighed magnanimously. "I guess we've both shared a lot of sleepless nights over silly things that happened a long, long time ago. Besides, I just knew Craig wasn't the sort to... well, you know."

The admission helped Nikki feel more confident in sharing her thoughts. Indeed, her wistful brown eyes must have intimated to Wendy at least some of what had transpired. Besides, like all the great debates of the intervening few weeks, it was all water under the bridge now. Soon perhaps Mrs Nicola Anderson and Mrs Wendy Bradleigh would themselves be thrust into the limelight to realise a destiny of which they were able to only vaguely discern at this seminal juncture in their lives.

Wendy folded her bag under her arm and held the door open, adding, "I dare say that neither Craig nor Brad will ever admit that, for good or bad, better of worse, it's not they, but we who have really determined who they are and where they want to go; and to actually get them there. We're the great unsung heroines of this campaign."

Nikki laughed. "Yes, you mean 'behind every great man there's a great woman'?"

"Great or small, Nikki, behind every man there needs to be a woman – they know it; and they know they wouldn't have it any other way!"

"Ladies… Ladies…" cried Gerry Roberts, searching about the foyer, "they're ready! We've got a result! Come on, quick!"

He grabbed their hands and together they all rushed into the main hall just in time to witness their husbands mounting the dozen or so steps that led onto the stage. Suddenly, everyone began to almost physically feel that part of the watching nation that was still awake drop what it was doing and join David Dimbleby in the election studio, his producer ordering the cameras to zoom in on the handful of figures assembled together beneath the august coat of arms of the Borough.

"I, Gordon Michael Thompson, being the returning officer for the parliamentary constituency of Gunsbridge South do hereby announce the results of the election for the member of Parliament for the said constituency to be as follows… Allsop, Jane Elizabeth (Liberal Democrat), 20542 votes…"

She'd lost it; but boy oh boy, what a fighter! She smiled disappointedly at her cheering band of party workers, both Nikki and Wendy sure they noticed a tear or two emerge discreetly from beneath the formidable carapace of her otherwise steely resolve. Both girls couldn't help but feel the sisterly urge to weep alongside the plucky, little lass. But where did that leave the contest now?

"Anderson, Craig William (Conservative Party), 20857 votes…"

The Tory cheers went up and Nikki held her breath. Her husband had found his missing one hundred votes after all! However, she found it impossible not to feel sorry for Brad that his audacious gamble with his career had not paid off after all. She glanced over and noticed him close his eyes as the room fell silent and the returning officer rediscovered his place in his notes.

"Bradleigh, Robert (Labour Party), 20875 votes…"

That magic number was the herald that brought the entire Gunsbridge South Labour Party to their feet, whether they were stamping those feet and ululating wildly in the Town Hall or still watching at home on their television sets. No other result really mattered just then.

"*So,*" Dimbleby puffed, "*there goes the once-safe Tory seat of Gunsbridge South,*" he said, and an appropriately-coloured message flashed across the screen in front of him. "*It had been held more or less continuously by the Conservatives since 1970 and has now been captured by Labour by a whisker after a truly hard-fought campaign there. What do you make of that, John?*"

"*Well, David,*" the tuneful voice of John Cole interjected, "*I think Neil Kinnock will take great satisfaction in that result, but I don't honestly think now it can prevent John Major from gaining an overall majority in the new Parliament…*"

Indeed, the mood had changed. By the time Gunsbridge South had announced that its recount was underway the studio panel had begun to sense that something dramatic was happening. Though various marginal seats were tumbling to Labour, overall the Conservative vote had rallied. Slowly, Labour campaign staff began to wake up to the numbing realisation that their leader was not on his way to Downing Street after all. Brad had guessed as much by now, but had good reason to push such thoughts to the back of his mind. To be sure, he had stood before many different audiences during his years in local politics, but somehow tonight was different. The television lights bore down on the new Member of Parliament and captured a man caught almost in a daze as he stood before the people. Then he noticed the etchings of joy and thanksgiving written all over the faces of his comrades on the floor. He blinked exaggeratedly, realising it was not a dream. He had done it! He had seized the prize!

"Ladies and gentlemen, Mr Returning Officer, comrades. It almost feels unreal to be standing before you tonight as the victorious candidate. But, here I am; and I intend to do everything in my power to use the office you have bestowed upon me to secure for all the people of this town the justice and recognition they rightly deserve, justice and recognition that I have endeavoured to work for during my eight years as a councillor in this town."

Again, applause and cheers broke out as he paused before concluding magnanimously, "I would like to thank my opponents for their own not inconsiderable contributions to the betterment of this town, and which has manifested itself in the earnestness and the tenacity that they have brought to this campaign; to Jane and to Craig especially, for chasing me almost to the very end for the privilege of serving this constituency as its voice in Westminster."

Maybe her husband had been chastened by the emotional cost of his victory tonight, Wendy hoped, watching him as he motioned to Jane Allsop to step forward, tears still cascading over her smooth cheeks as she thanked her campaign team.

"You'll forgive me if I cry just a little..." she sobbed, mocking her own emotions. "I cry with regret; but I cry with pride also. Pride that, whether we have won or whether we have lost, here in Gunsbridge South, my team have proved their mettle, not just here tonight, but in municipal elections each year. Things will never be the same again. We've proved what we can do when we really try."

Craig shared the applause that broke out when she concluded with a stirring *cri-de-côeur* for women of whatever political colours to go out and show their mettle also, and it led him to cock an eye down at his own precious nugget of female inspiration. He couldn't hide from her his own terrible regret, for she read it all over his blanching face. Meanwhile, their invisible antennae buzzed and the message crossed between them: the words of the Apostle Paul to the Philippian church, "*But one thing I do: forgetting what is behind and straining towards what* is ahead, I press on towards the goal to win the prize for which God has called me heavenwards in Christ Jesus." Gunsbridge South might be lost, but that other prize would still be beckoning him tomorrow. And tomorrow is another day, Nikki whispered to him lovingly. Tomorrow is a brand new day!

"Mr Returning Officer, whatever his politics, I have no doubt that Councillor Bradleigh will make a truly outstanding member of parliament for this town, and I wish him every success in his endeavours," he noted graciously. Brad mouthed a 'thank you' to him and looked on as he continued.

"The Conservative Party in this town has had its share of disappointments," he confessed, "…and surely none can be as disappointing as tonight's result. Even so, my fellow party workers have put in a first-class show under very difficult circumstances, and have given their all to my campaign over the last few weeks. To them, and especially to Sarah Packington – my superlative agent – to Gerry Roberts, to Des Billingham, and to my wife, Nikki, I say thank you. And – despite it all – be of good cheer. For there will be other nights when we will again be rejoicing and singing here in Gunsbridge, just as it now appears that John Major will soon be rejoicing as he prepares to form the government of the country for the next few years. For tomorrow is another day," he consoled them, staring once more into the eyes of the woman he adored, "tomorrow is a brand new day!"

****

THE GUNSBRIDGE HERALD
Friday, April 10th 1992
Special Election Edition   -   Still only 30p

MAJOR WINS HIS MANDATE – BUT ONLY JUST!
A jubilant John Major today received his mandate for another term of office after amassing the largest popular vote of any political leader in modern times, despite virtually every opinion poll during the campaign having consigned him to the political graveyard. Results now in give the Conservatives 336 seats, Labour 271, the Liberal Democrats 20 and other parties 24, the Conservative share of the vote holding firm at 42%, with Labour on 35% and the Liberal Democrats on 18%...
LOCAL BOY TRIUMPHS – BUT ONLY JUST!
The Deputy Leader of Gunsbridge Borough Council, Robert Bradleigh, successfully captured Gunsbridge South for the Labour Party with a majority of just EIGHTEEN votes, making it one of several Labour gains throughout the West Midlands taken on an average four percent swing from the Conservatives...
LOCAL BOY FAILS – BUT ONLY JUST!
For another 'local boy', Conservative candidate Craig Anderson, Gunsbridge South was only denied him by the slenderest of margins. Commenting on his close-run campaign, he noted that, despite the adversities that had dogged his campaign, he was satisfied that his local party had put on a "first-class show"...
LOCAL GIRL FAILS – BUT ONLY JUST!

Surprise performance of the evening was the impressive vote accumulated by the Gunsbridge South Liberal Democrat candidate, Cllr Miss Jane Allsop, whose third and most determined campaign in the seat so far brought her a close third behind her two main opponents...
WHAT NOW FOR LABOUR?
Despite their Gunsbridge triumph, this third failure to oust the Tories will surely prompt some in the Labour Party nationally to question what more the party can possibly do to make itself electable. Meanwhile, whilst Shadow Chancellor, John Smith, is odds-on favourite to lead the party in the new Parliament, in a special feature on Page Six our political editor, Julie Cameron, tells us who else we should be looking out for amongst Labour's other up-and-coming talent: Gordon Brown perhaps...? Or maybe even Tony Blair...?

If you have enjoyed reading this, why not continue following the story…

Ray Burston

The MAKING of the MINISTER

The sequel to The Making of the Member

In 'The Making of the Member' we followed the story of two young friends from an unsung 'Black Country' town in the industrial West Midlands as they pursued an arduous thirteen year quest to become its Member of Parliament.

By the time Tony Blair and New Labour completed their epic journey from the political wilderness to Downing Street, both men were also completing the first stage of their own political journeys.
Ahead of them there will now lie further years of struggle and disappointment, of danger and intrigue, of triumph and tragedy, as they seek to lay claim to their place at the heart of power within the British political system.

It is a struggle that will prove to be the making of the Minister.

Printed in Great Britain
by Amazon.co.uk, Ltd.,
Marston Gate.